ORB STATION ZERO

GALACTIC ARENA

BOOK 1

Rama Seti
and the Mission to Orb Station Zero
2199 AD

DAN DAVIS

Orb Station Zero
Copyright © 2016 by Dan Davis

All rights reserved. No part of this book may be used or reproduced in any manner whatsoever without written permission except in the case of brief quotations embodied in critical articles or reviews.
This book is a work of fiction. Names, characters, businesses, organizations, places, events and incidents either are the product of the author's imagination or are used fictitiously. Any resemblance to actual persons, living or dead, events, or locales is entirely coincidental.

For information contac :
dandaviswrites@outlook.com

ISBN: 9781519057174
First Edition: August 2017

For Liam. Brother, squad leader, ultimate space marine.

PART 1
ADAPTATION

CHAPTER ONE
RAMA SETI'S HEAD

THE FIRST time the UNOP operatives cut off Rama Seti's head, it was for a good cause. Perhaps, the most important cause in human history. The second time, three years later, it was in order to save his life.

The Tactical Surgeon knew that his target, Rama Seti, was not expecting to be beheaded in the middle of the night. The target's apartment was on the 37th floor of 6 Constitution Plaza, Delhi and Mr. Seti had the kind of security system that made high net worth individuals sleep soundly. Entry to the building itself was controlled and patrolled, funded by the residents' monthly fees. Even so, from the personality profile in his file, the Tac Surgeon knew the target was not a man to trust other people to keep him safe.

The target had invested in an automated body scanner, fingerprint and retinal scans combined with a password combination lock with a timer that didn't allow the door to be opened outside of 1400 to 1700, when the target took his deliveries. The apartment door was high carbon steel reinforced with six locking rods that bolted through the door and into the frame.

Yet the best civilian security on Earth would not stop United Nations Orb Project (UNOP) Tactical/Surgical Team 8 from breaking through.

It was 0300, local time. Suitable bribes had turned the heads and cameras of building security and the UNOP T/S Team 8 electronic specialist rendered the alarm system inert, gave a nod and the lock breaker stepped up and started work. While he drilled into the door by the main lock, the rest of the UNOP Marines covered him. The non-surgical team members carried assault rifles, armed with non-lethal electroshock rounds to take out unarmed civilians but also a selection of AP and hollow point magazines for local law enforcement and enthusiastic security guards if it came to it.

The locksmith put down his drill and turned to the Tac Surgeon.

"Five minutes," he whispered.

"Surgical team," the Tac Surgeon said into his internal mic.

"Come on up."

There were only twelve hours and thirty-four minutes until wheels up on the orbital shuttle and UNOP were remarkably keen to get the target's central nervous system onboard. So much so that they had offered a bonus big enough to upgrade the Tac Surgeon's already-booked Mars colony cabin to first class. Why they wanted this particular target so badly, he could not fathom.

The Tac Surgeon waited in the hall, half-heartedly reviewing the target's file while he waited. He had broken into dozens of homes in the last couple of years to perform tactical surgery and he knew that some people invested in security to keep their family safe. Yet the target, 28-year-old Rama Seti, had no family. None that counted, anyway. His parents lived on the other side of Delhi, he never saw them and had no other relatives. He had no children and the surveillance notes said all his sexual partners in the previous decade had been visiting prostitutes. The target must have paid them well, or perhaps they were just financially desperate enough to engage in intercourse with a man as morbidly obese as Mr. Seti.

The UNOP Marines locksmith carried on with his work, inserting a self-guiding wire into the hollow part of the door up toward the internal computer that controlled the time lock.

Previous targets had installed layers of high-tech security to protect their precious gold, jewelry, works of art or gemstones that they would not trust to bank vaults. But the valuable content of Rama Seti's apartment was cutting-edge technology for online virtual reality competitive gaming. The target was the founder and Chief Executive of Rubicon, a gaming cooperative with one-hundred members. The gaming system was known as the Avar and it was the ubiquitous online system the world over. None of the other Rubicon members was even based in India. Avar brought players the world over together seamlessly to compete in virtual worlds. Spectators and fans would join the players and watch in real time from the sidelines or even down amongst the players, unseen by them and each other and unable to affect the outcome.

It all sounded incredibly tedious to the Tactical Surgeon. Spending your life playing make believe when humanity's very existence was on the line.

"These virtual reality people are disgusting," he muttered.

"Sir?" The Marine next to him asked.

The Tac Surgeon did not bother to respond.

The target's most prized possession, the file said, was his custom Avar Chair. It cost more than the Surgeon's annual salary had back when he had been a junior resident in Austin. The headset, gloves and shoes of the device were engineered to the micrometer and the seat itself was designed to reduce the risk of bedsores. It aerated and cooled, massaged and moved so that blood flow was unrestricted. Vital for the target as he was recorded as being in the chair anywhere from eight to eighteen hours every day.

"Remarkable," the Surgeon muttered as he flicked through

his screen. "Goddamned waste."

"I'm through," the locksmith said. "Ready to open."

"Initiate entry," the Tac Surgeon said, yawning, and the locksmith heaved open the door. It swung out into the hallway without a sound.

The team members held their breath. They had experienced more than one night when unplanned alarms sounded, ruining their carefully laid plans and earning the Tac Surgeon a mauling from his UNOP commissioners.

But not tonight. The Marines swept inside with their weapons up, leaving one man to watch the hall and another to descend to cover the lobby and their exfil. The elevator door chimed and the surgical team trundled their equipment after the Marines.

The target slept on in his bedroom, oblivious, snoring like a broken air conditioning unit.

"That is not a healthy sound," the Tac Surgeon said, to no one in particular.

In the main living area, almost empty other than the obscenely expensive Avar chair, his surgical team laid plastic sheeting on every surface. Walls, floor, and ceiling were covered in layers of clear plastic. More team members rolled the heavily-reinforced and extra-large gurney into the target's bedroom.

The Tac Surgeon had personally performed thirty-four corporectomies and only the first half a dozen had been in a proper medical facility. And yet, even after so much experience in the field, performing the most complicated tissue removal procedure in medical history inside an unsanitary apartment made him deeply unhappy. It was sordid. Disrespectful to the medical profession. But UNOP paid better than anyone and they didn't care about his past run-ins with uptight Research and Ethics Boards with morals stuck back in the 21st Century.

He wandered after his anesthetists into the subject's bedroom where the rumbling and snorting echoed from the walls. It smelled of sickly-sweet sweat and the kind of rank feculence particular to the morbidly obese.

The anesthetic dosages had been prepared well in advance. All his team had to do was inject the patient and heave the disgusting fat son of a bitch onto the gurney, which was wheeled in next to the bed.

"What are you idiots waiting for?" he said in the internal comms system. "Get on with it."

"He's too fat," one replied, gesturing. "Adipose tissue at the neck too thick for the needles to penetrate. We are changing them now."

The Surgeon drew a deep breath but he stopped himself from shouting abuse at the morons. He would just kick them from the team after they got the target's nervous system safely back to the UNOP shuttle at the spaceport. While his morons changed needles, he peered closely at the young man's snoring face. The neck was indeed horrendously thick, perhaps ten centimeters of adipose tissue that he would have to cut away before even beginning the surgery proper. It would be a long procedure and he silently cursed all obese people the world over for being such pathetic slaves to their urges.

His anesthetists came back and injected their first round of sedatives while the others prepared to lift the huge mass of blubber onto the gurney.

Leaning over the target's body, he looked over his shoulder at the security team leader. "This will be the worst one yet. How anyone can allow themselves to reach a state like this is beyond me. And for a prospective subject, with his genetic potential, the waste of it is offensive to me."

"Tall guy, too," the Marines Lieutenant said. "Six-five, right? Taller than most of the others. That's weird, right? I thought they were identical."

"Environmental factors create the individual variation," the Surgeon explained, sighing at the ignorance of the military mind. "This one ingested more calories from a very early—"

The patient groaned and waved a fat hand up in the air. The surgeon jumped back, the slab of a fist whooshing past his face.

"What the hell?" the Surgeon shouted. "What did you give him?"

Both anesthetists approached to examine the groaning patient. "Just an involuntary—"

The target opened his eyes, took one look around, shouted in fear and threw himself out of his bed in a mass of quivering flesh.

The Tac Surgeon ducked aside as his surgical team scattered,

9

crying out as the man threw them aside as if they were children. The Lieutenant shouted to his Marines, drew his electroshock pistol and shot the man in his quivering, flabby back. It seemed to only drive the man into a wilder frenzy. He was a head taller than anyone in the infiltration team, even the Marines, and three times the weight. The target tossed the gurney over as if it was nothing.

The Surgeon fell into a stack of computer equipment, the cases of the machines tumbled down onto his head, slicing open his scalp.

In the end, despite the Marines' attempts to wrestle the stumbling, wild, half-drugged and stunned man, it was his own size that brought him down. The sedatives and panic helped to wear him out and within a few seconds, he was wheezing and slowing. He fell quite suddenly, falling across the upended gurney, buckling and snapping the steel tube frame.

Everyone stood looking at each other, breathing deeply.

"Help me up, you fools," the Surgeon commanded the anesthetists, who cleared the pile of fallen cases from him and heaved him up to his feet. "When we're done here today, you two incompetent fools will be finished."

"Men as overweight as this one are difficult to judge—"

"Save your excuses or I'll operate on you next. I'll take your legs and leave you in India, how would you like that? Just get him up and onto the gurney."

The gurney was beyond repair.

"Can't you operate on his bed?" the Lieutenant said.

The Surgeon did not bother to hide his contempt. "I need a completely stable platform for the procedure. Do you have any idea how precise you have to be when you sever a man's spinal cord? No, we'll have to call this off."

The Lieutenant scratched his jaw. "What about that giant-ass Avar Chair?"

The Surgeon hesitated. Then laughed. Perhaps the military mind was not so useless after all.

"Get your Marines to help heave him into it," the Tac Surgeon commanded the Lieutenant. "And hurry. We have a long set of procedures ahead of us and the shuttle launches in twelve hours."

While the target's mind was downloading, the Surgeon removed great chunks of body fat. The bio-waste bins filled up right away and the blood suction pumps kept clogging up. After a while, the Surgeon just started flinging globs of adipose tissue onto the floor. Most of the UNOP Marines found excuses to leave the room at that point but the Lieutenant stayed, seemingly unconcerned. Hours later, he woke the target up.

"What's happening?" Rama Seti mumbled.

The patient no longer had control of most of his body but the Surgeon had not yet severed the connection to his diaphragm. It was unlikely that the patient's eyes worked but he knew the young man could hear and probably retained a sense of smell, that most primal of senses. Machines beeped, plastic crinkled as the people around him walked here and there. A machine sucked and gurgled. Despite the apartment's expensive air-conditioning system, the room reeked of the hot metallic stink of surgery. It must have been really quite disorienting for the patient and the Surgeon felt a momentary, faint pang of empathy.

"We are in the middle of performing surgery on you," the Surgeon explained. "I have cut away much of your body, trying to preserve as much of your ganglia as I can but now I am beginning to sever your spinal column and the final links to your body. I prefer to do it with the patient conscious as any sudden incoherence on your part may indicate I am heading for a problem."

"My body?" the patient said. "Please, please, I don't understand, just let me go, take anything you want."

Some people in his team laughed while they worked.

"There's only one thing we want from you," the Surgeon said, playing to his small crowd.

The man said nothing for a while and the Surgeon stopped, scalpel in hand until he muttered another question. "What are you going to do with me?"

"You're going on a long journey, son," the Lieutenant said, to further titters from the surgical team.

"Please, do not tell him anything," the Surgeon said.

"It ain't like he's going to remember this, is it. You're going to zap his hippocampus, right?"

"Quite right. Yet I would rather not stress him unnecessarily with the enormity of his situation."

The Lieutenant chuckled. "Come on, Doc, there's no way this disgusting sack of shit is ever going to be selected to be a subject for Mission Four. What a lazy freak. He's going on a shelf somewhere at HQ until they incinerate him without ever waking him up."

"I'm sure you're right about this one. I can't tell you how sad it makes me that these will be his final moments of consciousness," the Surgeon said, trimming away remnants of tissue under his patient's chin. "I will be so glad when the mission finally launches. I am looking forward to a comfortable, quiet, semi-retirement on Mars. I would rather enjoy being a family doctor for a peaceful little colony town, you know?"

"What?" Rama Seti, blind, paralyzed, and soon to be little more than a severed head, muttered. "What are you saying? Please, don't do this. What's happening?"

"Alright," the Surgeon said, handing over his scalpel and taking the circular saw in its place. "I am about to remove the last sternocleidomastoid. I am afraid, Mr. Seti, that this will hurt quite a bit. Suction, please."

A motor whirred and the Surgeon carefully eased the tiny blade sliced into the target's last attached neck muscle.

Rama Seti screamed.

CHAPTER TWO
REALITY

TIME PASSED. AND RAMA SETI woke. He knew he was awake because the glare was like a scalpel in his retinas. There were people around him, he was sure. Shapes and sounds moved beside his head. It reeked of antiseptic and minty-fresh breath. He tried to move and to speak. Someone hushed him and sponged lukewarm water into his mouth which he licked up with a rough tongue. A cool hand stroked his forehead.

"You are currently disoriented," a voice said in his ear. It spoke English but the accent wasn't Indian. "Please remain calm."

Had he been in an accident? Was he in hospital? All Rama knew was that he had to find out what was going on.

"It's bright," Ram said, his voice sounded strange to himself. Rumbling, deep.

"You have been asleep, Rama." The voice was soft, comforting. As a mother or father might speak to a child. Ram was afraid of it.

"Where am I?" He couldn't see properly.

Ram's throat felt full of glass. Machines beeped steadily around him.

"A special facility, Rama Seti," the voice said.

"Who are you?" Ram's heart thumped in his chest.

"I am a medical doctor. My name is Dr. Fo. The others here in my team are biotechnicians, nurses, anesthetists and so on. We are all leaders in our field. None finer in the Sol System, I promise you."

Shapes and shadows loomed around him. Soft shoes swished on hard floors. The clatter of metal implements in metal bowls rang in the cool air that drifted across his face.

"Can't see," Ram said, fear rising further.

"We will rectify that shortly," the doctor said, a smooth, cool palm patted Ram on the forehead. "Eyes are complicated, Rama. Yours were a remarkably astigmatic and a little myopic. The muscles strained from a decade and a half of overuse of Avar headsets and we had to do a little extra work tinkering around in there." A finger tapped Ram on the bridge of his nose. "When we correct the calibration your eyes will be significantly improved, along with the rest of you. Here we go."

Ram blinked smears of light away and a grinning Chinese face leaned over his. The doctor was possibly middle aged but it was hard to tell. Probably a heavily-surgeried old bastard with newly-grown skin. Still smiling, the face pulled away.

He was on his back, probably on some sort of a hospital bed. The room beyond Dr. Fo's face was lined with large white tiles and soft light came from somewhere. Ram tried to look around but he still could not move.

Was he dreaming? Had his Avar malfunctioned? He wanted to wake up, wanted to get up, run, get away.

Yet he couldn't move, not even a little, not his arms or his legs. He couldn't move his head to look around.

What the hell was going on?

"Can't move," Ram said, his throat dry. "What happened?" His voice sounded amplified, as if it didn't belong to him. "Was I in an accident?"

"In a way," the doctor chuckled again, his cool hand patted Ram's forehead and then it rested there. "But you are all better now."

There was a faint pressure on the back of his head where it rested on the bed or gurney. Ram pursed his mouth and the skin there cracked into tiny crevices. He licked his lips, his tongue rasping against the ridges of dry skin. The wet sponge returned, dabbing cool beads of water into his mouth. He sucked the water down, the moisture spreading inside, freeing his tongue.

Why could he not feel his body? Nothing made any sense.

"Tell me what happened," Ram said. Why did his voice sound so strange? "Why can't I move?"

The doctor leaned down to look Ram in the eyes. He smelled of powerful soap and the whiff of mint.

"You are sedated, Rama Seti and your endocrine system is under our control. Your file states that you have a high resilience to emotional shock so I don't mind telling you that you were abducted from your home. An infiltration team escorted surgeons into your apartment in New Delhi where you were rendered unconscious and they removed your morbidly obese body. The only parts of you that we needed were your head, spinal column and as much of the central and peripheral nervous systems ganglia as we could get."

"Am I in Avar?" Ram said, his heart racing. His face flushed with the panic of it. "This can't be real. This is Avar, isn't it?"

"You were a professional Avar gamer, I know. But this is the real world."

Anger and fear surged through him and Ram tried to jump out of bed.

Nothing happened.

"You are attempting to move," Dr. Fo said with joy, looking at a screen next to him. "That is a marvelous sign. We have disabled your movement from below the neck, other than your diaphragm for conscious breathing and speaking. Just like when you plug into your Avar, yes? Just like when you enter REM sleep. As I was saying, we brought your head and spinal column here.

Plus a few of the important nerves, especially the solar plexus and so on. It makes fusing your nervous system to the new body so much easier."

Horror crept up Ram's neck into his face, warming it like spilled blood in an Avar-induced nightmare. And perhaps that was it. Perhaps he had finally succumbed to the Avar Psychosis that had claimed so many others of his profession. His cooperative colleagues had often warned him about it but he'd always disregarded their concerns. Ram always thought he could handle eighteen hours a day in the chair every day.

Maybe he had been wrong.

"What a second," Ram said, his voice deep and unfamiliar in his ears, panic rising in waves through his face. "Are you seriously telling me that you cut off my head?"

Dr. Fo chuckled. "Oh dear me, no. How could you think such a thing? No, no, no. We cut off your *body*. The procedure is called a corporectomy."

Ram's throat constricted and his heart thudded in his ears and he struggled for breath. It had been years since he'd had a proper panic attack but he knew the signs.

I have to get out of here.

A new voice, a woman's voice, close above him muttered a warning. "His catecholamines are spiking. I'll ease him back down."

The hot sensations drained from his face and his panic receded. They were controlling him, somehow, giving him drugs and he knew he should be angry about it yet he was relieved. It was nice, feeling calm.

"Why are you doing this?" Ram asked, straining to see as far around the room as he could. He could not see much. There were people there. Machines, beeping and humming.

"I will show you."

Even swiveling his eyes so far over in his sockets that the muscles ached, Ram couldn't see the doctor anymore. Instead, he noticed the soft glow of pale blue lights from high up around the room. The white ceiling above had a bluish tinge from the artificial lighting. There was no daylight.

Someone pulled a screen attached to a mechanical arm down over him. Ram looked up and for half a moment saw a reflection in the black of the screen.

The face was familiar. But it was not his own.

"Welcome to the new you," Dr. Fo said and the screen flicked on.

The image showed a man on a gurney, covered by a sheet up to the upper chest. A screen on a mechanical arm overhung his face.

That man was not Rama Seti.

It couldn't have been.

The figure was muscled as heavily as a bullock. The body of a champion bodybuilder only bigger, all veins and lumps and crevasses and ridges. A body resembling a relief map of the Himalayas. A body like the avatars Ram used in the *Galactic*

Games persistent world, and *Shield Wall* the European early medieval massively multiplayer wargame that had pretentions to historical accuracy but disregarded scale. A body that existed only in comics and animated films and maybe on the Artificial Persons that they designed for asteroid mining and outer system exploration.

A creeping horror crawled over his skin as he began to understand, at least a little, of what was happening to him.

Tubes, data cables, and fluid drips ran out from under the blanket and snaked along the floor out of sight.

In the image on the screen hanging over his face, the screen hanging over the face of the muscled giant on his screen.

Dr. Fo stood next to the bed, at the giant man's shoulder. He seemed diminutive in comparison.

"Do you like it? We matched the skin tone of the body to your own. It was paler than you before the procedure but it's trivially easy to do. You have a rather lovely natural color but it was awfully washed out from the lack of vitamins and UV." Dr. Fo chuckled, shaking his head. "Your diet was appalling, Rama Seti."

"That's not me."

On the screen, the giant's mouth moved as Ram spoke.

"You will experience a period of adjustment to your new self, of course," the doctor said, resting his hand on Ram's forehead. He saw it happen on the screen and felt the palm on his head at the same.

Ram struggled to comprehend what was happening.

"That's not my head, it's not me." Ram swallowed as he spoke.

The muscular figure on the screen was Indian but he had a handsome face, a strong jaw line. Prominent cheekbones.

Nothing like Ram's face at all.

"It is very much your old head that you grew all by yourself." The doctor stroked Ram's shorn scalp. Caressed it. "Rama, your face and head is the only external part of you that remains your own. You have been increasingly overweight since your early childhood. Not your fault, of course, it was your mother and father's fault. Your mother did it because she wanted to make you happy. You father, well. Never mind about him. My surgeons removed the excess adipose tissue from the face and especially the neck area."

"I'm thin."

Ram had never seen himself thin before. He had never looked in a mirror and seen a face that was tight. He had never seen his cheekbones. His cheeks had never gone inward, only puffed out like a cherub or a hamster or the other horrific terms of endearment his mother used to call him by. Ram watched on the monitor as a single, shining tear ran down one temple into the raised sheet that cushioned his head. The urge to wipe it away was intense but Ram could not move so much as one of the massive muscles that he now owned.

Ram's head looked smaller than he remembered it, with all

that fat taken away. In fact, it looked small attached to those huge shoulders.

"Wait a minute," Ram said, watching himself on the monitor speak the words. "Did you shrink my head or something?"

Dr. Fo chuckled. Even a couple of amused snorts came from the nurses and technicians as they worked around him.

"We have reinforced your skull with extra bone mass, in fact. As with the bones in your new body, we have increased the density and so increased the overall cranial mass. In terms of volume, we encouraged extra bone growth on the external side but of course, we did so subdermally. You have extra bone all around the cranium, face and jaw which has made your head around six percent larger. And it was already a deliciously big head to begin with. Indeed, the size of your big old head was one of the factors in your selection. You see, your new body is very large indeed, for a human, and having such a large head helps with the transplant process."

Your new body. Strange thing to hear. It couldn't be real, could it?

"I was always tall," Ram said, feeling the need to stand up for himself, for his old body.

Dr. Fo grinned and pulled out a screen. "You were a fairly impressive 199 centimeters tall, much taller than the Indian and Earth average. You certainly maximized your genetic growth potential. But now, you are 261.26 centimeters tall. In other words, in the top one percent of the tallest people who ever lived, although most of them were gangly weaklings, half crippled by pituitary tumors. You, on the other hand, may have the most muscle mass on a single body in history, even counting Artificial Persons. Although, this body is not natural. We designed it, we grew it, nurtured it so I suppose it's cheating but you are a human from the neck up."

Ram had a wave of unreality flush through him. The sense that the world could not be trusted, that he could log out of his Avar and be back in his apartment if only he could find a way of getting out.

"This is not happening," Ram said, hearing his now-deeper voice rumbling in his chest. A larger chest cavity, a larger throat and a deeper voice.

"I assure you it is," Dr. Fo said, gesturing at the room around them. Ram could see quite a lot with his peripheral vision but a single room could be modeled with perfect realism within Avar. "But if it helps you to feel better in the short term then please, go right ahead and believe that you are in some sort of VR device, while you acclimatize to your new reality and learn why you are here. No skin off my nose."

"Why?" Ram asked. "Who are you people? Where am I? I need to speak to my co-op. I need to speak to my parents, come on, you have to let me out of here, this isn't legal. This isn't legal, you can't do this to me."

He needed to get out, to get away from them.

"Rama Seti," Dr. Fo said, leaning over him. This time, the

man's face was not smiling. Not even a little. "You will find no allies in the judiciary realm. As for your friends and family, well, they believe that you are already dead. We will never let you go. Not ever. Of course, this is a violation of your legal and human rights but our purpose is so vitally important that we left ordinary ethical concerns behind us decades ago. Your rights as an individual are as nothing in comparison to what is at stake here."

"Bullshit. What could possibly be so important?"

"Rama, you are here to save humanity."

CHAPTER THREE
ESCAPE

RAM KNEW TRUE FEAR, then. He was in the lab of some crazed Doctor Frankenstein, cutting people up and sewing them together again because it was for the good of all humanity. Another lunatic who believed the rights of the individual could be dismissed in the name of science or progress or some other crazy shit.

Ram knew, also, what he had to do. He had to stay calm and he had to play along until he had a chance to escape. It might be hours or even days but he would escape and then he would call the police and he would upload his memory into Avar if he could. Show everyone what had happened to him. Then the mad doctor and his team of lunatics would get the justice they deserved for abducting him. For cutting off his body.

It still didn't seem real.

"Now," the doctor said, "let us get you out of my clinic so you can begin to contribute to the mission. I have been working on you for some time and, please don't tell the Director this but I'm keen to get you out of my door. First, we are going to adjust your bed so that you are seated in an upright position."

Dr. Fo turned away. The screen that had displayed Ram's body turned off, folded up and the arm moved up into the ceiling. The gurney bed hummed beneath him and Ram's head started to rise, slowly and steadily, into a sitting position. The higher his head got, the better look he got at the space before him.

The floors, walls and ceiling were huge white ceramic tiles with slight gaps between them. A steel alloy medical workbench around the wall opposite him held neatly arranged implements and wrapped packages. Shelves and cupboards of various sizes lined portions of the wall above.

Four biotechnicians in white coats sat at the bench on stark, uncomfortable stools tap-tapping on screens in front of them or on the wall. Trolleys with stainless steel implements, pre-loaded syringes and trays underneath full of tiny bottles and dressing packets encased in shining sterile wrapping. Medical machines on wheels displaying screens showing internal scans or stylized images of Ram.

Without the ability to move his head, Ram strained his eyes looking left or right for a way out, for anything that he could use as a weapon. His field of vision was limited but he thought one of the wall sections looked as though it might be a doorway. There was a fingerprint and retinal scanner keypad by it.

No one paid Ram any direct attention as his horizontal gurney turned into a semi-vertical, upright chair. All instead engrossed in at least one screen, tapping, whispering, adjusting settings or recording the readings. For some reason, none of them appeared to use internal augmentation, not even eye screens and gesture sensors. It was like stepping back in time to when 2D displays were the height of technological interaction. There was no reason for such a clearly well-equipped medical center to utilize such antiquated tech.

The chair whirred and clunked into a locked position.

Sitting fully upright with his feet near the floor, his head was higher than anyone who was standing. As if he was in a shrunken world, where everyone had been shrunk by a third and he alone was normal sized. But that was wrong. It was he who was the freak in the room.

There didn't seem to be any security guards. If he could get free, he could flatten everyone in the room with ease.

"The subject appears to be having a spike in his testosterone and epinephrine levels," Dr. Fo said and he glanced at someone unseen behind Ram's gurney chair.

"Suggests he is planning violence," the woman's voice said

from behind his chair. "I will pacify him."

A warm sense of relief flooded through Ram, from his neck, over his scalp and settled over his eyes. The sharp edges of the room softened. The white glare lessened.

"Drugs," Ram said after a moment, his tongue thick in his mouth. "You're drugging me."

Even though he was outraged, he had to admit to himself that it felt really good.

Dr. Fo frowned. "We avoid pharmaceutical substances for altering mood where we can, especially at this stage. Milena is adjusting your body's hormone uptake. It's tricky at first and it looks rather as though we are alternating between too much and not enough. Your body is our old model and the control systems are cruder than in our cutting edge subjects. There is also the fact that your mind is entirely untrained. You have little control over your thought patterns. Have you never attempted meditation? We will help you with that, too."

Whatever they were pumping him with, Ram had to admit it was delightful. He'd taken synthetic oxytocin and dopamine before but it was never as strong or as enchanting as whatever they were doing to him right there in the hospital room. Ram was quiet for a while as the people around him worked on his body. He peered down, moving only his eyes, as they prodded the tips of the monstrous fingers and toes. When the first sensations jerked through his body, it was a completely alien feeling.

He tried to remember that he needed to escape, that the people around him were his enemies. But it was hard to retain the thought, it kept slipping away into a warm and fuzzy feeling.

A biotechnician prodded the tip of his index finger and there was a subsequent reaction in his mind. Not one of pain, not the sensation of a needle being jabbed into his finger. It was akin to a blast of cold air, tinged with the color blue. The biotechnicians jabbed more needles all over his hands and arms, releasing a flood of warm, cold, green, red feelings, hisses of static and strange smells he could not identify before they were gone. And the sensations did not seem to be coming from his body but from somewhere else, either further outside himself, as if he could feel someone prodding the far wall, or else deep inside his guts.

"Subject is registering," a biotechnician said.

"Lighting up all across the board," another team member called out.

"Visual, aural but tactile, too. Hits on all digits."

"Excellent," Dr. Fo said, beaming up at him. "Very fast, Ram, very fast indeed."

"What's going on?" Ram said, his vision clouding with tactile sensation.

"We are helping your brain to mesh its new nervous system together," Dr. Fo said, peering down again at a screen in his hands so that all Ram could see was the shining black top of his head. "Your conscious mind needs help to realize what nerves go where as they connect to your brain. Your brain can keep your vital processes running already. Your breathing and heartbeat and so on. But skin sensation? Fine control? These are incredibly complicated processes, Ram. We have done so much work on you already, so much work, yes indeed. Everything is in place and you are almost complete. But we have to be sure that you are not overwhelmed by strange sensations so we block certain signals reaching your moment to moment awareness. And we are now carefully removing that block. Your body and brain are all linked up but your consciousness now needs to catch up. Do you understand?"

"I'm tasting strange colors. You've wired me up wrong," Ram said, a distant fear and outrage bubbling up again.

"A little synesthesia is perfectly normal. In fact, if you weren't experiencing it then I would be worried," Dr. Fo said, chuckling and went back to his work.

"I feel like I shouldn't feel calm," he said, wondering why he was admitting that to these people. "I should be feeling angry at you."

Shut up, you idiot, he told himself. He was babbling like a drunk.

Dr. Fo laughed. "Regulating your hormone uptake stops what would be your ordinary fear and anger getting in the way of our final release protocols and it's just easier for my team if you're dumb and docile."

Ram grinned, pressure on his temples pushing his brain together behind his eyes, like that time he had accidentally overdosed on 2C-B, alone in his apartment. Only, much more pleasant. Sweat broke out all over his face and body. "I feel like I'm tripping."

"Hmm," the doctor said. "Perhaps we are dosing you too much but we tend to err on the side of caution. Without hormonal sedation, your distress at what we're doing to you right now might create lasting psychological damage. Post-traumatic stress can have a significant impact on performance and poor Milena here has a tough enough job to do on your psyche as it is. Not a fully actualized personality, are you, Rama?"

Intellectually, he knew that it was ethically worse to be controlling the workings of his mind than it was to restrain and even to exchange his body for a better model. But the outrage he felt at the endless violation of his rights was distant. Diluted. Hidden behind the waves of pleasure and flooding skin sensations. His arms prickled with a kind of itchy delight. He breathed deeply, smelling the cleaning chemicals and detergents of the walls and the doctors and technicians. Smelling the human sweat and breath of the people.

Smelling the smell of the women in the room.

Ram wondered if the body they had given him had a dick. He could almost feel it but he knew it was only his imagination.

He looked down at himself. As far down as he could look with just his eyes. They had dressed him in a skin-tight gray vest and matching shorts. He thought he could see a bulge down there amongst the bumps and ridges of his huge thigh muscles.

In truth, it was difficult to see past his massive pectorals. It was not so different from the usual difficulty he had seeing his genitalia, only that was because of his great big rolls of flab getting in the way.

Perhaps they had not given him one. If the body was synthetic, grown as biological parts in a womb tank then maybe he didn't have one. The Artificial Persons they grew for space mining and stuff were often non-gendered. Or they were one or other but without working genitals. There were rumors about sex slaves but Ram had never especially believed the stories. Why would anyone bother to spend a fortune on growing someone when there were so many real people willing to sell their bodies cheap and enter contractual slavery? But Ram was afraid to ask. The worry was a distant one and was quickly buried under the continuing low pulses of pleasure flowing across his skin like—

Searing agony shot through his body. His hand plunged into fire.

Ram cried out, screaming at the burning, crisping of the skin on his hand, the bubbling, searing agony of it.

The pain vanished like a light switched off in the darkness.

Ram's cry died in his throat and he was left panting, glancing down as far as he could at his big-boned hands where they rested on the arms of his mechanized chair. They were perfectly unscathed, the technicians prodding them with needles.

"What the hell was that?" His heart was racing, the soft and calm feeling replaced by fear, exhilaration. He couldn't keep up.

I need to escape, he reminded himself. *Bide my time until I can escape.*

"You are responding marvelously, adapting remarkably quickly," Dr. Fo said, grinning. "In the ninety-fifth percentile, at least, I would guess. How curious."

"It's these older models," the unseen woman said from behind Ram's upright gurney, her voice steady, smooth and rich with a Latin timbre. "The nerve pathways are shorter, simpler. And the guerrilla corporectomy compounded the issue by leaving so much of his original ganglia in his birth body."

The woman's tone had been full of clarity and confidence and Ram found it arousing. Even without seeing her, Ram knew instantly that she would be forever out of his league. No one so self-possessed would give Ram the time of day. He wanted to see her, see what she was like. He was certain she would be physically attractive and he wanted her.

"Of course," Dr. Fo said, shaking his head. "You are right, of course. I am so forgetful. Look at his testosterone, Milena, it is shooting up again. I'm not sure what is causing it."

Footsteps on the tiles, light and careful. Ram glanced down.

"Pleasure to meet you, Rama Seti."

It was the confident woman. And she was indeed out of his league. So far out that it was a relief he wouldn't have to worry about playing any games with her. The young woman had a cascade of thick black hair, skin the color of milky coffee, huge dark eyes looking up at him, a huge, straight nose and lips like a goddess. Her body was fit underneath the tight black vest and loose black trousers, shoulders broad and muscular. She wore heavy boots, like a soldier. Her breasts were amazing. He knew he shouldn't stare at them but his vantage point was above her head and he could look right down her top and into her cleavage where her lovely skin went underneath the top of her vest. They looked perfect, smooth and round, dense and heavy and yet high and firm, standing straight up without any support. He could not take his eyes away.

"Hi," Ram said, grinning. "Nice to meet you, sweetheart."

Sweetheart? Why did I say that?

Ram felt what must have been his new penis and scrotum stirring between his legs and under the sheets. Maybe it was actually there after all.

"Testosterone spiking into the red," one of the technicians said. "Vasopressin too. I'll deal with it."

The woman raised her eyebrows at Ram who felt a flush of shame as his lust receded. He looked away.

"Hello, Ram," she said. "I have been with you for some time now, since before you were first woken. I have helped to smooth out your moment-to-moment experience by adjusting your hormone uptake. Before then, I have been getting to know you. Studying your genes, your history, your environment, your achievements and failures, your hopes and your shame. And I feel that I do know you because I have seen you at your best and at your worst and your most mundane. So you need not feel any sense of embarrassment with me. My name is Milena Reis. It is enormously satisfying to finally speak to you face to face."

Ram did not know what to say. What did she mean she'd seen him at his worst?

"It's satisfying?" Ram said. "To meet me?"

Ram wished he could move so that he could kick himself up the ass for being so catastrophically whatever the opposite of suave was.

Her mouth twisted into a wry smile. "You do not know how much is depending on this project. How much we have already invested in you. I have personally invested hundreds of hours in studying you, Rama Seti. Satisfying is putting how I feel about meeting you in the mildest possible terms."

"I still don't understand this, I'm sorry. Who are you? Like, what's your job? You're my hormone pimp?"

"I'm your driver," Milena said, nodding slowly.

"Oh," Rama said, recalling what the word meant when it was applied to a person and not software. "Okay. Where are you driving me?"

"A very long way from here," Milena said, a strange, half-amused look on her face. "But I am not that sort of driver."

Milena moved to the side of Rama's huge chair and tapped away against the side of it, out of his sight. The chair beneath him hummed into life and the thing rotated, turned ninety degrees. Ram got a view of the room and the people in it as it turned. Men, women, nurses, technicians, all busy working on screens and whirring machines. Still no security guards, as far as he could see. Hopefully, he was in a normal hospital or clinic and he could force his way out onto the street in no time. Just as soon as they gave him the ability to move.

"Are you going to let me go now, right?" Ram said. "Let me get up out of this chair, I mean?"

Milena and Doctor Fo walked around so that they both stayed in Ram's field of vision.

"Do you want to escape?" the gorgeous woman asked, tilting her head to one side.

Ram's heart raced. He knew they were monitoring his every breath so he tried to relax. "No," he said, feigning casualness.

Milena and the doctor glanced at each other but did not bother to address Ram's obvious lie.

"We have kept you immobilized until now because of the danger that you pose to yourself, to that body and to the valuable people and equipment in this room. If you lose control and destroy it, that would mean an awful lot of people's hard work has been wasted. So you must learn control, first of all. Then you may walk, run, jump, exercise, train. And then, finally, you may begin to fight."

"Fight?" Rama said, trying to stay calm. They were going to let him out soon but only if he pretended he was playing along, only if he proved that he was no threat.

Dr. Fo turned away, calling out congratulations and thanks to his team for their work.

"Come with me," Milena said. Under its own power, the gurney-chair rolled away from the center of the room to a corner that was free of machines or screens, taking Ram with it. He had never felt so helpless in his entire life. They could do anything to him and yet he could do nothing in return. When he got free, he was going to end them, one way or another. Whoever they were. "You were a fan of gladiatorial, person versus person Avar gaming, were you not?" Milena said.

"I was kind of into fighting games but not really. How is that relevant?" Ram asked, his chair rolling after her, the rubber tires screeching softly to a stop on the tiled flooring. He wondered if she had the ability to read his mind. Could she see that he was planning violence? He knew that it was possible to extract specific memories and knowledge but he didn't know if it was possible in real time. If she could read his mind then she might be watching him think the thoughts that he was thinking in that moment.

How could he hide his thoughts from himself? Don't think about escaping, he thought.

"I look forward to seeing your Avar abilities, that's all," she said. "We will now activate your body but before we start, you must know one thing."

"Okay," Ram said, trying to not think about climbing out of his chair and charging for the closed door.

"You must know that if you take any action that threatens anyone in this room or if you are in danger of harming yourself, we will switch you off. Dr. Fo can push one button that will remotely drop you in a nanosecond. Your skeletal muscles will immediately cease to function and you will collapse to the floor, unable to move even a little bit. Understand?"

Ram swallowed, his throat dry. "I get it."

He wondered if his hope for escape was truly gone. Was she bluffing? He didn't think she was.

"Good. Now, your brain has never consciously used your skeletal muscles," Milena said. "The relevant areas of that brain have been stimulated artificially while your corresponding muscles are simultaneously contracted. It is a crude method but we find it effective. But there's an error rate, Rama and it varies from subject to subject. Might be five per cent, might be fifty per cent but you could find your brain and your body has been wired improperly. Dr. Fo and his team might have been probing what they thought was your right biceps part but instead, they were tweaking your triceps. It's common for subjects on their first time in control to intend to bend their arm only to straighten it. I told a young subject once to clap her hands together and she punched herself in the nose. I'm not kidding. And it could be worse. What if they've aimed for your gluteus maximus but had a near miss? One subject a few years ago, when he tried to complete a standing jump he instead shit his pants. I'm not kidding. So, are you ready?"

"Ready for what?"

"Here we go," Milena said, unfolding a screen from her

pocket. She tapped on it, expertly, as if she was used to 2D physical interfaces. "Try standing. Get out of that chair."

Ram forced his hands down to the arms of his chair. With his eyes fixed on the keypad by the closed door on the far side of the room, he planted his feet on the floor and heaved himself upright.

Milena leaped back out of the way and Ram tipped forward onto his face. His arms did not respond properly and instead of bracing his fall they just tangled beneath his massive chest and his face smashed into the tiles with a crack. Breathing heavily, Ram rolled his head to the side and looked up. He didn't have the guts to try to move his body.

Milena roared with laughter and jabbed Ram's shoulder with her foot.

"You did it," Milena shouted. "I can't remember the last time someone did it their first time. Maybe never. Well, well." She jiggled Ram's shoulder again. "Did you see that, Dr. Fo?"

"Very impressive," Dr. Fo said from across the room. A few people clapped.

"Get to your feet, Ram," Milena said. "Come on, get up, I believe in you."

If I can get up, I can get out of here.

Ram pulled his hands under himself and took a breath. His arms were huge, the muscles so big they restricted how far he could bend them. He planted his meaty hands on the cold ceramic tile underneath his massive pectorals. He bent his knees up under himself and felt his toes grip the smooth floor.

He stood up, staggering and crashed into the side of his chair. He reeled off from it, staggering across the room with no control and banged into the wall. His face pressed against the cool white tile, breathing heavily.

"Whoa, there, whoa," Milena said, laughing. "That's some fine work there. You just have to watch out for that slight Coriolis effect, that's all. Try standing away from the wall."

Ram held himself away from it, stepping away, raising his arms for balance. His head spun and he wobbled but he kept his feet.

"I'm doing it," Ram said, excited.

"It's these older models," Dr. Fo called out. "They don't make them like this anymore."

"It's not the model," Milena said. "Ram has an iron will, don't you, Ram."

"I guess," Ram said, realizing that he had to learn to control his body before he made a run for it.

So, when Milena took Ram through exercise after exercise, he played along. Touching his fingers to his thumbs, flexing his knees, swinging his arms. Jumping, twirling, spinning. Ram hit his head a dozen times, bashing his elbows and knees. But each time he performed his tasks a little better than the last and he knew that he would soon be able to make his body do what he needed it to. He would have to find his way out of the medical facility and out into the real world. He wondered if he was still in Delhi or somewhere else in India. He could be anywhere on the continent, he supposed. A worrying thought but he would cross that bridge when he came to it. If he escaped and found himself in another country, he would have to find the Indian Consulate and then they would help him.

If they believed him. He was in a giant body, 261 centimeters tall. That was eight feet and five inches tall and with the sort of muscles that only existed on professional bodybuilders and strongmen.

A small part of him, he admitted, was thrilled.

"Where did this body come from?" he asked Milena after an hour or so.

She looked uncomfortable and Dr. Fo called out an answer. "Synthetically grown, obviously. Same way they grow organs and limbs for repair. Grown in tanks as arms and legs and organs and then assembled like a kit. Finally, when all is ready, the human heads are sewn on top."

Ram had a thousand objections and questions but he fought down his anger and played along, feeling the control coming. He might only get a single escape attempt and he had to get it right.

"It's just like practicing in Avar," Ram said at one point after performing twenty controlled pushups. "Repetition until you get it right."

That amused Dr. Fo, standing beside Milena to watch Ram while his team cleaned and cleared the clinic room behind him.

"Did it ever occur to you that Avar is based on real life and not the other way around?" Dr. Fo said. "You practice something, you get better at it, whether it's punching a guy in the face or scratching your balls just right. Avar is an incomplete simulacrum of reality. This is the real world young man and Avar is just a poor copy."

Before Ram could respond, Milena cut in.

"Learning is part of the animal experience that we call consciousness. It doesn't matter where our attention is focused, whether in the physical world or the virtual reality of Avar or in mindfulness."

"Very interesting," Dr. Fo said, with a straight face.

Ram decided that what he would have to do is charge Dr. Fo first of all and take him out. Just charge him down, flatten him. He was short, slight, he looked like he would have weak bones and Ram was sure he would be able to cross the four meters to the doctor in a couple of strides, hopefully before the little fellow would have a chance to trigger the mechanism for disabling Ram. If that mechanism even existed. And then Ram would grab the woman Milena as a hostage, force her to open the security door for him. Force her to open all the doors. Maybe force her to help him when they got to the street, summon a taxi for him using her ID and so on.

"We have enough readings now," Dr. Fo said. "Everything is working as it should be. Better, actually. So I officially confirm Ram's graduation into full mission subject. You poor bastard."

"Why do you say that?" Ram said, standing and looking down

on Dr. Fo and Milena, the top of his head near to the ceiling. It was amazing how tall he was.

Before Dr. Fo could respond, Milena cut in "It is just the doctor's terrible sense of humor," she said.

"That's true," Dr. Fo said, sadly, peering at the screen in his hands while he spoke. "Lost my marbles from the horror of all this. Plus all the radiation, of course. Crazy to be out here again, cooking my noodle in a gamma ray soup. Just goddamned crazy."

"Radiation?" Ram said. "What does radiation have to do with anything?"

Milena stepped forward, cutting off the doctor again. "It is time you are taken to Disclosure."

"Disclosure?" Ram said. "About what?"

He had to charge now, quickly. He looked down at the doctor, willing himself to flatten the old bastard.

"Don't even think about it," the doctor said, looking him square in the eye and speaking calmly. "We can read your neurotransmitters and hormones like a book, Rama. Like a transparent book, I might add."

Ram hesitated.

"You wouldn't get far," Milena said. "It's not just the doctor with a paralysis button. There are cameras watching your every move. Even then, we have Marines here who would stop you well before you could do any real damage."

"I wasn't going to do anything," Ram said, looking between them. "I wasn't, honestly."

They ignored him.

Dr. Fo placed a hand on Milena's lovely shoulder. "Look after him, my dear."

"Of course," she said. "Better than anyone."

The doctor looked up at Ram. "I fear I shall see you in here again rather soon. Nevertheless, I wish you the very best of luck."

Ram just stared at him, frozen by the insanity of it all. He still wasn't sure that he was truly awake. If he had to guess, he'd say he was experiencing a locked-in Avar Psychosis.

Whatever the truth, he sensed that he had lost the initiative and in his heart, he doubted whether he ever would have been able to crush a kindly doctor anyway. Even if the mad old bastard had cut off his body.

"Rama Seti," Milena commanded as she strode for the door. "Follow me if you want to find out why you are really here."

CHAPTER FOUR
MISSION ONE

I HAVE FULL CONTROL of a powerful new body, Ram thought as he stepped into the corridor. He decided to bide his time and wait for an opportunity to escape to present itself. They might be bluffing about the knock-out switch and the Marines.

Anyway, he really wanted to find out why he was there at all.

The door slid shut with a slight hiss and a soft pop as the air sealed in place. A stenciled design on the door said B3 RECOVERY SUITE 1.

"Come on," Milena said and headed down the corridor.

Walking just a few steps required a level of concentration that gave him a steady ache in the temples. His new body might not have been ready for violence after all. The glare from the white ceramic tiles on the floor, ceiling and walls did not help his mental state. Diffused green light came through latticed aircon illumination strips between the tiles low down and a bluish-white light filtered through higher up on the wall and ceiling. A lame yet effective attempt to make indoor spaces mimic natural daylight that featured in municipal and government buildings.

And yet he was walking. Moving under his own power, in a giant, powerful body. A body like an Avar avatar. The fact of it felt pretty great. He wished he could see himself in his skin-tight gray shorts and vest. On his feet, he wore these little, flexible gray shoes that gripped the tiles remarkably well. They were like rock climbers' shoes, he thought and wondered how long they would last if he had to make his escape through a desert environment or in a jungle.

"Are you really going to give me answers now?" Ram said, the top of his head a few centimeters from the ceiling.

"The truth, yes," Milena said, stopping at another door that said B3 CONSULTATION ROOM 4. It slid up, revealing a small room. Before she went in, she squinted up at him. "How are you feeling right now?"

"Fine," Ram said, trying not to think of escaping.

"I'm going to increase your dopamine uptake a little," she said, tapping on her screen. "It will make you more docile."

"No, don't," Ram said, anger flaring. "Honestly, I'm fine." A wave of contentment overcame him and he sighed, losing his train of thought.

"Come on," she said and he followed her into the room, ducking beneath the top of the doorway to peer inside.

A scrawny young man sat at a desk beneath a large, blank screen up on the wall. Milena walked in and took a seat. Ram stepped through the door, bending at the waist and holding onto the frame so that he did not fall over. The door slid closed behind him and Ram stood in the doorway.

"Rama," the scrawny man said, turning about in his chair. "My name's Diego. I'm part of the UNOP Mission Four Intel Team and I am your designated information liaison officer. Right now, my job will be to brief you on what you need to know about Mission Four and the Orb Arena Project. I'm the context provider, okay? So for now, my man, take it easy. Sit back, relax, watch this movie."

"Sit here," Milena said, pushing a mechanical button on the wall and a shelf-like seat slid out, big enough for his ass to perch on with room left over. Ram sat his vast bulk against it and held on. He did not trust his control over his body, yet.

Ram looked down at the man called Diego, trying to be casual about his examination. He was gaunt, quite small and Ram thought he could probably take the guy as a hostage with more ease than he could the woman called Milena. Maybe it was his cultural prejudice that made him hesitate to harm a woman but it was more the fact that she seemed like a fighter. He bet that if he grabbed her she would gouge his eyes out or yank a chemical spray out from her pants or something and mess him up. She had the lean musculature of someone well used to physical fitness. Trying to hold on to her lean body while she raged would be difficult.

The information liaison officer, though, looked like a little nerd. And Rama felt comfortable with little nerds. He knew enough of them in Avar to know that they were mostly physical cowards. Yeah, he thought he should probably take the little African guy as his hostage.

Just as soon as he got some answers.

The black screen up on the wall that Diego and Milena were staring at was not actually blank. The white specks were stars. A single star right in the center grew larger and larger until it resolved itself into a small white disk. The other two in the room with him were staring at it without speaking, as if it was somehow fascinating. Their silence was almost reverential. It kept growing, starting to fill the screen.

"What is that?" Rama asked, leaning forward. "Is it flat or is it three-dimensional? There's no way to assess the scale."

Diego grinned over his shoulder. "This thing is four thousand meters in diameter. Your file said you prefer Imperial measurements. That's like two and a half miles. Are you American? We have a few Americans here."

"I'm not American," Ram said, still looking at the thing on the screen. "I understand Imperial measurements because my idiot father is a Rajist. He thinks India was only great under

British rule three-hundred years ago and they want to take things back to that. You'd think an engineer would know better. This is four kilometers in diameter, so an asteroid? A small moon, maybe?"

Diego laughed and pointed at the screen. "This thing, man, ain't nothing natural. Watch this."

He tapped a pad on his desk and the image grew again, gradually. The resolution slowly improved.

"These images were taken from our first probe, the Hanno Mission, back in 2055," Diego said. "See, the Orb was discovered out beyond the orbit of Neptune. And in case you don't know, that's a long way. That old probe was ninety-nine percent propulsion system by mass. The rest of it was imagining, sensing and transmission equipment. You see, we don't know how long it was out there because it's not in orbit around the Sun, as such. It is holding position, relative to the Sun and the thing can change its outer hull from completely black, which is its normal state, all the way to a mirror shine like you see in these images here. We only saw it when the Orb began signaling us. It's not just able to change the surface reflectivity but actually to emit radiation in the visual and other wavelengths, flashing out coded signals for years. It was saying that it was artificial and we thought it was telling us to come visit. When the probe arrived, the images we resolved were astonishing. As you can see, it is a perfect sphere. Faster than our frame rates can catch, anyway. And it can emit tight bands of radiation in the visual spectrum, blue to red light and into ultraviolet and infrared. When the probe arrived they were expecting a hatch to open on the Orb and for little gray men to wave the probe onboard."

"Wait a second," Rama said, looking between Diego, Milena and the screen on the wall. "This is insane. I know all about this. I've seen conspiracy theory shows about this, read about it. The Alien Space Station conspiracy theory. Yeah, out at the edge of the Solar System. I've seen movies about this, I've even played an Avar on that thing, there was this deathmatch horror hybrid set on an alien space station orbiting Pluto. Some of my team were convinced it was a real thing, they'd send me blurry pictures and recordings of people saying they'd seen the aliens that built it, there's all this hacked data. Whole communities in Avar constantly talk about this. And you're trying to tell me that all that bullshit, all that alien conspiracy theory stuff, it's all real?"

Diego shrugged. "A lot of that theory is speculation, extrapolation based on incomplete data and ends up pretty much wildly incorrect. But sure people know about it. You know, this Project has been a worldwide effort for decades, over a hundred years since the Orb was discovered. Tens of thousands of people, at least, have had Full Disclosure over that time. Hundreds of thousands have worked on the project directly and millions have worked on it indirectly. Billions, probably, when you think about it, how our global, system-wide goal has been increasingly focused on the Orb Project. The Project is managed under the United Nations. In fact, you might say that the United Nations has only made it through the last century because of the Orb Project. The United Nations as an organization exists now almost entirely in order to run the Orb Project."

Rama ran one of his massive, synthetically grown hands over his bony face. "Billions of people have worked on this? I don't understand, how can that be possible? You guys are lying to me, right?"

"Thousands of companies have been contracted to supply goods and services over hundreds of years. Engineers have designed components for equipment, weapons, ships. Our explosion of human exploration of the solar system and everything that supports those efforts has been driven by the Orb Project. There's no way to keep something of this magnitude quiet. Today, millions of people, like your friends, are totally convinced the Orb exists. And it's an easy thing to believe, I mean, there are authentic images of it. Imaging from the observatories on Mars and the Moon. Private space telescope images, radio telescope recordings of the communications. Testimonials from people that worked on the project that you've seen. We've had elected officials and even heads of state talk publicly about it over the last hundred years and that's probably some of the stuff your buddies sent you."

"I can't believe this. How can it possibly be so ridiculed? I mean, I never really looked into it much, I just figured it was another one of those things like the scare stories about Avar or AI or Artificial Persons. Why doesn't everyone know about it, why isn't it openly admitted to, it doesn't make sense."

"You're right. Most governments and corporations have standing policies to deny it or they just keep quiet about it and so most normal people, like yourself, assume it's the crazy UFO nutjobs playing make believe again."

"UFOs are real too?"

"No," Diego said, chuckling. "Come on, man, no way. Look, the Hanno Probe arrived in orbit around the Orb in 2055 and we broadcast welcome messages to it. We broadcast stuff like we come in peace, we are earthlings. We showed them images of life on earth. Crazy, right? Even though they had absolutely no reason to think it, they were convinced the aliens would be peaceful." Diego laughed. "They were so naïve back then it's painful. But the idiots had their preconceptions confirmed. Because then the Orb replied. In English."

Ram looked at Milena then back to Diego. "Come on."

Diego grinned. "Seriously. It learned enough of our languages from our broadcasts and presumably already had decades of TV, radio, communications traffic to learn our languages."

"What did it sound like?" Ram said. "Can I hear it?"

"Oh, it didn't use sound, it used our own optical communications transmission frequencies to beam encoded messages back to us in the same digitally encoded format as we were sending to each other through the Deep Space Optical Communications Network. They thought the probe was malfunctioning until they realized what was going on. What it was saying."

"And?"

"It said." Diego paused for dramatic effect. "Send. Humans."

"It did not say that," Ram said, all thought of escape gone for the moment. All he wanted was to find out more, find out everything about this.

Diego chuckled. "The guys running the project back then just about shit themselves inside out."

"I can imagine," Ram said. He turned to Milena. "Did that Orb really say that?"

Milena nodded. "It has broadcast a lot more to us since."

"Woah, let's not get ahead of ourselves," Diego said, scowling at her before continued his story. "That was when they decided to launch Mission Zero. I mean, we only started calling it that later but it was the first manned mission to the Orb. Even before the probe proved beyond doubt what they were dealing with, our predecessors were already building engines, ship hulls and reactors like crazy. There were militaries involved back then, even before we found out what it was all about, and they were preparing for an invasion. Ships were being constructed in orbit before the probe had crossed Jupiter's orbit. As soon as the proof came through then the first ship was constructed specifically to carry a crew out there. Those guys on Mission Zero accepted it could be a one-way trip but they were willing to sacrifice themselves for the good of the species. A bunch of heroes, just like us."

"In fact," Milena said, cutting in. "The Mission Zero crew had a number of stated reasons. Duty, adventure. Most of the crew went in order to meet an alien lifeform in person. They wanted to be the first and they wanted to be remembered for all of human history. And they just wanted to meet an alien."

"Yeah," Rama said, imagining it. "Sounds amazing."

"Something went wrong," Diego said. "Still never totally clear what but there was a malfunction and an explosion that wrecked the ship, including the comms equipment. The crew was killed before they got near the Orb. The human crew that is. In order to minimize risk, there was a complement of Artificial Persons. No one knows how but those Artificial Persons completed the mission. They performed the deceleration maneuver and the orbital insertion. Incredible, really. The story of it got out and helped to accelerate the whole pro-human, anthropocentric crazies and the pro-Artificial Person terrorists. They were supposed to be incapable of so much as scratching their asses without precise instructions but the Artificial Persons actually repaired the comms and docked their shuttle with the Orb before their biological clocks gave up. And then the Orb beamed a message to the Zero ship. It said you passed the test. Now come back in thirty years. Come back in thirty years with your chosen representative and if they are worthy, you will receive great gifts of knowledge."

"Holy shit, great gifts of knowledge from an alien race?" Ram sighed. "What about the aliens, did the Artificial Persons meet them?"

Diego shook his head. "The Orb was apparently unoccupied at that time. But we had made it there, that was the main thing."

"But... what the hell? After we sent a manned mission beyond Neptune the aliens just told us to send someone else?"

Diego grinned. "These were all tests, man. Every step, every stage. What's thirty years to an all-powerful alien race? Maybe they live for thousands of years, I mean, they probably do, right? These tests the Orb was putting us through? It was to see if our civilization was capable of making the trip first of all. And when we could, I guess we triggered the start of the Arena System for humanity."

"Why thirty years?"

"This is the cycle. It is not exactly thirty years. It's ten thousand seven-hundred and fifty days. Our predecessors spent a long time translating what it was beaming at us through the ship's systems. The language and the coding used by the Orb were far from perfect, okay, it was using our systems but finding common meaning in language is difficult even for the Orb Builders. So our guys back then in 2079, they had to decode what it was telling us. And of course, it was our own cultural assumptions that led to our first great error."

"Show him," Milena said, sighing. "Just show him."

Diego pulled up video of a dignified young gentleman with neat gray hair, dressed in a dark suit and crisp white shirt and tie standing in a wood paneled room with Earth sunlight streaming in through huge windows on one side. He faced the camera, addressing an unseen audience but there was no sound on the video. There were men and women behind him in military dress uniforms.

"Okay, so, you can imagine the meetings," Diego said, spreading his hands and settling back into his seat. "The Orb told us to return with our chosen representative and maybe get this great gift of knowledge. Almost certainly the most significant opportunity in our history, right? So who, out of all of humanity, should be chosen to represent us? You see, the Orb instructed that in ten thousand days we send the very best of us. Well, how do we decide on the criteria for selecting who is the best of us? What is it about humanity that we want to show off? Presumably, we needed someone strong, decisive and yet empathic and compassionate. Communication skills were absolutely top priority. The scientists in the early Project pushed real hard for it to be a scientist. Someone who would be able to converse fluently in the language of the universe. You know, mathematics." Diego snorted. "They wanted someone who could talk about the molecular weights of elements as if they were ordering in a Chinese restaurant. But the scientists were drowned out by the corporate leaders who demanded they choose. After all, they paid for half of it, right? The politicians pulled rank on everyone as they had the tax dollars of billions of people plus the licenses to print money."

"For the love of God, leave off with your political nonsense,"

Milena said. "Get on with it."

Diego laughed. "Alright, so, months of arguing, horse trading and everything but everyone could compromise on the fact that it was a diplomatic mission. So, pick a diplomat. But what world-bestriding ambassador or negotiator would be willing to, effectively, give up the rest of his life in return for this great honor? Well, lots of them were on the table but this was the one they chose." Diego leaned forward and tapped the image of the man on it.

"Who is he?" Ram asked.

"Malcolm Diaz. American. Incredibly accomplished, started out a political scientist, came up with a revolutionary approach in Cooperation Theory pretty much right before he started employing it on the world stage. U.S. Ambassador to Indonesia during some rebellion, then at the U.N. negotiating a peace treaty in the Balkans. I don't even know all that he did but the Project decided this is the guy we want representing humanity. I've seen footage of this guy destroying his opponents in debates, on all kinds of topics. He could work a crowd but he always made the argument about more than winning the debate. He would destroy the opponent, entertain the audience and also inform everyone listening, make you see the whole topic through fresh eyes. The guy was a legend by the time he was thirty. And, in a tragic but suspiciously handy turn of fate, his wife and daughter had died in a helicopter crash outside Geneva. Bit of a coincidence, right?"

57

"They didn't kill his family just so he would take the job," Milena said.

"Oh no?" Diego said, raising his eyebrows. "You think we abandoned ethics after Diaz not before? Maybe you're right. Either way, he had no family to leave behind so Diaz was perfect. And why was he perfect again? Well, there's no diplomatic situation he can't talk his way through. He's the greatest communicator on Earth, okay?"

"You're building up to something," Ram said. "I can tell."

Diego moved the footage on and it showed the diplomat Malcolm Diaz with a large group of uniformed men and women walking through a dark corridor, lit by the cameras and other bobbing torches the people carried.

"That's Diaz and the Mission One crew boarding the Orb," Milena said.

"He had a tough trip," Ram said.

"It took nineteen years back then," Milena said. "Mission One left Earth orbit in 2090. They arrived at the Orb in 2109. It was rough on all of them."

"They're walking normally," Ram pointed out. "It's not microgravity on the Orb."

"The gravity there is approximately 0.9G," Diego said. "We spin our ships at two revs per minute or so to replicate that force but the Orb doesn't spin and we don't know how it creates the effect. Considering what else it's capable of, that doesn't seem like so much of a big deal."

The camera feed was cut from many on the heads of the crew members. The corridors were silvered but dark, like black glass. It was difficult to make out what was being shown on the screen. The lights from the crew illuminated the backs of the heads but not much beyond. They bobbed as they walked through the corridors inside the Orb. They appeared to enter a square chamber of some kind. One wall was semi-transparent.

The heads stopped moving and the crew busied themselves setting up equipment, talking in hushed tones about what the aliens would be like and how they would communicate.

The talking stopped as a single chime sounded on the Orb. The crew looked up.

Ram held his breath.

"Let's just skip through this bit," Diego said, clearing his throat and sighing, wafting a hand as he spoke. "The Orb chimes three times to let you know it's time. That wall fades and turns into a door. There's a Zeta Line test where the Orb stops anyone going through the smokescreen with a weapon. We'll get to all that stuff later."

Even the Intel Officer seemed tense and he was watching events from ninety years ago that he had seen before. Diego clicked through the footage until the aged Malcolm Diaz stood alone in a vast chamber.

Above, the ceiling arched over in a dome shape. It was like a half a bowl. Other than Diaz, it was empty. The light came from everywhere, diffused and evenly lit.

From the viewpoint of the camera, filming behind Diaz, Ram could only just make out the far side of that chamber.

"Why's it so blurry?" Ram whispered.

"There's a force field," Diego said. "The section of wall between Diaz and the crew? It's a plasma of some sort, we call it the smokescreen but we don't know what it is really. A window that can't be broken by anyone inside or out."

"It's empty other than Diaz," Ram said. "Where are the aliens? They didn't say hello when the crew boarded the Orb?"

Diego pointed at the screen just as the crewmembers on it noticed something.

A shape. A smear of color on the far side. It was hundreds of meters away from the camera but it was moving. Pale, yellow, on the dark background.

"An alien," Ram said.

Milena nodded. "Our enemy."

CHAPTER FIVE
ANSWERS

RAM DECIDED THAT HE WOULD find out everything that these people had to tell him, he would let it play out. If they were trolling him then it was the most involved, sophisticated scam he'd ever heard of. Either way, he wanted to see what happened to the ambassador on the screen. Then he would take action.

"I suppose that is my cue," Diaz said in the replay, half turning to the camera behind him. "Well, Captain Andrews, thank you and your crew for delivering me here. I only hope I can do my job as well as you all did yours."

The captain gave a little laugh over the comms. "It has been the greatest honor of my life bringing you here, sir. Tell them howdy from us."

The crew members laughed and Diaz squared his shoulders and strolled out farther into the vast space.

He had a long way to walk into the middle. Ram wanted to know how far it was but he did not want to break the spell by speaking. Even though the footage was a hundred years old, he felt almost as though he was there. Why had the people in charge of these events hidden such a profoundly important moment in human history? It was outrageous. Telling humanity what was out there in the galaxy, at the edges of their own system, in fact, might have stimulated millions or billions of people to be more engaged in the world. So many people had taken refuge in the shared dreamspace of Avar where you could live out any fantasy you wanted but if they knew what was out there, they might be doing great things in the real world instead. Ram might have become an engineer, like his father, if he'd known he could be building giant spaceships for meeting with aliens.

The crewmembers mounted larger cameras while Diaz walked toward the alien and the edited feed jumped up in quality. The cameras were trained on the growing yellow shape and they zoomed in.

"That's incredible," the Mission One crew said to each other as the image resolved on screen.

"There it is," an awed voice muttered.

"What is it?" another voice said before someone else hushed them into silence.

Zooming in past Diaz to the far side, an image resolved itself.

It was a circle. A wheel, rather. The shape of the alien was that of a thick, squat wheel with six spokes. Two long arms stuck out from the hub at the center perpendicular to the legs. A three-clawed hand flexed at the end of each arm.

It rolled toward Diaz. Lumbering.

"Six legs, you see?" Diego said, his voice tightly controlled. "Each leg ends in a large, flat, prehensile pad. The pads fit together almost without a gap between them to form the rim of the wheel shape."

Diaz got closer, smaller and smaller and the alien got larger. The perspective seemed wrong.

"How," Ram started. "How big is it?"

"Two point eight meters in diameter," Diego said.

"It must be twice as tall as Diaz," Ram said. He knew that 2.8 meters was over 9 feet.

Milena nodded.

Diego said nothing.

Out in the middle of that vast alien dome, Diaz drew to a stop.

The alien kept coming.

The two arms rolled over and over, sticking out from the central hub. Huge, long, knobbled arms ending in three-pronged hands. They stuck out to both sides, rolling over and over, with the legs and central hub closing in on Diaz.

"Greetings," Diaz intoned, his powerful voice picked up

clearly on his internal microphone. "I am Ambassador Malcolm Diaz and I am here representing humanity, which is my species and for my planet, which is called Earth, and all the lifeforms that we share it with."

The alien did not stop.

Ram found that he was chewing the nails of his new hands and he yanked his finger out of his mouth. He literally did not know where that finger had been.

On the screen, the alien did not slow down. Diaz' mic picked up the soft thump-thump-thump of the alien's feet on the black tiles getting louder as it cartwheeled toward him. The size of the thing was undeniable, now, bearing down on Earth's ambassador, a monster twice his height, many times his weight, with the long arms twirling and the hub seemingly without eyes, without a mouth or any features at all other than lumpen sockets where the limbs met the hub.

Diaz tensed. Took a step back, then another.

"What is it-" Ram started.

The alien accelerated the final few meters, charging Diaz. Faster than seemed possible.

Diaz seemed fit for an old guy but the ambassador barely had time to flinch and turn half back to the way he'd come before the yellow alien was on him. It leaned to one side, pivoting just as it reached the human.

One of the long arms slammed into Diaz, smashing straight down into his head and chest with incredible force.

The blow was fast, powerful and it happened so fast it was hard to make out. Diaz snapped in half at the spine even before his legs buckled. The man's chest exploded with the impact. Bright blood sprayed through the air in an arcing mist of red. His head was just gone.

The alien spun, turned, rolled back and smacked into the body again. It leaned over and slammed and slapped Diaz's remains against the floor a little while longer, gathering smashed parts to break further into pieces. Diaz' body was obliterated further with every blow. Shredded strips of Diaz' clothes hung sodden with chunks of flesh as the blood-splattered creature flailed into the gore, flinging it everywhere.

After a few moments, the blood spattered alien turned and rolled back the way it had come. Its footpads slapping wetly into the tiles as it went. Ram could just about see it left a trail of blood, a chain of oval footprints of shining red.

The crew members were screaming, in shock, in terror, in rage. The captain shouted at them to be quiet and gave the order to arm themselves with weapons from the armory.

Diego cut the footage.

"What happened then?" Ram said, letting out the breath he'd been holding. His new hands had been grasping the edge of the seat beneath him as if his life depended on it. "Did they attack the alien?"

"It was pointless," Diego said. "They would never have made it through the smokescreen with weapons, the Orb don't allow that, only organic material plus a little bit of tech, the extent of which we call the Zeta Line. Anyway, after the alien rolled away, the Orb did that three pips thing again, the three chimes? The smokescreen opened, the crew went in, some of the crazy ones looking for a fight. But the alien was gone, the arena was empty. They scooped up as much as they could of poor old Malcolm Diaz and then the Orb directed them back to their shuttle. It opened up the shuttle bay, they went back to their vessel and the ship was free to leave."

"What the fuck," Ram said, remembering to breathe. "What was that? The aliens just let them go? What the hell was the point of all that?"

Diego nodded, pursing his lips. "The Orb seemed satisfied with how everything had played out. Like you, our guys thought they'd been attacked, ambushed, that they'd been tricked and that war had been declared on us. But the Orb didn't seem concerned. It said to come back in thirty years and try again. It said that the other alien had won its gifts and next time we could win some of our own. I'm paraphrasing. The communication between our people and the Orb has always required varying amounts of computation before we could get close to what it was actually telling us. Although we're all learning. It and us, so that our AIs can translate almost right away with what we think is over ninety percent accuracy. But back then, as the ship headed home, the Orb began broadcasting more detail than we ever had before. Spilling the beans about the galactic civilization that it represents."

"An intelligent alien civilization?" Rama said, head reeling. "Those yellow cartwheel monsters?"

Diego shook his head. "No. Here's the thing you have to understand. The Orb was not built by the Wheelhunters."

"There's two alien civilizations?"

"What we didn't show you just now was telescopic images of the Wheelhunter starship arriving at the Orb two days or so after Mission One went into orbit around it. There was some kind of electromagnetic and gravitational disturbance tens of thousands of kilometers from the Orb, and then they picked up radiation emissions and the Mission One ship telescopes picked it up."

The screen flicked on, showing a dot that grew, in time-accelerated footage, to show a large ship in space.

The design was not one he'd seen before but it was recognizably a spaceship. Longer than it was wide, with engines at the rear but flatter than a human ship. It was more like some monstrous, chunky airplane design. It looked awesome, Ram thought.

"The creature that killed Diaz was the representative of an alien species that the Orb had invited, just as it had invited us. Only, the Wheelhunters come from another star system and the Orb brought them to ours."

"It was a competition," Ram said. "Right? Us and them, the yellow guys." He paused. "What does it mean? *Wheelhunters*? What do they hunt?"

"Us," Diego said. "In the arena. But it's not an official designation. First off, they called it XB-001, which is kind of cool but pretty boring. And the UNOP biologists argued about the name, what taxonomy they should use for it. Some people said it could be included in a new domain or kingdom but others went insane over the suggestion. You think Marines and martial artists are crazy, you should see biologists fighting. Anyway, while they were screaming at each other that it was *xenopoda rotaeflava* or Orb Station Zero Xenobiological Species 001, someone in the Project started calling them Wheelhunters, or just Wheelers and the name seems to have stuck."

"So the Orb Station is not built by the yellow aliens, the Wheelhunters," Ram said. "So, why are they there? Did they take it over? Or is it some sort of symbiotic relationship between the two of them?"

"Not bad guesses. But it's not just two species we're ultimately dealing with here, Rama. There are many intelligent species in our galaxy creating a vast interconnected network of civilizations. A true galactic civilization. They are all in contact with each other through the Orbs. And we were being invited to join that galactic network. The strange thing was that they had this specific method of interaction. We didn't understand it at first. It made no sense to us, a hundred years ago, our global culture back then had become obsessed with deemphasizing warfare as a means for resolving disagreements."

"What is it really, then?"

"Imagine this galactic culture which is made up of these alien species that have evolved on worlds separated by lightyears and by millennia. They must have wildly different physiologies, totally unique cultures, languages. And yet they managed to survive alongside one another. At least, they had a way of formalizing their differences. Of giving them an outlet, a safety valve. The way they keep the peace, out there across the galaxy, is to hold ritualized but deadly combat between individuals from each of the races. And we don't yet know who the Orb Builders are because they haven't shown themselves yet but what it has told us is that the Orbs facilitate everything. They are the nexus of that multi-civilization galactic network. There are Orbs in solar systems all over our galaxy, communicating, providing wormhole travel between systems. And hosting formalized combat between the civilizations. The one in the Sol System was given the designation Orb Station Zero. You know how military types like to start counting with zero, right? Well, we expect that humanity, if we manage to compete and win these combats, will be coming across a whole bunch of these Orbs, one in every habitable system, maybe. A galactic civilization, with us as full participants. That's the dream, anyway."

Diego finished and stared at Ram.

Milena, too, looked at him with what was either complete sincerity or the best poker face in history.

Was it some kind of test of his credulity? It was ludicrous, completely, but he had just seen the replay and it had been convincing yet he still wondered if he wasn't being trolled. It was surely the more likely situation. Even though he couldn't imagine why anyone would go to the trouble of trolling him so completely.

They were waiting for Ram's response.

"You can't be serious about all this."

Milena and Diego both nodded.

"We'd been misunderstanding the situation right from the start. They weren't asking us to send an ambassador," Diego said, leaning forward. "They were telling us to send Earth's champion."

CHAPTER SIX
SUBJECTS

THE DOCTOR HAD SAID Ram was good at dealing with trauma but he didn't know how anyone could come to that conclusion.

Ram had never experienced any. Not really.

When you're secluded in your home, there's nothing that can really trouble you. He had dropped out of school as soon as he started making money from Avar. After starting his own co-op a few years later, he had barely left his apartment. Even before then, when he was a child he had moved home just a couple times in his life. The first time was when they bulldozed his parent's suburban house for the New Delhi Spaceport.

Luckily, his parents had moved far enough that the Seti family weren't vaporized in a 4,000 degrees kelvin fireball when, three months later, the shuttle for the *Colony Ship Gandhi* went down on launch and destroyed a quarter of the city. That had been a trauma of a sort but mainly he felt relief for himself and contempt for the idiots in the government who had decided that placing the world's third largest spaceport next to a city was a good idea.

Rama was not sure he had ever left his apartment after he moved into it by himself.

But why would you? Everything you could possibly want could be delivered to your door. He earned his living entirely in-Avar. All his friends were in-Avar and always had been and he did all his socializing, learning and playing there, too. Whenever he wanted to visit somewhere in the world he could project himself to anywhere that had the setup. Every lecture theater and tourist attraction was available, for a fee, and you could see it all, hear it all as if you were really there, but without any crowds spoiling the view.

Ram was in Avar all the time and studies showed that virtual experience was practically as good for you as the real thing.

And what was that real thing, anyway? Outside his front door was nothing but millions of polluted, coughing assholes and urban bullshit for miles in every direction. Beyond that? A billion and a half Indian lunatics. And Indians were sane compared to the rest of the world.

No thank you.

Ram stayed safe inside his apartment, experiencing everything Earth and the Solar System had to offer in perfect safety. That was saying nothing of the endlessly rich game worlds that he and his cooperative played in, competed in, killed and fucked in. And that was the way he intended to live for the rest of his life.

Ram realized he was holding his head in his hands.

One thing he knew, staring at his enormous legs in their stretchy shorts, was that his new goal was just to make it out alive. Whether it was all true or not, these people were crazy. If they were trolling him, they were beyond nuts. Who knew what their purpose actually was, his actual life might be in danger.

And if they were telling the truth, well, then he was in real trouble.

"Let me get this straight," Ram said, without looking up. "You recruited me, abducted me, to be trained for a mission. A mission to fight aliens?"

Diego shrugged. "Only one alien."

Milena nodded. "This Mission, this Project is focused entirely on finding humanity's greatest champion and delivering them to that Orb."

"And you wanted me?"

Milena stood. "You've seen enough for the time being. The other subjects will fill you in on the rest. And you and I will have regular sessions from now on so any questions you have you can ask me. You'll move into the ludus and then your training will begin. First, you need to meet the Director and Chief Exec."

Milena opened the door and Ram stood, carefully holding on to the edge of his seat and then to the wall and door frame. He couldn't believe how tall he was. He could feel the potential of his enormous strength and it terrified and excited him.

"Thanks," he said to Diego.

"No problem," Diego said, spreading his hands and leaning back in his chair. "Listen, good luck, okay? You just be careful in the ludus with the other subjects. They're crazy, man. They're all crazy. You watch yourself with them. They're not Avar gamers. They're stone cold psychotics and lunatics. They're killers. You just stay safe, be nice and submissive to everybody, alright? Everybody. Survive your first few weeks at least and maybe they'll let you make it through to the end of the line, you never know."

"Alright, Diego, that's enough," Milena snapped from the corridor. "Let's go, Ram."

The door slid shut behind him and Ram followed Milena along the corridor, the gently curving floor curling up to the door at the far end.

He watched the way she strode forward, her rubber-soled boots squeaking every few steps or so. Her trousers clung to the top and sides of her perfectly formed ass. Ram stared until he remembered she could measure his hormones then flicked his eyes up to the ceiling scrolling past above him.

"You're taking me to the Director, right?" Ram said, clearing his throat. "I assumed this was a military project but if you have a director not a colonel or a general or whatever then I guess you're a private company?"

"In a way," Milena said over her shoulder, flicking her thick dark hair. "We offer an enormously high-risk investment, without dividends or chance of payoff for decades or perhaps centuries."

"Doesn't sound very attractive," Ram said. Strangely, the floor of the corridor was slightly arched, running down toward the center and then up again at the far end where there was a closed door. "Are you a cooperative? Something this big has to be a consortium of cooperatives, right? Where are we? This place is underground, isn't it. Am I still in India?"

Milena stopped at the door at the far end of the corridor with the words DIRECTOR ZUMA on it.

"You are not in India," she said.

"How big is this facility?" Ram said. "Are we in China?"

"I will let the Director explain," Milena said. "If she chooses to."

Ram was about to ask what was going on when the wall section before him drew up into the ceiling, revealing a room beyond.

It was not the antiseptic white of the hospital room but an ornate and antiquated study, like you would find in an English-style country home.

He followed Milena into that plush room with a huge antique

looking desk in the center. A bookshelf filled the rear wall with old-fashioned books jammed into them every which way. There was even wall-to-wall carpet in a deep, subtle mauve under the legs of the chairs.

Strangely, the furniture was all bolted to the floor and the shelves had strips holding the books in place, as if someone was afraid they would escape.

A beaming, middle-aged woman, stood up from her leather-bound chair behind the desk. She wore black military fatigues and a woolen hat, her tight, black dreadlocks curled up behind.

"I am Director Zuma," she said, in a powerful but finely controlled voice. "You are Rama Seti and I am very pleased to meet you. I would come round there and shake your hand but I don't yet trust your self-control. May I present Chief Executive Zhukov."

Zhukov was a tough-looking older man in a gray business suit, standing stiff as a board in the corner of the room by a dark brown antique table with an old, 3D model of Mars on top. Zhukov had small blue eyes, a big nose and square head. He looked like someone who could commit a murder and then sit down to enjoy a five-star meal.

"Mr. Seti," Chief Executive Zhukov said, speaking English the same as everyone else in the base yet his accent was so profoundly Russian, Ram had to concentrate to understand his meaning. "It is gratifying that you survived the procedures."

"Thanks," Rama said. "I'm pretty gratified, too."

"Milena, please take a seat," Director Zuma said and sat back down in the creaking leather chair behind her desk.

Zhukov was neither offered nor took a seat for himself and Ram was left standing in the center of the room, looking down on everyone.

The Director leaned forward on her desk. "I believe you tend to go by Ram with your friends. May I call you Ram?"

"Are you kidding?" Rama said.

"Ram it is," Director Zuma said, inclining her head a fraction. "And I understand your anger. I wanted to meet you right away, hoping to help you transition to your full and willing engagement with the Project. And as our Chief Executive says, we are awfully glad that you survived the transplantation. We need you."

Zhukov grunted, a sound meant to convey his contempt for Zuma's words. Director Zuma, however, paid the man no attention.

"That's what I still don't understand. I'm nobody."

"I beg to differ," Zuma said. "You are precisely what we need."

"I know my emotional state is being chemically manipulated to keep me docile but this all seems crazy. I'm not exactly qualified for fighting, am I. At least, I wasn't. Before you grafted me on this giant body. I have no experience in saving humanity."

Zuma pursed her lips. "I agree that at first glance, it may first seem like you are an unusual choice. But I have high hopes for what you can do for us. All of us. High hopes indeed."

"I believe," said Chief Executive Zhukov, talking over the end of Zuma's sentence, "that your admission into the Project for what will be a minimal return on investment is a waste of time, attention and resources. However, we had a recent fatality and Director Zuma has called in the last of her favors in order to activate you, hoping to make the best of this situation. Although the Director and I disagree about your presence here, I am willing to give her this last chance to prove that the course of action she has steered us on is the correct one. If she is wrong, she will have to consider her position."

Director Zuma nodded, seemingly unconcerned.

"I think I've worked it out," Ram said, looking back and forth between them. "This is a mental institution."

"You feel uncomfortable at us expressing ourselves openly. Let me explain," Zhukov said. "We practice a policy of the fullest possible disclosure here at the Project and particularly during this mission. Honesty, both professional and personal, is the greatest benefit for delivery of successful practical outcomes. The nature of the Project leads us to think in terms of secrecy, deceit and competition. It is inevitable that these modes of thinking bleed into the day-to-day work of the Project. My policy of openness and transparency counteracts those destructive tendencies. Do you not agree, Director Zuma?"

"I have doubts," Zuma said. "My opinion is that we already give up most of our freedoms and I suspect morale would improve if we allowed interpersonal deception to be practiced more widely, as it is in normal society but I continue to adhere to the policy to present a united management structure for our heads of department and their teams."

"Seeing as you guys are into telling the truth, can you tell me what my cooperative has been told about where I am?" Ram said. "And my parents? Because my co-op relies on me, completely, for arranging practice and competitions. Oh, we have the *Gunpowder Dragon* semi-finals next week."

Chief Executive Zhukov opened his mouth to answer.

The Director hurried to answer instead. "As far as the world is concerned, you are dead. Your headless body was found and the investigation came up with no leads to explain your murder. Probably Avar gaming related, seeing as it is big business, but basically, the case was quickly closed. Your cooperative, Rubicon? They have recruited another member to fill your place. They have fallen in the rankings. Your funeral was held. Your parents and a few of their friends attended, plus, we assume, your cooperative members attended via Avar projection. You are legally dead."

Ram closed his eyes for a long time. The others in the room, the perpetrators of the massive violation of his rights, waited silently. Ram wondered what he would be feeling if they let his hormones behave naturally.

He took and released a slow, shaky breath.

"No chance you made a mistake and you can let me go home?" Ram said, quietly, opening his eyes.

Zuma picked up her screen. "You are an elite Avar

cooperative leader. You have led your cooperative to the finals of a number of combat based international tournaments."

"That doesn't mean I am good at combat myself. I play team games," Ram said. "I have a good team. Mostly I manage the strategies and deal with the administration, financials and moderation these days. Less time for practice, my skills aren't what they were a couple of years ago."

Director Zuma nodded. "It is time to move beyond denial. You put a fantastic team together, built it yourself. You attracted gamers with potential, molded them, inspired them, shaped them in a world-class unit. A hundred Avar players in your cooperative from all around the world and you were involved in recruiting them all. You made excellent judgments about their character and potential ability based on their gameplay and meetings in-Avar. You have attracted an enormous amount of sponsorship, advertising and subscription fees. Your cooperative has done fantastically well. All because of you."

"Even then," Ram said, delighted but astonished these people had even heard of him. "There are literally thousands of better players than me. Thousands of Avar players who are more famous and with more dedicated fans. Why not recruit those players into whatever this Project is?"

"Do you know how many of those players are jacked up on drugs? How many have used augmentation, biological and technological implants, nootropics, stimulants?"

"Sure," Ram said. "If you want to break the top ten thousand you pretty much have to use all those strategies. There's no drug testing in Avar."

Director Zuma nodded. "Why did you not chose to utilize these strategies?"

Ram would have shrugged if he could have done. "I probably would have, eventually."

Zhukov stirred in the corner. "You were afraid," he said. "Of taking your life to the next level."

"Yeah, I was," Ram said, trying to glare at the Chief Executive. "Have you seen how long those people last? Even if something doesn't go wrong with the enhancements, they burn out. You're not on top for long."

Zhukov grunted, amused. "You were eating yourself to death anyway. Your objections make no sense."

Ram looked at Zhukov. But there was nothing he could say.

"You studied in your spare time," Zuma said, speaking loudly with a quick glance at Zhukov. "You took extensive courses in mathematics, ancient languages, engineering." She raised her eyebrows suggestively. "You wrote an anonymous paper titled *Strategic Massacres in Ancient Warfare and How to Apply the Concept to Galactic Conquest 7*. That paper changed the nature of the metagame, forever. It makes for a stimulating read."

"I was just a kid when I wrote that," Ram muttered. "And all that research I did, all those courses I attended," Ram said, looking at the wall of books behind Zuma. "I didn't do it because I'm a scholar or anything. I only did it to get better at Avar."

Zuma beamed and jabbed a finger up at Ram. "I am so happy that you said that. I too studied to better achieve my ultimate goal. My mother took me from Durban when I was four years old. I joined a Brazilian security co-op when I was eighteen. I saw some shit, Ram, and I did some shit I am ashamed of. But I knew I could do more with my life. I read these books here behind me and other books like them in order to be a better soldier and a better human being.

"Knowledge makes everyone better at what they do, no matter what it is. There are no limits to knowledge and wisdom. The more you know, the better you can perform. Many of the other subjects here, your new comrades, were elite soldiers even before they joined us with their enhanced bodies. But we have also had subjects in the past who were elite athletes, extreme sports pioneers, astronauts and, of course, hand to hand combat champions. You, however, are different. And I am confident that your difference is exactly what we need at this moment."

"Knowledge and wisdom," Zhukov said, scowling across the room at Ram and tapping his temple, "counts for nothing without strength of will. In all life but especially here. If you are to survive beyond your first day or two, then you must remember that."

"You are far from weak, Ram. I have watched you. I have seen you storming the gates at Dar-Kudan in *Dragon's Dominion*, the first person to do so alone, after your whole co-op died in order to get you there. You personally captured the final flag in the international tournament of *Hannibal's Revenge* five years ago, atop the Capitoline Hill. And this year you came out of nowhere to defeat the champion of the *Galactic Games* in one v. one combat. With barely any time to practice."

"I didn't know I had fans in the secretive underground base demographic," Ram said, attempting a lame joke. "But if you know me that well then you know I don't have many wins on that epic scale. Our fans like me because I go all out. I am never in the middle of the table. Nine times out of ten, I lose and lose hard. I go out in the early rounds, I don't hold back. People watch me on the remote chance I'll do something great. I rarely do."

"You are an all or nothing kind of person." Zuma stood up and jabbed her finger at Ram. "And that is precisely what we need. You see, Rama. In this Project, there are no prizes for second place. Either we win everything. Or we die."

"Okay," Ram said. "But just remember when I die that I told you my epic failure rate is eighty percent."

Zhukov grunted. "Better odds than ours."

"We will take you to the ludus, your new home." Director Zuma came around her desk. "When you meet your new comrades, the other subjects, try to not let them see your fear."

As a group, they headed back into the corridor and kept going. Zuma and Zhukov walked on both sides of him and Milena behind.

Ram considered that he was chest, shoulders and head taller

than all of them and probably weighed a hundred kilos more. He could destroy all of them in seconds if he wanted to. But then what?

At the far end of the corridor, a wall panel one the side slid up, revealing a big rectangular room with a door at the other end, like an airlock.

"What is this?" Ram said.

"Security," Milena said.

Director Zuma smiled up at Ram. "Our subjects are precious indeed and we can take no risks with you. Also, your new comrades are, almost by definition, violent people. We do not want them to get out."

The door behind them slid shut. The door in front did not yet open. A mechanical hum thrummed through the walls and a red light above flashed. His heart raced and his face tingled. He'd had panic attacks before and he knew he was freaking out.

"Don't be alarmed, Ram, I will make some adjustments," Milena said, tapping on her screen. "You will feel better almost immediately."

The panic receded, replaced by a certain calm, almost contentment.

"Oh, that's nice," Ram said, sighing. "You know, I feel like I should be angry at what you're doing to me."

"Of course, you should be," Director Zuma said, looking up at him. "You would not be human if you were not. We all want to be free. Humans all have this overwhelming desire to hold on to the illusion of free will. It is perfectly natural that, when the veil is lifted, you should feel the need to rebel. Intellectually, at least, even if we subdue your emotional response."

"Free will is not an illusion," Ram said, the rush of happy hormones loosening his tongue.

The room hummed on, the red light above flashing.

Director Zuma laughed, even Zhukov made a sound that could have been a chuckle. But she ignored his free will assertion and changed the subject.

"You are a late addition to the program. We experienced the loss of one of our subjects and so Chief Executive Zhukov gave me clearance to activate you. The others have been training together for at least three years. Three years of bonding, interpersonal conflict and resolution. Of competition, cooperation and rivalry resulting in an established hierarchy. You coming in is going to disrupt all of that. The leaders are going to have to put you in your place. Are you ready for that?"

"No," Ram said. "No, I hate that kind of thing. It's bullshit."

Zhukov sneered. "This is why we do not take on shutaways. There is no substitute for real world experiences, none. There never can be. Avar is a simulacrum with far too much control by the user. The real world has orders of magnitude more variables and you cannot simply unplug at will."

The door in front hissed, the red light above switched off. A clear but gentle ping sounded three times.

"It is unfortunate that you are incapable of being socially

competitive," Zuma. "Your relationships here will be difficult. Do remember that it is your real world performance that you will be measured by. Performance in training correlates closely with the interpersonal hierarchies within the ludus."

"Work hard and I won't get bullied?"

"You catch on quickly." Zuma beamed. "Shall we?"

Red lights flashed and the huge door separated into the walls, floor and ceiling, revealing a large room beyond. The floor, walls and ceiling were all black.

"Welcome," Director Zuma said. "To the ludus."

Beyond the doorway, it opened up into a rather narrow, long room. It was somewhat tube-shaped, like the fuselage of an intercontinental airplane. The room was empty of people but filled with exercise machines. The benches, cables and weights looked like a torturer's playground in a medieval dungeon.

"Where is everybody?" Ram asked.

"The ludus training facility is quite large, featuring six sections," Executive Zhukov said. "The subjects are sparring in the adjacent section so while we wait until they finish, we will show you what you will be competing with. And introduce you to Bediako." The Chief Executive looked up at Ram. "That should make you quake in your boots."

"I think you'll find Ram is made of sterner stuff," Director Zuma said.

Ram's sensation of unreality kept growing. The group turned to the left and marched along next to the wall, striding by machine after machine toward the door at the far end.

No one spoke. Perhaps Rama was projecting his fear onto the people around him but it was as if everyone was holding their breath, anxious about what was to happen.

The door hissed open and they stepped through into a narrow corridor that sloped sharply upward to a higher level. From up ahead came the distant sound of grunts, thumps and shouts. Ram tried to control his breathing.

The corridor ended up ahead in a kind of balcony. As the slope leveled out again, the wall opened, showing a long, tubular room very much like the one they had just left.

The group stopped at an opening in the panels. Director Zuma leaned on a low railing to look out down below. Ram stopped behind her and looked down into the open space of the room below the balcony.

His heart sank.

Instead of rows of exercise machines, covering the floor of near enough the whole room were two rows of six enormous, rectangular padded mats.

On the mats, people fought.

A roomful of monstrous great people, grappling and sparring, all unarmed. It reeked of both fresh and stale sweat. The walls echoed with the sound of grunts and the hard smacks of heavy bodies slapping into the mats under their feet and the wet slaps of skin whacking against skin.

All of the giants had undergone the same nervous system

transfer procedure as Ram. They had the slightly shrunken head appearance that Ram had on his own body. All those heads were shaved or had hair shorn close to the scalp.

Another ten or so normal sized people walked around the room, observing, giving instructions, recording the fighting, and handing out water and towels. Though the height of the members of both groups varied, the normal sized people mostly reached no higher than the chest height of the fighters that they were advising.

He counted twelve of the giant men and women, although two of them were not fighting. They wore tight, thin shorts and vests of stretchy black, white or gray material. Some were stripped to the waist. They fought in pairs. One of the giant women stood at the edge of the matted area near the balcony as if waiting her turn. Another walked around, watching but not fighting.

The waiting woman's pectorals and shoulders were just as pumped, her hips just as narrow as any of the men's.

Taken all together it was a heaving mass of wrestling and striking. It was pairs of bodies coming together, breaking apart, breathing heavily and smacking back together again. They were huge and full of incredible strength. But for all their violent fury, they were not fighting to the death. The enormous men and women helped each other to their feet after they fell. In between grappling, some exchanged words. One pair laughed even as they fought.

But the intensity was astonishing. Their skill and speed were frightening and he could barely follow what was happening.

Did they really expect him to be part of this group?

"These are our subjects," Director Zuma said, speaking over the sound of it all. "The eleven toughest and greatest fighters in human history. It sounds hyperbolic, doesn't it and yet it is true. These people were the most elite of the elite fighters even before they were gifted these bodies. And that one there, the old man carved from teak, keeping out of the combat? That is Bediako. Our Chief Instructor in the ludus."

Walking between the enormous sparring mats, calling out criticisms and bellowing commands at the pairs in a voice as loud and raw as an antique machine gun. Some of the fighters hunched as if to protect themselves or flinched away when he stalked by them. Though the body of the man was powerful and rippling with muscle, his face was hideously scarred and lined with age, his head not shaved but as naturally bald and smooth as a plastic egg. His skin was so dark that it was almost black and his teeth and eyes flashed white as he roared his contempt at a woman on the mat next to him. She bowed her head and muttered an apology, though she herself had the aspect and bearing of a god.

"Chief Instructor Bediako," Zuma said. "We have your newest subject here and he is dying to meet you. Please attend to us upon the balcony." Director Zuma spoke at a normal volume, not loud enough for her voice to carry the distance to the man and be audible over the racket. Clearly, they wore communications implants.

The scarred old man looked up, scowling. There was undisguised irritation in that glance. Open hostility, even. Zuma raised a hand in greeting but Bediako looked away, growled something to his staff and stalked underneath their balcony, heading toward Ram and his new bosses.

"Do your best to not be alarmed by his appearance or his demeanor," Milena said softly beside Ram. "If there's one thing Bediako despises, it is weakness."

"Okay," Ram said, wondering if she could tell how terrified he was. Of course she could, he decided. She was measuring his hormones in real time, she could see his cowardice projected onto her screen.

The wall panel at the end of the corridor slid up and the giant Bediako strode out. He was even more intimidating up close than he had been from far away. For one thing, he towered over everyone else in the small group. Ram was of a height with him, taller, even but Zuma, Zhukov and Milena reached no higher than his lower chest.

"Here he is," Director Zuma. "Our newest subject. Rama, meet the eighth wonder of the Solar System. This is the great Bediako. He is our ludus instructor, training program designer and chief assessor of our entire training program and has been so for a great many years. He is also the only man who survived humanity's toughest contest. All that you learn here will be from this man. Bediako, this is Rama Seti."

"The replacement," Bediako growled, his voice like a sandpaper bag full of ball bearings. He looked Ram up and down. "In the old model body. The failed design. Why are you wasting my time with this, Zuma?"

"Yes, yes," the Director said, seemingly unconcerned at being spoken to in such a way by her subordinate. "But we have to work with what we have available, do we not? And now, despite everyone's objections and dire predictions, he is here with us and you will welcome him into the fold. Our other option is putting him back on the bench and that seems like an awful waste of the resources getting him to this point. If you give Ram a chance you will find him a suitable candidate."

Bediako grunted, his bulging eyes flicking up and down Ram's body. He felt incredibly vulnerable and that look was loaded with evil intent.

"I saw his file," Bediako said. "He has the least experience of anyone ever recruited to the Project. If he lives through his first week with us, perhaps I will give him the time of day. Until then, I have real subjects who deserve my attention."

Bediako bowed his scarred head, turned and strode away through the way he had come.

"He seems nice," Ram said.

Ram looked past Zhukov's bulbous head and down at the fighters beyond. A small group of four had broken off their sparring and gathered near to the balcony, looking up at him.

All wore tight shorts and tight vests, showing off their insane musculature and enormous stature. Bediako strode up to them from underneath the balcony and spoke a few words, too low for Ram to hear. The group of five looked up at Ram as one. Their neck muscles bunching and flexing as they moved.

One man among them seemed to be the center of their attention. The others, even Bediako, all seemed to be turned toward him in some subtle way and they looked at him with something like devotion, hanging on his word.

That man was not the tallest or the bulkiest. Indeed, though he was muscled beyond the normal human range, including pharmaceutically enhanced bodybuilders, he was positively slender compared to Ram's new body.

Yet he was the most frightening looking man there.

He had a face like it had been hacked out of granite with a shovel. His nose was flat, his cheekbones wide. The man's short black hair glistened with beads of sweat. He looked like a mix between Mongolian, Italian and some sort of mechanized battle suit made flesh.

That man fixed Ram with an intense stare and, when he was certain Ram was watching, drew his thumb across his neck.

He sneered, spoke some unheard insult about Ram and spat to the side. The others all laughed, watching Ram like tigers observing a mouse. Their eyes were full of contempt. Two of the four were women. Though their bodies were just as huge and muscled as the men next to them, they were obviously female. Both sexes' genitals could be discerned outlined through the tight, thin material of their shorts. Ram silently hoped that his own new penis was as massive as theirs were.

The others laughed at whatever the frightening one had said, their massive shoulders rolling up and down with the sheer hilarity of it. The frightening man did not laugh.

His top lip curled up at one side.

"Ah," the Director said. "That is Mael Durand. Milena would say that Mael has a pathological compulsion to be the top dog in any room. His drive to succeed is equaled only by his urge to destroy the competition. He is our greatest hope. The elite of the elite of the elite, and so on. Our Subject Alpha. I recommend that you stay as far away from that man as you can for as long as possible."

That man sneered up at Ram the entire time, even while the others turned and filed away to the far side of the long room.

Subject Alpha, Mael Durand, mouthed a brief, silent sentence across the room, all the while sneering and quivering with rage.

"I'm going to kill you."

CHAPTER SEVEN
DRIVER

THE CHIEF EXECUTIVE AND Director stepped in front of Ram, breaking the line of sight down into the room.

Ram took a deep breath and tried to shake off the feeling of terror.

"We leave you in Milena's capable hands," Director Zuma said. "Do precisely as she says, listen to everything and trust that she will only ever have your best interests at heart. Good luck. I believe in you, Rama Seti. You are exactly what we need. Your contribution to this great project will have a great and lasting impact. There is no doubt in my mind that you will survive your first week. None at all."

While she was speaking, Zhukov walked away without saying anything. Director Zuma nodded at Milena and followed the Chief Executive.

"I'll take you to the mess hall," Milena said. "It is time you began nourishing yourself, with food and with the company of your peers. Then I must leave you. There are no drivers physically in the ludus but I will be monitoring your life signs remotely, plus we can speak whenever you wish to with your microphone. Just speak and I'll pick up. Unless you are in the barracks. Visual and audio are cut off at night."

"Cut off," Ram said, absently, thinking of that guy Mael Durand.

"That's right, you'll be alone with the others so your priority must be in making allies with one or more of the subjects. It might be your only hope."

Ram stared down at her. "Who are you, Milena? Are you a psychologist?"

"I have studied psychology," Milena said, tilting her head. "As well as biology, neurology and other disciplines. My qualifications focus on human behavioral biology and positive psychology."

"And those subjects are relevant for a driver?"

She smiled. "Driver is a colloquialism. My job title is Subject Operator."

"And I'm the subject that you operate."

"Your new body is a powerful device. It is engineered to a

degree of astonishing complexity. When your biological systems are fully integrated between your old CNS and your new body you will have complete control over your nervous system. But the situations you find yourself in will be very dynamic, very high intensity and so you will benefit from my support. I will make real-time adjustments to your central and peripheral nervous systems through manipulation of your endocrine system. And that will increase your combat efficiency."

Ram thought it sounded like being a slave. "You'll have remote control of me?"

"No," she said. "Well, not like that. They tried it and it doesn't work. Reaction times were slow and the vestigial will required from the Artificial Person conflicted with the operator's commands. They lacked the capacity to understand what was happening. But I am here to support you, give you more power when you need it. If you were a racing driver, I would be your race engineer, feeding you info and strategy. I am the corner man to your boxer. The CIC Commander to your special forces soldier."

"How did you get this job? Did they kidnap you from your bed like they did with me?"

Milena smiled at him. "I knew what I was getting into when I was recruited, back when I was young. I really never had a life outside UNOP."

"But you're young now," Ram said. There was no way she was older than thirty. Maybe thirty-five at the most.

"You are attempting to flirt with me," she said, nodding. "That's good."

"No, no. I really meant it." Ram's face grew hot.

"Forget ever feeling embarrassed around me," Milena said, looking at Ram intently. "I know everything about you. I have been watching you, watching your Avar competitions, reading your correspondence, even learning about your food and grocery deliveries and other purchases."

"That's pretty weird. I feel violated right now."

"Of course you do," Milena said. "What we are doing to you is completely unethical."

Down in the sparring room, most of the subjects and support staff had gone, just a couple remained to clear up the towels and water bottles.

"Is that Mael guy crazy?" Ram said, lowering his voice even though there was no one around. "He's crazy, right?"

"Mael Durand, our Subject Alpha has a severe problem with almost all people. A simple way of saying it is that he is mentally disturbed. In the past, he would have been called a homicidal maniac or a psychopath or a sociopath or another euphemism for his violent and pathological behaviors. In this Project and on this mission, we prioritize physical ability and violent creativity over stability."

"So that's what the Intel guy Diego was saying?" Ram said. "I'm in danger?"

"Don't listen to Diego," Milena said. "He's afraid of physical conflict. Even vicariously, it scares him but that clashes with his profound ideological beliefs about personal freedom. Don't let his nonchalant, casual demeanor fool you, he's quite brilliant and quite passionate. Everyone here is and Diego is more brilliant than most. But he struggles to come to terms with the ethical consequences of what he is participating in. If anything, he's getting worse and his advice, therefore, is inaccurate."

"I'm relieved. I knew all the subjects couldn't be psychotics. You wouldn't put me in real danger."

"Well, many of them are," Milena said. "And you are in danger. Everything Diego said was true but you shouldn't listen to him about being submissive in the ludus. In fact, if you don't stand up for yourself then you put yourself at further risk. The subjects value physical prowess, mental fortitude. To have their respect you must display these traits. You need to stand up for yourself or you will probably be beaten, or worse."

Ram rubbed his eyes. "Sounds like a British boarding school."

Milena shrugged. "Not an inaccurate analogy. Any small group of physically isolated people, separated from the normalizing influence of the variables in a freer society will develop a culture of pathological brutality. Creating a group of peers, overseen by a small elite of powerful authority figures will do this. Whether it is a prison, a sports club, a school or even a whole culture, we see the same stressors expressed through a pathological need to impose hierarchies within the group.

Bullying behaviors are a natural consequence of our social instincts where we need to create a tribe of individuals that have a range of interpersonal influence or kudos. However, the fact that this is natural and even predictable doesn't make it easier on the people within those groups. So you'll suffer and you'll have to fight, socially and physically, for your place in the hierarchy. When that is established, the worst of them should leave you alone, more or less."

"What if I'm no good? What if I can't cut it?"

"I know what you are thinking," she smiled, radiating sympathy. "You have used failure as a tool for extricating yourself from situations that you found difficult or undesirable. It is an awfully common behavior and when someone learns how effective it is, usually at a young age, they can come to rely upon it. Possibly, you discovered the tactic during your brief time at a real world school. Perhaps your tutor instructed you to perform some menial or physical task, such as sorting the color pencils or carrying chairs to another room. You were extremely bright but lacking practical experience so, in a fit of childish resistance you threw down your efforts, sabotaging yourself. When confronted by your tutor, you lacked the courage to admit that you acted out of conscious decision and instead claimed that you accidentally ruined your activity. It could be that you shed tears, overcome by the emotion and stress of the situation. I can imagine your elation when the tutor told you that she would clear it up for you and to run along back to class where you once more felt comfortable with your computer. Do you recall anything similar to that happening when you were a boy, Ram?"

"No," Ram said, picturing the scattered computer scrolls spinning across the corridor floor at his feet and feeling the warm urine spreading down his trousers. Through the absolute, abject shame he remembered his joy at being sent away, alone, to clear himself up. It was a victory, of sorts, over the power of the tutor. "I don't remember anything like that."

"Of course," Milena said. "Only rarely can a single incident form a lasting neurosis but a viable tactic, oft repeated, can become a pattern, a crutch, a place of refuge and it is something you, Rama, turn to in stressful situations."

"Doesn't sound like something I'd do," Ram said. "I'm always trying to win."

"Your entire Avar career is somewhat an extension of this behavior pattern. Your supposedly heroic, all-or-nothing Avar play style? Sometimes, you see a great opportunity and you go for it. But over half the time, you destroy yourself in spectacular fashion. It is a means of avoidance. Of resistance to your own potential greatness. You kill yourself, kill your chances, before someone else can do it for you."

"I think that's a little unfair," Ram said. "Anyway, I'm not trying to actualize my life inside the games. I'm performing. I'm performing for my fans."

"Your entire life is inside Avar," Milena said, which was certainly true. "And if you're not fulfilling your potential inside the games, you're certainly not doing it inside your apartment, eating yourself to death."

Even in his normal life, Ram felt very little, emotionally, most of the time. And since he'd woken up in the white walled prison they'd kept him sedated even further. But it was safe to say that she had hurt his feelings.

"I feel like dramatically storming out of the room right now," Ram said.

"Thank you for proving my point," Milena said. "Listen, I'm not trying to rile you. I am on your side. Believe it or not, it is in my professional interest to help you feel as positive and fulfilled as possible."

"Oh yeah?" Ram raised his eyebrows. "Sweet."

"Emotionally and intellectually fulfilled," Milena said, smiling. "Your physical fulfillment will be the responsibility of Bediako."

"I hope not," Ram said. "I understand what you're saying about me always finding a way out of committing to something difficult. I think that's probably true for a lot of people. But this is crazy. I never asked for this. Is it neurotic to grab at a way out of this insane situation? I can fail to progress in the training process and then I won't have to fight."

Milena tilted her head and ever so slightly sucked in one side of her lower lip. "I'm afraid that in this case, the only way you are permanently dropping out of the Project is if you are killed."

"Killed."

"This is a Project with standards, physical and ethical, that are probably unique in human experience," Milena said, shrugging.

"No shit," Ram said.

"We are just talking about facts here, Ram," Milena said. "The fact is, if you do not make maximum effort in all training endeavors then you will die. Your usual, fallback position of conscious failure, of self-sabotage, will by necessity be the last time you are ever able to apply that tactic. You must get over it immediately or else you will fall at the first hurdle. And yes, I mean fall as in get snuffed out. Not getting killed is up to you. Probably the best you could hope for is to be so severely injured that you can take no further part in future assignments in a supporting capacity. This is what happened to former subjects like Bediako. His replacement artificial body lets him keep up with his subjects but it won't last long before it degrades, as would yours if you were lucky enough to get one. So, yes, your violent death may be certain. But I think we should focus on ensuring you survive the training process for as long as possible and that means believing in yourself and fighting as hard as you can. Are you willing and able to do that?"

His eyes tingled, grew hot and he blinked away the moisture leaking into them.

"Sure."

They walked down into the sparring room in silence. Ram, the top of his head only a couple of centimeters from the ceiling, looming over her like an adult over a child. He felt like the rooms were too small for him, his height was absurd. He weighed tons. And yet his body quivered with potential energy and power and he felt an urge to run, to sprint forward to see how fast he could go, to see how high he could jump and what he could punch through or tear down. He was jittery, surging between scared of what was to come and thrilled by the knowledge of what was happening.

"The social dynamics in the ludus are brutal," Milena said as they approached the door at the far end of the room. "Barbaric, even. But you have to remember what our objective is. We must do whatever is necessary to win the next fight. It is vitally important for the continuation of our species wherever we are and perhaps even all the species on Earth."

"Because we're fighting to get some of those gifts of knowledge, I get it," Ram said.

"This will be humanity's fourth visit to the Orb," Milena said. "Each time we leave the structure, break orbit and head back to the inner Solar System we get a little more information via a broadcast from the Orb itself. Last time, at the conclusion to Mission Three, when we translated their messages to us we understood, finally, what was at stake. What had been at stake for the previous hundred years without anyone realizing it."

"What is at stake?"

"We told you that the Wheelhunters are not the makers of the Orb. They do not occupy it or control it. They come to the place every thirty years just to fight us."

"Sure but where from?" Ram said, thrilled.

"We reason that it is a star system relatively near to ours, though it is not clear where they originate," Milena said. "We reason that each time the Wheelhunters arrive at the Orb, they do so through the power of the Orb bringing them to us."

"Yeah, wormhole right?"

"That's what we call it but the physicists are not sure what it actually is. Clearly, due to the fact that their vessel appears while throwing off a shower of particles and radiation, we assume it is some sort of wormhole that the Orb controls. Although, perhaps it is even a space-folding ship-based drive that the Orb provided to the Wheelhunter species as a reward for winning some previous combat, with us or with another species somewhere else in the galaxy, on another one of their borders perhaps. Whatever the process, it is currently beyond our understanding, although our scientists all have their pet theories that they love to talk about, endlessly, over dinner in the mess hall."

"Obviously, the Orb is way more advanced than us," Ram said. "By hundreds or thousands of years. Or millions. But what about the Wheelhunters? Their ship looked kind of like ours, right?"

"We don't know about their society but the Wheelhunters appear to be barely more advanced than us in terms of ship technology. It stands to reason that their society, like ours, puts their most advanced foot forward. So the wormhole brings the Wheelhunters to the Orb because the giant yellow aliens want something from us. Something they're willing to fight for. Remember that the Orb told us it exists to enable a kind of combat based diplomacy in the galaxy? Well, the Wheelhunters, starting with poor old Malcolm Diaz, have been winning the rights and the ability to star systems near to our own. We assume they have been given systems with habitable worlds, or ones that are potentially habitable, with which to colonize. So far, humanity has lost the rights to three star systems near to our Solar System. As far as we can tell, the victor of the next combat will determine who gets the Solar System itself."

She watched him, waited for him to process.

"I don't understand," Ram said. "We're already here. It's ours."

They stopped at the closed far door, which was stenciled with the words D3 MESS. Ram could smell food.

"Think of it like a bet," Milena said. "We're betting our solar system on the outcome of this game. Winner takes all. What will it mean if we lose? Will the Wheelhunters sterilize Earth? Take our bases and colonies? Or will they enslave us, take us away to work for them? Will they just tax us, in some way? Or will we just carry on as we are? Perhaps we'd have to share our land? We have no idea."

"Humanity would never allow that," Ram said. "None of those things."

Milena nodded. "We might not have a choice. That's why, as soon as the precise nature of the existential risk became clear at the end of Mission Three, the major corporations and nations got together to begin constructing a war fleet, space-based weapons, planetary defense systems, recruiting crew, specialized ground combat soldiers and space marines. If it comes to an invasion, we'll be as ready as we can be. But what if the Orb is here to enforce galactic law? Maybe we'll be annihilated for breaking the convention."

"But we never signed up for this," Ram said. "This is crazy."

"Indeed," Milena said. "But imagine what will happen if we win. If we can learn to beat the Wheelhunters. We will be invited to colonize distant systems. The Orb might give us wormholes that lead to those systems, as it seems to have done for the Wheelhunters. Imagine the technological leaps we will make. We'll be a part of a galactic community. Who knows where that might take us. This is a matter of life and death."

Ram took a slow breath, filling his enormous lungs. He held it for a moment. Then breathed out as steadily as he could.

"But only if we win," Ram said.

"Win and we win a future amongst the stars," Milena said, nodding. "Lose and we lose everything. Come on, let's get you started. Time to do your part. They're eating dinner. The next ring section is the mess hall."

She jerked her thumb at the D3 MESS stencil on the door.

"Ring section?"

For the first time since Ram had met her, she seemed a little nervous. "This isn't a base under the earth. Not in Antarctica or

Siberia or the Himalayas."

"Don't tell me. I already figured it out."

"We are on a ship called the UNOPS Victory. A ship heading out to the Orb Station. We have a long way to go yet but we are closing rapidly on our destination."

"I knew it," Ram said, shaking his head. "A spaceship? It must be enormous. This is way bigger than anything I've even heard about. This must be bigger than the Mars colony ships."

"The UNOPS Victory is easily the biggest vessel to travel to the outer system. They're completing bigger ships back in Earth orbit now, ready for defending the planet should it come to an invasion but they don't have to propel themselves half the width of the solar system. And there are armed ships with fighter fleets and manned weapons platforms being sent to Mars and out to Saturn. But we are leading the way. I can't tell you how many exactly but we have well over a hundred people on board."

"UNOPS?" Ram said. "People keep saying that. It's United Nations...?"

"United Nations Orb Project Spaceship," Milena said. "You'll hear people here refer to the Project as a whole as UNOP, using both words interchangeably. But we all call our beautiful ship the Victory."

Ram looked around the room with new eyes, shaking his head. "So many of my friends told me this was happening. I never believed them. How is it possible? It feels like we're on Earth."

He banged his hand on the black ceramic tile of the wall. It was cool to the touch.

Ram smelled hot savory food wafting out of the room beyond. He felt a pang, not of hunger, exactly, but of the urge to stuff himself senseless. How long had it been since he had eaten? Hours, certainly.

"The apparent gravity is provided by rotating the ship." Milena took out her screen and unfolded it. "Here's an image of the *Victory* from one of our drone fleet. Our shielding masks the internal design somewhat but the *Victory* is constructed of six adjacent rings around a central core. Each ring has six sections. Each section is a tube, like a rocket body, joined end to end. Each ring of six is joined to the one next to it. The rings are designated A through to F and the sections are numbered. So we are now in the Ludus Training and Sparring room section which is D2. And next up, D3 is the Ludus Mess and Nutrition section. D4 is the Barracks and Living Quarters section and so on. Other rings are Administration and Flight Control, Life-support, Medical, Research and Communications. The central core contains the Engine Room, Reactor Compartment, Astronomy and Navigation and so on."

"I'm in space," Ram said. "I'm in actual space."

"Try to keep up, Rama," Milena said. "Through that next door is the ludus mess hall, so go in and start filling up on calories. I'll stop blocking the hunger signals now so you have an appetite. You'll need to eat thousands of calories per day just to maintain that muscle mass and on top of that, you'll be exercising rigorously. You'll spend much of your downtime eating and drinking protein nutrient shakes."

"Sounds amazing," Ram said. "Eating is the one thing I do at an elite level. You're not coming in?"

"Don't worry," Milena said, patting his arm. "I'll hear and see everything, other than at night. There's a device in your ear and a microphone in your jaw, so I can speak to you anytime I want and all you need do is whisper and I'll hear you. There are cameras everywhere other than the barracks and even there I will keep watch on your vital signs. Nothing you say or do goes unnoticed or unrecorded. Good luck. Show no fear, especially to the subjects who will be your enemies. Remember, you need allies from the rest. Survive, Rama. Survive."

Milena hit the door control and turned and walked away. The door slid up and a wave of voices, clanking and clanging and the comforting smell of boiled rice poured out, crashing into him.

The room - ring section - was half the length of the one behind. Obviously some internal division. Twelve huge people sat around at the six benches in the room, shoveling trays of food into their faces. At the far end on either side, staff served mountains of food from vast trays. In the opposite wall was a door with the words D4 BARRACKS on it.

Normal sized support staff stood and sat amongst some of them or stood at the edges of the room. Ram recognized the instructor Bediako sitting at a table surrounded by a group of assistants craning their necks to see the screen he was pointing at.

The talking, laughing, shouting, mass of sounds faded as every face turned toward him. Some were surprised. A couple even smiled. The insane one called Mael stared with dark eyes like a shark closing in on a flathead mullet.

Ram did not know what to say. So he just stood there.

The food they were serving included vats of a spicy stew and trays piled with rice that smelled delicious. His stomach rumbled for the first time since he had been kidnapped and beheaded. It was enough to force him over the threshold and into the den of monstrous killers.

Show no fear to my enemies, Ram thought.

He forced his face to form a smile and stepped inside.

PART 2
ALLIANCES

CHAPTER EIGHT
SURVIVE THE LUDUS

THE WARRIORS WITH THE MASSIVE bodies and their undersized heads almost filled the mess hall. The giants, his fellow subjects, all eleven of them were there and the grim, scarred instructor. Most of them sitting at the benches, halfway through pounding down mountains of brown rice and piles of black peas with flatbreads. Six men and five women wearing skin tight, figure-hugging shorts and vests in white or gray or black. Some wore nothing on their top half, their skin taut with bulging muscle. Most had shaved heads or else hair that was so short it might as well have not been there.

The normal sized people filled the gaps between the subjects, some sat with the fighters while others stood in groups at the edge of the hall.

The one named Mael, the one who had laughed as he'd run his thumb across his neck in the sparring session, grinned while he chewed, looking at Ram from under his eyebrows, radiating hostility. The other subjects sitting at his table grinned along with him. They reminded Ram of a pack of baboons.

Others in the mess seemed uncomfortable. Yet no one spoke. It was as though they were waiting for something.

He looked at the instructor Bediako, expecting and hoping that the scarred man would deliver a welcome speech or at least introduce him to everyone. Instead, the man stared across the hall with open contempt and even amusement. Saying nothing. Waiting to see what Ram would do or just enjoying his discomfort, the bastard.

I need to make allies, Ram reminded himself.

"Hi," Ram said to the room. He cleared his throat. "Nice to meet you all. I'm Rama Seti. People call me Ram."

"Ram?" the one called Mael said to those around him. "Ewe is more the like of it." He laughed, a deep, booming sound and the others chuckled. "You understand what I am saying? That he is like a sheep." He laughed again and pounded the steel tabletop with the palm of his huge hand, knocking over drinks that a couple of the normal sized assistants moved to mop up.

Ram swallowed. He needed to make allies specifically to

defend himself against that psychopath. Clearing his throat, he looked around, wondering how to do that, exactly. Deep down, he had the overwhelming urge to simply log out of his Avar.

A huge, graceful warrior woman sighed on the nearest table and she stood, unfolding herself like a dancer.

"Rama," she said, her white teeth shining out of her dark skin as she walked toward him. "My name's Sifa." She stuck out a hand when she got close enough. "Sifa Kiyenge."

Ram was taller than she was and he was broader. While Ram's muscles were bunched and rounded as if he'd been assembled with a mound of boulders, this woman called Sifa was sleek and dark and shining, her long muscles running with striations and veins and sinews stood out at her neck and inside her elbow. She looked like an athlete that could run a hundred klicks per hour all day long and fling herself into a fifty-meter long jump. She also had strikingly beautiful eyes, a crooked nose and a mouth as wide as the Indian Ocean. He tried and failed to avoid staring at her incongruously large breasts but they were right there underneath him, straining against the thin, stretchy fabric of her tiny white vest.

Ram had never had a fetish for gigantic, musclebound women but he could feel one coming on like a rocket taking off for orbit. Even if she hadn't been sexy as hell he could have kissed her just for saying hello to him. Instead, he just took her hand and shook it.

"Thanks, I'm Rama Seti," he said after unsticking his tongue from the roof of his mouth.

She smiled and a few of the others laughed. Ram remembered he'd already introduced himself.

"We know who you are," Sifa said. "We've been so looking forward to you joining us, Rama."

"You have?" Ram said, relieved but worried about being trolled by these people. Why was she being nice? Was she about to kick him in the nuts or something?

A hulking white man seated at the bench behind her spoke up. "Get some food, bro," he said, gesturing with a fork toward the back of the room. "It's nothing but hard work here and you'll never be able to eat enough. Trust me, you'll be needing energy."

Sifa leaned in toward Ram a little and whispered to him while he looked down at the curves of her soft, dark skin of her breasts.

"They have planned a sparring session after this. I expect you will have to fight."

Ram not only had no fighting experience, he'd never even had a playground scrap before. The idea of fighting with the monstrous, elite warriors around him was profoundly unsettling.

Everyone was staring at him.

"Er, yeah," Ram said, aware that his nervousness was obvious. "Sure. No problem."

The white man stood. "Sit here, mate, come on," he said, pointing at their bench. "I'll get you something."

"Right," Ram said, thinking that he should decline and go get the food himself. Yet the sanctuary of a bench seat two steps away beckoned and he wanted to dive right into it as though it was a port in a typhoon. "Thanks very much."

"My name's Te," the guy said. "Te Zhang." He did not look Chinese and had a bold, swirling tattoo on the side of his face and flat, wide features and a great big forehead. "Take a seat, seriously, chill out."

Te Zhang strode toward the rear of the room where the food was.

The remaining woman at the table before him looked up expectantly, as did the remarkably attractive woman called Sifa.

Ram eased his massive body onto the bench and Sifa sat down beside him. The bench was big, made for the huge subjects but still Ram had to squeeze himself into the space between the bench and the tabletop. He rested his massive arms on the top, moving carefully. Still afraid of his body.

The conversation in the room slowly started up again, people began eating and ignoring him, though there was plenty of muttering and thrown glances.

Opposite hunched a dreadfully pale woman, enormous, with a hard, bony face, eyes so light blue they were almost white and the stubble on her head was a shining blonde. Her nose looked like it had been broken a thousand times and her cheekbones were as sharp as ice skate blades. Her mouth would probably have been beautiful, it was wide and her lips were full and colorful but that mouth was also smeared with black bean paste.

"Alina," she said, glancing at him in between spooning rice

into her mouth.

"Nice to meet you, Alina."

She grunted, spooning more into her mouth. Rice littered the tabletop.

"Wow," Ram said, trying to break the tension, "you guys get a lot of food here. That's great."

Alina glanced up and scoffed.

"Give it a few more days for the nerves governing your digestive system to fully wake up and for the intense exercise to burn through you," Sifa said, sitting beside him. "You will be as hungry as we are. No matter how much you eat, it is never enough. They measure everything here. Our calorie intake is monitored, our energy expenditure is monitored and yet we are always hungry."

"You don't understand. That's how I've felt every day of my life," Ram said, feeling himself smiling.

Sifa smiled sympathetically. Alina snorted in derision without looking up.

The tattoo faced Te Zhang came strutting back between the benches with a tray that was fully loaded with brown rice, black bean stew and flatbread. Ram's stomach growled as Te set it down on the table along with a huge cup and took the seat beside him. The bench, some sort of high strength aluminum alloy, groaned and bent under the weight. All the furniture was integrated into the tiled floor and was engineered to support a group of people whose collective weight must have been well into the metric tons.

"Eat up, you idiot," Te said, then shoveled his own meal into his mouth. "That tray had your name on it. That two-liter bucket with the drinking spout is your protein and micronutrient drink. Get used to it, because you'll be downing them three times a day, at least."

Ram picked up his spoon. The rice smelled good. The bean thing smelled good. There was so much of it and Ram was supposed to eat it all. He was so excited that he was beside himself. He savored the moment.

"Strange, is it not?" Sifa said, leaning her rock-hard shoulder against his own. "Being in a new body. We all had time to prepare, mentally, for the change when we volunteered for it but you just woke up like this, yes? You had no idea, this is what I heard. Yes? So this must be even worse for you. The sensations are all there but they are not right, they are like you are behind a filter. You are looking through a window smeared with oil. You make out what is beyond but it is not like really seeing it clearly. Well, don't worry. It fades, in time, that sense your body is a machine for your head to operate, that you are a great big monstrous thing sitting here with you riding on top? That will be gone and you will be you, in no time at all." She leaned in even closer, pushing herself against him. "But only if you eat up all of your food, Rama."

Ram stared at her for a moment, not sure what to say. He nodded his thanks and spooned a mound of rice into his mouth.

It was his own mouth, of course. Or so he assumed. What had that Dr. Fo said about increasing the bone mass and density in his skull and jaw? Presumably, his teeth had been toughened in some way so that they didn't get knocked out of his head. Maybe his teeth were not his own.

The rice tasted good. Better than good, after a couple of mouthfuls Ram shoveled more in, tearing fistfuls of the bread to scoop up the bean mixture. Ordinarily, Ram knew it would have seemed bland beyond belief. There was barely any salt and the spicing was so light as to be non-existent but it was sprinkled with the greatest seasoning of all. Gluttony.

"So," Sifa said between mouthfuls. "You're from India? I've always wanted to go there. What is it like?"

Usually, he revealed his nationality to prospective members of his Avar cooperative and no one else. They were the only friends he had but when they found out or guessed where he was from, that was always the next question. Probably it was the same for everyone, from every nation but Ram thought it was a stupid question.

"Good question," Ram said. "What's India like? I never really left Delhi my whole life. I traveled all around the world and our solar system using Avar. But in real life, no, I rarely leave my apartment on the thirty-seventh floor of a residential building. It's one of those ones with the vertical gardens that are never properly maintained and they dry up so you get yellow grass on the walls. And the water recycling system breaks down every few months but it's a pretty nice place. The power supply is completely reliable."

"Oh," Sifa said, tearing off a chunk of her bread and dipping it in Ram's bean stew. "I guess that makes sense. You were an Avar champion, right?" She popped the soggy bread into her mouth, smiling at him.

She had spoken in the past tense. Ram was an Avar champion in a former life but he was that no longer and it hit him that his life in a competitive Avar cooperative was over. Forever. He'd been snatched out of his life and was hurtling away from Earth as fast as was humanly possible.

"Yeah," Ram said. "An Avar player. That's what I used to do. Before I was here. Immediately before. Feels like only yesterday."

"What games did you play, mate?" Te Zhang asked, before slurping down his protein shake.

"Action and strategy stuff, mainly," Ram said. "That's where we had most of our following, where we made most of our money."

"How'd you make money playing games?" Te asked, eating and not looking up.

The woman Alina sat beside him as if she was not listening at all or did not care. Her pale shoulders were truly remarkable.

"Tons of ways to make money in Avar," Ram said. "We sold subscriptions to fans who watch us compete and train. You got a range of purchasing options, from paying by the hour to full access. We even sold one on one time with us at a virtual location of the subscriber's choice. And we sold advertising space, merchandising, sponsorship. We did pretty well, actually."

"Let me get this straight," Te said, frowning. "So people spend, what a year's wages for an ordinary bloke to invest in this amazing kit we strap into and you can do practically anything you want with it. And they don't just decide to watch you train, they actually pay you for the pleasure of doing it? Why aren't they all just fucking each other, all the time?"

Ram laughed. "Yeah, good question."

"Forgive Te," Sifa said to Ram. "He's a technological barbarian. Listen, Te, the spectators enter the Avar space as an observer, they can't be seen by the players or interact with anything or affect the outcome of the competition or the training. It is comparable to when Bediako watches us when we're inside our units."

"I know bloody how they do it," Te said, scowling. "I'm not an idiot. I just can't for the life of me work out why anyone would waste their time watching gamers play games instead of playing with themselves." He grinned, pleased with himself, rice mashed between his teeth.

It took Ram a moment before he realized what Sifa had said. "You have Avar on this spaceship? Are you serious?"

"It is not the full Avar system. Not even close," Alina said. "We are networked no wider than one part of the ship's systems and we do not have time for visiting anywhere enjoyable. They run combat simulations where we trial tactics and techniques.

Over and over."

"It's no fun, man," Te said, talking with rice spilling out of his mouth. "Not like roaming a persistent fantasy realm with your friends hunting goblins or dragons, right?"

Ram paused, his spoon halfway to his mouth. "I played historical stuff, you know, battle simulations," Ram said. "Ancient Rome, medieval China but mostly contemporary military combat."

The big white woman paid attention when he said that. "Did you know that the Avar system was originally created by the Project?" Alina said

"What Project?" Ram asked.

Sifa laughed. "This Project."

"UNOP," Te said.

Ram shook his head. "It was developed by Tomo, a Japanese guy, working pretty much alone, at first, in his parent's basement."

Alina shook her head. "That is a cover story. Avar was developed by a Chinese and American conglomerate, commissioned by the Project's Board of Directors to come up with fully immersive simulation technology to train subjects in fighting the Wheelhunters."

"That's crazy," Ram said. "Tomo is a legend."

"This is correct," Alina said, her accent thick. Russian, probably, or something along those lines. "Tomo is a fiction. He was created by a marketing team."

"No way," Ram said. "I know all about him. I've seen interviews with him, hours of them."

Alina leaned over her food, gesturing with her spoon. "Fact. Tomo was played by at least three different actors. The first Tomo threatened to go public so they killed him and from then on digitally inserted animations of his face onto a new actor's body. A third actor provided the voice, mimicking the original Tomo. A few months later they claimed he had that fatal skiing accident and the legend was complete."

"That's crazy," Ram said. "Why would they do that?"

"Avar gathers data on the users," Alina said, looking at Ram with a particular scrutiny. "The system is used to test theories and techniques on millions of players all over the world. Not just with fighting aliens but to measure mass behavior and innovative solutions and group thinking by harnessing the computing power of the Avar network and millions of human brains. But they also use some of the games as part of the selection process for UNOP, as they did with you. And you Avars lapped it up because they sold you a lie about Tomo building encryption into the system. Anonymized, untraceable users. Do not make me laugh. You fools sold yourself to the Project and to the corporations and governments of the world."

"I can't believe this," Ram said, looking between the three new friends at his table. "You're a conspiracy nut."

Te laughed and he clapped Alina on her massive back. "He got you pegged in, like, four minutes, Alina. That's got to be a record, right?"

Alina scowled at Te while she scraped the last morsels from her tray.

"You may mock the truth as much as you wish but it remains the truth."

"Hurry up and eat all your food," Sifa said, leaning into Ram. "It will be time to fight soon."

Ram finished and sat upright, glancing around the mess as subtly as he could. The subjects were talking quietly, a few people laughed every now and then. The support staff sat here and there, reviewing content on screens between mouthfuls.

"You were right," Ram said to Sifa. "Eating was a strange experience. Sensations are as though they are happening behind a screen, a filter. Not unpleasant, exactly. Unnerving."

Te Zhang laughed. "Just wait until you take your first shit."

Sifa sighed. "Forgive his crudeness. I would say that he means well but he does not."

"Hey," Te said, sitting up straight. "I'm totally serious, man. It's the strangest thing, first few times. It's akin to dreaming about laying an ostrich egg."

Ram laughed. "Okay. I'll look forward to it."

The subjects in the mess hall were throwing Ram looks, glancing at him, whispering and smirking, frowning. Mael and the four others with him muttered almost continuously.

Sifa elbowed him. "Do not worry about them," she said. "They are merely curious."

"You should worry," Alina said, staring at Ram. "Worry very much."

"Worry most about Mael," Te said, lowering his voice. "And his crazies."

"Yes, this is correct," Alina said. "Mael is capable of killing you. He is devoid of mercy."

Sifa dismissed that with a tut. "Don't listen to her. You stay by us and we will protect you."

"No," Alina said. "Do not trust us. Do not trust anyone but yourself here or you will die."

"Okay," Te Zhang said, jerking his thumb at Alina. "Don't trust her. Me and Sifa are on your side, man, we'll stick up for you."

"I am merely being honest," Alina said, shrugging her massive, hunched shoulders. "It does not reflect on our individual ethics. The carefully cultivated culture of competition here overwhelms our attempts at prolonged unity. Everything they do and say is designed to manipulate us."

"Hard to argue with that," Te said.

"Have you considered how strange it is for Rama to be here at all?" Alina said. "He will be useless as a fighter. The obvious conclusion is that they have decanted Rama Seti as a method for obtaining percentage point increases in performance from the group. Especially from Mael, of course. He will expend energy putting Ram in his place at the bottom of the pecking order and the increase in Mael's testosterone and so on will increase his combat efficiency."

"Alina," Sifa said. "Rama is here to help. He is one of us now. And even if you are right, we should help to protect him all the more. Ignore her, Rama."

"He is not one of us," Alina said. "He will never compete on our level. They gave him an oversized body fifty years past its use by date and he has no combat experience. None."

"I'm right here," Ram said to Alina, his heart racing. "I can hear what you're saying."

Alina turned her sharp blue eyes to him. "This is not your fault. In fact, I feel sorry for you. You will die, soon."

Ram hesitated, unsure of how to react. More worrying was that his new friends, Sifa and Te, would not meet his eye.

A chime sounded and everyone in the room stood. Everyone got up and made their way through to the sparring hall. Mael Durand, Subject Alpha, strode out first and the rest gave him plenty of room.

"What's happening?" Ram asked Sifa, looking around.

He really was the tallest and probably the bulkiest of the whole group, just as Milena had said.

"Come on," Sifa said, leading him toward the exit. "Time for an evening training session. Usually, it's light activity, stretching, relaxation, mental exercise. Today will be different."

"Because I'm here. They need to put me in my place."

"Words of warning? Do whatever Bediako tells you to do. Do not think that speaking back to him or resisting his will shall be tolerated. Do not try to stand up to Mael. It will make him even more violent. If you have to fight him, simply let him knock you down and hope that Bediako stops him before he kills you."

"What?" Ram asked, panic rising. "What?"

But she patted his upper arm and walked through the door.

He followed, out into the practice hall where the group of subjects gathered in a rough half circle around Bediako.

Most of the subjects leered and or looked grim, blaming him for the extra session no doubt. But Ram barely noticed the others, because Mael Durand, Subject Alpha, stood with his head lowered, looking through his eyebrows at Ram as he approached, grinning like a maniac.

CHAPTER NINE
FIRST TEST

"THIS EVENING OUR REPLACEMENT subject finally joins us," Bediako said when Ram joined the end of the rough semicircle of subjects. His voice was harsh, like a belt sander churning through a bag of bolts. "I know some of you are unhappy about the new member of our ludus. Unhappy about having a new comrade at all and also unhappy about the individual himself. I also know that considering what is at stake, our happiness as individuals is unimportant. That is why you will all join me in welcoming Rama Seti to our ludus. Come on up here, Rama, and tell us all about yourself."

Ram stood on the edge of the group and stared at Bediako,

wondering what he should say, if he could escape, somehow.

Whatever happens, he promised himself, I have to survive this.

"Come here, now," Bediako said, scowling. "If speaking to a small group of peers makes you nervous then you will not enjoy the rest of your time here. Not at all."

Mael laughed. An evil cackle that came from deep in his gut. Most of the others laughed or smirked too. Ram stood up straight and strutted as best he could to stand beside Bediako, their laughter still ringing in his head.

It felt strange, looking around at those men and women. Shaved heads, short hair, mountains of muscle under thin vests and shorts. Hard faces on almost all of them, unfriendly eyes, downturned mouths. Fighters, soldiers, killers. A frightening bunch.

Someone sniggered.

"Right," Ram said, nodding. "Okay. Hi. My name's Ram. Er, Rama Seti but just call me Ram." He could not think of anything else to say. "I guess you don't want me here but it's not as much as I don't want to be here myself. It's pretty amazing to be on a spaceship and everything and find out that aliens are real and all but I think even in spite of all that, I'd rather be at home. I don't know what to think and feel about all this. I'll have to do what I can do."

Ram faltered, knowing he sounded like a weakling and a loser. He was about to mention his Avar career before he realized that would make it. So he paused, wondering what he could say that would make him sound impressive to the toughest group of warriors in the system.

"Very informative," Bediako said after a moment. "Thank you for that speech, Rama Seti, and the insight it gives us into your character. Emotional stuff, I think I might have shed a tear."

Most people chuckled and Ram walked toward his place at the end of the line, flooded with shame and also relief that it was over.

"Where do you think you're going?" Bediako roared.

Ram flinched, turned back.

"I think we'd all like to see what you're made of," Bediako said in a reasonable tone and looking him steadily in the eye.

Murmurs of assent. Ram did not think it would do much good to explain that he was made of naan and soda and probably something squishy, like shit. So he said nothing and stayed in the center next to Bediako.

"Any volunteers?" Bediako said.

About eight hands shot up. Almost everyone.

Mael was one of them.

Te was another and Sifa, too. Alina was not even looking in his general direction

"Mael," Bediako said and Ram's guts churned. "Put your hand down, you maniac. We don't want Rama killed on his first day, do we? Well, we know that you do." Almost everyone laughed. "Te Zhang, put your hand down, we don't want your bleeding heart leaking all over my ludus. Sifa, I know what you want to do with him, put your hand down. Aziz, yes, you will do."

The biggest man in the line of subjects stepped forward. Ram was taller but the man walking toward him was big boned and bulky and had a jaw like a bulldozer's bucket.

"Allow me to make the introductions," Bediako said. "Eziz was a junior wrestling champion in a previous life, weren't you, Eziz? Until he got banned for killing the adult Olympic silver medalist in the ring." Bediako said, chuckling. "Can you imagine, it, Rama Seti? In a sanitized, protected wrestling match, a fifteen-year-old Eziz broke the neck and skull of an adult champion. They made him join the armed forces for punishment and he started his career as a professional killer. In fact, it was more of a calling, I would say. A gift. As you can see from the size of his head, Eziz was almost this big before he got his new body. Weren't you, Eziz? Never much of a talker, though."

Eziz's dark eyes glinted in the low light, half hidden under the slab of his eyebrow ridge. He moved with a strutting solidity, like a gorilla and took a hunched stance a few meters across from Ram.

"Eziz, this is Rama Seti," Bediako said. "He sat on his fat ass his whole life and never did anything of note."

Bediako stepped back a few paces and the rest of the subjects stepped back away.

"Alright," Bediako said, "are you ready, Eziz?"

The monstrous man leered, his eyes locked on Ram's, hunched and bouncing on his toes, his long arms dangling.

"Are you ready?" Bediako said to Ram.

"Er, wait, no," Ram said, looking between Bediako and Eziz. "What are the rules?"

Bediako laughed, as did the others.

"Alright, let's go," Bediako shouted and clapped his hands.

Eziz crouched lower and shuffled forward.

Ram instinctively took a step backward. Were they expecting him to fight? On his first day? On a full stomach?

"Ram."

Milena's voice sounded in his ear, from inside his head.

"Ram, it's Milena. I'm watching you right now. I am monitoring your vitals. Do not be afraid. They will not allow you to be seriously hurt."

"Okay," Ram said as Eziz circled. The other subjects called out advice for Eziz or Ram but Ram's heart was pounding so hard that he couldn't hear the words, just the hum of the noise.

"Don't speak, just listen," Milena said, talking quickly. "Eziz will toy with you, try to humiliate you before he beats you. Your best hope is to hit hard, surprise him. Show everyone you mean business. You will not win. Do not think that. Do not have hope for victory. But you must fight, right now. Here he comes, watching him. He's a grappler, so you have to punch him. Punch, kick, strike. Go for his face, his eyes."

Bouncing lightly on his toes, Eziz shifted rhythmically, as

though he was dancing.

Ram had never thrown a punch in real life. In Avar, he had fought thousands of battles. Unarmed combat, swords, guns and energy weapons, Ram had used them all. He'd crushed battalions, he'd smashed armies. But it was all in Avar. Throwing a punch should be the most natural thing in the world, instinctive and also he'd performed the move thousands of times in virtual practice. He knew in theory what you had to do. But doing it in Avar, when the only consequences was a little tap of sensory feedback, was a world away from what he was facing in that moment, with a monstrous great elite wrestler coming for him.

Eziz feinted forward and Ram jerked back, causing much amusement from the others. Ram got halfway through a sigh of relief when Eziz changed direction, breaking rhythm. The room spun and Ram crashed into the floor, on his back. When he looked up, Eziz had already retreated, grinning and waving at the others.

"Get up, Ram," Milena's voice sounded in his head.

"What happened?" Ram muttered, like an idiot as he climbed to his feet.

"He tripped you," Milena said. "Come on, Ram, you have to fight him."

Ram glanced at the crowd as Sifa shouted encouragement.

"Watch it," Milena shouted and Eziz was on him again, feet pounding on the mat. Ram threw his hands up, stepping back and to the side. He realized with surprise that he had caught Eziz's hands in his own.

Eziz was surprised, too. He froze, just for a moment, before, twisting Ram's arms down and round. Ram found himself spun about with Eziz's arm across his throat and the weight of the big man on his back, bearing him down to the floor.

"Ram," Milena's voice came through, calm and clear in his head. "He has you in a rear choke hold. Force his hands apart, reach up and separate his grip."

Ram fell to his knees, Eziz pushing him down, panting hot, spicy breath into Ram's ear. Reaching up to his own throat, Ram grasped Eziz's massive wrists and tried to pry them apart. It was like trying to bend an iron bar or pull apart a steel chain. But it did ease the pressure on his neck.

"Good, Ram, keep it up," Milena said. "Now, hunch your shoulders. Push your chin into your chest. Keep pulling his hands apart."

With the pressure of Eziz on his back, all Ram could see was the floor underfoot, the slight wrinkling of the black padded mats. Ram blindly followed Milena's instruction and felt the pressure of the choke ease off further.

Eziz twisted and slammed a knee into Ram's kidney. The blow was more a surprise than painful but it distracted Ram's attention enough to find Eziz slipping his arms up higher, one tight into his neck and the other on the back of Ram's head, pushing it down.

Ram knew he was going down.

"Don't give up, Ram," Milena said. "Reach up to the back of your head with your right hand, find his fingers. Do it now." Ram's vision darkened, blackness rolling in from the edges. But he obeyed Milena's insistent voice. "Grab his fingers, hard, bend them back. Snap them off, Ram, tear them from his hand. You're bigger than he is. You're stronger. You hear me, Ram, you're stronger than he is, just rip his hands off."

Ram felt where Eziz was forcing his head down, grabbed the first two fingers and pushed up as hard as he could.

It turned out, that was pretty hard.

The bones in Eziz's fat fingers snapped, with a series of crunching, grinding pops. Eziz roared in Ram's ear and released the choke on his back.

Ram got to one knee, breathing deeply. He had done it, he had broken free.

"It's not over," Milena said. "Watch out for—"

Eziz thumped the back of his skull and Ram went down. The world went black.

Bediako rolled him over and stood looking down at him. The instructor did not help him up and he stood right over him, suggesting Ram was supposed to stay down. That was fine, so far as Ram was concerned. People were clapping and jeering.

"Eziz," Bediako shouted, though he kept looking down at Ram. "You useless bastard, go to medical right now. How you got selected for this project, I will never know."

"He was supposed to be untrained," Eziz said from behind Bediako. "I was just having fun."

"Talk to me again after I've dismissed you," Bediako said. "And I'll break every bone in both your hands."

Milena's voice was a whisper in Ram's ear. "Stay down," she said. "And well done. Very well done, indeed." It sounded as if she was smiling.

The laughing and jeering died away and Bediako stepped back. "Alright, thanks to that shameful display, we are not done for the day. You people clearly need more practice, if a complete novice can incapacitate one of you. Now, pair up. You know your drills. Zhang, you start showing Rama Seti here some fundamentals. Mind he doesn't snap your neck or something."

The line broke up and Te and Sifa pulled Ram up off the floor.

"You didn't die," Te said, grinning. "That's something."

"I broke his fingers," Ram said, feeling the tender parts of his neck.

"He was not expecting that," Sifa said. "Where did you learn grappling?"

"Just now, actually," Ram said, rubbing the back of his head where Eziz had thumped him. "What did he hit me with? A shotgun?"

"Your good old fashioned front kick, mate," Te said. "Cracked one right at your light switch, didn't he."

"I guess," Ram said.

137

"How are you?" Sifa asked.

"Fine," Ram nodded his thanks. "I mean, I think I took my first shit just now and you were right, it was a pretty strange experience."

Te laughed. "A day of firsts for you, isn't it," he said. "All you got to do now is make it through your first sparring session and then your first night."

Ram looked at the group of subjects as they separated themselves out from each other. At the far end of the room, Eziz turned back in the doorway, holding his injured hand, before he stepped through the door. His eyes were full of malice and then carried on. Mael whispered something to his partner and they both glared at Ram as if they were wolves and he was an injured lamb.

"What do you think my chances are of seeing tomorrow?" Ram asked Sifa and Te.

They traded a look.

"Ask us in the morning," Sifa said.

CHAPTER TEN
DARK NIGHT

THEY TRAINED FOR another half hour. The whole time, Rama felt sure he was about to get jumped by one of the others. Every time he looked over his shoulder, Mael was leering at him.

Still, Ram spent the session attempting to learn basic striking and grappling techniques. He thought he had done well but Sifa assured him that he had not.

Bediako dismissed them and Ram stuck close to Te and Sifa as they gathered to head for the barracks section.

"So, listen," Ram muttered to Sifa at the end. "What exactly do you mean the ludus barracks are unobserved? I'm not sure how to make it through the night without any protection against him."

Ram watched as Mael walked off toward the mess hall in silence, trailed by the other subjects and the support staff, all chattering and making a huge, excited noise. He was like a famous actor or an Avar champion getting chased by his fans.

"Everywhere onboard is covered with cameras, okay?" Sifa said. "Everywhere on the *Victory*, you are filmed, recorded. Monitored. Measured. But not in the ludus barracks. That time is for us. Private time."

"Sounds nice when you put it that way," Ram said.

"It's not, bro," Te said. "Think about what it's like to spend your time with a bunch of killers and no oversight. No one to come rescue you. No one to break up the fights but us."

"Do not be so dramatic," Sifa said, punching Te on the shoulder. "It is not all bad. We are tired and the nights are long but we need not feel lonely."

Te grinned and Sifa smiled. They followed the rest of the subjects toward the mess and the barracks beyond.

"We'll watch your back," Te said. "Me, Sifa. Even Alina, maybe, depending on her mood."

"You'll help me watch out for Eziz?" Ram said. "Call me crazy but I reckon he is plotting revenge for his broken fingers."

"Eziz is a dangerous man," Sifa said. "But he is a follower, not a leader. I think he was ranked as a private in the military."

"He lacks the imagination to instigate something alone," Te said. "The one you need to watch out for is Mael. He isn't afraid of using the darkness to hurt you."

"Why are you helping me?" Ram said. "What's in it for you?"

"We're just good people, mate," Te said, grinning.

Sifa tutted. "A few of us resist Mael's demands, his bullying, his violence." Her beautiful face twisted into a cold anger. "We must stick together to survive."

"I can't believe this," Ram said. "Aren't we going to fight the aliens? What's with this infighting? It doesn't make any sense. We should be on the same side."

Sifa nodded. "I think so too."

"We're unusual for not following this techno-primitivism anarcho-competitivism bullshit. But this is how they do it. The right level of conflict, designed to produce the highest performance. It's not about creating harmony for us. It's not about us being happy or feeling comfortable."

"And many of the subjects and crew are military or ex-military," Sifa said. "This is how they do things."

"Alright," Ram said. "I understand, I get it."

Ram was tired but amazed by his new body and what it was capable of. The sparring had been difficult but the most fun he'd had in real life, maybe ever. He was aching, exhausted and the thought of sleep was welcoming. On the other hand, he was afraid of being alone and unobserved.

"So there's no cameras in the barracks," Ram said. "Can we still speak to our drivers?"

Te chuckled. "Man, if Milena was my driver then I'd be

missing her, too, bro."

"Your poor driver, Te," Sifa said. "She's beautiful."

"She is," Te said. "She's no seven-foot-five African goddess like you, babe. But Milena? Oh, man, she's something else."

Sifa laughed. "There is no contact with the drivers in the barracks, our communications are shut off," she said. "So if you want to speak to sexy little Milena before tomorrow then do so now."

Milena came through in Ram's internal speaker. "They're right, Ram. We should speak about tonight." Ram found a quiet place at the side of the hall outside the barracks door and leaned against the wall.

"What, you're just listening to me all the time?" He said, feeling violated all over again.

"Watching you, too," she said. "That's my job. I'm here to help you."

"Alright then," Ram whispered. "You're going to help me get through tonight. You're going to give me advice on how to deal with Mael and whoever else decides to put me in my place tonight."

"The main thing is to relax," Milena said. "They won't kill you on the first night, probably, so just make sure you stand up for yourself. Hit back, at least once. You might get barely one opportunity before they get you so try to break someone's nose or gouge out an eye, maybe. No matter what it costs you."

"Thanks for the pep talk," Ram said, his heart hammering.

"Sweet dreams," Milena said in his ear. "

"Come on, Ram," Sifa said, waving him over. "We will take you in."

"Into the dungeon," Te said, grinning. "We call it the dungeon."

"No we do not," Sifa said. "No one calls it the dungeon, don't be ridiculous."

She slipped her arm inside Ram's and drew him after the others. Her arms were rippling with muscle, shining and dark and her shoulders showed striations, so low was her body fat. Where most of the others were hulking monsters, gorillas or rhinos, Sifa was like a cat. A big cat, admittedly but there was a fluidity to her movements that was bordering on inhuman. Te strode a pace in front of them, his V-shaped upper body half as wide again as Sifa's.

The subjects in front streamed through the empty mess hall and then through the heavy security door at the rear into the barracks beyond. Bediako's assistants were standing around, wishing everyone a good night and filing back the way they had come.

Sifa squeezed Ram's arm. "All of us in this ludus, everyone here is training so that, whoever is the best of us, is in the best shape they can be when they fight the Wheelhunter. If it takes our deaths to achieve that goal, then it is acceptable to me. I can say that in truth. My driver agrees with me and I believe her. Te Zhang believes it, too, correct, my dear Te? Everyone on the

Victory, I bet, believes themselves as a means to an end."

"Mael thinks that we are the means to his end," Te muttered.

Sifa inclined her head in acknowledgment.

They stepped through into the barracks room. The door was large and bulky, like a blast door on an old battleship. Ram wanted to ask why there was so much heavy security but he was afraid to ask. He was getting tired of all the questions.

"Thanks, I appreciate you helping me out, explaining things to me," Ram said. "I got to say, the idea of dying for a cause I never signed up for is pretty strange. I'm not sure if I want to be here at all but I guess escape is off the table now."

Sifa stopped him in the doorway, grabbing the flesh of his arm in a grip of steel. "If I was in your position," she said, all her charm and warmth suddenly gone, "taken against my will, then I would still give myself, my life, body and soul to this project. This is for our species, Ram. For our culture, for all the cultures that make our civilization. Everything that humanity has accomplished in thousands of years may be lost if we do not give of ourselves to making this mission a success. I will suffer any hardship, experience any pain and humiliation and loss necessary to contribute to that. But all this does not mean I must be rude to my comrades and colleagues. Taking the time to befriend you, instruct you, help you, these things take little of my time or my energy and cause no harm. More than this, by helping you, we help our mission. Come on."

Ram pulled his arm away. "Fine," he said. "I get it. This is all very important."

She tutted and turned away. Ram knew he needed to keep her as an ally, that he should apologize for being sarcastic or flippant but he couldn't bring himself to.

They stepped into a long room with doors down both sides, eight doors aside and one at the far end. The center aisle was a communal space with three benches running down the middle and five of the rest of the subjects already stood and sat around, chatting. Mael was not one of them.

"Your room is the last one on the left," Sifa said, speaking brusquely.

"It belonged to your predecessor and no one wanted to swap rooms," Te said. "They're all the bloody same, anyway."

They got halfway through the center of the long barracks when Mael squeezed himself through the doorway into his room, in the center of the right-hand row, half blocking their way. Sifa and Te stopped.

"You," Mael said to Ram, his face contorted into a sneer.

He wore nothing but a pair of tight shorts, he was rubbing some sort of oil or lotion over himself. His body was ludicrously over muscled, his pectorals were vast, his deltoids like upturned bowls carved from solid olive wood. He wasn't as bulky as Ram was, nor even as big as Eziz but his body was astonishingly perfect, with a kind of symmetry and proportion to his physique that made him stand out even amongst a room full of giant freaks. His arms were crisscrossed with veins resembling a river system seen from orbit and his thighs were as thick as redwoods. Mael wiped his hands on a rag and tossed it back into his room.

All the others fell silent and gathered in the central area, a couple of half-stripped subjects leaning on their doorframes to watch the confrontation. The heavy barracks door behind was closed. All twelve of the subjects were there. Ram looked around for Bediako or the ludus crew members who could help him, protect him.

There was no one but the subjects.

Mael laughed. "Alone, at last."

The quality of his musculature was noticeable, even to Ram. Mael's muscles popped out all over, they seemed dense and solid. Clearly, Mael had received the deluxe version of the tank grown synthetic bodies.

"Thanks for being so welcoming," Ram said, trying to sound calm.

"Who do you think you are?" Mael said, speaking softly. He kept his distance but his body almost quivered with tension, as if he was aching to leap forward.

A couple of the guys near Ram backed away slowly.

The feeling of unreality crept back. Ram felt as though he was in Avar, acting out a script. As if what was happening was set on rails and he was just going through the motions.

"I'm Rama," he said. "You're Mael, right? I met Te Zhang and Sifa and Alina. And I met Eziz, didn't I, Eziz, how you doing there, fingers all fixed up, right?"

Eziz, leaning against the next doorway, scowled. His heavy, black eyebrows knotting together over his nose. A few of the others snorted and laughed at the audacity. Or the foolishness, perhaps.

"You are right," Sifa said, stepping forward, placing one of her dark, perfect shoulders slightly in front of his. "We should introduce ourselves. Bediako should have done it earlier but is it up to us to make our own community here. We should take it in turns, yes?"

Mael took a step forward himself, flexing his back and latissimi dorsi muscles. "He won't survive long enough for it to matter if he knows our names," Mael said, his accent heavy with rounded vowels. "He won't survive his first week. Look at the body they gave him. It's a fifty-year-old design, it didn't work last time and it won't work this time. What were they thinking, bringing those fucking things on the ship? Is that really the best the Project has got, are we so poor with resources that we have to share our space with that? With that thing? Put any one of one of you on that body and you'd be the bottom of the heap so what the fuck is this moron going to do? You saw him sparring with Te Zhang, he's like a child. Like a disabled fucking child and they just handed that freak body to him, like winning a lottery. And the prize he has won is a painful death."

A deep anger rose from Ram's guts, his face flushing hot. He wanted to stride over and punch the guy but he was rooted to the spot by fear. He knew he should at least shoot back an insult but he did not know what to say so he just stood there like an idiot, like a coward.

"Sure," Te said, shrugging and stepping up to Ram, clapping him on the shoulder. "You're right, Mael, you're right. Doesn't mean you have to be an asshole, does it?"

The room seemed to take a collective breath.

"He doesn't deserve to be here," Mael said, jabbing a finger at Ram. "His presence puts the mission in danger. When he dies, we will all be better off."

With a final sneer, he turned and barged back into his sleeping quarters.

Ram breathed out in a long sigh.

"So that's our buddy Mael," Te said, attempting levity. "Who wants to say hello next?"

Four of the remaining subjects unfolded themselves from where they sat or leaned and stomped off. Two went into Mael's room, two of the others into an adjacent room, banging the doors shut behind them.

Te pointed at the ones who stalked off with him and turned to Ram with a lopsided grin on his tattooed face.

"The Chinese woman who went in with Mael was Jun. She was some sort of special forces super soldier in her past life. Not sure what because her file is redacted to fuck and she doesn't talk about it. So we all reckon she was an assassin of some sort, right, like political murders from the Chinese Terror a few years back, remember that? She's the smallest subject here but she's fast and she's ruthless. She'll smash your face in without even changing her own expression. She might be a robot, we don't know."

The others around laughed, nodding.

"And you already met that miserable bastard Eziz, he was from Turkmenistan, originally. Great wrestlers, those guys, they love it. They all have those long arms and big heads, must be something in the food up there. You just stay away from him altogether. He was even better with an assault rifle that he was grappling in the dust, I think he just likes blood and shit. And did you see that big white chick? She's an American called Genesis. Crazy name, right? Religious parents. She's a killer, though, another special forces soldier, a United States Marine special forces unit so secret she still won't even tell us what it was called. She spent her twenties in the jungles and mountains in South America fighting for the forces of capitalism over the corrupt, communist, totalitarian assholes. How many people do you reckon she killed? Hundreds, definitely. She liked to use a big knife to cut people up, she's totally insane. Black guy's called Gondar. Ethiopian army, you might have heard of him from the news a few years back when he took on all those terrorists who had taken the airport?"

"I don't remember that," Ram said.

Alina spoke up from across the room. "He was one of those kept ignorant and enslaved by the Avar network and he knows nothing of the world."

"Oh yeah, I forgot," Te said, waving down Ram's objections.

"Anyway, you got to watch the footage, it was broadcast live and he went through twenty or thirty of them. Proper ninja shit, guns, knives, hand to hand. The guys running UNOP recruited him straight from the hospital after. I think now he worships Mael Durand as the chosen one so he must be another nutcase. Stay away from him, he'd kill for Mael without thinking about it."

"Okay," Ram said.

"They all would," Alina said, without looking up.

"Hi, I'm Alejandra," a woman said, strutting over and taking Ram's hand. She had a big, crooked nose and a closely shaved head. "I am sorry you had such a poor welcome. I hope that you do not die."

"Thanks, I appreciate that."

"Didem," another said, a sturdily built woman with coffee color skin and big, hooded eyes. She stepped up close and put her head so close to his that her face was touching his body as she muttered at him. "You should not make friends with anyone here. Everyone will betray you. Sifa and Te are the weakest of us all, they cannot protect you. Save yourself, give yourself to Mael and you might make it through."

"Er," Ram said, wanting to ask what she meant but she nodded and stepped back.

"Javi," a black haired man said, stepping up with a lopsided half-grin. He had a face like a coyote. "You made a real bad choice signing up for this. Oh, wait, you didn't. Never mind, good luck to you, friend. Listen, you stay away from Mael." He lowered his voice and leaned in slightly. "And you stay away from Alina, too. She's even worse. Seriously. I'm not kidding."

Ram wanted to ask why but he already turned away.

"Yeah, hello," Ram said, looking around at the faces of those that had remained in the central common area, feeling that he needed to say something but being overwhelmed by how much he wanted to express. "I know this is strange for you. And I know I'm here because someone you knew died. I never wanted to be here. They never asked me. But now I am here, all I can do is do my best. Everyone expects me to fail, I know that. And maybe I will. But I will do my best to live up to your standards. I'm just going to give it everything I have."

"Well said, mate," Te shouted and clapped. No one joined him but he did not seem to care and he kept clapping enthusiastically for a good few seconds.

"You're one of us now," Sifa said when he stopped, grinning.

"No," Eziz said from the doorway to his room. He stood leaning against the frame, his voice a rumble so deep it was felt as much as heard. His broken fingers had been fixed in no time at all but it was not his body that had been wounded. "No, he is not. He never will be."

Eziz turned and slammed his door.

I have made a couple of allies, Ram thought, staring at the door as the air yet rang with the slamming of it.

But he knew they might be weak and he had no idea how far

their friendship would go. And the one thing he did know for certain was that he had managed, on his first day, to make a lot of powerful, psychotic enemies.

CHAPTER ELEVEN
DEFEND

TE SHOWED Ram his quarters while Sifa went to hers.

"We usually have more time before lights out," Te said, "but with that extra sparring session taking up our down time, it'll be dark soon."

"That's my fault," Ram said as he stepped into his new home. "Sorry about that."

"Nah, that's Bediako's fault," Te said. "That fucker's a bastard."

A rectangular room dominated by a giant slab of a bed along one wall. Underneath were pull-out bins for storage. A plain desk and chair took up half the opposite wall and laying on the desk was a screen. Another door led to the shower and toilet. It was completely bare, totally sterile.

"This is lovely," Ram said to Te. "So homely."

He knew he would have to make it through the night in that box. He'd have to make it through the night and then all the nights after.

"How do I lock the door?"

"Bloody good thinking," Te said. "You got your head screwed on straight, you have. Sorry, just a little UNOP subjects humor for you. Yeah, mechanical lock here operated by your thumbprint, there's the scanner by the door. I'd recommend that whenever you are alone in here, sleeping or showering, you lock it up. There's a little red light that shows on your door when it's locked."

Ram sighed and it came out shaky. "I have to lock myself in every night?"

"You get used to it. Anyway, Mael and those guys are just excited to have a new boy to fuck with. The routine here is boring but if you can last this next few days, they'll forget about you in a few weeks."

"Weeks, sure, I can make it through a few weeks." He looked around the space that was a quarter of the size of his old bedroom in Constitution Plaza. "Stuck in here."

"You can do what you want to the room, decorate it with whatever you like," Te said, before slapping himself on the head. "But you don't have anything to decorate it with, do you, mate.

We all brought personal effects with us on the trip, pictures of home and trophies and music and shit. I would have thought the bastards could have at least stolen some of your stuff when they kidnapped you."

"Well they only kidnapped my head," Ram said. "Maybe they had to travel light."

"Good point. Fuck it, anyway, it's all just stuff. Who needs it?"

"Do you think we could pop back so I can get my silk dressing gown?" Ram really did miss that thing. He used to wear it every day. It might have even still fit him, though it might have been a bit short.

"Sure, man, no problem. Earth is five billion kilometers in that direction. I'll get the ship's captain to swing her about."

"There's a screen on the desk," Ram said, sitting on the bed. The mattress was thin but made of some sort of gel that adjusted to his shape and supported his weight. It was comfy. "What can I do with it?"

"Not a lot," Te said, pursing his lips. "It's just on a section of the ship network. Still, you can read anything about anything, watch a million years' worth of instructional and entertainment video, listen to a billion years' of audio on anything you can think of. Just can't contact no one, can't create nothing."

"Games?"

"Nah. Nothing like what you're used to. Mostly it's a way of wasting time, relaxing, you know. Helps to unwind in the evening but we don't get much downtime. Anyway, it's funny, when you can't interact with other people on there then it starts to lose its appeal. I only use it every now and again these days."

"What do you use it for?"

"Pornography," Te said. "And if it's not porn, sometimes I watch the old footage, you know, of the previous three missions. That feels like the day job, though, because we study them anyway, I just. I don't know, I can't help but wonder about the aliens. I find them pretty bloody mesmerizing. The way they move, cartwheeling like that? And their arms are so weird, twirling and flexing like puppets. And they have no head, or eyes or mouth. Freaks me out, big time but I can't help but watch anyway."

"What do we know about them?"

"I don't know how much they told you so far," Te said. "Truth is, we don't know a whole lot, not as much as we want to. They're faster than us, stronger than us. Tougher, too, thick skin. We don't know how thick, though. We have unproven hypotheses about their physiology. UNOP biologists have been studying their DNA for decades now but that only gets us so far."

"Wait a minute," Ram said, rubbing his eyes. "They have DNA? How is that possible?"

"Sure they do, bro," Te said. "I mean, look at them. Like I said, their morphology is pretty different from earthlings but check it out."

Te tapped the screen and brought up the video of

Ambassador Diaz and paused it a second before it swiped the man to pieces. Diaz's face was frozen in a state of terror. Te cut Diaz out of the picture and dragged the Wheelhunter image so it filled the screen. The creature still as a statue, leaning over like a bike taking a corner, one arm scything down toward where Diaz would have been, the other held out and up for counterbalance.

"Check it out, man," Te said. "They've got six legs and two arms. The legs have feet and the arms have hands. The limbs have joints and they have a rigid core inside that function in the same way as bone. It has skin on the outside, internal tissue that corresponds to our own skeletal muscle, expanding and contracting on opposing sides of a limb. Totally incredible, isn't it, think about all the possible ways a lifeform might look. In all the galaxy, all the possible planets with all the variables and then all the chance occurrences over billions of years from the origin of life on those planets up to now. Imagine all the possible forms that life might take. There might be intelligent blobs of slime or things like articulated bundles of sticks or beings a centimeter tall or ones as big as a skyscraper. And there must be species out there amongst the stars that are stranger than we can imagine, forms and function that no human has even dreamed up, surely there must be, that's reasonable to assume. So what are the chances that we end up fighting something as relatively similar to humans?"

"I don't know, what are the chances?"

"No idea but they got to be pretty slim, right?" Te said. "This has all kinds of implications. Maybe DNA is not some crazy chance occurrence that happened only on Earth. Okay, so there's a bunch of ways organic molecules could potentially encode data for it to be passed on to the next generation of organisms. So you would expect that other planets might evolve life based on these other molecules combining in unique structures. But when they scraped the remnants of alien skin from the remains of our predecessors, they found this goddamn thing has DNA. So maybe DNA assembling is just a standard thing the universe does whenever the conditions are right. You know, increasing complexity from the big bang, into stars then heavier elements, organic molecules and water, planets with complex geology and then from that you get strings of chemicals and the RNA and DNA chains with cells and then increasingly complex life based on that DNA, you know. Just as the stars are made from hydrogen and helium, life in the universe is made from nucleic acids. That's just how it goes."

"Sounds plausible," Ram said.

"Others say we can't draw conclusions from so small a sample size. And one that isn't random. The Orb Builders brought the Wheelhunters to our solar system, right? Maybe they matched us together for combat because we are so physiologically similar."

"Okay," Ram said. "That sounds plausible too."

"Here's the one that boggles my noodle, right. So they're so similar to us, relatively speaking, that it's too much of a coincidence. So what if they're not even natural beings at all?

Speaking for this theory is the fact they don't seem to have any means of procreation, as far as we can tell. Maybe they were created from us, using our DNA and twisting it somehow. Imagine that."

"Yeah, that would be incredible," Ram said. He yawned.

"Oh, man," Te said. "Look at me yakking on at you. You got to sleep, mate. Tomorrow, you'll have a session with your driver, first thing in the counseling rooms on the ludus. They usually give you bit of a medical, too. Juice you up with your steroids and estrogen blockers and human growth hormone shots and all that and take your blood to sample, nothing to worry about. Then you got to eat and it's resistance training. We're all looking forward to seeing what that old model body is capable of. I bet you can deadlift more than Mael. I got to see that, can't wait. I got money on you, son, you got to get your rest. Light switch is by your head when you lay down, right there. Rest well."

"Thanks. Thanks for helping me. I don't know what it would have been like today without you and Sifa."

"Anything that helps the Project, right? One of us has got to smash that Wheeler or everything humanity has ever done will be for nothing. Now shut up and go to sleep."

"Feeling pretty tired now," Ram admitted, rubbing his eyes. They were so dry he could barely keep them open.

Te turned just before he left. "Don't forget to mechanically lock your door behind me, it's this fingerprint pad right here." He tapped the wall by the door and Ram gave him a thumbs up.

"Alright, night-night, pumpkin."

Before locking the door, Ram lay back on his bed, just for a moment, overtaken by a mighty yawn. The lights around him dimmed automatically, on a timer or trigger by his yawning. The mattress molded itself to the weight and size of his body and supported his head.

His head was the one part of him he had left. Even his head had been tampered with. Dr. Fo had increased the volume and density of the bone in his skull and jaw. They had implanted him with communications devices and systems for monitoring his take up of hormones and who knew what else.

He had a vision of his old body, left rotting in his apartment in Delhi. He saw the great mound of fat and skin that had been him, that belonged to him, laying there with no head amongst his computer and Avar equipment. All his ergonomic furniture, custom printed desks and his precious Avar chair. He missed slipping into his custom headset, and he missed the familiar feel of the straps and foot and armrests that had supported him, held him, for so many years. He missed it so badly that it hurt.

Pure imagination but he could see it so well in his mind's eye. His body rotting right there in his apartment, polluting all the electronic equipment until the stench alerted his neighbors or the building supervisors or security guards. Maybe one of his regular delivery people had called for help when he failed to answer his door. Whoever broke in would have found his headless corpse. His gigantic body, his folds of fat finally exposed to other people. They would have seen everything. Had the police shown his body to his parents? Surely, if so, they would have done it remotely, that was something, at least.

He felt more shame at his body, rotting there until it was discovered, than he ever had when it was attached to him. The reek that would have come off his rotting old, leaking, decomposing, gut-stinking body, was shameful. Someone would have had to deal with his body, get it ready for cremation, maybe washing his skin down. Someone would have had to throw out the blood and guts that had been Ram and clean the place up for the new tenants. Perhaps his parents would have inherited the place, that was good. They might want to rent it out or sell it. He supposed that they didn't really need the money but at least it was something. A pang of loss twisted his guts. He had loved that apartment. It was his, he had worked hard for it, he had made it his own in every way. It was his sanctuary where no one could see him or hear him unless he was in Avar.

All gone.

He raised his new hands, turning them this way and that. There was no denying that Ram had been given quite the upgrade. What they'd done to him was unforgivable. They'd restricted his life, conscripted him into a service against his will. It was as great a violation as you could get, other than murdering him outright. It was like being put in prison for a crime that had never happened. They had no right but they claimed they could throw out morality because the survival of the species itself was at stake. Or even all species on Earth and maybe even the artificially manipulated human and animal lifeforms that humanity had designed and created to carry out tasks all over the solar system. It was worse even than that, though, because if all the people were gone then that would mean all their culture would be gone. Everything that humanity had ever done, every person who ever had a thought, every painting, every war and every song would be gone forever and it would be as if humanity had never existed at all.

So maybe they had a point. Maybe Ram was being selfish by objecting to what was being done to him. Maybe it really was his duty to sacrifice himself for the good of the species. There was something good and noble in that. A way of being truly useful.

Although, it was a shame that no one would ever know. Even if he survived, which seemed doubtful, he would never be able to leave the Project and he could tell no one what he had done, where he had been. It would be nice for his parents, his friends and his fans if they could know why he had died.

Either way, there was nothing that he could do about it now he was on the ship. Incredible that he was in space at all. He'd always wanted to see the solar system but from an early age, he'd known he'd never pass the physical requirements for colonization. He would have had to become wealthy indeed to pay for private passage somewhere and even then any colony or station would have required him to undergo extensive surgery to remove the fat and skin from his body. Even if that had been done he'd have had to have proved his underlying psychological issues were addressed so his addiction to eating did not continue.

He wondered what there would be for breakfast. He was drifting off to sleep but there was something he had to do first. He would remember what it was in a minute.

But visiting Mars would have been nice. Ram liked visiting the colonies through Avar. The underdome plazas of the crater communities were his favorite, showing that familiar yet not familiar sky and Sun of Mars. Seeing Phobos pass overhead twice a day. Even now that he was actually in space, he was heading far from any human colonies. Heading out to beyond the fledgling outposts around Titan and the tentative, Artificial Person staffed research station on Triton. Ram suspected that he would not survive the intense training that he was about to face. And if he did, what would life be like for him? He would be a permanent slave for UNOP in some way until his mighty Artificial Person body fell apart in just a few years. The best he could hope for was a life like Bediako, big but physical health suffering and mind rapidly deteriorating.

He yawned, rubbed his eyes. Had an urge to go through his usual nighttime habits, power down his equipment unless it was updating and have a final snack. Lately, he'd been devouring a pack of spiced baked soya beans. He missed them.

Ram missed Avar.

Every day of his life, for twenty years, he had spent time in Avar. Most days in the last ten years he'd spent almost all his waking hours in Avar. Either practicing, playing competitive matches, or meeting friends and colleagues, attending lectures or traveling to virtual environments in second worlds or visiting real world places in real time. He'd been experiencing his time on the ship as a prolonged Avar excursion and that was okay. That was making things bearable. But by now, if he could, he'd be switching up to go somewhere else. He'd go play some crazy zero-G deathmatches in *Delta4Niner*, maybe man a machine gun nest in the squad based tactical shooter *Indonesian Civil War 7* or chill out with his buddies for a couple of hours in their favorite tavern in 15th century Germany.

On the spaceship, though, it would always be the same program. And, in the morning, it was about to get a whole lot worse.

He woke, heart hammering in his chest. Hands held him down. A great weight on his chest. There was something over his face.

Couldn't breathe.

Ram bucked and writhed but his hands were pinned to the wall behind his head. Someone held his ankles.

"Shhhhhh..." a hot voice hissed in his ear. "You do not deserve to be here."

Mael.

Ram stopped moving. There was a cloth or something tight over his face but he could just about see shapes moving beyond it. Ram could just about suck a few mouthfuls of air through it.

"That's it," Mael's voice whispered. "Do not fight this."

Were they going to kill him?

I'm bigger than any of them, Ram remembered.

Ram heaved himself up, pulling his elbows down, drawing his feet up. The men holding him were not expecting his strength, perhaps, or not expecting him to fight so hard. But Ram got one hand free and lashed out with a fist, catching someone on the head or somewhere hard. It hurt Ram but the other person cried out in pain or surprise. Exhilarated by his success he kicked with one freed leg and thrashed it about until he connected with someone else, knocking them down. I'm doing it, Ram, thought, I'm fighting them.

Then someone hit him. The blow to the stomach was like being run over by a train. It knocked the wind out of him, stole his breath. They grabbed his limbs again, pinned him.

"I told you not to fight this," Mael said.

They hit him again, the shock traveling through his body. They punched or kicked his chest, then his stomach again. Ram's instinct was to curl up into a tight ball but they held him stretched out. Someone threw the towel or something over his face again and held it tight across him, pinning his head down no matter how much he struggled. He could not have been more vulnerable.

Hands began grasping at his hips, tugging down his shorts, fingers digging into his skin.

Mael's voice shouted. "What are you doing?"

The hands at his hips withdrew.

Eziz answered. "I want to fuck him."

Ram shouted but a blow crunched into his stomach. It crushed his breath to dust.

"And we will," Mael was saying. "We all will. But let's not rush things. Plenty of time. It's better this way. There's months before we reach the Orb. What else are we going to do at night? Leave his face."

Again and again, they hit him in the body, the arms and legs. He struggled to suck air through the towel over his mouth, eyes and nose. Someone punched him in the balls so hard he though his new testicles would be ruptured. They dragged him off the bed, kicking and punching him. Ram curled up in a ball, finally, and they rained blows down onto his back and kidneys. A final flurry knocked him senseless.

When he came to, his attackers were gone. His door was closed.

Ram found himself on the floor between his desk and his bed. He gingerly touched his head and chest. It hurt, all over his body. And yet the pain was nothing like it should have been.

One of the benefits of being barely human anymore.

He climbed back onto his bed, wincing and breathing hard. He pulled up his top. The ridges and furrows of his abdominal muscles were red and purple with bruises all over, mottled like an old bowl of tarka dal he once left out for a month without noticing.

He looked at the door. Imagined throwing it open, storming out after Mael and the others. Imagined finding Te and Sifa and Alina and demanding their help.

Instead, he lay on his side and curled up, pulling his blanket over himself.

He did not know how he would do it. But he knew that he would hurt them back.

CHAPTER TWELVE
HELP

"HOW WAS YOUR FIRST night in the barracks?" Milena asked as Ram sat down.

They were meeting face to face in a section on the opposite side of the ludus ring. The room was small, set up as a counselor's office. Ram took a seat in a chair made for his size and Milena reclined in the comfortable one opposite.

He looked at her closely, peered into her eyes. Her head tilted professionally to one side, her eyebrows raised in open enquiry. They probably taught that expression in counseling training, as if she was interested in what he was going to tell her and as if she was prepared to listen and be empathetic. But it was bullshit. She wasn't there to help him. She was trying to present a poker face but he could see anxiety in her eyes, he was sure. She knew, no doubt about it, she knew.

"I can't fucking believe you can sit there and ask me that," Ram said, crossing his arms. They were so heavily muscled it was quite uncomfortable and he uncrossed them. "You're monitoring everything that happens to me. You tell me how things are going."

"You're angry because something happened last night," Milena said. "Yes, we monitor everything. I noted your adrenaline and cortisol spiking, your heart racing and all the other signs that you were undergoing some exertion. What happened?"

"You know what happened," Ram said, shuddering. "I don't want to talk about it," he said. "This place is crazy. Is this really the best way to come up with the best fighters on Earth? Really? It's like one of those college fraternity clubs from America. It's like an army barracks. It's like a school or something. Who are these people? How can something so important be entrusted to maniacs like these guys? Isn't there a better way?"

Milena looked Ram square in the face. "Mael attacked you."

"Of course he did. Him and his gang," Ram said. "The others even said he would, like it was inevitable, like what happened to that woman Samira. Why put me in with someone like that? Do you want him to kill me?"

Milena chewed her lower lip. "Why would we want that?"

"I have no protection in there. Make allies? Make allies, you said. Those people were useless. No way they couldn't hear what was going on, did they bother to help me? Did they fuck. You have to help me. You're here to help me, right? So don't just tell me to get allies, I need you to tell me, right now, how I can defend myself against those psychopaths. What's going to happen tonight is that I will get another beating and worse and then what are you people going to do? Why bother to bring me out here if you're just going to leave me to get beaten to death in my first week? This is crazy."

"You're bigger than Mael," Milena said, tapping on her screen. "Bigger than anyone in the Sol System. Stronger, too, probably."

"He's a trained fighter," Ram pointed out, feeling a little less annoyed, suddenly.

"So are you."

"In Avar?" Ram laughed at the very idea of it. "He's done it for real, his XP is all IRL. It's different."

"It's not so different. Avar was designed to be useful in the real world, it provides analogous experience. It has been proven that proficiencies in specific skills in Avar translate to proficiencies in the real world. You know this. You just never put any of your thousands of hours of Avar training into IRL practice before."

"Exactly," Ram said. "And look what he did to me."

Ram pulled up his top to show her the bruising Mael and the

others had caused.

But the mass of mottled purple that had covered his abdomen that morning was gone, other than a touch of redness here and there across the rippling muscles of his stomach. For a moment, Ram wondered if he had dreamt the whole attack. His confusion must have shown.

"If you were expecting to see wounds," Milena said, "you should remember that your new body has remarkably accelerated tissue repair capabilities."

"To help when we fight the Wheelhunter," Ram said, pulling his vest back down over his abs. He was almost disappointed that his bruises were gone. They had been pretty spectacular and he'd never really had any proper injury before and he'd been as bizarrely proud of them as he was of his new genitalia.

"No," Milena said. "A Wheeler fight would never last long enough for the healing effect to be noticed. And it was not designed to heal major injuries but instead to facilitate faster recovery from the exertions of training. You experience little delayed onset muscle soreness after training, muscles recover faster when overloaded, skin stitches together rapidly if you get lacerations in sparring and so on. If you break a bone or worse then you'll heal quicker than normal, sure enough but you're still out for days or weeks the same as anybody else."

"Yeah, like Eziz, his fingers. He was one of the ones that attacked me last night." Ram did not wish to give voice to what Eziz had threatened to do to him.

"He is one of Mael's true believers. He knows, for certain, that Mael is humanity's best hope. Stay away from him."

"Sifa and Te told me about the others. The Chinese woman called Jun with the neck like a guar. The American woman called Genesis looks insane, an Ethiopian guy Gondar. They all attacked me together last night along with Mael and Eziz, I'm sure of it.

Milena's face was stern. "Stay away from all of them."

Ram couldn't believe what he was hearing. "That's almost all the subjects in the ludus, there's no way I can avoid them, you must know that."

Milena shook her head, her hair shining in the artificial light. "You should have listened to Te and locked your door. That's an easy fix from now on and that will keep you completely secure after lights out."

Ram sighed. "Yeah, alright, fair enough. I fucked up there, I admit it. So I'll be fine at night but what if they come for me outside of that?"

In truth, he felt as though he could deal with a beating, even being beaten to death. He realized just how frightened he had been about being raped by Eziz and maybe the others.

"You might mock but I also recommend that you continue to seek protection from Alina and her allies, Sifa and Te Zhang. They are united by their opposition to Mael's methods and from the fear of living and training with him. Alina does not lead in the same way that Mael does, she is simply astonishingly capable and intelligent and, although she may not seem it, empathetic. But she's also disinterested in dominating and leading. A natural draw for Sifa and Te who have no military background and also, somehow, appear to have at least a little compassion in them and chafe at authority. They believe in Alina's ability to beat the Wheelhunter and they are horrified at Mael being humanity's greatest hero."

"What about the others?"

"Yes, Alejandra, Didem and Javi. They all have a tendency toward social isolation or they flip back and forth between the two camps. Really, they do what they can to stay safe from Mael's violence."

"It still seems crazy to me that he is allowed to behave like this, dictate the whole show. Doesn't Director Zuma want the rest of us to be safe?"

While she tapped away again at her screen, Milena shrugged, pausing with her shoulders up. "Why would she? All she needs, all the Mission and Project needs is to produce a single great fighter who will defeat the alien once we reach Orb Station Zero."

Ram sighed and sat back.

"Te Zhang has this theory about the origin of the Wheelhunters. He says maybe they were manufactured by the Orb itself, through manipulating human or earthling DNA."

Milena smiled. "A persistent theory amongst the more credulous guys in UNOP but it has been pretty thoroughly discredited. What about the fact that the Wheelhunters arrive in a ship, through a kind of hyper-advanced space warping drive? We see the alien spaceships arriving at the Orb, so it's not as if the Wheelers are on the ship. And yes, they have DNA and RNA but their cell structure is different from eukaryotes. I'm no cell biologist but I'm told there are minor but unmistakable differences in cell structure. They have something equivalent to but different from mitochondria so you can imagine the knock on implications for cell function. Even more than that, the Orb has explained that we are fighting for the right to colonize nearby systems. The Wheelhunters are being given star systems to colonize every time they beat us."

"That's just what the Orb tells us," Ram said. "What if it's lying? What if your intel people are messing up the translation?"

"For decades we've been building the biggest optical and radio telescopes we can technically achieve and we're looking closely at our nearest Sun-like stars. We're even sending microprobes toward these neighbors, accelerating them to ten or even fifteen percent the speed of light toward where these stars and their systems will be when the probes reach them. Indications so far are that all our nearest sun-like stars have either terrestrial planets around Earth masses or gas or ice giants with moons that are within an acceptable Earth mass within the habitable zone for their parent star."

"Every star near us has planets we could colonize?"

"As far as we can tell," Milena said, nodding emphatically.

"Tau Ceti has three bodies we could colonize right now, if only we could get there. A rocky planet with a surface temperature allowing liquid water and a breathable atmosphere. It has a moon around an ice giant that is .91 Earth mass and has abundant water and breathable atmosphere. Another planet in the system has an atmosphere but it is very cold. Still, we could live on it inside habitats, as they do on Mars. But it is more than habitability. Our investigations suggest that there is electromagnetic activity of non-natural origin in some of these systems. So, whole new systems that could be ours if we beat the Wheelhunters. If we lose, they get the Solar System. That's what the Orb Station tells us. Why should we doubt it?"

"And we're risking the future of humanity on Mael?" Ram said. "A madman?"

"Mael, Alina and the rest of you, yes," Milena said. "But all of you are just the end point. There is a hundred years of the Project behind you and the blood and toil of thousands upon thousands of people over those decades. All working toward this aim, many without even ever knowing about it. Did Zuma give you her line about how UNOP is a spear? Her heavy-handed metaphor?"

"Don't think so."

"She likes to tell the subjects that, figuratively, you are the point of the spear. We on this ship are the shaft of the spear. The leaders of Earth and the rest of the solar system are the ones grasping the spear and thrusting it toward that Wheelhunter that will be waiting for us inside the Orb."

"And Mael is the best of us? That guy is insane."

"He suffers from significant psychopathology, yes," Milena said. "As does Alina. And yet they are the two best-performing people ever studied in this program. Which you can take that to mean they are the best fighters in human history."

"You admit he's crazy," Ram said. "Not just him, either. The others who attacked me, just because he said so, probably. Even Alina seems, I don't know, like she's not really here. Like she's schizophrenic."

Milena tilted her head to one side. "Why would you assume that fighting prowess corresponds to sanity?"

Ram opened his mouth. Then he closed it again.

"Alina has her share of neuroses," Milena said. "More than most. But she was assigned an experienced driver to help her through the fluctuations of her emotional state. That's the main issue with her performance. She has performed as well or better than Mael in most tests and assessments. She has demonstrated faster reaction time, faster hand speed, better decision making. She has lifted more weight, pushed heavier loads. She has run at a faster pace, for longer than Mael ever has."

"So how come she's not the favorite? Because she's insane?"

"She's not insane," Milena said. "No one would get on this ship if they were assessed to be a danger to the mission, not even Mael. She is inconsistent, that's all. Alina is extremely intelligent but also has an overabundance of empathy. She has a tendency to overthink things and also to experience repetitive thinking. Combined with what I assume are unresolved emotional problems, this leads to her lacking focus. Her performance is unpredictable."

"You said you assume she has unresolved emotional problems? You don't know for sure?"

Milena shrugged. "I'm not her driver. I'm not privy to their discussions so I don't know her specific conditions and I'm not diagnosing anything. I'm just telling you what I have observed of her, generally."

"Even still, it just sounds as though you're saying she's as mental as Mael."

"She might be our Subject Alpha if it weren't for her inconsistencies," Milena said. "But Mael is different. He is absolutely driven. He buys into our mission with every fiber of his being. He will drive himself as hard as he can in order to be humanity's best hope for victory. The traits that make him like this also contribute to his aggressiveness, his dominating behaviors. His inability to let perceived slights go unpunished."

"Why don't you just fix him?" Ram said. "You guys have the most incredible medical technology ever, I bet Dr. Fo could do something. Doesn't his driver control his hormones?"

Milena sighed. "If only it were so simple. A lot of these behaviors come from what I would guess was an abusive home environment when he was a child and I also know he has certain brain regions that are underdeveloped. These could be genetic or brain damage from childhood but there are areas of his orbitofrontal cortex that do not work as they should. And yes, it would likely be possible to repair some of the brain damage. We could restrict his testosterone uptake. Yet we could not oppress these socially disruptive traits without impacting his performance. In fact, if anything we should do everything we can to make him more aggressive, within reason."

"The more of an asshole he is, the greater the chance for saving humanity?"

She nodded. "A crude way of putting it but not inaccurate."

Ram leaned forward and rested his head in his hands. "So what should I do? How do I survive another beating?"

"If he'd wanted to kill you last night, he would have done. He might not actually have any homicidal tendencies toward you."

"That supposed to make me feel better?" Ram said. "Is he a rapist?"

Milena pursed her lips. "I suggest that you properly lock your door every night. Even then, do not be alone if you can help it. Attempt to woo Alina into friendship, although be careful not to annoy her because she would make a bad enemy. Te and Sifa might protect you. I believe they are engaged in sexual activity on most nights, although I don't know if they are romantically involved. You might attempt sharing a room with one or the other of them, or both of course, if they allow it."

"Is Sifa trustworthy? She seems so friendly, it makes me wonder."

"Wonder if it is an act?" Milena said. "She certainly uses her sexual charisma, extensive physical touching and so on, in order to manipulate others. The extent to which it is a conscious strategy versus her normal behavior, who knows."

"You think it might be a tactical thing? What's her endgame?"

Milena shrugged. "What we do know is that every one of the subjects, including you, is ultracompetitive. She might be messing with people's emotions on purpose or just screwing around, having fun. A couple of the subjects have been hurt or offended by her sudden lack of attention after a liaison. Perhaps she is callous or oblivious or perhaps she does not invest herself emotionally in sex."

"She sounds pretty great. But she's kind of intimidating." Ram looked down at Milena. "Sexually."

"Or you can attempt to begin a relationship with one of the other heterosexual women, though most have arrangements that you might be disrupting that might cause you additional problems. Of course, depending on how fearful you are, you could attempt to strike up a relationship with one of the homosexual men. Javi, I believe, could be persuaded if you treated him right."

Ram sat up straighter. "Are you kidding? I'm not gay, I couldn't do that."

"Why not? Are you saying you wouldn't trade sexual favors with a man to save yourself from being beaten to death?"

Ram drummed his fingers on the arms of his chair. "Which

way does Alina swing?"

Milena sighed. "You'd be willing to have sexual intercourse with her, even though Alina has remarkably masculine features and physiology. If you can see past that, why not widen your options and give yourself to the men, also? We're all people, does it matter what shape our genitalia is?"

"I don't know, yes, it just does," Ram said. "And Alina is a woman, she has a woman's voice. And, you know, she doesn't have balls. Does she?"

"Only one way to find out," Milena said. "I'm not certain but I believe she has no especially strong feelings for men or women, although she has had relationships with both. She is not an especially sexual person and engages in it somewhat unemotionally."

"You're a psychologist, you must know I'd rather not prostitute myself."

She stared at him in disbelief. "You'd rather not? It's rarely a first choice for people, Rama. You don't have to enjoy it, it's a transactional relationship. You can perform your own cost-benefit analysis by asking yourself a simple question. Is your life worth less to you than a fistful of blowjobs? Anyway, your nighttime bodyguard relationship does not have to be based on sex. You could attempt to find some sort of reciprocal relationship with anyone willing to risk the wrath of Mael in return for something you can provide."

"Okay, good, great." Ram leaned forward. "What can I

provide?"

"I don't know, what can you?"

He sighed and sat back. "I don't know. Maybe nothing. I'll have to have a think about it."

"Well, think fast, Ram, because our time is up. You have to return to your fellow subjects. I believe it's resistance training this morning." She stood and folded away her screen.

"Oh man," Ram said, standing too. "Te Zhang said he's got a bet riding on me lifting more weight than Mael today."

Milena paused. "Interesting dilemma."

"What is?"

"You might find that that body of yours is stronger than Mael's. Demonstrate that fact in front of everyone then it might win you more renown, more kudos, more social capital with Te and Sifa and Alina and the others. It might even translate into increased protection for yourself. But showing Mael up like that might drive him into a rage, might tip him over the edge into wanting to truly damage you."

Ram rubbed his face. "What should I do?"

"I think you should go for it. Give it everything you have. Go quickly, you do not want to be late for Bediako. He's almost as dangerous as Mael."

CHAPTER THIRTEEN
BREAKING

THEY HAD ALREADY BEGUN when he arrived. The subjects and attendants filled the long room, the ring section that contained the physical training equipment. Some were pounding away on treadmills. Others were sitting or lying inside bench and frame devices, pushing or pulling bars or handles attached to straps and wheels. The room resounded with grunting and clanging and whirring. Already it stank of sweat and warm plastic.

Bediako stood in the center of the action with his human-sized support staff gathered about him like cubs around the mother bear. Ram strode up to Bediako.

"Your timekeeping is appalling," Bediako said, giving him a cursory glance but pausing, allowing Ram a chance to object or make excuses. Some distant memory of his early life in the crèche and nursery school rose up and set off a long-dormant survival instinct. Ram was about to speak but he held his tongue, sensing that it was a trap. Bediako made a tiny grunt before continuing. "How much resistance training experience do you have?"

Ram knew he had to make an impression. He had to prove his strength, prove he was tough. Still, he knew that being dishonest would do no more than catch him out down the line.

"None." It was the truth.

Bediako shook his head. The assistants all appeared suitably horrified.

"You mean in all your precious Avar time you never taught yourself weight lifting? Why not?"

Ram was about to explain that there was no reason to do such a thing within Avar, where you use an avatar with whatever traits you want but again he sensed he was being led into a trap of defending himself, at which point his answers would be used against him. So he just gave what he hoped was a neutral answer.

"Just never did it."

Ram watched Sifa laying on her back on a bench within a cube frame, heaving a weighted bar up and down over her as if it was nothing. He stared at her chest.

"How you came to be in my ludus, I will never know," Bediako said, as if he had a bad taste in his mouth. "Now I have to train you on how to lift weights when I do not have time to spare to teach you everything from scratch."

"It's just lifting heavy stuff, right?" Ram said, staring at Sifa and not paying enough attention to the words coming out of his mouth. "How hard can it be?"

Bediako spun about, glaring. The assistants froze. The subjects in earshot likewise ground to a halt.

Ram knew he'd made an error.

Bediako stalked over to Ram. Even though Ram had to look down slightly to maintain eye contact, he was suitably intimidated. "Really?" Bediako said, in a voice so low it was little more than a growl. "You're asking me to show you how hard it is, Rama? Is that what you want to know? I would be delighted to demonstrate. Here, take a seat in this leg press machine. You will learn today what hard work really means."

Rama was put through his paces. Pushing, pulling, heaving, squatting, lifting. The weights were great slabs of iron strung together, lifted by pulleys as well as resistant, elasticated rods and stretch cables. Ram heaved, strained and sweated for hours. His arms, legs shoulders burned like fire. Again and again, he felt he could not go on but Bediako was always there in his face, forcing Ram to do more, lift again, push another repetition. Ram almost quit a dozen times, a hundred. But every time he reached the end of his tether, he found another layer of strength.

Milena was in his ear.

"You can do this, Ram." She said it a hundred times. "You

can do this. Don't give up. This is how you beat them, they want you to fail. They want you to be weak because it would confirm their preconceptions. Every rep, every set, you show that you are one of them. Push through the pain. Your body is capable. Your body is a miracle of science. Your body can do anything. Your body can go on for hours. I'm helping you, increasing the right hormones when you need them. You can do this, you have to fight. Push harder."

At some point, he realized the other subjects were standing around him. Some muttering, a few others speaking to him but he could not make out their words. Most were silent, standing like grim, giant statues.

After some time Bediako pulled him upright, someone swiped a towel across his face and hands guided him to a new machine. Some sort of frame over and around him.

"This is the deadlift." Bediako's voice. "Grasp the bar, bend your knees, point your toes this way. Hips back, shoulders back. Do not round your spine. Push your belly out, tense your core. Push your heels down." On and on, Bediako's voice barked out instruction. The weight on the bar grew and grew. Ram's forearms ached, then they burned. His back spasmed and his grip faltered, dropping the bar. His audience cried out, disappointed. Ram's vision swam, misted, blurred.

"You can do this." Milena, in his head. "You must focus for this final effort, for this final weight."

"Why?" Ram was not sure if he spoke aloud or just thought

the word.

Milena answered anyway. "No one ever lifted this much, not ever. So you must concentrate. Breathe."

Bediako roared at him to try again, shouted to grasp the bar and to lift.

Milena in his ear. "Push, come on, everything you got, Rama. You can do this, you can do this."

It was like pulling up a building by the foundations. The weight of it dragged him down, all through his body, arms, back, thighs. He moved it off the floor and up and up. His legs shook. A jolt of agony shot through his back. His fingers slipped, hands opening, the bar sliding down toward his fingertips. His neck, his shoulders quivered with the strain. Eyes squeezed shut, sweat poured into them but the cries of encouragement swelled him.

Ram pushed up with his legs and pulled with everything else.

His knees locked out and he stood straight. He held it up for a second before it slipped from his fingers.

Ram fell. Hands caught him. Carried him out.

***

When he woke, someone was there, over him.

"It has been a good while since I saw someone hospitalized for weight training."

"Dr. Fo?" Ram said, blinking.

"Welcome back to my lair." Dr. Fo cackled like a madman.

Ram rubbed his face and looked around.

"What happened? Where is everybody?"

"Oh, I don't know," Dr. Fo said, shaking his head. "Something about breaking a record. Why you barbarians insist on killing yourselves attempting these arbitrary goals, I will never understand. They told me you were different from these brainless thugs, they said you were an educated man, wise beyond your years. Clearly, they were mistaken. As usual."

"I feel fine," Ram said, flexing his arms. "Can I go?"

"Yes, yes," Dr. Fo said, waving a hand. "Your body can process stress chemicals rapidly. Your skeletal muscle will be sore for a few more hours. But you are mostly undamaged, all we did is rehydrate you. You're free to go back to the training ring."

"I'd have preferred to stay here for a few more hours. A few more months, ideally. But okay, I'll head back now. Must be time for food anyway. Thanks, Doctor."

"I will take you," Milena said, stepping forward as Ram stood up.

She was smiling.

"What happened?" Ram asked.

They spoke while they walked through the ring sections.

"You were magnificent," Milena said, grinning. Her smile was really something.

"I broke the record?"

"Two records," Milena said, touching her fingers on his arm for a moment as they walked. "Heaviest weight ever lifted and the most mass lifted over four hours, adjusted for the reduced apparent gravity on the ship."

"I beat Mael's record? That's great."

"The heaviest weight was Alina's record but yes. But they weren't just onboard records, you beat every human who ever lived."

"What about Artificial Persons? The ones engineered to do asteroid mining and stuff."

Milena would not meet his eye. "Obviously, not them. I meant human records."

"But I'm not human," Ram said. "This body is not human. It was grown, right? In an artificial womb or whatever, like vat meat."

Milena sighed. "Alright, so it's a gray area, Rama, just accept that you broke a sporting world record and be happy."

"Yeah, sure, okay, Milena. Take it easy."

"I'm nervous," Milena said. "Mael is angry, as you might expect. Who knows what he will try tonight."

"But you told me to try harder," Ram said. "You were playing with my chemistry the whole time, you pretty much forced me to beat him. Why did you do that if it was only going to make things worse for me?"

"It should force Alina's hand," Milena said. "She will protect you now. Now that she sees you are worthy. And Sifa and Te will see Mael's anger. You should have more protection from now on."

"Should? Great. Thanks for looking out for me."

"Don't act like a child," Milena said, her eyebrows diving toward her nose. "Remember where you are right now. Remember where you are going. Why we're all here and what is at stake. Stop feeling so wounded, so sorry for yourself. Accept this situation. Adapt. Learn. Survive. I will be with you as much as I can be. Go, now."

She pushed Ram through the door into the ludus. On the other side, the ever-present, always-lurking ludus staff escorted him back to the barracks. Bediako was nowhere to be seen.

When he stepped through into the barracks, the subjects there in the central common area gave him a round of applause. They clapped and banged their table tops and a couple of people even cheered.

It was startling and almost overwhelming. Even Mael and Eziz were clapping and grinning. He was touched, thinking that he had won them over with his efforts.

Until he realized most of them were doing it mockingly.

"Hospitalized for weight lifting," Gondar cried out, laughing hard. "That body is a wonder."

Te and some others shouted him down and congratulated Rama for breaking the record. Ram mumbled his thanks and looked for somewhere to hide. He decided to just go straight to his quarters.

Alina sat hunched at the nearest of the three central benches, watching a screen. Her enormous shoulders rounded, her voluminous trapezius muscle bulging right up to her ears. She glanced up as Ram rushed by her for the relative safety of his room. He wanted to test the locking system, immediately.

"Rama," Alina said, sticking out a palm the size of a dinner plate. "Wait. Come, sit here. You broke my record. Sit with me, I said."

"I don't know what happened," Ram said, sitting down. "I never even tried weight lifting before."

Alina's gaze pierced his own. "Your driver drove you senseless with hormones. I saw. We all saw."

"She did. It was like I was in another world. Separated from this one."

"These hormonally induced states are powerful. When my driver, Noomi, first took me to levels like that? It reminded me of the late stages of the labor of childbirth. A powerful altered state of consciousness."

Ram found it difficult to link the hulking, masculine figure sitting opposite him with the act of childbirth. "Oh really? You have kids back on Earth?"

Alina's eyes hardened. "You think I would abandon children to come on this mission? What sort of person do you think I am?"

"I don't know, I mean, I'm sorry, I spoke without thinking. You don't have kids, fine. Trying to get to know you, that's all."

"Ah, I see now," Alina said, nodding. "You were trying to change the subject away from yourself. My driver said that you do that."

Ram glanced around over his shoulder. No one was paying much attention. "How does your driver know what I do?"

"The drivers all talk to each other. They all have access to information we do not. I bet there is a great deal of information that they know all about which is actively hidden from us." She lowered her voice. "My driver, Noomi, has an inquisitive mind. I am certain that they have access to information that we do not have."

Ram leaned in a little. "Like what?"

Alina lowered her voice, leaned over the table further. "Like where they actually get these bodies from. No synthetic body ever grown in the tanks looked and performed like ours. And like why there's so much security on this ship, so many Marines that they hide from us. And like why, when Mael killed Samira six months ago, are they only waking you up out of stasis now."

Ram stared at Alina. "What did you say?"

Te and Sifa came over together to sit at the table with him and Alina.

Six months?

"How are you feeling, Rama Seti?" Te asked, trying and failing to keep a straight face. "Did she bring you down off that epi-cortisol cocktail? Oh man, you were so off your tits on hormones, you were in another dimension, bro. The juice dimension, right? On the other hand, you're officially the strongest person who has ever lived. What's that feel like? Got to feel pretty good."

He had been on the ship in stasis for at least six months?

Alina tutted. "You cannot say a thing such as that with any degree of confidence. There are countless untested people throughout history who may rival our strength, many outliers."

Te hesitated, clearly wanting to argue. Instead, he laughed. "The human with the heaviest officially recorded deadlift, then, is that alright?"

"But is he truly human?" Alina said. "Are any of us?"

They all stared at Alina.

"Not this again," Te said, finally, throwing his hands up.

"Where is your body coming from?" Alina asked Ram.

"What? I don't know?" Ram said. "Where did your body come from? Or yours?"

Six months of his life spent unconscious?

"They were grown for us," Te said. "Same way they grow meat, same way they grow replacement limbs and organs. Same way they make Synthetic Persons, by growing the tissues in the tanks using our stem cells."

"We do not know that," Alina said. "All we know is what Dr. Fo tells us and what our drivers tell us and what they tell our drivers."

"What else can it be?" Sifa said, flexing her arms in the double front biceps pose, causing her already thin top to stretch further across her breasts. Her nipples were erect. "Look at us. They grow these specially designed bodies in wombs tanks for us, they perform a transplant and here we are with these bodies that are essentially synthetic versions of us."

She lowered her arms, giving Ram a quick wink.

"Yeah and here we are," Te said, nodding. "They grow the bodies in the tanks then sew our heads on later, Alina. Nothing to be concerned about."

"Wait a minute," Ram said, lowering his voice and glancing over his shoulder. "Alina, you just said something about Mael killing someone six months ago. And me being in stasis. Six months ago on this ship? How long exactly have you all been here?"

"Since we left Earth orbit?" Te said, blowing air through pursed lips. "Mate, that was like, two and a half years ago."

Ram closed his eyes.

"How can that be?" Ram said, holding his head. "They said they cut off my head in my apartment. I just woke up here a few days ago. What in the fuck did they do with my head for two and half years?"

"This is what I am saying," Alina said, pointing at Ram but speaking to the other two. "Director Zuma and Executive Zhukov claim to have this policy of telling truth, always. But they do not tell us everything. That is a lie by omission. A lie, all the same, is it not? They deceive us as a matter of course."

"I can't believe this," Ram muttered, rubbing his hands over his shaved head. "Six months was bad enough but…"

"Maybe they do," Sifa said, her voice harsh. "But what more do we need to know in order to do our part? There are thousands of people back on Earth who worked on this project, worked to get us here. Tens of thousands. Hundreds of thousands. Not just on Earth. Researchers on Mars and who knows where else. All working on their own jobs, all part of the larger project, even if they never heard of UNOP. What about the other people on this ship, do you think they know everything? The engineers work on the propulsion system, the navigators do their jobs. The Marines protect us. You think that we are special just because our jobs are near to the end of the mission?"

"Yes," Alina said, deadly serious. "Of course we are special. It is ultimately we who must fight the alien."

"You only think that way because it's probably going to be you that does the actual fighting," Te said. "The rest of us are here to make you do it as best you can, right? We're backup. We're redundancy."

"And you are happy with this?" Alina asked.

"I signed up, same as you," Te said. "I knew what I was getting into. You went through the same vetting and assessment stuff, right?"

"Yes but he did not." Alina nodded at Ram. "So we are so many, us twelve, we are training partners for the one who is the best. And also we are redundancy. So, Ram was redundancy for Samira. They kept him on ice or something like that until he was needed."

Ram couldn't believe it. "So you're saying my head was in a freezer for all that time? So yeah, it's like you were saying, Alina, why hook me up now? Why didn't they tell me this? My funeral must have been years ago."

"Yes, you make my point," Alina said. "Why, after we have been eleven subjects for the preceding six out of the last thirty-three months do they want to make us twelve again? And also, you know, if they had Rama Seti's head back there this entire time?" She trailed off.

"Maybe they have more," Te said, staring unfocused at the wall as if he could see right through the bulkheads of the *Victory*.

"Indeed," Alina said. "How many heads do we have? And what will happen to them if they are not needed? That is not acceptable to me, ethically."

"That's what we're saying," Te said. "Ethics don't really matter for UNOP. Not with what's at stake. Anyway, it doesn't sound as though Ram was conscious when he was on ice, right, bro?"

Ram shrugged. "Can't believe it. How long until we reach Orb Station Zero?"

"Nearly there," Te said. The other nodded. "Three months left for the outward journey. Few days in orbit and then we burn for home."

"Do not think about home," Alina said. "Only victory."

"You know what Rama has got that we haven't?" Sifa said, slyly looking between them. "Why they might have woken him up now, right at the end? What are we doing again tomorrow?"

"Yes, possibly you are correct," Alina said. "That could be it.

Perhaps they decided the group must improve our performance in this area and produced for us an expert."

"Expert?" Ram said.

"See, Alina," Te said, clapping her on a massive shoulder. "You're always looking for a nefarious purpose behind everything. A secret cabal, a conspiracy. But there's always a perfectly reasonable explanation for everything."

Alina scoffed at that.

"What are you guys talking about, what are we doing tomorrow?" Ram said.

"We know for certain that you will enjoy tomorrow's activity," Sifa said, patting him on the arm. "It's Avar practice."

CHAPTER FOURTEEN
INTO AVAR

THAT NIGHT, WITH THE door to his quarters properly locked, Ram lay awake listening to the hum of the air conditioning and power units, the major and minor vibrations that harmonized throughout the ship constantly.

He could hear the occasional and faint murmur of voices through the walls between the rooms. If he could hear voices from the room beside him, surely that meant the night that he had been attacked, the others in the barracks who he had considered his friends had decided to not intervene. Perhaps they had not been woken by the commotion and but more likely it meant that his new friends would not protect him, as Milena had suggested. So if Mael and the others broke in or came for him somewhere else, Ram had to be ready to fight for himself.

Unless he could change their minds about him. If he could show how much value he could add to the mission through the Avar session the next day, perhaps they would help him next time.

On the other hand, he knew now that he couldn't trust anyone on the ship.

Ram checked the date on his screen again. He couldn't believe that he hadn't done it before and it had taken a chance comment for him to find out. Milena had not bothered to tell him. Dr. Fo had not told him, even when given the opportunity, so it must have been a deliberate deception.

It had been 33 months since they took him from his apartment. 33 months since they had left Earth orbit. They had cut off his head 33 months before they had woken him up.

Almost three years.

He lay on his back on his bed and hunted through content on the screen, searching articles and videos on recent world history that had been transmitted to the *Victory* in flight. There was too much information to take in and reading text from a 2D screen was so painfully old-fashioned that he found the process irritating. The *Victory* used hardened computer chips and ancient operating systems in space but kitting out even the non-critical personal devices with it smacked of a conservative, almost ascetic mindset. No doubt it was that smug Director Zuma and her love for ancient books, the ludicrous, affected bastard that she was.

It was the same old shit, anyway. Pro-human terrorism sweeping the globe with attacks on Artificial Persons labs in North America and Europe especially. The pro-human movement was a strange collaboration between religious lunatics of various denominations, leftwing civil rights fanatics, biological purists and tedious moralists. Some focused on blowing up labs, others on freeing APs to go live in remote sanctuaries where they could live out their days in mindless, idiotic peace as if they were rescued farm animals. Corporations everywhere were investing in space technologies and more and more people were clamoring to their governments for additional colonies to be set up on Mars and on moons, asteroids and artificial space stations. There were the same old objections raised, how emigration from Earth would not solve Earth's problems, there were hysterical Left Behind groups who demanded that the disadvantaged of Earth could not be left to become even more of an underclass after all the best and brightest were selected for colonies and research outposts.

Ram looked for references to Orb Station Zero and the United Nations Orb Project. He was amazed at how much information was in the public domain but it was swamped by the sheer volume of data. There were so many conspiracy theories, especially related to humanity's sudden and rapid leap into becoming a spacefaring civilization, that the UNOP content was just one set of data amongst the relentless opinions of billions of people, everyone shouting and no one listening.

He struggled to wade his way through the ocean of bullshit but he could not keep his eyes open for long. He stuck his hand down his shorts and had a half-hearted attempt at jerking himself off but he wasn't in the mood and, anyway, it felt weird. It was like someone else's dick in his hand. It wasn't even his own hand, for that matter.

Soon enough he was woken up by the light in his room brightening automatically and a chiming alarm tone growing louder and closer together. The noise stopped when he stood up.

Te Zhang banged hard on his door and shouted through it to hurry up, have a shower and come eat your fucking anabolic breakfast, mate.

After showering, he stood naked in front of his steamed up mirror, trying to reconcile the sight of the monstrous bodybuilder physique and how he thought about himself. He gave up and got dressed. Someone was filling his drawers with fresh clothes when he was out. At least the barracks was five star rated.

When they sat down in the mess hall, Ram noted how the room was divided physically between those that were in Alina's camp versus Mael and his band of bastards. A couple of subjects held themselves apart so presumably they were not taking sides.

"Big day for you," Te said, spraying crumbs from his mouth while he tore into a whole loaf of bread. "We're all expecting great things."

Ram swallowed a mouthful of micronutrient tablets and washed them down with the protein drink assigned to him.

"In Avar?" Ram said. "You've all been in your Avar dozens of times in the last three years." He did not bother to keep the bitterness from his voice.

Milena would have heard that and yet she said nothing. She had not spoken since he left the barracks and yet Ram knew she would be listening. It was an odd feeling, being watched and listened to during every waking hour. Was this how his ancestors felt about their gods? Always on edge, watching what they said.

"We have been using Avar," Sifa said. "Even before we were transplanted onto our bodies, Avar was a vital part of the selection and training process back on Earth. We have hundreds of hours in Avar."

"How do you train with it?" Ram was excited to be going into an Avar device. He'd never been out of one for more than a day or two since he was a kid and he was itching to get back into one. The urge to link himself up and disappear into a second world writhed through him and he tried to remember that he had to be sure to impress everyone, as much as possible. Other than brute strength, it was the only possible thing he could excel at in the ludus. "What are the programs you use?"

"It's not the kind of shit you're used to," Te said. "We don't get to fly fighter planes or do giant ancient battles or whatever."

"That's a shame," Ram said and he meant it.

"I know, man," Te said. "We should get them to sort us out

some free hours on them things, we've argued we should get downtime, visit simulations of a tropical beach or a forest or something at least, surely that has a therapeutic effect, right? But no, Bediako and Zuma just want simulations of the alien fight. Over and bloody over again. We change the variables, change the tactics. We get smacked down, we respawn, we try something else, we get smacked down. We're all really good at getting killed. But that's all we get to do."

"You will love it," Sifa said, grinning. "Hurry and eat your breakfast."

"Drink your protein shake, bro. Get that shit down you."

Later, they gathered in the Avar section of the Ludus Ring. Just looking at the machines, in two rows of six along the center of the room, gave Ram a thrill. The chairs were hugely bigger than the normal ones, even his own custom made one in his apartment, designed to support the weight and mass of his flesh in comfort. The other equipment was in proportion. The gloves attached to the chair arms, the boots at the foot of the chairs, the glasses and headset sitting ready to be lowered onto the heads of the users. Most commercial chairs were sold in flashy colors but in the Avar section of the *Victory*, everything was done in tastefully black synthetics and edged in delicate silver.

"You know the drill," Bediako said, his voice echoing around the Avar machines. "We'll run individual simulations to start and team sessions at the end. The usual variables. Take your seats and do not disappoint me again."

"Why was he disappointed?" Ram whispered to Sifa.

"When is he not?" she whispered. "That's your chair over there."

"The dead woman's chair," Ram said. The one called Samira who had died six months before.

"What are you assholes gossiping about?" Bediako shouted at Ram. "Sit in your chair, Rama Seti. Or perhaps now you've had a taste of the real world you're afraid to go back into the fairy tale one?"

What's real about all this shit? Ram wanted to say but he knew an argument would be giving the bastard what he wanted so he held his tongue.

The chair and equipment were first class. The materials, the finish spoke of enormous investment, clearly custom made with extraordinary care. The joins between the softer sections and the harder ones blended so smoothly that it was difficult to determine with the naked eye. Every surface was scrupulously clean, as if it was new, which was certainly not the case for his own Avar chair. Ram had paid a fortune for his device, choosing the top of the line at every opportunity, taking the best available for every optional extra. He'd scanned his body in a hundred poses, standing, stretching - as best he could - sitting, laying down. His chair was molded for his body, for the rolls and folds of fat that spread in all directions when he lay down. He'd chosen the very best massage components and software which would help him to avoid bed sores and circulatory conditions. Even so, his home chair was not as sleek as the one under his fingertips.

"Rama Seti." Bediako's voice shook him out of his revere. "Are you going to sit in that chair or fuck it?"

"What? No, I'm going to—"

"Sit down, you idiot," Bediako roared.

Ram eased himself into the chair to the sound of laughter. It was irritating. He had wanted to look professional but already he was looking like an idiot.

Everyone else was getting hooked in. He slipped his hands into the gloves and the boots. They had redesigned the chair for him. It all fit perfectly. Every finger was fully enclosed and touching the inside surface of the gloves and nowhere was too tight. The headset must have been molded to his head when he was unconscious because it slipped on like a second skin and the temple contacts aligned perfectly with his subdermal implants. He should have thought of it earlier but the chair seemed so new because it had been repurposed to match his new body.

Everyone seemed to be jumping straight in so he pushed down on the activation switches inside the little fingers of both hands simultaneously and focused on clicking his implants on. Ram had logged into Avar more than four thousand times in the previous decade so it was like stepping into an old pair of shoes or sliding into a hot bath. Although, for Ram, there was no equivalent activity that was as familiar and as comfortable to him as the slipping out of the real world and into the virtual one. The "shared dream" of Avar, although the famous marketing slogan fell down as a true analogy because the second world was fully programmed and hosted by a powerful server rather than a human mind.

Avar was a multiuser space, though, that was the "shared" part and Rama uploaded into the lobby while the others joined, faded into existence into a square room with dark walls. Bediako was there with the others, already shouting out orders as the figures filled the room.

Everyone's avatar was an exact copy of their real life body. Which was almost unknown in the Avar world, unless you were on one of the servers that demanded such a thing and they were pretty niche. Even if you made your avatar in your own form then you would make improvements. Make yourself thinner, bigger, taller. Change your hair or features. Most people went further and changed their form entirely. You weren't limited to your own gender, of course but nor would you need to appear fully human, depending on the competition. Some in Ram's co-operative favored anthropomorphic animals of various kinds, especially in social situations. In the deep servers, you could find avatars of the most insane and terrifying forms imaginable, often doing unspeakable things to each other.

But as he spawned in the loading space, everyone around was an exact copy of themselves in the real world even down to the thin, stretchy clothing covering their ludicrous musculature. The Avar generated lobby had twelve doors around the four walls, each with the subject's name on it. He saw his own, SETI, on one across from him.

"Finally," Bediako's avatar said. "We'll start off with the Wheeler dialed down to thirty percent and you can take it from there. Listen to your drivers, they've been working on your approaches and they'll have suggestions ready to feed to you. Rama Seti, we're all expecting great things. We are all prepared to be impressed." Laughter, both good natured and nasty, filled the Avar space. "Now, go on, get out of here and tear those things apart."

Te and Sifa patted Ram on the shoulder as they went to their doors. Everyone was opening them with a waved hand and stepping through into a large open space, their avatars froze and faded into nothing, the doors closing behind them. Loading points. Conscious of Bediako's contemptuous, amused glare, Ram waved open his own door and stepped through.

The loading was smooth, no stuttering at all and he came out into a space he recognized at once.

An exact replica of the arena in the Orb, just as he'd expected it to be. The domed ceiling was far above and the far side was barely discernable.

"Ram," Milena's voice in his head. "How are you?"

He wanted to confront her about being kept unconscious for 33 months or whatever but he was too angry to do it virtually. Ram would wait until he could look her in the eye and see her squirm about lying to him. That was the least he could hope for and he meant to have it.

"Great," Ram said. "So how do we do this?"

"I'm sure you can guess," Milena said. "I'm sure the others explained it. This is a combat simulation. You versus the alien entity."

"Just like that? No discussion of tactics or training on how to fight from Bediako or one of the others?"

"I'm here to tell you about tactics. And you'll have plenty of time to learn how to fight. I think we're all curious to see how you do without any training. Now, go to the middle of the arena."

Ram started walking, out to the center. The curving edges of the circular walls around him arced up into the domed roof above. It was like being a tiny ant walking around underneath an upturned bowl.

"You think I'm going to apply my Avar fighting experience to this simulation."

"Exactly. But more than that, I'm excited to see the extent to which your virtual experience will carry over into your real world body."

"Yeah, you know, I'm not sure about that. My usual avatars have specific powers and abilities that have no real world counterpart. In one of them, I had the ability to jump a distance of twenty meters without tiring. Another one I had arms that were machine guns in a dieselpunk fantasy version of the Great War. I fought with swords and assault rifles in zero-g vertical structures. I've been a rampaging bear, fighting groups of armed peasants in medieval Europe. You think this stuff has any real world application then you're deluded."

Ram reached the center of the space and waited for the game to start. Everyone else must be in their own virtual spaces, running concurrent simulations.

Milena scoffed. "Stop making excuses. Stop preparing for failure. I've seen you play with avatars just like the body you're in now and I've seen you do amazing things with them. Your body, the one reclining in an Avar chair right now? That is simply another avatar for you. Or that is how you should see it. You have the skills, you have the experience. You simply must now apply it to this form, within this simulation and out in the real world, on the *Victory*."

Ram looked around at the huge half dome arena. The light was strange, glowing artificially from no specific light source.

"Easy for you to say," Ram said. "If I die in Avar then I respawn. Or I turn off the Avar and I'm fine. That's not going to happen when I fight an alien, is it."

Milena paused before replying.

"Ram, you know there's no chance you'll fight the alien. For all that I believe in you, and I truly do, you have no chance to perform as well as even the lowest performing subjects on the ship. I'm sorry but that's the way it is. You will, however, be fighting them in sparring and I want you to know that you needn't be afraid. We have a world class medical staff here, as you know. If you get hurt, even seriously, you'll wake up in the medical ring again. That's just like respawning, right?"

Ram sighed. "That subject Samira was killed by Mael and she didn't recover, did she. And there were those terrorist attacks on the facilities before, back on Earth. Training accidents with potential subjects. This isn't exactly a risk-free situation, is it."

"Yes, it's terrible. Now shut up and look. There's your opponent."

Across the arena, a fifty-meter section of the smoky, swirling wall faded, like a bubble popping in slow motion.

And there was the creature.

It rolled through the wall opening, which closed behind him and it rolled forward. Seeing it on the screen and seeing it before him was completely different. On the screen, it had looked like a bizarre and absurd creature. In person - for Avar was as close as simulacrum as was possible - it was a wholly different feeling.

It was a creature from a nightmare. An unnatural, unknown entity, something with no relationship to anything on earth. Three meters tall, from footpad to footpad. It was massive, weighing perhaps half a ton to a ton on Earth, a little less in the lower gravity of the Orb and the ship.

"That thing is really something," Ram said. "Looks like a psychotic wind turbine fucked a bunch of bananas."

"You have a couple of minutes before it reaches you but you should prepare for when it does."

"What's the deal with the parameters Bediako was talking about?" Ram said, stepping a few paces back and forth while swinging his massive arms around. He kept his eyes on the Wheelhunter the whole time. It was mesmerizing.

Milena, her voice calm, sounded inside his head. "The Wheelhunter top observed speed was estimated as forty kilometers per hour. It accelerates up to that speed in three seconds. Its impact damage is estimated at a range between a thousand and three thousand newtons, depending on the point of impact. Without downgrading these abilities, you would have no chance of survival. Even at thirty percent of baseline speed and strength, you will probably be killed immediately, first of all. In the game."

It rolled forward, its feet flap-flapping against the smooth black floor with a solid flood.

"That all sounds great. So, what do I do? What abilities does it have?"

"Abilities? It is not constrained by the restrictions they design in enemies in commercial Avar games. It can do anything that it can physically do based on observations of the previous three missions. The version you see before you is programmed with the range of movement that we have seen but we can change the variables so that it can do more than we have seen. But really, we can merely predict based on the limited examples we have and then extrapolate potential behaviors from there. For example, the Wheeler tends to accelerate once it closes to around thirty meters and that is usually how we run these simulations. That doesn't mean that it will next time."

"Great."

The Wheeler was still around a hundred meters away so Ram stepped backward. The great yellow thing rolled on.

"That's right," Milena said. "Keeping your distance is a perfectly viable strategy."

Ram kept walking backward. "Do they get tired?"

"No one knows. The battles never last long enough for us to know what stamina it has but presumably the wheel design improves efficiency. It may have limitless endurance for all we know."

Ram was approaching the wall behind him so he moved sideways along it. The Wheelhunter rolled onto its side, like a bike taking a bend in the road. The arms rolled over and over, the long fingers with their oversized knuckles flexing.

"So I can run around this arena all day and the simulation won't get tired?"

"I can change the parameters if you wish. I can make the Wheeler slow down, tire, become weaker. We do these things with regularity, testing every variable. The AIs have been running simulations for years, with and without human controlled subjects. We have so much data but few factors to feed in at the start. There are so many potential variables that it is difficult to draw firm conclusions."

"But what are the best strategies assuming that we have seen everything that it can do?" Ram kept his distance and the alien matched his pace. "Surely there are common solutions?"

"Depends on the parameters we set for the alien. Depends on the skills of the subject. With the current settings and your lack of ability, you may as well attempt to tackle it head on."

"Inspiring, thanks. Okay but it doesn't have a head. What are the weaknesses?"

Ram slowed his retreat a little, allowing the alien to gain on him. It came to within eighty meters.

"We don't know if it has any. Our assumption has often been that the ball and socket joints are the weakest parts of the anatomy."

"What about the central section? Is that its head?" Ram slowed further, ready to react if he had misjudged the distance but he thought it was about sixty-five meters away.

"The hub is surely where the control takes place. If it has a brain, and it must surely have something like that, then presumably that is where it will be and is well protected. It has eight joints around the outside of it for one thing. That's a lot of sturdy bone structure. Imagine a pelvis with eight limbs and a brain and all the other organs inside. Must be tough to damage them."

Ram was beginning to understand why everyone who had faced it before had failed.

"Alright then."

When the steadily cartwheeling alien reached forty meters away, he took a deep breath.

"Come on, Ram," Ram said, speaking to himself. "It's just

Avar."

He sprinted toward the Wheelhunter.

In his chair, in the Avar room, on the spaceship *Victory*, his body would be barely twitching.

His simulated body was powerful and he charged the distance in just a couple of seconds. The alien covered more than half the distance for him and the thing was upon him. The huge, flat-topped footpads rolled up over Ram's head height, crashing down toward him one after the other, as if mechanized, a conveyor belt. Each foot was bigger than Ram's head, solid and heavy enough to crush his skull like an eggshell.

The skin covering it was a crazy, slightly mottled canary yellow, with mustard splotches and darker patches like an old banana. Tiny bumps, nodules small and large, covered every part. Ram reached up and caught the edge of the next footpad. His hands wrapped around two edges and pushed back, trying to stop it.

It was too much. The weight and momentum of the thing rolled on, pushing down, buckling Ram's arms and knocking him down before he could react. He looked up in time to see a three-fingered hand, each finger with three bony knuckles, come whipping down into his face. The blow knocked him down hard, he fell back off his feet and hit the ground hard, smacking the back of his skull onto the black floor.

The last thing he saw was the underside of the footpad crush his face.

"No!"

His vision whited out and when he came to, he found he had respawned. On the far side of the arena, the wall faded open and the Wheelhunter rolled out again.

Ram was breathing deeply, his mind forgetting momentarily that none of it was real.

"That wasn't bad." Milena's voice in his head. "I've seen worse first attempts."

Ram quickly shook off the horror of the first person death experience.

He had a lot of practice.

"If it wasn't for your passionate encouragement, Milena, I don't think I could go on."

She did not laugh. She was all business. "Next time, try moving your body to one side as you grasp the underside of the foot."

"Alright."

"And if you give me a little warning, I can help you by simulating what I would do in real life with your hormones. I'll adjust your strength and speed, replicating the surges of adrenaline and testosterone I can provide to you on the *Victory*."

"You sure can."

"Shut up and concentrate," she said.

Time passed strangely in Avar. Another way in which the technology is like a dream state. One can sometimes spend what seems to be hours deep within only to find mere minutes have passed in the real world. Likewise, a full day could pass in the blink of an eye but your Avar settings or your rumbling belly will let you know that you should eat, drink and urinate. That first session in the Orb arena simulation, Ram went without a break for eight hours. Another record on the UNOPS *Victory*.

Inside, he and Milena ran through techniques, different approaches, angles of attack. Milena paused the Wheeler in motion a hundred times so Ram could get a close look at the way it moved, its point of balance at any one moment, the range of motion in each of its joints. He died thirty-four times but it was never enough.

"I have to stop," Milena said, yawning in his ear. "And so should you. You need to eat regularly to maintain your muscle mass. It's dinner time."

"Already? Can we just try one more thing?" Ram had not done enough, he was sure. He had died so many times, he had barely landed any significant kicks, punches or holds on the alien all day.

"I'm sorry, Ram," Milena said. "I never could keep up with you. Not that anybody could. We'll pick it up again in a couple of days. Tomorrow I think you have sparring. Real world sparring. You should get some rest."

He hesitated. He really wanted to have some sort of victory to go back to the barracks with. He needed it. "I'll be okay by myself for a while, you can go eat."

"No," Milena said, her patience clearly evaporated. "I'm

about to disconnect you. You won't be able to play. And listen, I hope you're feeling pretty good right now. You should be. You've done some good work here today, I can't wait to work on more tactics with you. But this is the virtual world and you've got real world problems to deal with. Just now, while you were training, one of the other drivers came in and told me that Mael and his followers are going to try to injure you tomorrow. They'll break one of your limbs, put you in the medical center. Maybe worse."

"Fuck." Ram forgot the alien.

The arena gamespace dissolved and Ram found himself in the empty lobby.

"What should I do?" He disconnected, transitioned back into his body.

"You're going to have to try to hospitalize one of them first, before they can do you. Scare them off."

"Hospitalize one of them?" Ram sighed, suddenly feeling tired. "In sparring? Come on, seriously?"

"If you have to do it in sparring, I suppose you might get lucky. But I'd suggest you try breaking into one of their rooms tonight, break a leg or an arm, smash their face in a little. Maybe Jun's, she's the smallest and she sleeps heavily."

"You can't be serious."

"It's time for you to stop hesitating. Stop looking for a way out. This is your reality, they have their sights set on you, you must attack first. Considering what happened to Samira, it might be the only way you get out of this alive."

CHAPTER FIFTEEN
LOVE

THEY APPLAUDED HIM when he walked into the mess hall. Most of them were laughing, some kindly, some with open malice. Clearly, it had already become a sort of in-joke with the subjects to do this. It was clear that they lacked proper entertainment.

Eating at his bench, Mael fixed Ram with his typical leer and leaned sideways to mutter something to Genesis. The American woman laughed and nodded deliberated at Ram, curling her lip as she did so. Ram turned his back on them as he marched to retrieve his food.

All the while, the place between his shoulder blades itching at the thought of them stabbing him in the back with a plastic piece of cutlery.

"Thank you for the sarcastic applause," Ram said as he sat down at Alina, Te and Sifa's table with his vast mounds of food. Pasta with a chili tomato sauce plus a loaf of unleavened bread the size of Alina's anterior deltoid. "What did I do this time?"

"What do you mean sarcastic?" Sifa said, as if she was genuinely confused.

"You were in that thing for eight hours straight, man," Te said.

"So?" He wasn't really listening. The thought of having to attack one of Mael's men was distracting.

"We do four-hour sessions in Avar," Sifa said.

"Four hours?" Ram asked, glancing at Mael from under his eyebrows. "How come it's so short?"

Te and Sifa exchanged a look. Alina had her massive upper body hunched over her dinner and kept pounding it down without looking up.

Sifa answered. "Our Avar performance peaks after the first hour and then starts dropping after three. A lot of us are clutching it out from even before then."

"Why's that, though? It's not as if you can get tired in Avar."

Te scoffed. "Are you crazy? It tires your mind, doesn't it? You're still thinking, focusing, hard for hours. All your focus, all your mental strength focused on the moment. All the mental computations your brain is carrying out is focused on what is happening right now and also projecting into the future, constantly assessing variables and recalculating, adapting. It is a hyper-alert state. You know what we mean, you've been there."

Ram nodded. "Okay." He glanced sideways at Jun, who was guzzling her protein shake. Could he really break into her room and snap her leg in the night? He didn't think he had it in him.

"He doesn't understand," Sifa said to Te. "Rama Seti, all of us here, apart from you, are used to fighting in the real world."

"Sure." Jun might have been the shortest subject but she was still around 7 feet tall and she was stocky like a rhino. And she could easily throw him across the room and break him in half if she caught him.

"Real world fights don't last long," Sifa was explaining. "We're from all different fighting leagues and we are used to specific rules. Some of them have three rounds that last for two or three minutes each. Others favor ten or fifteen rounds but usually they get boring by the end so they're not so popular. Eziz and Te used to do unlimited fights, no rounds, no time limit. How long did they last, Te?"

"My record was forty-one minutes but a few went over an hour. Most were between one and twelve minutes long. At those kinds of intensities, it doesn't matter how fit you are, you just get too tired."

"Physically tired," Ram said, pointing with his spoon. "You don't get mentally exhausted."

"But we do," Sifa said. "Which is why we are limited to four hours in the Avar. We are not used to concentrating at that intensity for that long. And yet you do it so easily. Obviously, it's your experience doing it for a profession but it is still impressive. We were watching you after we finished, you were really going for it. You died so many times, that takes a toll, too, even though we know it's not real. So, that's why we were applauding you and it was not sarcasm."

"I see," Ram said, cautiously. "It is easy for me, you're right and I could have kept going. Reason I didn't is because Milena pulled me out."

"Oh yeah?" Te said, nudging Sifa. "I wish Milena would pull me out, know what I'm saying? Tasty little piece, that bird, yeah you guys know what I'm saying."

Sifa elbowed him in the chest. "It is good that she stopped your session, she is taking care of your mental health."

"Listen," Ram said, leaning forward and lowering his voice. "I have to tell you something. It wasn't that. She said the other drivers had warned her about something. An attack. On me. Mael and his crazies are going to do me, probably tonight. They're going to cripple me, put me out of action. Fuck me up for good."

Alina tensed at once, her head shot up, blue eyes burning bright. "They cannot stand to see anyone but Mael succeed," she said, her voice a hiss. "They are fanatics. It is for the human race, they say. All morality must be put aside so that the great Mael can save humanity from destruction. The fools. Is that what humanity is about, is it?"

Te whispered back at her. "Alina, you know my feelings about those fuckers but I kind of agree with their thinking. We all do, right? That's what we're doing with this whole mission. We're all putting everything aside, our futures and our ethics included, so that humanity can keep on making whatever stupid decisions it wants to make."

Alina looked for a moment as if she wanted to crush Te's face in.

Instead, she relaxed, rolled her head with her eyes closed. When she opened them, she appeared in control of herself again.

"You can each of you do what you wish," she said, speaking deliberately. "I am not putting aside my own humanity in order to save everyone else. I will not do so."

Te clearly disagreed and started to say so but Sifa placed one huge, long-fingered hand upon his arm and he fell silent.

Ram ventured a question. "If you feel that way, Alina, if you don't mind me asking, why did you even sign up to this?"

She snorted a mirthless laugh. "Believe me, Rama Seti, I ask myself this question more every day that I am on this ship."

Sifa spoke in a low, even tone. "Forget ethics, what about this warning from Milena?"

"They can't get into my room," Ram said. "Not with the doors locked."

Alina jumped in. "Electronically controlled locks are worthless. They may be able to override the doors."

Te sneered. "Shut up, Alina, Mael can't do that. If he could do that he would have done it already, stop trying to bring him into your little circle of paranoia, will you?"

"I had locks on my apartment back in Delhi. Best money could buy, pretty much. Somehow I still ended up here."

"Alright then, mate, what are you going to do if they do come for you?"

Ram sighed. "Try to hurt one of them before they come for me. I reckon I can land a few blows, maybe hurt someone bad enough that I gain their respect."

Te and Sifa shook their heads. Alina turned away in disgust.

"Bro, seriously."

"You would only make it worse."

"Right but Milena says I have to try."

"You couldn't hurt any of them, no offense, brother. They'd fucking mash up your biscuits."

"You need to protect yourself," Sifa said.

Ram sighed. "Yeah, okay. Maybe I can, I don't know, maybe I can stay somewhere else tonight?" Ram tried to avoid looking at Sifa but he failed.

"Oh, I see, man," Te said, chuckling. "You want a go on my girl, here, is that it?"

Rama mumbled denials. Sifa smiled and reached across the tabletop to pat Ram's hand. Yet she did not volunteer any actual help beyond perhaps sympathy and a hint of affection. He did not blame her for not jumping to defend him, to put her own body in the way of his. They barely knew each other and Ram was clearly not worth saving. His continued presence on the mission was far from vital and he couldn't help but conclude they had consciously left him to be beaten the last time.

He smiled as if he was being understanding, though he was deeply disappointed that he would not be having sex with her.

"Stay with me tonight," Alina said with her mouth full of pasta, not looking up. "Survive the night, at least, if they try this thing."

"Are you sure?" Ram said. "Thank you for—"

"It is no solution," Alina said, cuffing the tomato sauce from her lips. "If this plan to break you is true, as the drivers say, if Mael is denied on one night, he will get you on another. We have seen this. Many years now, we have seen this."

"He'll just have stay with you every night, eh, Alina?" Te said, nudging Sifa who grinned. "Maybe you should get married."

Alina did not smile. "If not in the night, Mael will get you somewhere else. The steam room, the ice baths, the counseling rooms, medical, the corridors. It will not end unless something happens. Something must change. You both know this. We all know this."

"What can we do, then?" Sifa said. "We don't want you to get killed, Ram. Samira was bad enough. Even though you're not really, you know, one of us."

She was right, he had no reason to be there. Still, hearing her say it did make him feel bad.

Alina kept her voice low but the tone of it made Ram's hair stand on end. "Perhaps it is time that I destroy him."

"No," Sifa whispered, horrified.

Te leaned in, face darker than usual while he muttered. "Alina, you'll bloody kill each other."

"And where will that leave humanity?" Sifa whispered, her voice an angry hiss. "The people on Earth, the colonies, maybe all life on our home planet for all we know. You need to save yourself for the Orb fight. As much as I dislike to admit it, if it is not you fighting the Wheelhunter, we must have Mael as Subject Beta. We need you both. Humanity needs you both."

"Perhaps I will crush Mael's skull before he sees me coming," Alina whispered, staring at her hands, still holding her cutlery. "I would need some sort of weapon stronger than his skull, however, which makes this plan difficult to carry out. I could obtain a bone saw from the surgical section or someone could fetch it for me."

"Do not," Sifa warned.

"This is crazy, why don't the bosses step in to help me out?" Ram asked, lowering his voice. "If Milena knows and the drivers know then why doesn't Director Zuma and that guy Zhukov and whoever else step in and stop it? Are they willing to let me die?"

Te shrugged. "Seems crazy, sure, but that's the way they are. They're into the whole Techno-primitivism thing. If every one of us gets killed in the ludus, by each other, then they would know that whoever is left at the end is the most worthy and should be the one put forward for the final fight. Director Zuma is the one pushing it. It's the ultimate meritocracy. They're willing to sacrifice individuals if the mission succeeds. We're all expendable. And I hate to say it mate but you most of all. For Zuma and the rest of them, the end always justifies the means."

"For all of us, subjects included," Sifa said, nodding. "We have to think that way, do we not? When one considers just what that end is, what it could be."

"That's right," Te said. "Thinking anything else is just wishful thinking. It's childish."

"No," Alina said. "No, I do not think this. Even if our fate would be to become extinct, it does not absolve us of the sins carried out by the leaders of UNOP. The lives destroyed, the Artificial Persons and the cloning and the experiments on thousands of nonconsenting people all over the world."

"What Artificial Persons?" Ram asked but Te spoke over him.

"We have to be alive in order to have any ethics at all," Te said. "At least if we win there will be humans around to feel guilty, to be guilty about the things we did in order to survive. We can grow into a better species but only if we are capable of killing that creature."

"We will become better than we are by behaving worse and worse every year? Why even bother to keep us alive if we act as robots? Do you think I should let him kill Rama Seti, would that be for the best? You people disgust me." She took a deep breath and climbed from her seat. "Come now," Alina said to Ram and strode out of the mess hall.

"Do not worry," Sifa said to Ram as he got up to follow, shoveling as much pasta and bread in as he could. "She is often this way. On and off, friend, enemy. Reasonable, emotional. She is not a stable person. Another day or three and she will be well again. You will see."

"Sure," Ram said, staring down at her.

Was it better to lock himself into an enclosed space with an unstable woman or risk being attacked by a gang of lunatics intent on disabling him?

Just then, Mael and Eziz and the others began streaming to their rooms and the other rooms with open doors showed nothing but dark masses in the shadows. They were arguing, laughing, shoving each other's massive bodies as they did so.

Ram quickly followed Alina to the barracks and into her room as the lights lowered in the communal area and closed her door behind him.

"What happens now?" Ram said, sitting on the edge of the bed, folding his hands in his lap. He hoped she would want to go to sleep.

"Now?" Alina said, pulling a mound of blankets from the bins underneath her bed. "Please remove your clothes."

She tossed the blankets on the floor and stood before him with her hands on her hips.

Ram knew what she expected. She was not exactly his type. Her pale face was bony, with large features, none of which were especially feminine. The blonde hair on her head had regrown from a recent shaving but it was still so short it could not be grasped, not even by normal sized hands. And her body was a hulking great masculine machine. A lumpen, veined, swollen mass of muscle on muscle. Not even simply a male body, it was close to masculinity personified. The upper body was broad, her pectorals were vast slabs. She had no width to her hips but her thighs rippled with musculature.

And yet, Ram did want to have sex with her. As far as he knew he had little in the way of homosexual tendencies but she was there before him, offering herself to him and he wanted her. Was it simply the fact that she had female genitals? Or, at least, he assumed she did. With the figure-hugging nature of her clothing, it certainly looked like it. Was that all Ram needed, then, he wondered? Anything vaguely human shaped would do, so long as it had a vagina? Perhaps it was the fact of his loneliness and need for comfort and for protection that was directing him to seek solace wherever it was offered. It was absurd, really, that he would not entertain doing the same with one of the men in the ludus.

It was a shame that she did not have any breasts at all. That would have been nice.

The thoughts rushed through his mind while he glanced up and down her body but Ram's hesitation was evident to Alina, who was prepared for it.

"I am sure that this is not the kind of body that you would

seek under normal circumstances," Alina said. "And that you want Sifa, of course."

Ram began to object that he did not know what she was talking about but she hushed him up.

"She is a beauty," Alina said, sitting on the edge of the bed next to Ram. "Everyone wants to have intercourse with Sifa, that's why she was famous in the first place."

"She was?" Ram said. "IRL? I mean, back on Earth?"

Alina shuffled herself closer to Ram so that their shoulders pushed against each other. Ram was bigger than her but not by much. They did not look at each other. "You did not know about Sifa, truly? She was a star. Of course she was. She was better than almost any man or woman. And she won so many tournaments but she won them with style, you know? Yes, indeed, she knew how to play the game, how to win the big money. Obviously, she was beautiful. Tall, just like that. Most important, she had those big tits. Adored by so many fans. So much money. So much to give up, to come here."

Alina was right, Ram did want to have sex with Sifa but he had enough tact not to admit it. "You didn't have anything to give up?"

"Not tits, that is for sure. No, I gave up nothing."

Ram did not believe her for a moment but he didn't want to push her. "Okay."

Alina's skin was warm against his own as she half turned, brushing against him. "So, do you wish to do this or not?"

"Well, I was taken against my will. But you know I am here now so I think I have to give it my best shot. It's for the survival of the human race and, well, I don't have any other option but to be here."

Alina scratched her chin. "I am asking if you wish to have intercourse now?"

"Oh. I mean, yeah. I guess."

"Very well." She stood and removed her vest and shorts. Her body was exactly as he'd already seen, through her thin clothes and from catching a glimpse or two of her wandering out of her room after a shower. No one was body conscious in the ludus. Yet it was different, seeing her stepping right up in front of him. Her abdominal muscles were huge with deep canyons in between the square sections of muscle. She had no hair anywhere on her body. "You must disrobe also."

"Sure." He peeled off his vest and his shorts. Alina looked down at him.

"Do you believe you will be able to achieve and maintain an erection?"

"I'm not sure. I haven't used this before. Oh, wait. Yeah, I think it's okay."

It was strange, at first, having sex with someone so powerful but Ram got over it rather quickly.

In fact, an intense feeling of warmth and joy spread through him. Compassion, empathy, an intense desire for physical contact, it came on him like a wave, like a series of waves building higher and higher.

Her skin was smooth and delightfully, surprisingly soft under his fingertips as he ran his hands over the ridges of her muscle.

It was the best he ever felt.

"What was that?" Ram asked after, when they lay entangled, hot and sweating on the floor. "Is it these bodies? That was so intense. It was overwhelming. Do you know what I mean? That was amazing."

"Thank you. I am very skilled." She spoke with a straight face.

"No kidding." Ram sighed and arched his back.

"And yet I cannot claim responsibility for the intensity of the pleasure, which is in fact due to the hormonal intervention of our drivers during our intercourse. Your hormones from your driver and mine from dearest Noomi, my own driver. Surges of dopamine, oxytocin, whatever else they do for us. It is very nice, yes? Better than drugs."

Ram, bathed in the afterglow of a powerful climax, took a moment to process what she had said. "Wait, what? But I thought we were cut off in here? No driver communication in the barracks. How could they do stuff to us?"

"They say they cannot hear or see us, though I have my doubts. But the drivers, they monitor our readouts. They know us and our behaviors. It has become a convention to do this for us. I do not know who started it, probably Sifa and Te, they are sexual, sensual people. Perhaps they asked their drivers to increase hormone secretion during their lovemaking. Whoever it was first, now all of our drivers turn up the sex hormones when our readouts indicate we are experiencing increased sexual arousal. You understand? Most of the time it is masturbation, I suppose but it also makes the intercourse more enjoyable and palatable, especially when most of us do not find the others physically or emotionally desirable in any way yet we experience intense sexual urges."

"I see." Ram felt violated in some way. His privacy intruded upon so that even when he was at his most intimate and most vulnerable, he was being manipulated chemically.

Still, he was tired and still shrouded in happiness, so he just tucked the feeling away for the time being.

She stood, looming over him in the low light. "I will sleep now. If Mael attempts to force the door overnight, do not fight him. Leave him to me. Now, the bed is too small for both of us so you will sleep upon the floor." She lay flat on her back on her bed and turned out the last of the lights.

"Alright, fine, sure." Ram wrapped the blanket about himself as best he could as he lay down on the cold tile floor. "Well, good night, Alina. And, you know, thanks for helping me out, letting me stay here and be safe and everything."

She was already snoring.

CHAPTER SIXTEEN
BEATEN

NEXT MORNING, RAM WAS wary. All the pleasure from the night before was gone, it seemed like a dream, like it had happened to someone else.

All morning, creeping out of her room, he stuck by Alina and watched his back. But Rama knew that he was not in charge of his own destiny, not even close. He had been conscripted into service and he was treated as a prisoner or a slave and he could not go where he wanted, he could not escape. So he had to eat with the others, on edge the entire time, glancing at Mael and Eziz and Jun and Genesis. They knew that he knew. Ram could tell that they knew, that everyone knew what was going on. He was going to be attacked by the others, there was nothing he could do about it and they were loving his fear. They were getting off on it, they were laughing and whispering.

Alina ignored it and Ram tried to emulate her and imitate her shadow as they were called from the mess into the morning training session.

Bediako roared across the training area, calling out the pairings for the sparring bouts. "Rama, you'll be facing Te Zhang first of all. Te, do not take it easy on him, you will not do him any favors in the long term."

"I know," Te shouted back, before adding, under his breath, "you big fucking prick."

"And for the love of Jesus, all of you," Bediako roared. "Stay on your goddamned mats today, alright? This is about area control as much as anything. Anyone crossing into another pair's space will get PT-X'd, I swear to God. Now get to work."

Ram chanced a whisper to Te. "PT-X?"

"Physical training until you collapse. Usually circuit training with whatever exercises you personally hate the most, for hours, until you run out of juice or dehydrate to the point of collapse."

"That's crazy. Aren't we supposed to be staying in peak condition?"

"Just stay on your mat, alright, Rama? Come on, mate, let's see what you're made of."

Ram was a giant amongst giants, and yet he could not stay upright against Te's throws, could not block his strikes, could not resist his arm locks or leg hooks.

"You going easy on the fucking new guy, Te?" Bediako said, after Te had thrown Ram to the floor for the eighth time.

"No way, boss," Te said. "I'm messing him up good."

Ram climbed to his feet again. The clashes with Te hurt his pride, not his body. He didn't feel much pain at all, even when punched or crashed into the mat.

"I do not expect you to win in sparring," Bediako said, standing before Ram with his arms crossed over his chest. "I do not expect you even to stay on your feet for long. Despite your advantages in height and mass, your body is an obsolete design. Believe me, I know. I trained and fought with the same model as you. Even with a lifetime of combat training to boot, I lost. No matter what supposed upgrades they've installed in you, your muscle tissue is less efficient than everyone else's. Your nervous system is slower. Your endocrine system is primitive, to say the least. But you can do better than this, Rama Seti. You can make a better punching bag for my warriors. Te is going soft on you, despite what he says. Don't deny it, Te Zhang, you goddamn pussy. The one thing you might be good for, Rama, is being taller and heavier than anyone else, making for a better dummy analog Wheeler. Maybe I'll dress you up as one, what do you think about that? Dress you in a yellow leotard and strap some spokes around you? I'm just kidding, son, don't worry. Okay, time to change it up. Te, get out of here. Hey, the African queen, you come and manhandle our useless Wheeler dummy, here, see if you can't knock some life into him." Bediako stomped off, calling out the next pairings.

"Don't worry about it," Te said before he walked away. "He's trying to rile you up."

"It's working," Ram said, shaking with anger that he could do nothing about. Everyone on the *Victory* was a psycho and Ram wanted off.

"Ram," Sifa said, striding over and tossing her towel and other things to the edge of the mat. The other subjects were swapping around, starting again.

"Te's right." Milena's voice came through, her tone soothing. Condescending. "He's ridiculing you because he thinks anger is the best motivator. He's also doing it to encourage Mael and the others to perform better, hoping that they will humiliate you by fighting better, demonstrating the gulf between them and you. It will work, too. Another thing to consider is that Bediako used your model body, as he said. His loss weighs heavy on him, it is perhaps the defining event which shaped his character and his behavior ever since. Bediako does not want you to succeed. If you do badly, his failure is even more justified. He can blame it on the model body he was given. If Mael or one of the others beats the Wheelhunter, then Bediako will know it was the new and improved body that won it. Do you see?"

"Of course," Ram said, irritated. "Don't patronize me. I don't need you explaining the obvious to me, alright?"

Milena said nothing. Ram almost apologized but he didn't.

"Finished arguing with your driver?" Sifa said, speaking brusquely. "Come on, try to put me down. Use your weight and height to overtop me. Grasp my hands, try to bend me backward, push me down, harder."

She wore her usual tiny, thin, skintight shorts and a tight vest that squashed her breasts against her body. Her nipples were hard.

"Focus, Ram," Sifa said, not smiling as she usually did. She was all business. "The Wheeler is too strong for blows to damage it, as far as we can tell. You know that grappling will feature in how we defeat it and you struggled with the technical aspects of what you tried to achieve in your Avar session. You have to learn how to position your body, how to distribute your weight. Come here and take my hands."

Sifa held him, pulled, twisted his arms and pressed herself against his body. Her skin was hot, smooth, firm. The only soft part of her body was her chest and even there her nipples were hard as they brushed across his arm.

"Hold on a sec," Ram said and broke off, turning his back so she would not see his erection.

"What's wrong?" Sifa asked.

"Just wait a minute," Ram said and he crouched to his towel and opened his water bottle keeping his back to her. "Milena," he mumbled into his bottle. "Are you there? What the hell is going on? Can you help me out?"

"Oh dear," Milena's voice came in clear. "Are you

experiencing unwanted tumescence?"

"It's not funny," Ram muttered. "Help me out, here."

"I have increased your testosterone uptake which is increasing your sparring performance but also giving you a touch of irrational anger here and there. And your body has elevated levels of vasopressin along with it. Let me just sort that out for you. Give it a moment and don't worry, my dear, it happens to all the boys when they grapple with Sifa."

Bediako shouted across the room. "Rama Seti, what in the shit is wrong with you, you goddamn lazy asshole, get up off your ass and get to work before you get PT-X'd."

"You ready now?" Sifa asked when he stood up. She glanced at his crotch.

"Sure," Ram said. "Sorry."

"You need to learn this," Sifa said. "Right now. Who are you going to spar with next? One of the others who will break you? Come now."

She threw him to the ground a dozen times. It was astonishing to Ram that for all his enormous mass and strength he could do little to resist Sifa. The tall, lithe woman looked fast and agile so her speed was totally expected. The way she twisted and slipped from his grasp made sense. But she was also able to push him back and overpower him in simple clinches.

"Muscle mass is not necessarily related to muscle strength, you know. And anyway, grappling is mostly technique," Sifa said when he complained of this. "It is angles, it is geometry and physics. Your strength means nothing if you cannot bring it to bear. Assuming I am standing motionless when you push me away, what is the limiting factor in how much force you can use on me?"

"Don't know," Ram said, frustrated. "How thick my bones are?"

"A poor guess. It is how much of that force you can transfer to the floor."

Ram shook his head. "I don't understand."

"If you used all your strength, your feet would slide across the floor. Your shoes have non-slip soles and we have these mats underfoot. But you know from the Avar that the floor of the Orb arena is some kind of smooth metallic or ceramic surface? It provides more friction that you would expect and they've replicated it as best they can with the floor tile surfaces throughout the *Victory* but it's still a flat surface. You will find that pushing your hands hard against a wall causes your feet to slip away. The force you can exert overcomes the amount you can transfer into the floor. So what is the use of all your mighty strength if you cannot use it? Technique is everything."

Ram nodded. "I understand. Can you show me?"

"What I can, I will show. But it takes a lifetime to learn. You have six months."

"It's not like I'm going to fight the alien, right?"

"Indeed." Sifa glanced across the mats to where Mael was elbowing Genesis in the face. "But there are other fights you must win."

"Rama Seti," Bediako shouted. "You lazy piece of shit, you time wasting, fat, useless fuck. You might be used to pissing your own life away but you are mine now, you belong to me and you will not waste my time, nor the time of any of my real fighters. Stop fucking talking and move your fat ass or I'll kill you myself, I swear it by all that is holy. Move it!"

Ram and Sifa continued for an hour. When Ram was covered in bruises and drenched in sweat, Bediako shouted out the next partnerships. Ram waited for his name to be called. But Bediako waited, saving the words Ram feared the most for last.

"Alright, let's see how you shirk your way out of this one, Rama Seti," Bediako shouted. "It's time for you to fight Mael."

Ram felt everyone's eyes on him as he walked, a condemned man, to where Mael stood waiting.

Bediako clapped his hands together with an echoing slap. "What are you bunch of lazy shits waiting for? This is not a spectator sport. Get on with your own work."

Mael's grin was as wide as his face. "Here we are at last."

"Look," Ram said, from as far away on their sparring mat as it was possible to be. "I know you want to prove a point or something. But think of the greater good here."

Mael sneered. "Oh, I am. You are weak. They gave you an obsolete body. You were born with an obsolete mind and lived a wasted life. By your presence here, you weaken us."

"I am trying to learn—"

Mael darted forward and smashed Ram's jaw, throwing him down. Ram rolled and stood, turning to face Mael. But his opponent came instead from the side, stamping on Ram's knee before he could react. He threw out an elbow, hitting nothing but air, swinging again and limping back. Mael punched him in the kidney, hard as a blow from a horse.

Melina was shouting in his ear but he couldn't focus on what she was saying.

Ram knew he was being toyed with and the knowledge filled him with rage. The fire of it flowed through his limbs down to his fingers and toes. He threw out an arm and somehow connected with something solid. He followed up and grabbed what he realized with surprise was Mael's neck. Ram squeezed with all his might and pulled the man toward him, throwing his greater weight down on top of him, wrapping his arms about Mael's chest. Mael twisted and they both fell, Ram on top, his head smashing into Mael's face and crushing his nose. Ram butted him again, hard and tried to get an arm free from Mael's grasp. He punched Mael in the side of the head and in the face. Ram had time to feel a thrill at how well he was doing.

The voice in his ear came through. It was Milena, calling out a warning.

He caught a fragment over the sound of his own breathing and grunts of exertion.

"He's toying with you," Milena was saying. "Just stop. Stop and get away from him."

Underneath Ram, Mael was laughing. Ram punched as hard as he could at the awkward angle and held Mael down with the rest of his body and yet Mael was laughing like crazy, even as Ram's fist crashed repeatedly into his neck and jaw and temple.

Ram was defeated by that laughter. Still, he kept fighting, as hard as he could. But Mael wrapped his legs around Ram's, threw his hips over and Ram found himself on his back looking up as Mael, still laughing, rained blows into his face.

Ram found his arm in Mael's grip for just a moment. Ram strained against Mael's hands but it was no good.

His forearm snapped, halfway between wrist and elbow. The pain shot up and died away, echoing through his shoulder. He threw a punch with his other arm. Mael grabbed that fist with both hands and started to twist, trying to break it too.

Rama wasn't thinking clearly. Milena shouted without meaning in his ear. He felt as though he was underwater or in a dream, powerless to stop what was happening to him. Helpless in the face of incredible power.

He had a flash of memory of himself as a boy, fighting his father. He remembered the familiar futility of trying to do anything. But Ram had grown quickly as a boy, overtopping his father when he was still in junior school. Then, in his memory of that one fight, the last ever play fight with his dad, he threw out a hand that thumped into his father's face. There had been blood streaming from his father's nose and mouth and Ram's head echoed with his father's furious cries as he beat Ram unconscious. You unnatural freak. You're not my son. His mother screamed off to the side for his father to stop.

"Fight back," Milena shouted in his head.

Ram punched Mael with his broken arm.

The pain of the impact was incredible, throwing waves of nausea over him. But it was worth it to see the shock on Mael's face as his nose was broken, blood exploding everywhere. He only had a moment to enjoy the sight of it before Mael retaliated, opening up with a flurry of blows into Ram's face.

They slammed into his cheeks, his lips and teeth,

His world became a sea of stars that faded into an infinite blackness.

CHAPTER SEVENTEEN
MISSION TWO

"I THOUGHT THAT WHILE YOU recover from your injuries, we can still do useful work," Milena said the next day. They met in the special counseling room in the ludus ring.

Ram's face was a terrible mess and he had four broken ribs. Dr. Fo assured him that he would be completely healed inside twenty-four hours.

"We can do useful work?" Ram said. "Do I have to write an essay on why I'm the most useless subject in the UNOP's history?"

"Yes, very amusing," she said. "I think I'd have you write ten thousand words on why you suffer from so much self-doubt."

They sat opposite each other in the counseling room, Ram on a metal stool, her in an upholstered armchair, though it was as much bolted to the floor as every other piece of furniture on the ship. He wished he could have a chair as comfortable looking as hers.

Ram attempted a smile at her self-doubt joke, though it hurt to move his face much and the joke was painful too. "Why I'm suffering from self-doubt? Are you serious? I thought you were supposed to be a psychologist, Milena. You know what my problem is, don't you? I was abducted, I had my own body removed and placed on a synthetic monster. I have lost years of my life from being kept unconscious and since you woke me up I've been in genuine physical danger from my supposed peers who I am also locked up with constantly. I'm not only a prisoner in body but in mind, with you manipulating how I feel and what I think constantly, even when I'm having an intimate moment with another person, in private. I can't get away from you. In fact, I only find out after that it was you, sitting in an office somewhere on the ship, getting this body to release hormones to make me horny. And despite all this, the single reason I'm here is to be a punching bag. I have to be honest, I think a little self-doubt is to be expected, don't you?"

Milena sat quietly after he had finished. "I apologize. I know you've been through a lot. What UNOP has done to you, the great bureaucracy, is clearly unethical. Personally, everything I've done with regards to your endocrine system has been to help you.

That might not mean a lot to you but my intentions have been good. In fact, that's why we're here today. I want to help you to engage fully with this project."

Ram rubbed his chest. His bruises were fading but still he was sore all over. "I haven't been fully engaged?"

She tilted her head to one side. "Ram, you know you haven't. You've been looking for a way out since you got here and that's understandable. But I know you, remember. I know you through unethical means, yes, but I know you. And I know that you have been running whenever things are hard, you've been doing it your whole life. Well, it's up to you to decide if that's how you want to continue with the life that you have left to you, now, on the *Victory*, on this mission. You don't have much freedom left but you can choose how you perceive your reality and it is in your power to do that. That's one thing that I can't help you with, not really. I can jack you up on testosterone and make you bullish and confident but that wouldn't address the underlying problem and you would not be in control of yourself."

He sat quietly for a few, long moments. "Alright, so, what are we doing?"

She nodded, sat back. "You're going to review the events of the Arena Combat Phase of Mission Two from sixty years ago. Diego the Intelligence Officer is on his way over to take us through it. One of the AI's flagged up that you have not watched the replays of the previous missions."

She waited for him to respond.

"I read about the missions on the networked screen in my room."

"We know but you stop the footage before it plays. No need to try to explain, I know why you don't watch them. It's an avoidance tactic. It is your fear of witnessing the horrific reality of this situation."

Ram touched his face. "Actually, I witnessed that in the mirror this morning pretty well."

"What I want to do in our next Avar session is to run through the replays of the old missions in the simulated Arena. Many subjects find it useful to see precisely where the previous missions went wrong."

"Sounds great," Ram said.

The door hissed open and Diego the Intel guy stepped in. He was a small guy, small shoulders and kind of hunched. But his teeth shone in his dark face when he saw Ram and the smile seemed genuine.

"Diego, just in time," Milena said.

"Hey, man," Diego said, jerking his head in greeting and sitting on a wall perch he pulled out. "Ouch, your face." He winced. "Once, when I was a boy I walked thirty miles through the bush to the next town just to see a girl. On the way, I saw a rotting goat lying by the side of the road. It was all bloated and swollen after heavy rain and then lots of sun, half caved in and exposing the innards. Your face right now kind of reminds me of that goat. Anyway, let's do this." He clicked on the wall screen.

Ram didn't think it was all that funny. His face was the only thing that was left of the real Rama Seti, the thing that made him unique.

"You know, guys," Ram said. "I could just watch this by myself in the barracks, I don't need to be talked through it."

Diego and Milena exchanged a glance as the screen flicked into life.

"What?" Ram said.

"You have a tendency to avoid difficult, graphic images," Milena said.

"Well, yeah because I'm a normal person."

Milena slowly raised a hand to point in his face. "Exactly. Which is a serious problem. If there's one thing we can't have, it's you being a normal person. You have to put aside your compassion and empathy to get through the next few months."

Ram sighed. "How do you suggest I do that?"

Milena shrugged. "We can always do a lot of that chemically. But it would be better if you could do what you can to stop caring about the physical and emotional wellbeing of yourself and your new colleagues."

"I don't care about them," Ram said, lying. "But I'm not sure how I can stop caring about myself."

"You don't care about dying in Avar. Try to cultivate that."

"But—"

Milena spoke over him. "Good, let's do this Diego?"

"Right on," Diego said. "Check it out." He scrolled through

a few clips and pulled the one wanted onto the screen. "Mission Two Arena Combat Phase took place back in 2139. That's almost sixty years ago, in case you're suffering from memory loss due to brain damage in that smashed up head of yours. You know about the selection process?"

"Yeah, after the Mission One disaster they recruited military personnel from all over the world. I'm not sure how many thousands of people they went through but they ended up with this guy at the end of the mission, a Brazilian."

"Rafael Santos, known as Onca," Diego said.

"Yeah, the briefings just call him Onca, what's with that?"

Milena sat up, a little smile on her face. "We Brazilians enjoy our nicknames. Onca is jaguar. His friends called him that from when he was kid, even before he joined the military because he was quiet, solitary and an absolute killer. A perfect ambush predator."

Ram raised his eyebrows. "Oh yeah, so what's your nickname?"

She smirked and sat back. "None of your business."

Diego cleared his throat. "Onca made Major in the 1st BF Esp., which is Brazilian Special Forces, by the time he was twenty-eight. That unit specialized in counter-terrorism and all the usual special forces ninja stuff. Their motto is 'Any mission, anywhere, anytime, anyway.' And Onca certainly lived that. A lot of his service history is still classified, even now and even from us, so we expect he got up to a lot of off the books work, probably assassinations but who knows. Enough of his missions were conventional, in the special forces sense and he quickly became a legend within that community. Everyone who worked with him, and he worked with a lot of people, always said he was a genius. He could do it all, long range shooting, close-up stealth, urban, jungle, amphibious, airborne, everything. Just an enormously gifted, natural soldier."

Ram was tempted to make a joke of some sort but he remembered he was about to see this legend get graphically murdered so he held his tongue.

"Anyway," Diego continued, "like a lot of the guys back then he retired early, when he was about thirty and set up a private outfit called the Sabre Rubro. A cooperative made up of other ex-special forces that was commissioned immediately by the Brazilian Government to crack down on the pro-human terrorists cropping up all over. I don't know if you know your Brazilian history but when the crazies were out in the Amazon, no one really cared that much but when these cells started taking over company buildings in Sao Paulo state, well, you can imagine the reaction."

"What companies?" Ram said.

"Biotech, pharmaceuticals, same as usual. Onca's Urban Security Co-op bounced around these towns, storming buildings and shooting terrorists. Amateur recordings everywhere on our system, you got to check them out, here I'll bookmark some for you. Anyway, his team gets called into this giant siege operation at the HQ of Abora Biopharma, huge firm utilizing unique Amazonian compounds for use in the medical industry. Specifically, they developed solutions for the synthetic amniotic gel for the exogenesis tanks being first rolled out worldwide at that point. This helped to spur the interplanetary resources boom back then."

"They helped make the Artificial Person asteroid miners and colony support workers," Milena said. "And they were, and still are, a significant member of the UNOP Commission."

"Got it," Ram said.

"Cameras of the world were on this siege. Millions of people watched live when Onca's Sabre Rubro went in. You can see it from a dozen angles from all sides of the compound, from choppers and drones and satellite. But it was a trap, really. All the disparate, warring factions in the pro-human movement had come together to sucker Onca's guys in by posing as a new group, Sangue Puro. There were dozens of terrorists there, heavily armed. They never had any genuine demands. They were never going to let any hostages go or expected to get out themselves. The crazy bastards inside fell back to a central area then blew up the whole bloody, goddamned building, man."

"I think I read about this before, maybe."

"It was pretty famous, my friend. Four hundred and twenty dead, plus injuries, including all the terrorists and the Sabre Rubro Co-op. A nation in mourning, new laws passed to crack down in insurrection, the usual. In the meantime, we have

Onca."

Diego threw up a still image on the screen. Onca, bandaged and in a hospital room on Earth, unmistakable sunlight streaming in from somewhere.

"He knew something was wrong by how the terrorists fought and he ordered his team to abort but the communications were cut off. As the structure was detonated, he took shelter under a stairwell and survived in the rubble for three days. When they pulled him out and told him all of his men had died, the UNOP recruiters got to him and offered him a job. In space, probably a one-way trip, doing something profoundly important for Brazil and the world. The jaguar pounced. He blitzed selection, made it onto the mission, became and retained Subject Alpha status. And so we come, to the hero on the Orb."

They cut to the Orb staging area where Onca was waiting with his boarding team.

The staging chamber, which Ram had viewed before, was a hundred-meter per side cube of a room with the large door in the center of one side and what they called the smokescreen the opposite wall. It was a fifty-meter square, semi-transparent and was the barrier between the room and the vast arena itself beyond. The slowly swirling, gray screen was lit by the strange feature of the Orb where the ambient light came, seemingly, from the surface of the walls and floors and ceilings so that every person in the room, including Onca himself, was cast in a remarkably even, soft white light that cast no shadow.

He was dressed in full combat gear. He wore a helmet with visor, body armor, assault rifle, sidearm on one hip and a huge combat knife holstered on his chest.

"They didn't know," Ram said, glancing at Milena. "The Orb doesn't allow weapons in the arena."

Diego responded. "That's conjecture, really. All we know is that it rejected these weapons, as you are about to see and it rejected the augmentations and weapons we tried during Mission Three. Who knows what the Orb will do in future? It's hinted that armed combat might be a possibility in future bouts, if we ever get there."

"Who's conjecturing now?" Milena said. "Just play the film, Diego."

The playback resumed. The boarding crew was tense. No doubt, they were all thinking of Ambassador Diaz's disastrous Mission One.

Onca, though, the Subject Alpha called Rafael Santos, seemed to be the calmest of the lot, simply standing as if he was waiting in line at a grocery store.

"Did they dose him like you dose me?" Ram said/

"They didn't use hormonal adjustment technology for Onca, no. He didn't need it. During his career, he had other nicknames, like the O Louco which means sort of like the Madman or the Crazy One. And the Lobo Feroz, the Wild Wolf, things like that."

"Oh, so, he goes totally nuts in battle?"

Milena stared at him. "No, it is a joke, because he is always so calm."

"Like when you call a great big man Tiny," Diego said, helpfully.

"Thank you, Diego," Milena said. "So, Onca was a man completely in control of his emotions. His greatest gift, perhaps, was his mental toughness. His psychological fortitude in the face of extreme stress. For whatever reason, his brain structure and chemistry, his genetic predisposition plus his environment and then his military training and experience, all combined with his very conscious personal philosophy meant he was able to remain alert but fully in control of his actions, even under intense fire. In effect, he was able to slip into a flow state with ease. In fact, it might be fair to say he existed in a flow state at all times, whether in or out of combat. Everything seemed to come easily to him."

"So he was a pretty chill guy," Ram said.

"Chill as a jaguar, anyway," Diego said.

"Mental toughness, a conscious toughness, is merely half the battle," she said. "Because you must also be strong emotionally. Mental toughness and emotional toughness go hand in hand."

Ram felt sure Milena was leaning on him pretty hard to pick up what she was saying as it applied to him. She was not particularly subtle about how she manipulated Ram. But then, perhaps that was the point. She wanted him to know, wanted him to take ownership of himself.

"You're telling me I need to get a grip on my emotions."

"Exactly," she said. "You are mentally prepared and bought into this Project, into this Mission, I can see that. You have reasoned that you are committed but I am afraid that over the next few months before we reach that Orb, you will fail on an emotional level. You will face many tasks that will overwhelm you physically and emotionally and all the reason in the world won't save you, not really, if your emotions cloud your judgment. An uncontrolled emotional response will disrupt your thinking and reasoning and also, neurotic thinking patterns will generate an emotional, physical response. Either and both of these states are self-replicating, they reinforce each other, sets you off into a negative state of mind. When you are in that state, you make bad decisions and then you will fail, at training and at anything. At life. When you fail, you become angry. Everyone experiences anger and self-pity when they are pushed beyond their breaking point but you must train your emotional response to stressors. So, ultimately, yes. Get a grip on your emotions. I would prefer it if you didn't get badly injured."

Or worse.

The words seemed obvious, seemed like they flowed into the silence even though they were unspoken. *Badly injured or worse*, everyone in the room must have been thinking it.

Ram swallowed down a quip and instead asked a genuine question.

"I thought you were controlling my hormone uptake and my moods anyway."

Milena tilted her head. "I am and I will. But do you really wish to live like that? Like an infant? A puppet on a string?"

"When you put it that way, no. Not at all."

"Onca was a master at connecting to short-term goals, like focusing his emotional attention on the short term, while focusing his mental toughness on the longer term, the bigger picture. He allowed them to carry him through times of intense stress with what seemed like ease from the outside. Now, watch what an emotional shock he had to face right before stepping into the arena." She pointed at Diego. "Play it."

On the Orb, the boarding crew was silenced by the sound of a clear, pinging chime ringing out in the chamber.

Without a word, Onca stepped up to the swirling smokescreen.

The Orb played a low, discordant tone that made Ram flinch. The crew in the replay flinched, too. They began arguing about what it meant.

"Lower the audio, Diego," Milena instructed. The replay continued in almost silence while Milena narrated. "They had to work it out as they went along but they had prepared for this, to a certain extent. We call it the Zeta Line now but back then, they didn't know."

Onca handed over his weapon to another marine and stepped back up to the swirling sheet of semitransparent plasma that Ram knew from his reading would part to allow the Subject Alpha through into the Arena.

Nothing happened.

"That noise, the negative tone?" Milena said. "It keeps sounding every time he steps back up to it."

Onca removed his helmet and stepped back to the screen. It did not part.

The support crew seemed agitated but Onca simply stripped off his body armor. It was a remarkable outfit, clearly molded perfectly to the marine's extremely impressive physique. It was presumably a complex and multilayered textile-like material, flexible at the joint and movement areas at the true waist under the rib cage but rigid around the chest. Onca pulled off a large, throat-protecting gorget piece from around his neck, unstrapped grieves and leg armor. Still, the screen would not part.

Not until he was stripped to his thin underclothes and his boots did the chime sound.

One of his marines stepped up and handed Onca back his assault rifle. The discordant note sounded and the plasma smokescreen whipped shut faster than the eye could see. Even when the rifle was swapped for the sidearm, a large caliber hand cannon type semi-automatic tactical pistol. The Orb sounded the negative tone once again.

Onca, impassive, handed back his weapon and in return took a large, evil looking combat knife. It was serrated on the lower half of the back blade, had a wicked curve to the top half of the front blade and was as long as Onca's forearm. He brandished it as he stepped up to the screen again.

The discordant note sound.

He handed his blade over so that he stood there in no more than his thin, stretchy underclothes, wearing black military boots.

The Orb chimed again.

For the first time, Ram saw Onca's head drop, just a little. Surely, he realized in that moment that he had no chance of victory against the giant alien. And yet he stood straighter after just a moment.

He turned and nodded to his crew, who called out to him.

"Turn the audio up," Milena said, her voice flat.

"Is there anything you want to say, Onca?" A woman on the playback called out.

Onca, his face impassive, looked over his shoulder. He shook his head, once.

The woman called out again, a slight edge of desperation in her voice. Ram guessed she cared a great deal for the man who was about to die. "Anything we can tell them? This will be declassified one day."

Onca seemed to sigh and started to shake his head again but he stopped. "*Diga-lhes que eu fiz o meu dever.*"

He marched right into the arena, the screen closing behind him.

There were a couple of minutes that Diego sped through, while cameras were set up close to the smokescreen and the view beyond was somewhat hazy because of it, though they had removed the swirling with post-processing, the Intel Officer explained. The 400-meter interior of the arena took a while to walk across. And to roll across.

"What did he say just then?" Ram asked Milena.

She shrugged. "He said to tell them I did my duty."

Ram didn't know why, exactly, but that brought a lump to his throat and the warm promise of tears to his eyes. It was stupid because Ram had always somewhat poured scorn on concepts like duty.

On the screen, Diego slowed the replay. Ram noticed that the Intel Officer was not himself watching the action unfold.

The Wheelhunter dwarfed the human. Onca was perhaps a little over average height. He was in amazing shape yet rather lithe and was only maybe ninety kilos. The Wheeler, on the other hand, weighed half a ton at least. It rolled onward, cartwheeling in that deeply unnerving way it did, the great footpads flapping on the floor, over and over. The knobbled, long arms with their three-fingered, clawed hands rolled over and over.

When the gap between them closed to around thirty meters, the Wheelhunter lurched into a crazed, spinning acceleration. It covered the distance in under three seconds.

Onca feinted to the right then leaped to the left, rolling smoothly over his shoulder and jumping up into a fighting stance, moving into an attack.

The Wheeler had tilted slightly away from him, deceived by the feint. It recovered immediately, swerved toward the human and lashed out with its wicked, long arms.

A two-meter, ball-jointed arm with three long claws on the end can deliver an incredible force. It delivered that force across Onca's chest, neck and the top of his head, almost instantaneously. The force tossed Onca sidewise in a tumble, as if he'd been hit by a racing car. As his body tumbled, the top of his skull, sliced by the claw, spun away like a china plate. His destroyed throat sprayed bright blood in a mist of pink through the air of the arena. The body crashed into the floor and slid another couple of meters, leaving a red stain along the black surface.

Still, Onca was not done. He should have been dead but his body did not understand that yet and he struggled to his elbows and knees, blood welling from his chest, neck and head and spattering onto the floor beneath him.

The Wheeler, however, had not stopped. Ram had to bite back the urge to shout a warning at the replay as he watched the great monster cartwheel up to the tiny human and whip its arm down onto his back. The force of the impact must surely have killed him, snapping his spine and crushing the rest of his torso. More than that, the claws tore out chunks of flesh and bone and organs as it smashed and ripped him with a wild, frenzied series of whip-like blows.

When there was little left but shredded flesh, the Wheeler paused for a moment, as if inspecting the remains. It then rolled away toward the other side of the arena, leaving a chain of red oval footprints behind it.

Diego cut the footage, not meeting anyone's eye.

Ram let out the breath he didn't know he had been holding. He didn't know what to say.

Milena was watching him closely. "My point in showing you this right now," she said, "is not really about tactics or training techniques. This is really to help you understand what the other subjects are going through. This man is a worldwide legend in special forces, even though they mostly think he died in that demolished building. You can imagine the metrics collected during the selection and training process and we're fairly confident that Onca was the best non-augmented, non-genetically engineered, old fashioned human soldier ever tested. His numbers are off the charts. And you saw what happened to him. The subjects onboard are pushing themselves and each other this hard for a reason. They are terrified of themselves failing. Terrified of this mission failing. We can't let it happen. And that's the real difference between them and you, that they have fully committed to sacrificing themselves. Not just them but everyone on this ship, more or less. We have to remove ourselves, our personalities, our emotions, our identities from what we need to achieve. However we do it, we must all put ourselves away. It sounds corny and old-fashioned or perhaps authoritarian and communist but the term I always come back to is, the greater good. Have you heard this way of saying it? For the greater good?"

Ram nodded, thinking about Onca.

Tell them I did my duty.

"If the greater good was for my country or for the state or for a corporation," Ram said, "I would laugh in your face. Even if it was for my own parents. But we're talking about the whole human race. You can't get any greater than that, I guess."

"Do you think you can commit to losing yourself for all of them back on Earth and elsewhere in the system?"

"Alright." Ram shrugged. "I'm in. All the way. No more self-pity, no more complaining or any bullshit. I'll do my duty."

PART 3
SURVIVAL

CHAPTER EIGHTEEN
THE PRICE

"HOW LONG HAVE YOU been here now, Rama?" Director Zuma asked him from behind her desk.

"Two months," Ram said, knowing full well that the Director would know precisely how long he'd been here. "Two months since I have been awake. Obviously, I was kept unconscious for thirty-three months before that."

Ram glanced over his shoulder at Milena, seated in the corner behind him but she did not even bother to look up from her screen.

The interview, in the Director's own office, was Ram's

opportunity to demonstrate to the top brass that he had truly bought into UNOP, to the Mission Four objectives and his own part in all of it. He knew that he was a tiny cog, he knew what he was giving up in order to be part of the great machine. He knew what the stakes were.

And now he had to prove it to them.

Director Zuma spread her hands across the top of her desk. "I know that has been a source of anger for you and quite rightly, too, in my opinion. I hope you understand why we did not reveal that fact to you immediately upon waking. It is most unfortunate that you found out by yourself rather than being told but there you go, these things happen, all water under the bridge now, isn't that right? Of course it is, and you are doing so well now that you are all settled in. Very well indeed. Look at your performance statistics, aren't they wonderful? You must be proud of yourself."

"I appreciate you saying so," Ram said, and he kind of did, "but I'm bottom of the group in almost every category."

"Number one in applied strength, strongest person ever, they tell me. Often you're doing well in the Avar simulations. That's nothing to be sniffed at, as they say. So, you are bottom everywhere else and by some margin. But so what? You should be proud of yourself. You are making a great contribution to this mission and to the Project overall. I could not be happier that we chose you."

She stared at him with a smile on her face.

"Great, thanks. That's great to hear."

"Nasty business with Mael a couple of months ago," Director Zuma said. "I was very sorry to hear that you spent so long in the medical sections."

Ram shrugged. "The pain suppression inbuilt in this model body is pretty good. Dr. Fo is a genius and Milena helped with all her hormones and drugs so I didn't suffer much. I was back to ninety-five percent in six days."

"What a marvelous attitude you have. Mael is a problem for you, for many of you, I know that. And I want you to know that I do not like the man, for who he is. For what he does. His behavior is appalling, barbaric. I know that tensions are high in the ludus and that low-level physical altercations are occurring regularly. You are doing well to maintain your own safety in difficult circumstances."

Low level, she said but everyone had been beating the living shit out each other for weeks. "All part of the job, right? We have to focus on the big picture. Our own personal issues, our own safety is of no concern when our planet, our solar system is at risk."

"You've accepted it fully? How wonderful. You are quite right. Yes, that's the spirit, son. You could not be more right. And keep up the good work," the Director said. "Thank you for taking the time to stop by and see me today. I will let you have your weekly meeting with Milena now."

When Ram and Milena were in the corridor and the Director's door slid shut, Ram mumbled to her. "What was the point of that little audience?"

"Come on," Milena said.

They walked in silence through the white-tiled corridors until they got to Milena's counseling room and Ram took his usual, oversized chair across from her normal one. It was nice to sit down in comfort and he stretched out his legs and reached up. He was hungry and aching all over. He felt quite good.

"Seriously, what was all that about? Why did Director Zuma bother to ask me to go see her today?"

"Perhaps she is worried about you." Milena seemed distracted.

"Didn't seem like it. She told me she thought I was doing great."

"You may have noticed that what people say does not necessarily tell you what they are thinking. Zuma tells you that she will always tell you the truth and then proceeds to do nothing but lie to you."

Ram sat up straighter. He had never seen Milena express such bitterness before. Not so explicitly.

"What's she lying about?"

Milena looked around the empty room. "Nothing. She is simply concerned about you and your endless questions. And how they distract you from your true purpose here."

"What endless questions?"

Milena sighed. "You know what questions. About why you were left unconscious for months before being woken up. About why you were really chosen. About how many people are onboard the ship, its exact dimensions and capabilities, how many marines we have onboard and what armament they bear. What our course is, how many ships are we building back on Earth, what communications and automated weapons platforms are there in deep space. You can understand why these sorts of questions make a soldier like Director Zuma nervous, right?"

"No, I don't understand. I'm not going anywhere. I don't have any way of communicating with Earth and telling the world all your secrets. And I wouldn't do it anyway."

"You wouldn't?" Milena tilted her head. "Do you not consider it an ethical duty to inform the people of the world of our impending destruction?"

"Well, yeah I guess I do," Ram admitted. "I think we should tell them. But information about the Orb is already out there and no one cares. There's no point me doing it by myself, who am I? No one knows me, I'd be ignored."

Milena smiled. "Admitting you would break our rules if only it could be successful is the kind of thing Zuma is concerned about."

"Fine, don't tell me about all the big secrets, whatever. But you can tell me about myself, can't you, at least? Tell me exactly what was done to me and I'll stop asking. You claim to subscribe to this whole honesty policy but your get out is that you can withhold information if it negatively impacts the mission. Not telling me means either your whole policy is bullshit or that the truth is somehow totally devastating. Or maybe both. Why not just lie? Just tell me anything, bullshit me convincingly and I'll just stop asking."

"I'm afraid we just don't do that, Ram."

"You know what I think it might be? What you're doing is a way of modifying my behavior so that I commit more fully to abandoning what's left of my own desires, my own freedom and self-determination. You obviously know that withholding information makes the subjects paranoid. You're driving Alina crazy with all the secrets, she thinks all kinds of mad stuff. Of course you know all this, so it must be by design. The increased tension and distrust within the group dynamic enhances performance, right?"

"Did you not mean it when you said to the Director that your own safety and security and needs were unimportant compared to this mission?"

Ram sat back. "Okay, I know, I'm being ridiculous. I'm acting like a child, demanding stuff I can't have because I don't understand. But I'm not a child and I want answers. I can't shake the feeling I'm being lied to about everything."

"But are you truly willing to sacrifice yourself for the survival of humanity?"

"Sure. We all are, right? I meant it. I get it. You need Alina or Mael to be the best they can be, peaking in performance at just the right moment in three months' time as we reach the Orb. I'm committed. I get it. I've studied the recordings from the previous fights. You've watched me get instantly killed by Wheelhunters at a hundred percent in the Avar sims so I know what a mountain we're facing. I know even those two will have the odds stacked against them. But we have to make it work, we have to get Alina into the right space and I'm willing to help her get there."

Milena pulled absently at her bottom lip while she contemplated Ram. "How is she?"

"I'm sure you know better than I do how Alina is. Don' t you speak to her driver? Don't you have her readings or whatever? You can look into our chemistry, our brain function."

"You are the one having sexual intercourse with her on a nightly basis."

Ram laughed, though he didn't find it funny. "You know it's not nightly. Not even close. Thanks for all the surges of vasopressin, by the way. Could you dial up the oxytocin next time? I can't get enough of that stuff, makes me feel so content."

"You have to go easy with oxytocin. Any more and you'll be falling in love with Alina."

"Nonsense."

"Are you the biochemist or am I? Anyway, your oxytocin is spiking plenty enough every time you look at Sifa."

"It spikes by itself or do you spike it? I never know how much of what I'm feeling is really what I'm feeling. How much of my day to day life is you making me do and think what you want me to think?"

"Will you believe any answer that I give? Or will you assume I'm telling what will elicit the best performance for the mission?"

"I think I recognize the truth when I see it."

She had the good grace to resist laughing in his face.

"Please, Ram, tell me about Alina."

"Are you actually worried about her? Because you should be. I don't know her, not really but she seems stranger than usual, the last few weeks. Talks about freedom all the time. About Artificial Persons, about how they are slaves and how we are all slaves, ultimately. How there's no free will for anyone. For the Artificial Persons and for us most of all."

Milena nodded as he was talking. "Has she told you anything about what she's planning?"

"No. And I'm being honest, here. What is she up to?"

"Her driver, Noomi, and me, we are concerned about her."

"What does Bediako think? What about old Director Zuma back there?"

"Alina's driver and I would rather keep our concerns to ourselves at the moment."

"Is that even possible on this ship? Why would you do that?"

"Our concern is that she would be removed from participation in the mission. Neither of us wants to see that and nor do you. Despite the fact that she has begun sleeping more often with Sifa rather than with you, she is still your best protection. She is the only person who can stand up to Mael, one on one."

"And I'd rather she be the savior of humanity than Mael."

"You would?" Milena said. "And would you help her to achieve that?"

He hesitated, feeling the question was heavily loaded. "Sure."

She looked at him for a while. "What is playing on Alina's mind, would you say?" Milena asked.

Ram scratched his chin. "Who knows?"

"I think maybe you know."

"Are you testing me to see if I will give up her secrets? It seems you know all about it, whatever it is. You'll just have to believe me when I say I don't know. Or don't believe me, up to you."

Milena looked at him for a long moment.

He held her gaze, realizing that he was right. Milena clearly did know what was wrong with Alina and she was testing Ram, trying to find out if he knew too. He did not. Alina remained as much a mystery to him as she had when he first met her, even though he'd had sex with her plenty of times.

Milena looked away and spoke to someone not present in the room. "Alright, bring her in."

The rear door slid open and Alina ducked inside the room.

Behind Alina came her driver, Noomi plus the intelligence officer called Diego. They were like children beside her. The three of them hurried inside the room, taking the last three chairs, the door closing with a soft thump after them.

"What is this?" Ram said, staring between them. "Were you listening to all that?"

Alina nodded a greeting at Ram as she sat next to him.

"We don't have much time," Milena said, leaning in and speaking hurriedly. "We must be quick before we are discovered together."

"Isn't everything on this ship monitored?" Ram whispered. "All the time?"

"I set things up pretty good," Diego said. "I have totally hacked the security systems throughout the ship, no one knows. And I gave us a cover so we can meet unobserved. Our monitoring devices are showing all of us as being where we're supposed to be right now, don't worry."

"Before we go any further," Milena said," we must remember that the mission has to come first. And we must retain control of our emotions."

"What is this?" Ram asked. Alina looked him square in the eye. Her driver was a Nigerian woman called Noomi, slim and tall. Not a million miles away from Sifa's physique yet Noomi had a hard, somewhat unkind face.

"Always it seemed suspicious to many of us," Alina said. "The way that Mael could kill Samira so easily, without her fighting back in any way. It was obvious that Bediako, Zuma and Zhukov and the others were hiding the truth from us. A few weeks ago, one of our friends onboard finally decrypted some of the reports. They described how Samira had been remotely paralyzed just as Mael moved in to attack her. She was unable to defend herself. And he killed her."

Ram looked at Alina, as he knew she had been close - and physically so - with Samira. But the Russian giant sat hunched in her chair like a gargoyle.

"Why?" Ram asked.

Alina shrugged her enormous shoulders. "My performance was degenerating. I cared too much for Samira, did not focus on training so much, stayed awake all night with her rather than rest. Without me pushing him, Mael's performance also dropped."

Noomi cut in. "Mael was exhibiting erratic behaviors too. Everyone knew what he was but they thought they could control it. They had kept a lid on his tendencies for a year, they hoped they had solved it but it was not to be. His compulsions had been buried, dormant. But he needed to commit a murder."

"I don't understand," Ram said.

Milena picked up the story from Noomi. "The ship's AIs and the mission leaders evaluated possible courses and concluded that the most efficient changes in performance would be to have Mael kill Samira. He would be cured, for a while at least, and once Alina got over her grief, she would fight even harder to be the one to beat Mael. So that is why they arranged it."

"I never heard exactly what happened."

Alina snorted. "Neither did we until recently. They got Mael to isolate her in her quarters, locked the other doors, then hijacked Milena's hormone control of Samira to make her angry, confrontational. But Mael did not need encouragement. Just to make sure their precious hero would not be damaged, they remotely paralyzed her. He beat her to death. She would have been conscious but unable to move while he savaged her."

Ram wiped his hands over his face.

"They?"

Milena answered. "Director Zuma, Bediako, probably Chief Executive Zhukov."

"And now they have you in their sights," Alina said.

So he's not given up trying to hurt me now, Mael's really trying to kill me?"

"Not yet," Alina said. "If he was, truly, you would be dead already. But they have decided to sacrifice you. Give Mael what he needs once again. And I would train harder and so would he. The cycle would continue. I would see your death as a personal affront."

"I appreciate it. So what do we do about it?"

"Nothing," Alina said. "Yet."

"We cannot let on that we know, or else we may be removed from the mission," Milena said.

"I can't believe that they would go through all this with me. Transplanting me, waking me, training me. Only to then kill me. Doesn't make sense."

The other three exchanged a series of looks. Milena opened her mouth. Closed it again.

"What?" Ram said. "Come on, what?"

"We found the reports," Milena said, indicating Noomi.

"Diego decrypted them. There is no doubt that your entire purpose on this ship, in this Project, on this mission, has been to create certain outcomes for the primary subjects."

"Speak plainly," Alina said. "Rama Seti, they woke you from a coma, gave you this body, for one reason alone. So that you may be killed by Mael."

CHAPTER NINETEEN
SACRIFICE

RAM LOOKED AROUND the small group.

"But I just saw Director Zuma, she just told me that I was doing well, that I was exceeding their expectations. I have been working harder than I ever worked before at anything and I've been killing it."

He sighed. He realized how much he'd been taken for a ride and his sigh turned into a bitter laugh.

"Those assholes. The sole reason they kidnapped me, gave me this body, brought me to the outer solar system, trained me... was so that Mael could kill me? Come on, that's got to be the biggest waste of resources of all time. What would be the point of that?"

Milena unfolded her screen and began to read aloud. "This is from the final report sent to Director Zuma to review before you were selected. By the way, your designation was Omega-14. Our projections indicate that the proposed Subject O-14's lack of experience will increase Subject Alpha's objective performance across the board. Alpha's deep-seated contempt for unearned positions of authority will have a significant impact on the social environment of the subject group as a whole. O-14 is of Indian ethnicity and this will have a number of benefits. Alpha is moderately racist, holding negative views on mainly those he perceives as of North African, Middle Eastern and Central Asian descent. Further, O-14 has an almost identical natural skin color to Subject Omicron - that was Samira - likely to cause Alpha to recall his homicide of Omicron. We believe Alpha is repressing guilt about the death, at least on some level, which will cause tension and confusion for Alpha, destabilizing him further. Due to synergies in personalities, it is predicted Subject Beta will befriend O-14 and, with the right social and hormonal encouragement, engage in a sexual relationship. O-14's pornography record shows preference for women similar in appearance and personality type to a pre-bonded Epsilon - that's Sifa, as if you couldn't guess. Epsilon prefers her sexual partners to be significantly weaker willed than she is and so this is another possible pairing opportunity. After Epsilon rejected Alpha during training Stage 2, this may increase conflict between them. If O-14 is bonded with an upgraded body type 2115-C then his strength rating should create a specific point of conflict. Escalation of this conflict should draw in other subjects to both sides. We anticipate Alpha will kill O-14 within the first three months of his activation and thus inspire a jump in performance similar to the Omicron leap and plateau. Other possible outcomes all lead to varying degrees of performance enhancement. See attached Gantt chart for proposed project timescales. Anyway, it goes on and there's sixty pages of detail but you get the idea."

Ram realized that his jaw was hanging open. Everyone was looking at him but he was unsure where to start. Outrage was there but it was buried beneath a lot of confusion and denial. "I was already on the ship at this point? I was selected from what? Who else was there to choose from?"

"There are forty-eight backup subjects onboard this ship in a persistent coma."

"Backup subjects who have undergone a corporectomy," Alina said, as if she had a bad taste in her mouth.

"Forty-eight?" Ram wasn't sure he heard her right. "They brought almost fifty heads into the outer system?"

"They wanted to cover many variables. Each person has a specific range of skills, experience and traits."

"But what happens to the heads that don't get put onto a body?"

Alina answered. "They will never wake up."

"Are they all like me? Taken against their will? If they never get revived then they have been murdered."

"If they are considered at all by UNOP then it would be as necessary sacrifices for the good of the mission, for the great project as a whole," Milena said. "What are fifty people compared to billions?"

Ram nodded, though the thought of comatose, beheaded people nearby on the *Victory* was too disturbing to think about. He had been one of them. Could have remained one, if not for the conclusions in that report.

"It doesn't even mention my Avar experience," Ram said, astonished.

"It's in the appendix," Milena said.

"I'm just a sacrifice."

"Afraid so."

Ram felt defeated. Director Zuma had lied to his face, telling him he'd been recruited for his Avar experience, recalling his virtual achievements as if she was impressed and the whole time she had known that his purpose was to be a murder victim. Even that morning, she'd given him a pat on the back and further encouragement, as if she was impressed. He couldn't believe it.

And despite his disadvantages and worries, he'd been doing well in the training, he thought, giving it everything, all day long, every day that he had been in the ludus.

And it was for nothing.

"Why did you even tell me this? I mean, you're telling me it's all planned out, since before I woke up here. What are we going to do about it?"

Alina leaned over. "You can change your fate. We all can."

"No shit," Ram said, irritated by her condescension. "I'm not letting them do this to me."

"Yes," Noomi the driver said. "And you can change the fate of the other prisoners on this ship."

"What prisoners?"

Alina punched Ram in the shoulder, then grabbed him by the upper arm, shook him a little. "Did you ever think where your body came from? Where all our bodies come from?"

Ram glanced at Milena. She looked annoyed, for some reason.

Alina shook Ram's arm.

"Yeah, course," Ram said. "Dr. Fo said we're grown from synthetic tissue. Synthetic bodies grown in pods, in womb tanks like Artificial Persons only ours were grown without heads and then ours were grafted on."

Alina sneered, her face twisted in disgust. "You can grow muscle tissue in a pod. You can grow bones and organs. But growing a whole person is different. The brain controls so much and computers, software, can mimic enough of the brain functions to get a body grown. But a computer is not a human brain and the resulting body is never in good enough physical shape for the needs of UNOP. It needs to be moving, to undergo compression and tension and torque and exercise or else it is not fit for purpose."

"So whose bodies were they?" Ram had a sinking feeling down in his guts.

"Watch the screen."

Up on the wall, Diego played what looked to be security camera footage, recorded from various vantage points, mostly high in the corners of a room. Ram saw shapes moving around a long, tubular interior, seats and beds and exercise equipment. People. Great big people. At least half a dozen of them. The scale was easier to make out because there were normal sized people in amongst them. The room was long, narrow, with familiar dimensions.

"This is on the *Victory*, is it?"

"These are some of the bodies grown for the subjects."

"They're Artificial Persons, right? Genetically engineered to be this big but without consciousness," Ram said.

Noomi—Alina's driver—spoke up. "Whether they have consciousness is debatable. Certainly, they appear able to experience suffering." She sounded extremely bitter.

"Appearances can be deceptive," Milena said.

Noomi glared at her. "Surely, you don't mean that."

"We do not have time for ethical debates," Milena said, looking hard at Noomi. "Drop this, now."

Noomi looked ready to argue for a moment before giving a single, tight nod.

Ram turned back to the wall screen. "That place looks like a mental health institution. Is it a live feed? Is this happening now?"

Diego shook his head. "This isn't a live feed, man. They'd be more likely to notice a hack in an active system. This is archive recordings from last year. After *Victory* was well underway. I only have access to a few clips someone saved in a subfolder but it's enough to see what's been going on."

"But they're still on the ship now?" Ram said.

"Yes," Noomi said.

"Some of them," Alina said. "Some have been culled for parts."

"We did not know," Noomi said, clenching her fist. Not until you were woken up. They hid it from us."

"That is the military style compartmentalization of knowledge," Milena said, speaking softly. "Need to know."

"Well, I needed to know," Noomi said. "Keeping these people like this is an abomination."

Diego pursed his lips. Obviously, no one agreed with Alina's driver that the APs were people but no one called her out on it either.

Milena sighed as she clicked through the footage from different angles, different cameras that were synced together and explained while she did so. Some of the big people were seated, drawing with huge crayons on colored paper. Others sat on the floor stacking blocks and pushing toys around. A couple of others exercised in resistance machines or on aerobic devices.

Milena went and stood by the screen. "The Artificial Persons on the *Victory* are tank-grown, back on Earth before we left. As I'm sure you know, one great benefit to the use of ectogenesis tanks allows them to be gestated for way over nine months. With proper muscle stimulation in combination with the accelerated metabolism they can reach a physical developmental stage equivalent to a nine or ten-year-old human child in just over a year in the tank. That's from inception, too, it's amazing what they can do now. And then when they are removed from the tank they are reared in a facility like this where they can get the full-time care they need and can fulfill their genetic destiny. You are quite right about the limitations on their mental abilities, especially in terms of self-awareness and complex cognitive processes."

"Oh man," Ram said. "I didn't know they get to draw and paint and play games. They look like giant, developmentally impaired children."

"Precisely." Alina sat up straighter, on the edge of her seat. "They never tell the public this information. They would have us believe the Artificial Persons are pulled from the tanks fully grown, blank slates, biological machines."

"This is why the pro-human and pro-AP activist movements are willing to take action," Noomi said.

"Terrorists," Milena said. "They're terrorists and this is a distraction."

Everyone ignored her.

"They're all so huge," Ram said. "Already muscled like

bodybuilders, like the subjects."

"Other than daily sessions like you see here, where they practice fine control, they spend hours per day in strength training, muscle building, flexibility and stamina training. When not exercising they are eating and resting."

"I can't believe it," Ram said, looking at Alina "Just like us."

She nodded, her face clouded in darkness.

"There's a big guy," Ram said. "Even bigger than the others."

Milena and Diego nodded at him. "We assume that is the model that they utilized for transplanting you onto."

Ram sighed. "Man, look at him. Playing like that. As if he's enjoying himself."

"It is a travesty," Noomi said, bitterly.

"No," Milena snapped. "It is necessary. Think about what we are facing, as a species. Rama, we're not showing you this to make you feel bad. I do believe that the Artificial Persons have no self-awareness, they are not conscious, they certainly have no free will."

"How can you say that," Noomi cut in. "The reports Diego hacked say that despite being tank grown in artificial wombs, there are still individual differences. This one, Rama Seti's one, liked coloring the best. Coloring and painting and he would become irritable and uncooperative when faced with prolonged physical training."

"Same as me, then," Ram said. He looked down at his hands. "What I am now, this thing that I am. It's more him than it is me."

"No," Milena said. "Who you are, your sense of self and your awareness, it is all in your brain. Who you are is still you."

Ram didn't quite believe her. He certainly didn't feel like his old self, from back when he was living in in Delhi, living in Avar. But then, had he really been living at all back then?

Diego shifted in his seat, cleared his throat. "Our normal inclination is to refer to the AP units as individuals, using he or she and thinking of them as living creatures. When actually it can't be proved that it was alive in the first place. Not in any technical sense."

"If you buy that falsehood, Diego, then why are you here with us now?" Noomi said. "I do not believe that you believe it. It is not an argument, it is not philosophy. It is spoken to shut down argument. How about you prove that you are alive? He looks very much alive to me."

Diego nodded. "But you know they are designed with an underdeveloped prefrontal cortex. That they effectively have no true self-awareness. No consciousness. No free will, not even the self-reported awareness of it. They are simulacrums. It is likely that we are projecting, anthropomorphizing these creatures. Seeing things that aren't there because they look like people, act like children."

"This is immoral." Alina stood, crossing her pale, veiny arms across her chest. "Perhaps I will refuse to fight unless the remaining heads are euthanized and the bond-ready, ectogenetically grown simulated humans are kept alive for the duration of the mission instead of being used for parts or replacements."

"They would laugh in your face," Noomi said. "I'm sorry, darling, it's the truth."

While they were talking, Ram rubbed his hands over his face and paused to look at them, turning them over to look at the veins on the back snaking under the skin. Veins that had belonged to someone else, that had pumped someone else's blood into someone else's heart.

"I can't believe this," Ram muttered, without thinking. Everyone turned to him. "I'm sorry, this is just crazy. So you all want to save the Artificial Persons on the ship from being culled for parts, is that it? Are you all pro-human terrorists or something?"

Ram noted how all eyes in the room flicked to Alina.

"They're people," Alina said, shrugging. "It is obvious. No matter what scientists say."

Noomi placed a hand on Alina's biceps.

"I disagree," Milena said and Diego nodded in agreement.

Diego spoke quickly, rushing to get his words out. "Look, whatever they are, I agree with you, Alina that creating them, farming them and culling them like this seems cruel. But when we signed up for this, we knew we were giving up any ethical concerns we might have had. The ends of this mission are so important that the means are justified. We are all expendable if the mission is a success, we agreed to that. This Artificial Person thing? It's fucked up. Sure, totally. But you're wrong about our cabal here, Rama. These Artificial Persons are not why we're here. We are not even here to save our own lives. We simply want to ensure the success of the mission and we don't believe that sacrificing our lives to Mael will do that."

"To answer your question," Milena said to Ram. "We are not attempting to save the Artificial Persons." She held up a finger to Noomi, who bit her tongue. "Not right away. We're showing you these images in part so you understand how much you've been lied to, how much you are a pawn, just as much as that Artificial Person there on the screen. We're here save ourselves and to save the mission."

"Yeah, and you are one of the people who lied to me," Ram said, astonished. "You withheld how long I was in a coma for, you knew I was going to be used, you must have known."

"I did what I had to do for the sake of the mission," she said. "But now I have additional data, I realize my decisions weren't actually for the greater good."

"Additional data that they're going to kill me?" Ram said. "I appreciate it and everything and I really don't want to die, certainly not to that evil fucker and I don't want to give Zuma and UNOP the satisfaction but if I'm so useless, why don't you just let them? Surely, I can't impact the mission much either way and then you're not risking anything."

"It is not merely you," Alina said, her eyebrows knitted

together.

"We're all on the hit list," Diego said. "Look at this. When I hacked this data I saw how we were all amongst those indicated to be targets for Mael's psychotic outbursts."

"All of us, as in...?"

"All of us in this room," Alina said. "And some others who we felt we could not trust with this information. Mael's cronies are in the firing line also, for example, but they are our enemies just as he is. Others would possibly join us but we cannot be certain of how they would react and so they are not here. And you will not tell them."

"Sifa," Ram said. "Te Zhang."

Milena inclined her head, confirming.

"Why would they sacrifice any of you guys. Me and Alina I can kind of understand, maybe even our drivers because of association with us? But why Diego?" Ram asked, looking at him. "You're not even in the barracks. He doesn't even know you, does he?"

"There are a number of intelligence officers on board who can provide similar analyses but it seems as though Mael has complex, racist feelings about African people and killing me may be a way to make him feel good about himself."

"That's insane," Ram said. "And I know I'm expendable, much as I hate to say so but they told me that from the start, near enough. But, what, all of you are in line to get murdered, too? Just to keep Mael happy? That can't be right."

"Zuma has set herself upon this road," Milena said. "She's staking everything on pandering to Mael's every killing urge. Samira wasn't his first murder, just the first on the ship. And we know his pattern, it is rather typical for a serial killer. Mael's urge to kill will only intensify and then his frequency will increase, culminating in an orgy of violence that Zuma hopes will peak when he fights the Wheeler. If she holds that view, and it certainly seems that she does, then all of us are expendable. Why me? I was Samira's driver and now I'm yours. As well as that, he finds me physically, sexually attractive and we know that alone has driven him to kill in the past. Alina, obviously she is lined up to be one of the last, should Mael need it. There are others on the list. There are hundreds of decision trees detailing potential sequences but all of us are on most of them."

"We are running out of time," Diego muttered, tapping on his screen. "Our absences will be noticed shortly."

"What are you planning on doing about it?" Ram asked. "What can we do?" He looked around at each person in turn. "We have no leverage, no way to change anything with strikes or protests. If Director Zuma is willing to help him kill then no matter what we do, they'll back Mael all the way."

Alina looked down at Ram. "Not if he is dead."

CHAPTER TWENTY
PUNCHING UP

THEY WERE PLANNING TO KILL the Subject Alpha. They wanted Ram to help them. For all he hated and feared the man, his instinct said that they were crazy.

"You can't kill Mael," Ram said. "You said we weren't going to endanger the mission."

"Mael is the one endangering the mission," Alina said, eyes wide. "Zuma and the others are enabling him to do so but with him gone, they will have to change their focus."

"His stats are consistently better than anyone else's, including yours," Ram said. "You say you want the mission to succeed. That's why Zuma is doing all this in the first place. I'm not saying

I want to die but everyone says he is a legend in his own lifetime. A combat genius and that's what the human race needs if we're going to survive. He has only become greater since joining the project and this mission."

"But why has he improved to such an extent?" Milena said. "No one doubts his abilities. But Director Zuma, Chief Executive Zhukov, Bediako and the others are making this whole mission about him. Every opportunity, every adjustment, it's all designed to improve his performance at the expense of everyone else's. What if Alina was able to get the same kind of support? Wouldn't she be consistently better than Mael? Even our lives are just tools."

"Maybe they're right," Ram said. "I hate Mael, too, alright. And I hate Zuma and the rest who did this to me but if it's true that we get one shot at the alien before it's curtains for the Sol System then none of that matters. You all signed up for this at some point, right? Now you're getting cold feet? Right at the end of the whole mission, out here at the edge of the system? What is it, nerves? You want me to join this rebellion or whatever but you have to stick with your teammates or else the team falls apart, you included. I've seen it happen in Avar many times. Best thing to do is to suck it up."

"Suck it up? You're going to be killed, Ram. That's what we're talking about here, and not just you." Milena took a deep breath and let it out slowly. "I know you don't care about Artificial Persons and you don't really know us very well yet. We signed up for this, so in some way perhaps we are responsible for your abduction and confinement, guilty by association. But are you willing to die, you, yourself, for the mission? You'll never know what happens. You'll just be dead and you'll never know whether we won or lost. You'll never know what great gifts are given to humanity in victory. And if we lose, everyone else will be dead, too but you will miss out. Humanity will be holding hands and stepping into the abyss together but not you. You'll have already gone out in ignominy. And you'll never even see the fleets of alien ships that come to bombard us or enslave us or whatever they're planning. You'll never find fame or fortune, in the real world or in Avar when we get back to Earth. You're willing to give up your future, whatever it is, just to avoid rocking the boat?"

Ram rubbed his face. "You made some pretty good points, I guess." He wondered what they would do if he said no. What would they do if he left and went and told Zuma what they were planning? They were waiting for him to make a decision. "Alright. Fine, let's kill the bastard. How are you going to do it? They have those remote switches, right, to paralyze us at the flick of a switch. You attack him, you'll get dropped."

Alina snorted. "Diego?"

Diego was nervous, edgy, checking his screen repeatedly. "That's right about the remote switches on you guys but I'll temporarily disable them when Alina makes her move on Mael."

"Why not just flick Mael's switch?" Ram asked. "You can drop him and Alina can break him."

"We'd like to," Diego said. "But the only way I can get access is through the emergency system. It's an all or nothing version so if I push the button, all of you guys will be equally out of action and there's no point doing that, right? On the other hand, I can block anyone from turning you all off, should things go wrong. But individual subject deactivations are operated by their drivers, by Director Zuma, Dr. Fo and the Captain of the Marines."

"The Marines can switch us off?"

"Their primary responsibility is guarding the ship against hostile alien boarding actions but they also provide internal ship security. There's no need for them to interact with the subjects but they have been called in to subdue the Artificial Persons and also crew members, mostly when boozed up guys fight in the mess hall."

"They're the police."

Diego grinned. "The most elite and heavily armed police in the system. When you jump Mael, you'll have to finish him immediately. As soon as the UNOP Marines show up, they'll take you down. And, guys, we're out of time now, we got to wrap this up or we'll be noticed."

"Wait, let me get this right. The knockout switches in the back of our heads are disabled," Ram said. "Once that is done, how are you going to get Mael alone, away from his cronies for long enough to take him out of action? Those assholes are always with him in the barracks and mess. He has his driver sessions in the ludus ring."

Alina nodded. "I need you to help me with isolating him."

"Ah," Ram said. "You need me."

Alina scowled. "I don't need you."

"We need each other," Noomi said.

"We can save all our lives," Alina said. "I will fight the Wheelhunter and I will win. But only if we do it my way."

"Unfortunately," Milena said. "Her way means that you will likely suffer a severe beating."

Ram shrugged. "Just another day at work. What do I do?"

Alina came closer. "Mael is due for his counseling session tomorrow at 1400. When he's in the middle of it, challenge Eziz to a sparring match. Or simply attack him. While everyone is watching, I'll slip out and surprise Mael. Milena will neutralize his driver so there will be no endocrine support for him, while my dear Noomi here will crank my hormones up across the board, yes?"

"So I end up in the infirmary again and you end up, what? In prison?"

"With Mael dead, they will have to move their attention to me."

"You're sure you can kill him? Sounds like a lot of variables."

"Real life is all variables, Rama," Alina said. "This is not an Avar game. If you let the fear of the variables control you then are truly a slave." She pointed at his chest, his heart. "You are the only true variable, the only variable that counts. Anyway, at the very least, if I can tear out his eyes, crush his throat or do heavy damage then his recovery period will be so long that I will become Subject Alpha anyway."

"We must go," Diego said, standing and folding his screen away. He placed a hand on Alina's mighty arm. "I will pray for you. Good luck."

"You two should return to the ludus separately," Milena said to Alina and Ram.

"Noomi and I will go now to the ludus counseling rooms for a short time before I return. Give us a few minutes, Rama and if I do not make it for lunch in the mess, I will see you at the afternoon training session."

While they gave them a few minutes' head start, Milena pulled Ram aside.

"Outside this room and outside this moment, our conversations and our comms are monitored, you understand? Don't even hint about this discussion when you and I speak remotely. If you start speaking in code, even if you think you're being clever, the algorithms will pick up on it. You understand?"

Ram looked down at her. "I'll keep my mouth shut, don't worry."

Milena nodded, leaned in and drew him down to her so that her lips brushed his ear as she whispered. "We should not trust Alina. Nor Noomi."

Before he could ask her to clarify, Diego kicked them out into the corridor. They walked the rest of the way in silence.

She left him at the airlock to the ludus ring and Ram went

on alone, arriving at the mess just in time for lunch. Almost all the other subjects were there, too.

"Good session?" Sifa asked as he took a seat at the table, trying to appear calm.

"It was fine," Ram said. "Perfectly adequate."

He wondered if he could tell them what Alina was planning. Instinct told him he should but conspiracies failed when people couldn't keep their mouth shut. If he told them and they told Zuma, what would happen? Maybe nothing to Alina, she was too valuable, but Ram might find himself nothing but a head again. Or worse.

"Uh-oh," Te said, nudging Sifa with his elbow. "Check him out. Something happened in there with you and Milena, didn't it, you dirty bastard. While you're boffing Alina at the same time. What a different experience that's got to be. Must be like eating strawberries and cream on one side and dragging sandpaper across your arsehole on the other."

"Te Zhang," Sifa said. "You had sex with Alina more than once."

"Exactly. I know what I'm talking about, don't I."

"What did the Director want to see you about?" Sifa asked.

"Not much. She just said well done to me for surviving so long, basically. Thanking me for my contribution, summarizing my meager achievements. I guess now that I think about it, she was pretty much doing my obituary in advance."

"You are such a drama queen," Sifa said, laughing.

"Speaking of boffing Alina," Te said between mouthfuls of mashed potato. "Are you guys still going at it? Or has the magic worn off?"

Sifa tutted. "You don't have to answer that, Ram."

"We're not really doing anything except sleeping. She never really spoke to me anyway and now she just sleeps."

Sifa and Te exchanged a glance.

"What?" Ram asked.

"Nothing, mate."

Sifa cleared her throat. "We are hoping Alina does not have another bad episode."

"A what?"

Te waved his fork in the air, flinging a splatter of mashed potato across the ludus mess table. "You know, one of her episodes."

"I don't think I know what you mean."

Sifa frowned. "Did Milena not even tell you? That Alina occasionally reverts to her old ways."

"As a pit fighter?"

"Mate, come on. You didn't read her file? It's on the system, same as everyone's."

When he had scanned her file, he had felt intrusive. "It's almost entirely blank."

"Man, maybe they restricted your access or something because you were a conscript, I don't know. Anyway, you know she was Russian military, right? Special forces. At their training

299

facility, they had artificial people in the program. Basically used them for live fire exercises and that kind of thing, they'd use them for dummy hostages or dummy bad guys and then do breach and clear drills with real ammo. Or they've tested different bladed weapons and hand to hand stuff so the trainees would know what it felt like to fight while your hands and arms are drenched in hot, drying blood. I don't know, probably it's half bullshit. Enough of it's true anyway because Alina tried to break them out or some mad shit and she got caught. Thrown out. She ran before they could try her. The story goes that she was a member of some pro-AP group when she was still enlisted, or she set up her own organization or maybe she just got involved after she ran. They carried out a few raids and terrorist actions but her little band got killed, arrested. I suppose she gave up on all that and ended up becoming a superstar in the pit fights. But every now and then she goes all intense and quiet and shit and then she goes nuts over dinner and all the time about the poor arties. You know what I reckon? I reckon she was in love with one. Definitely, I mean, think about it."

Ram found that he was sweating all over. "Guys, can I tell you something? You have to promise—"

Alarms blared, sirens rising and falling and the light strips around the edges of the room flashed red. The doors to the mess slammed shut and echoed with a thud that said they were locked.

Everyone jumped to their feet, ready to fight or flee, looking at each other and at the staff for clues. All anyone saw looking back was confused faces.

"What's going on?" Ram shouted over the noise. Half the subjects and crew in the mess were asking that question. The other half were just looking worried.

"No idea," Te said, shrugging. Same as everyone else.

"Milena?" Ram said but there was no response. "Te Zhang, I can't reach my driver."

"Same here," Te said. "Must be something big, right?"

People started calling suggestions to each other.

"Solar flare? This far out? Don't be an idiot."

Genesis, typically loud like all Americans, thought she had the answer. "Gamma ray burst or something cosmic like that, for sure. Like X-rays or whatever, right?"

Jun sat looking down at the floor, which was toward the outer hull. "I think we hit something. An asteroid."

Eziz turned on her, his face twisted in contempt. "An asteroid? Are you serious? Do you know how fast we are going right now? We'd have been destroyed, moron. Perhaps, though, we are about to hit something."

"There's an electric field around the ship pushing asteroids away before they make contact."

"You don't know that, we don't know anything about this ship."

"It's fucking standard, alright, that's what all ships have now."

"Hey, check out the professional astronaut over here."

"Fuck you, Gen, alright."

"Maybe the aliens are attacking us. The Wheelhunters, maybe they're heading us off at the pass."

"That's just crazy, man, that's complete nonsense," Te said. "They want all of us in here because they're up to something. I bet this is just to fuck with us. Part of the training."

"Wait," Ram said. "We're not all here, though. Alejandra's not here. Alina hasn't come back from her counseling. Where is Mael?"

"Weekly assessment session," Te said. "Why do you ask?"

Ram's heart skipped a beat.

It was Alina's plan was to attack Mael at his assessment the day after.

"Are you sure? It's not his driver session until tomorrow."

The alarms kept blaring. Around the mess, crew and subjects argued about what was going on.

"Mael forced them to rearrange his session because he wanted to keep talking to Alejandra. The things they do for that bastard, it's ridiculous. Imagine if one of us wanted to change our timetable, they'd laugh in our faces. But with him, it's like he owns the—"

"So he's in the assessment area, with Alejandra?" Ram said, heart racing.

"That's what I'm saying, mate. Do you think this alarm is about him?"

He grabbed Sifa and Te, one hand on each of their shoulders. "Alina wasn't really at her counseling session for most of it, she was with me at mine on the B-Ring. She was heading to the ludus rooms when I last saw her.

Te and Sifa looked at each other.

"Fuck."

The mess hall door cycled open. The frantic shouting stopped instantly and everyone turned to watch, alarms still sounding above.

A squad of Marines entered, assault rifles in hand. Four soldiers, normal sized, but fit people but moving with fluid efficiency. They were in full combat gear, headsets and body armor, no doubt augmented internally. They moved with perfect synchronization, though whether it was due to augments or good old soldierly practice, Ram couldn't tell.

The four took up positions around and beside the door with their assault rifles pointing down but held at the ready.

The Marines were met with shouted demands from the subjects.

"What's going on?"

"Why the alarms?"

"Are you here to protect us or are you here to watch us?"

"Are those live rounds in your weapons?"

"No way," Genesis said. "They wouldn't kill us. Those look like nonlethal rounds."

Ram remembered she had been a soldier. Some of the other subjects nodded in agreement. Most of the subjects had a military background.

The Marines said nothing, simply held their posts standing at the ready by the door that led out to the sparring room. With their helmets on and visors down it was impossible to read their expressions. The subjects remained pensive but gradually grew bored and sat back down again. Some of them started eating again.

Without warning, the alarms stopped blaring and the lights returned to normal.

The silence was deafening.

Te, Sifa and Ram sat looking at each other. Ram knew that Alina had been caught, she had failed and that their conspiracy had been uncovered before it had got going. He kept glancing at the Marines, wondering if they were going to arrest him. What would the punishment for that kind of thing be on a spaceship? If they were willing to kill Ram just to make Mael happy, then what was stopping them from executing him for an actual crime. Or was conspiracy to commit murder even a crime on a ship that actively condoned it? He was too nervous to speak so he sat drumming his fingers on the table. He hoped Milena was alright.

Someone called out a heads up and Bediako strode in with his assistants trailing behind him like ducklings behind their mother. His dark face was thunder as he planted himself at the head of the room, stuck his fists on his hips and glared at all of them.

A few of the braver people in the room demanded to know what was going on.

When he spoke, Bediako's voice shook with anger. "Alina attacked Mael. She killed Nurul, Mael's driver. She killed Alejandra. Mael is wounded but it looks as though he'll recover in a few days. Few hours, maybe. He's the toughest bastard in the galaxy."

Sifa called out. "And Alina?"

"Are you kidding? Stupid bitch went up against Mael and Alejandra at the same time, what did she think was going to happen? The crew called it in while they were fighting and Dr. Fo flipped Alina and Mael's switches, otherwise, Alina would have been killed. She's in the infirmary but if she pulls through, I'm going to kill her myself. Now, finish your lunch. Don't think this gets you out of training this afternoon. We're doing triangle chokes and leg locks."

Ram stared at Sifa and Te. They shook their heads, shocked. Ram wanted to tell them that Alina had planned an attack but that she had gone off schedule, gone crazy, maybe. Instead, he kept his mouth shut and shrugged along with everyone else.

Mael had changed his schedule at the last minute and Alina had seen him, taken a chance, maybe. Whatever, she had failed and now there would be an investigation and their nascent conspiracy would be revealed. Ram's involvement would be uncovered and he would be punished.

Even if he was not, Alina's failure meant that if Ram didn't come up with a new plan soon, Mael would certainly kill him.

CHAPTER TWENTY-ONE
ATTACK

"I SHOULD HAVE KNOWN," TE SAID later that night in his room the barracks. The three of them sat in Te's room, Ram on the chair, Te on the bed and Sifa sitting curled up on the floor reading from her screen.

It was shortly before lights out and Ram would retreat to his own quarters soon. He needed to tell them about the conspiracy but was still unsure about what way they would jump, whether they would help him or immediately denounce him.

"You should have known what, precisely, Te Zhang?" Sifa

said, looking up from her screen. "That Alina would have a violent episode? But we did know, we all did. Did anyone care? You did all you could."

"Can you imagine how fast and how quiet she must have moved to kill Alejandra and kill Mael's driver before Mael could react? All that without Mael moving quick enough to stop her. I would love to have seen his face when she acted. Would it be fear, do you reckon?"

"I doubt he'd be afraid of anything."

"Yeah I bet his amygdala is all fucked up," Te said. "Still, I'd love to see the surprise on his stupid ugly face."

"I would love to see the whole thing," Sifa said, sighing. "The whole footage of the incident. For training purposes."

"They'll never show us that," Te said, laughing.

"Maybe," Sifa said. "Do you think what Bediako said was true? They're going to kill Alina if she recovers? As punishment for murdering Nurul and Alejandra?"

Te scoffed. "No way, mate. Mael kills people all the time and they don't do anything to him. They'll just heal her up and bring her back. Probably it'll make Mael fight even harder, I bet they love it. Don't listen to Bediako, man, he's all mouth, no trousers."

Ram laughed. "You're kidding, right? He's terrifying. He's the biggest person here apart from me and he's the lone person to have survived a fight with the Wheelhunter. He's actually faced one of them, for real."

Te shrugged. "Yeah? And so what? He lost. You saw the fight, right? You've analyzed it. You been there in the Avar replays?"

"Not really," Ram said. "I read about it."

"It's brutal. You know how they told him to last as long as he could and the thing just ran him down and ripped him apart? I mean, he did okay, I guess. But he didn't do well enough and the fact is, he couldn't take any of us on now. So you don't need to be afraid of him, mate."

"Why couldn't he take us on? He knows his stuff. Even Mael listens to his advice."

"Advice, yeah. But think about it. If he was so good, why is he not fighting? Why is teaching instead of doing?"

"Because he's got an old model body."

"Exactly."

"But I've got an old model body."

Te scratched his tattooed face. "With upgrades."

Ram wanted to tell them about the conspiracy, about the AP bodies they had all been transplanted onto. They hated Mael and yet they both truly believed in the mission, in the Orb Project as a whole. Both had given up their lives to carry it out and they might turn him in, they really might.

Still, maybe he could sound them out a little.

"Upgrades?" Ram said, trying to seem casual. "So they tell me but I'm not so sure anymore. I think they've been lying to me since the start."

Te shrugged. "Probably. They lie to all of us. But do you know what your biggest problem is, mate? You lack self-confidence, son. You're taking the piss out of that old school body they stuck you into but that was the body you used to smash multiple world strength records. Them be facts."

"They could have doctored the records, they could have doctored the weights. All to make me look good, make me think I was doing well. All just to anger Mael."

Te looked annoyed. "Now you're just being paranoid. That body is amazing. Bediako is slow because he's on his second synthetic body. The body he fought the Wheelhunter in was destroyed. They recovered what remained and stuck his head on a new body and downloaded his mind back into the reconstructed brain sections. But the nerve damage is done. Old Bediako is slow as hell. I bet if he really exerted himself he'd end up rupturing something. I'm betting he'd have a stroke. His head would pop. That's why even you could beat him, you big fat bastard."

"I'm so fat I'm going to throw you across the room in sparring tomorrow," Ram said. "Again."

Te laughed. "That's the spirit, bro."

"I'm going to go get some sleep," Ram said, standing. "I know he's probably still recovering in his quarters but I hope Mael doesn't take revenge for Alina's attack tonight. He didn't look badly injured, did he. Just a bit beaten up. And the thing is, I shouldn't tell you this but Milena said he's pretty much planning to attack me anyway. And now, I'm the one closest to Alina, it would make sense for him and the others to try something tonight, what do you think? I'm going to sit up all night, be ready to fight if they get through my door."

"Want Sifa to sleep with you?" Te said, jerking his thumb at her.

Sifa looked up. "I think that's a good idea," she said, unfolding herself and standing up. Even so simple a movement could be elegant and beautiful when she did it.

Ram looked back and forth between the two of them. "Okay."

She followed him to his room, further along the barracks as the lights faded into a soft glow. The common area was empty but still he kept one eye on the three huge central tables and another on Mael's closed door.

When he got into his own sanctuary, Sifa slid in behind him, shut the door with a bare foot and peeled off all her clothes without another word, looking him in the eye the entire time.

Having sex with Sifa was a world away from the businesslike coupling he had been experiencing with Alina. There was no romance involved with Sifa, certainly. She was no dewy-eyed girl losing herself in the moment. They were not making love or anything like that. But the handful of times Alina had commanded Ram to screw her, she had remained distant throughout, as if he was simply a sex toy with a sturdy base. Sifa, on the other hand, seemed to be present in the moment as she sat astride him, looking down to make eye contact every now and then, clawing and pawing at his skin and squeezing his shoulders and arms, pushing down on him. Her dark skin was sleek and shining with sweat as she bore down on him, throwing her head back and arching her spine.

Ram tried to be good at the sex. He wondered if Milena was tweaking his hormones back in her office or in her quarters. The thought of it was suddenly hot, almost as though Milena was in the room with Sifa and him. Sifa's driver, on the other hand, was a German named Oskar, who seemed like a twat. He hoped Oskar wasn't all up in Sifa's hormones but he probably was, the dirty little prick.

"Focus," Sifa whispered, smiling at him.

"Yeah," he whispered back.

No matter his wandering thoughts, it was hard for him to take his eyes from her beautiful face, from the way her lips twitched and curled as she reached another height of pleasure and then another. And then there were her breasts. It was crazy that the UNOP surgical team had made a combat body with pretty big tits but there they were. Ram had, for years, never expected to see and feel real life breasts again and yet there they were, in his hands. Although, the breasts were as artificial as Sifa's whole body. Indeed, the hands that cupped them were not really Ram's hands either.

A thought at the back of his mind intruded and then would not go away again. The thought that this might be the last time he ever slept with anyone. His own death seemed so close at hand. Whether it was that night or in the morning or on another day soon, Mael would get him and that would be it. The Director and everyone else behind the scenes would not only allow it to happen, they had made it happen, had planned it and implemented it. He was living out someone else's plan. A plan drawn up by an AI and signed off by the UNOP leaders. Ram was no more than a cog, deep in a machine, spinning and whirring away in the darkness without ever seeing the output.

"Hey," Sifa said, placing her hands on either side of Ram's face and turning his head gently to have hers while she peered down at him, a small smile on her lips. "Where are you going?" She kept riding him, slowly, leaning over and her breasts bouncing beneath her.

"I'm sorry," Ram said. "I was—"

She leaned down and kissed him, squashing her lips against his. Ram had rarely ever kissed anyone before. A girl or two at school, back when he was a boy and not quite yet grown to truly repulsive volume but those girls didn't count. And since then it was only really the call girls that he ordered every few months when the need for real life human contact overcame his deep shame at his body. And that didn't count either.

Was it his first real kiss? He was about to tell her but stopped himself. It would be a truly weird thing to say so he said nothing. On the other hand, it might be that she would want to hear it. She might like to hear it. Still, it was embarrassing.

Sifa moved her mouth away from his, just a little and she looked deep into his eye.

"Rama," she whispered. "Stop going away from the moment. I can feel you drifting. Drink it all in, moment to moment, be here. Like in fighting. You think too much. Do not think. You must feel."

"Alright," Ram whispered back, their voices little more than breathy whispers in the low light.

"Feel that?" Sifa mumbled, placing his hands on her breasts.

"Yes."

She moved his hands to her muscular ass as she ground her hips down and back and forth onto him. "Feel that?"

"Uhuh."

"Stay in the moment," Sifa whispered into his ear. "Stay with me. Stay with me, stay with me."

They came almost together, the waves of it rushing through Ram as they clung on to each other with fingers grasping, their sweating skin sliding over skin.

"Thank you," Ram said.

Sifa laughed a little and nudged him with her elbow. "Thank you, also. We must sleep now, we must rest for tomorrow. I wish we could sleep naked in a bed together, a real bed. Well, a giant sized bed. But these things are too small and you are definitely too big."

Ram made a bed upon the floor, sighed with satisfaction of the madness of it all and closed his eyes.

It seemed like not a moment had passed but then his door lock beeped, startling Ram into consciousness. Sifa lay on her front in his bed, her back rising and falling with steady breaths, black skin shining in the darkness. A noise again. Was someone doing something to unlock his door from the other—

The door burst open and Ram jumped to his feet against the rear wall. Sifa crouched up on the bed, arms up ready to defend herself.

A bulging body filled the doorway, shadowed face swollen and purple, misshapen but easily recognizable.

"Come out, both of you," Alina hissed. "We must act quickly."

CHAPTER TWENTY-TWO
UNSTOPPABLE

"WHAT'S GOING ON?" RAM SAID, tiredness fading as his heart started thumping in his chest. "Why aren't you in medical, Alina?"

He glanced at the screen on his desk, faintly illuminating the on-ship time.

0327

There was no way Dr. Fo would release her in the middle of the night. The *Victory* ran on a very tight schedule and night time was for sleeping.

Alina's face was swollen and purple and black, with cuts at her lips and eyebrows and cheek that had been stitched-up and glued together. She held a roll of wide medical tape and a bandage in one hand.

"You escaped," Ram said in the darkness at the back of his room. "You broke out of medical."

"Being there had served its purpose. Come."

Ram glanced at Sifa. She was just as shocked as he as she stepped down off his bed.

"You intended to get put in medical?" Ram asked. "Why would you do that?"

Alina turned and strode back into the common area. Ram scrambled after her but Sifa beat him to the door and they both slipped through. It was still the low night lighting in the space between the bedrooms. All the other doors were shut.

"This is not good, Rama," Sifa said, all trace of softness gone from her. "Do we stop her?"

"I don't know," Ram muttered. He wanted Mael dead, he knew that much.

Alina threaded between two of the three tables that ran down the center line of the long communal space.

She was going for Mael's room.

"No," Ram hissed. "You'll get yourself killed."

Sifa darted forward after Alina but the bigger woman turned and held up a palm to Sifa. "Do not concern yourself. Mael is in no condition to offer resistance. Not now."

"Wait, he was not badly hurt," Sifa said, voice low and urgent. "He looks better than you do."

Sifa turned to Ram for confirmation but Alina crossed the last few steps and threw open Mael's door. It was not locked but perhaps he had never imagined needing a lock. Who would ever be dumb enough to open his door without an invitation?

Ram held his breath and Sifa stood tense beside him across the common area from Mael's quarters.

Alina stopped in the doorway and simply stared inside, shoulders hunched up. She marched into the darkness of Mael's room. Ram held his breath, waiting for the sound of struggle to start. If Alina had lost just a few hours before and now was already badly injured, then Mael would overpower her easily. And his followers outnumbered Alina's group.

Soft rustling, then a resounding thump. Alina backed out, bent over and dragging Mael's unconscious body out through the doorway by the ankles. She pulled him all the way out and into the space between the wall with the rooms and the long tables in the center.

Mael was awake, his eyes fixed on Alina, his face screwed up into a fury so intense that his face with crimson and veins stood out all over his forehead. Alina had stuffed the bandage into his mouth and then taped it in place so that he could not cry out.

"You've flipped his paralysis switch," Ram said. "How did you do that?"

"Dr. Fo obliged me," Alina said, standing over Mael.

"How did you get him to do that?" Ram asked.

Alina did not respond to him but instead addressed Mael below her.

"I wish we had more time together, Mael Durand, you disgusting waste of flesh. We have locked the doors thoroughly but the Marines will be forcing their way in here soon. Your minions I have also disabled, they are lying in their rooms right now, as helpless as you are. They are followers by nature and once you are dead they will be mine, believing in me as their champion. You know, Mael, it would have been very pleasant to have had a few hours with you, alone, just me and you and a few small, serrated blades and pairs of pliers. Sadly, time is a luxury unavailable to people like us so I will have to beat you to death with my own hands."

"No!" Sifa shouted. "You must not. Whatever your differences, you must think of the mission. The mission is the only thing that is important."

Te threw his door open and stepped out, his mouth falling open. Alina paid him no mind.

"But I am thinking of the mission, Sifa. Once your head is smashed into a pulp, Mael, I will be Subject Alpha. With the support focused on me, I will achieve higher performance than you. And I will beat the alien. Anyway, do not concern yourself with such things. Just know that your time is over. You lost. You were not the strongest. All you need do now is die like the worm you are."

She lifted her knee high and stamped down on Mael's face with her heel, crushing his nose in a shower of blood.

"Alina, no," Te and Sifa shouted together.

Ram stood looking at the scene, wondering if he should stop her. His own life would be safer if Mael died, surely. But it seemed as though Alina was also insane. Would she rule the subjects as Mael had, killing those who she took issue with?

Had she not already started?

Alina lifted her knee up high and stamped down again, smashing Mael's chin with a blow so powerful it broke his jaw. The sound of it was like a steel bar being snapped inside a vat of Jell-O.

Across the common room, Te held back Sifa who, though she hated and feared Mael, believed him the greatest warrior of them all. Sifa wanted to stop Alina. Was Te holding her back because he disagreed and wanted Mael dead or was he simply trying to protect his friend from Alina's murderous rage?

The door to the barracks resounded with a series of bangs. Someone on the outside, trying to break in.

"I think the Marines are coming," Ram shouted.

He wasn't sure if he was warning Alina so she would stop or so she would hurry and kill Mael before they could stop her.

Alina's next stomp down on Mael's jaw snapped it lose. Snapped it with such force that it tore the skin under his ear, blood pouring out as it was torn away.

It seemed unreal. Sifa and Te cried out at the sight of it.

The pounding and scraping on the door sounded like they were attempting to lever it open from the far side.

"Do not go anywhere," Alina said to Mael, who's eyes were mad with agony and fury. She kept talking but it was not to anyone present in the barracks. "Diego, are you still in control? Very good. Allow them to open the barracks door, let a few in. And execute stage two."

"What are you doing?" Sifa shouted.

"You may wish to take cover, my friends," Alina said. "And brace yourselves against something."

The barracks door slid open with a juddering, grinding clatter.

Alina ducked behind the bench closest to the entrance just as four marines ducked in, their automatic assault rifles firing as they stepped through. Ram leaped to the ground, scrambling toward the nearest room.

Not before he was hit.

Two shots slammed into his shoulder and arm in immediate succession. The force knocked him sideways. Pain shot through him even as more rounds clanged all around, spattering into the ceramic tiles and bouncing about, hitting the benches, the open doors.

No blood on his shoulder. Two more rounds hit him, pain jolting through him. The rounds had hit his leg but the pain writhed up and down his whole body.

Non-lethal rounds. Electrical slugs. Of course, they had to

protect their investment and they couldn't risk damaging the ship through firing proper bullets.

Ram crawled toward the nearest bedroom door but it was shut, no doubt locked and the doors were designed to be secure against even a subject's mighty strength. Still, there was nowhere else to go.

Alina roared. A huge sound from deep inside her belly, so loud that Ram could feel it rumbling through the air and the tiles under his chest. He risked a glance over his shoulder and saw her rising from her cover behind the bench.

The non-lethal rounds were fired on semi-auto, groups of slugs smacking into the bench seats, the tabletop, the legs. Cracking into the floor and walls.

The four marines stood in front of the open door, spaced apart from each other and all hunched behind their weapons, firing in bursts. Even as Ram watched, the door behind them slammed shut, cutting off the other marines lined up in the doorway beyond.

Te and Sifa were ducked down behind the second table, relatively safe.

But Alina was roaring and rising and she leaped up onto the top of the bench, coiled like a spring and jumped forward. The slugs smashed into her chest, her arms and legs and her face. It was as if she felt nothing. They did not slow her.

Ram felt strange, lightheaded. Perhaps the rounds that had hit him were more than electrical, perhaps he had been hit with a drug or something similar.

Alina covered the distance to the marines in a second. Two of them in the center scattered in opposite directions. The other two backed away into their corners either side of the door, still firing.

But nothing could save them now.

Alina reached the first marine and punched him in the face, crushing his skull, breaking his neck and sending him back in a ragdoll heap into the door. She spun and caught the next one by his helmet and yanked him backward off his feet and into her grasp, wrapping one of her mighty arms around him. The marine looked like a child compared to her. Alina drew his combat knife and sawed into his throat, spraying blood.

The other two kept on shooting her. They must have been down to their final few rounds as they were pinging single shots into her body now, conserving ammo.

And it was working, finally. She was slowing, her movement strange.

Or was it Ram's imagination? He climbed to his feet, the pain from being shot already faded into nothing. Yet he felt strange, like he was in an airplane or roller-coaster simulation.

Alina threw her knife into one of the marines. It curved strangely in flight but sank to the hilt in the marine's face, smashing through their visor. Alina turned and bound over to the last one and smashed her down with the weight of her body, finishing her off with a palm strike that crushed her skull.

Silence.

Not quite silence. The other marines outside the door hammered and scraped at it. Alina's breath echoed.

Mael's coughing from where he lay on the floor, spattering blood out of his ruined face and dislocated, shattered jaw. Unable to control anything but his own breathing, he must have been drowning in the blood leaking from his wounds.

Te and Sifa stood up from their cover behind the second bench.

"Alina," Ram shouted. "What are you doing? The marines are going to get through that door-"

He broke off when his stomach lurched and he felt like he was in a car, going over the brow of a hill. Blood rushed to his head, his body was lighter.

The ship's simulated gravity, created by spinning the rings, was fading fast.

And then, Ram's feet left the tiles underfoot.

Sifa and Te clung to the tables. Mael's body rose into the air, his eyes still wild and staring up with fury.

"The gravity," Te shouted. "Hold on to something."

Alina worked quickly with the bodies around her. She took rifles from two of them nearest to her, even as they all rose gently off the floor. Expertly, she unloaded the magazines and allowed them to float away but she stripped more magazines and loaded them into the rifles, stuffing a couple more into the waistband of her pants.

"What the hell is she doing," Te said, clinging to the bench table.

"We need to stop her," Sifa hissed. "Ram, we all rush her. Ready?"

"No way," Ram said, holding himself away from the ceiling with one hand, fingers gripping the edge of the lighting strip. "Did you see that? She loaded live ammunition into those assault rifles. How fast do you think you're going to move in microgravity?"

By way of answer, Sifa jumped upward. That is, she pushed herself toward the ceiling but she did it with so much power that she shot up and crashed into the ceiling with a crack. She bounced off, clutching her head.

Alina busied herself pushing the marine's bodies toward the door. She glanced round at Ram, saw him staring.

"Come take one of these assault weapons," she said.

Ram hesitated. If he took one, he'd essentially be agreeing to fire it. At who, the marines? If he was even just holding it when they finally broke in, they'd assume he'd been with Alina all along and no doubt they'd terminate him immediately.

Alina sighed at his indecision and pushed herself off the wall, heading toward Ram. She had perfect aim, gliding the ten meters with ease and alighting beside him with a weapon in each hand.

Across the other side of the room, Mael had somehow been rolled over so that he was face down. The blood pulsed out of his face and neck in a series of red orbs, shining in the low light.

"Ah," Alina said, tutting. "I hoped he will have drowned by now. No such luck for Alina, eh?"

Ram realized suddenly that she was happy. She was enjoying herself.

"Here, hold one of these." The huge woman shoved one of the weapons into his chest, which he took without thinking.

She pushed away from Ram, drifted over toward the floating form of Mael. His legs were drifting apart from each other, as were his arms. Alina stopped herself with a deft touch on the ceiling above and braced herself, wedging her mighty shoulders between the wall and ceiling.

"Do not kill him," Sifa shouted. "Think of the mission. What's at stake. It is not too late."

She brought up the assault rifle, which looked like a toy in her hands.

"It is too late," Alina said. "For him."

She fired a three-round burst at close range, straight into Mael's forehead. His neck jerked back and a fan of debris and pink blood shot up as his body turned and twisted down toward the floor.

Alina laughed. "Look, Ram," she said. She pushed herself from the ceiling down to Mael's body, which she straddled with her knees. As she had done with Ram, in his room at night. "Ram, look, his skull is unbroken. They made him well." She prodded the wound with the muzzle of her weapon.

Ram felt himself getting heavier, his guts being pulled

downward inside his body.

"He's still not dead?" Te shouted.

"You still in there, Mael?" Alina said, laughing again. "Look, he has his eyes open."

"ALINA."

A voice boomed from the address system in the barracks.

"PUT DOWN YOUR WEAPON AND STEP AWAY FROM HIM"

"That's the Director," Sifa said. "Listen to her."

"You did this, Zuma," Alina shouted. "You wanted to make the best warrior, the one best at winning at all costs. Willing to kill everyone. Here I am. Your warrior. Winning."

Ram drifted down toward the ground.

"NOT LIKE THIS," Zuma thundered. "DISARM. NOW."

"Diego?" Alina said. "Have they taken you?"

"Please," Sifa said. "This is crazy."

Alina shook her head, brought up her gun. "It is over, Mael," she said. "You lost."

The barracks doors opened and the marine poured through, firing as the came through. The rounds cracked and smashed the tiles all around.

Live rounds.

Not shock slugs like last time.

Alina fired a long burst into Mael, the rounds ripping into his face and head, this time showering blood and brains and skull all over the floor and wall.

She had neglected to brace herself properly and though the gravity was returning, she flew up and away, backward, still firing wildly. When she crashed into the other side of the room, the marines stopped firing. Presumably, they had been given orders to hold fire.

It was too late for Mael. The Marines could not save him.

The gravity came back as the rings were spun up to speed. It happened slow enough for Ram to land quite gently on his feet. Sifa and Te likewise stood, looking between Alina and Mael.

"Put your weapons down, now," the leading marine shouted his voice artificially amplified with some augment tech. "Now, drop them now."

Ram dropped his and put his hands up, stepping back.

"Fine," Alina said. "All I wanted was him. You are all safe from me."

She tossed her assault rifle to the ground and then tossed the spare magazines down, clattering beside it.

The bedroom doors unlocked and the other subjects came charging out. Finally released from their paralysis. Jun, Gondar, Genesis, Javi, Didem and Eziz They saw the body of their leader, his and head face shot to pieces.

They saw Alina and Ram with weapons at their feet.

Full of fury, they charged.

CHAPTER TWENTY-THREE
BATTLE

GENESIS AND JUN CHARGED Alina, straight at her with no thought of tactics, unless their tactic was to rush her before she could react.

Te and Sifa were shouting to stop but Gondar and Javi rushed them, leaping over the body of their fallen hero and bounding up to them in just a few strides. Gondar's and Javi's faces were contorted with fury, obviously assuming they were with Alina. Ram wanted to shout a warning to his friends but he had his own problems.

Ram faced the fury of Eziz, who leaped the bench in between them and came on like a Hell demon from a horror game. Didem was hot on Eziz's heels, growling bloody murder like a maniac.

"Wait," Ram shouted, backing up as far as he could. "Just hold on a—"

Eziz feinted high and right then dove for Ram's knees, trying to take him down. But Ram expected it and jumped up, pushing off the wall and coming down with a knee driven into Eziz's midback.

Didem was on him, wrapping her arms around Ram's neck and both her legs around Ram's waist. Ram was bigger, though, and very much stronger so her grappling alone was never going to bring Ram down.

It didn't need to.

Didem was doing no more than slowing Ram down while Eziz recovered from the knee to his back. The Turkmen wrestler rolled into Ram's legs, tangling him up and taking him down with Didem clinging to his back.

Ram knew he was in trouble. He was breathing heavily from the effort and Didem was constricting his neck, still growling maniacally.

On his feet, he was bigger and stronger than either of his attackers. Maybe stronger even than both combined. Ram was taller, had at least ten centimeters reach on Eziz and much more than that on Didem. But on the ground he was vulnerable. All his muscle made him bulky and inflexible where Di was lithe as a snake. She was increasing pressure on his throat, trying to choke him so he threw his head back, hard, and cracked her in the nose, trying to get his hand up between her arm and his neck to provide a barrier.

It was a mistake. The vast gulf in experience between him and the others was barely comprehensible to him. They had years of wrestling experience to draw on, he had a couple of months.

His skull walloped her hard but a single blow to the face for any of the subjects could never be more than a distraction. And Di wasn't even distracted. By throwing his head back, all he'd done was expose more of his throat to her thick forearm and she used the gap to slide her grip up higher, right up under his jaw and she tightened her grip.

Fighting for breath, Ram's heart hammered in his ears, his vision began to cloud and darken from the edges as less oxygenated blood reached him.

Eziz heaved his shoulder into Ram's knees, driving him sideways, twisting and pushing to bring Ram down. The wall was just behind, he knew, if he could lean on it, he might keep his feet. Ram shuffled backward, trying to keep upright, Di choking him. His advantage was his greater mass and strength, he knew he had to use it before they took him down. Ram pulled Di's arm away from his throat with both hands, leaned forward and threw her over his shoulder and crashed her down on to Eziz's back.

Ram, freed for the moment, jumped back and looked toward the shouts and sounds of fighting. His mind was whirring, freewheeling, he didn't know what he should do next. Te and Sifa grappled Gondar and Javi. Neither was doing well, both being pounded between the tables, back to back, bloodied and struggling.

The marines were shouting now, screaming at Alina, at all of them to stop, to cease immediately or else.

Gen and Jun pressed Alina hard, both striking, circling but Alina changed direction and jabbed a front kick up into Gen's face. It knocked her back and Alina dived for the floor, strangely not going for either of her opponents.

She got to her knees, holding the assault rifle she had earlier dropped.

Zuma's voice shouted over the speakers, warning them all to stop at once.

Alina snapped her rifle up to her shoulder and opened fire, shredding the heads of Jun and Genesis in two short bursts. There was little blood but he distinctly saw both their skulls exploding into pieces and clouds of pink matter erupting from them as they fell. The noise was terrific, painful inside his ears.

Ram ducked low, hugging up against the wall. He glanced back for Eziz and Di, expecting to fend off another attack but Di had dived for the wall herself, laying facedown along it and Eziz...

Eziz had scooped up the other assault weapon, the one Ram had thrown down.

He took aim at Alina.

Ram, without considering why, leaped forward from his crouching position and shouldered Eziz aside.

But he was too late. Eziz was already firing when they connected, firing on full auto. The weapon whirred into action, clattering rounds flying so close together it was a continuous sound, like a zipper or a sheet of plastic being torn apart but a thousand times louder, the noise alone shattering his senses.

Ram rolled against the legs of the nearest bench, cracking his head against a steel-hard edge. Alina returned fire from the far end of the room, the bullets scattering everywhere, the room filling with noise and the acrid stink of explosive propellant.

Screams, shouts from both ends and the center of the room. Ram wasn't sure where he was, exactly and who was where, until he risked peering out from behind one of the steel bench legs near his face.

The marines opened up from the doorway, firing off tight bursts, but over and over again. The noise in the enclosed space was appalling, rounds were sparking off the walls around the squad of marines.

Ram was certain he would be shot again. Utterly certain he would be hit but this time with the live rounds instead of the electronic slugs from before. They ricocheted underneath the bench next to him. Shards of ceramic, sparks from the metal bench and dust sprayed over him, the stink and debris filling his throat as he took big panicky breaths. The rounds were still firing from both ends of the room but the rate of fire grew ever more sporadic over the next few seconds.

Through all the shouting voices, he heard Sifa bellowing some battle cry that became a cry of pain or anguish before it was cut off. The acrid smoke in the air combined with the stink of fresh blood and the cloying foulness of shit.

He couldn't cower in fear while his friends were dying around him. Clearly, he was nearer the door than the rear of the room so he crawled toward the middle bench, keeping as low as he could, keeping his eyes squeezed tight, lest he get shrapnel to the eyeballs. Hoping to find Sifa. Almost immediately his hands, out in front of him, slid into sticky, warm liquid. Even before he pried open an eye, he knew he was crawling in a pool of blood.

Ram crawled forward into it, through it. The cloying stench of blood and the acrid tang of smoke filled his lungs but the shots had almost ended so he chanced lifting his head and torso up a few centimeters to look for his friends.

There were bodies everywhere. The one closest to him had dark brown skin but not much of a head.

A burst of fire ripped into his shoulder, neck and head, knocking him face down into the spreading slick of warm blood.

PART 4
ASCENDANCE

CHAPTER TWENTY-FOUR
AFTERMATH

THERE WAS PAIN. Voices. Dreams of gunfire and blood. Time passed.

"No!"

Someone hushed him, stroked his head.

"What happened?" Ram said, trying to sit up. He was conscious but couldn't see clearly. Someone was there and he was asking them a question. "Were we talking? Where am I?"

The figure resolved into a beautiful but exhausted face.

"What do you remember?" She held him down with one hand on his chest.

"Milena? I remember... blood. On my face. A... training accident?"

"No," Milena said, her voice tight with strain. "Perhaps it is good that you do not remember. You are in the medical ring, recovering from surgery to repair damage caused by injuries sustained in a firefight. Bullet wounds."

"Wait," Ram said, his tongue feeling wrong in his mouth. "I remember. Bits and pieces. What happened to the others?"

"Dr. Fo?" Milena said. "Can he be released?"

The tiny doctor sidled up to Milena. "Rama Seti," he said. Dr. Fo looked awful. Huge black circles under his eyes, his skin a shade of gray-green you only normally got on universal camouflage patterns. When he spoke, the doctor's voice was flat and lifeless. "I am glad to see you conscious."

"Doctor," Milena said. "He has memory problems."

"Of course he does!" Dr. Fo snapped. Then he slumped again, too tired to maintain irritation. "We can hope you make a full recovery, back to combat efficiency at any rate. But don't expect all your memories to be coming back. Good luck to you. To all of us."

Dr. Fo slouched away. Ram sat up to watch him go and noted the doctor's white coat was soaked with blood. Before he shuffled through the door, he took off a plastic apron and dumped it into a bin beside it.

"Where's everyone else?" Ram asked Milena.

He knew it was bad when she did not meet his eye. Ram reached up and felt his shoulder, his neck and his head. The stubble under his fingers told him his head had been freshly shaved, a day or two ago, and was barely starting to grow back. There were long stitched wounds over his scalp. The large clinic room smelled powerfully of disinfectant. Two medical personnel were tossing blood-soaked bundles of bandages into biohazard waste sacks. A row of three steel gurneys lined the far wall, an orderly or some such wiping them down with liters of cleaning fluid. The floor beneath spattered pink with diluted blood.

"Who died?" Ram asked.

Milena couldn't look at him. "Ram, it's not good. It was chaotic in the barracks, they lost control. We lost control. Thousands of rounds. Alina was an expert shot. So was Eziz."

"Just give it to me straight, don't draw it out."

"They all died."

Ram looked at her. "Come on. Not those guys. Those giants. Not these bodies."

She chewed her lips before answering. They were red, chapped, skin missing on them. "There were so many rounds fired. The investigation is almost complete and I have viewed the footage many times over. Alina and Eziz obtained assault rifles with hundreds of lethal rounds and between them shot almost everyone. They aimed for the head. The marines shot Eziz and Alina and they shot to kill. And everyone caught stray bursts, including you. You took a couple to the side and back of the head, here and here, but they were glancing shots."

"How long?"

"Must be around thirty hours now. No, more like forty. Dr. Fo and his team have been working without pause, fighting to save everyone we could. It looked for a while like Te Zhang would pull through but they could not save him."

"Sifa?"

"She suffered a number of wounds to the chest trying to drag Te into cover. She would have survived that but Eziz very deliberately shot her. Some number of rounds entered around the base of her skull, destroying her hypothalamus. Bone and bullet fragments traveled through to the front of her brain. She certainly would have felt nothing."

"Good. That's good."

"I am sorry."

"So the mission is over," Ram said. "And all because of Alina."

"Alina, yes," Milena said, nodding. "She was the catalyst. She was the perpetrator. But it was not just her, as you know. The Director and the Chief Executive are investigating now, the preliminary report being wound up now but it is already clear what happened, to a large extent. It's all right there, on the cameras."

Ram lowered his voice, leaned toward her. "Do they know about... you know. Us? What we talked about right before...?"

She looked up at him then. "Everything we are saying now is being recorded so there is no need to whisper. And yes, they know. They know everything. I told them even as the actions were taking place. Our concerns about becoming Mael's victims obviously became irrelevant as soon as Alina killed him. But we were cut off. Diego had hacked the security systems, blocked communications. He stopped the ship's rotation. Alina's driver, Noomi, intentionally or accidentally took her own life in an explosion in the medical ring. She improvised a device that burned through the reserve subjects in storage, incinerating them before the fire suppression systems could stop it."

"Reserve subjects?"

"The backup heads that were kept in a coma state, do you remember? We know that she had particular ethical concerns in that regard but not to such an extent that she would risk so much to see their exploitation permanently ended in such a manner, That's not all. The explosion damaged oxygen storage tanks in the connecting wall which blew the fire into the Artificial Person section and destroyed all but two of the remaining AP units."

"The bodies for spare parts and stuff? She wanted us to liberate them but instead she accidentally killed them?"

"A hastily planned terrorist incident does not usually go as intended."

"Noomi was a terrorist? A real one?" Ram said. "How did she get on the mission?"

"How can we ever know what intentions someone harbors in

the deep of their soul? If there was any sign before, it would have been picked up and she never would have made it onboard the *Victory*."

"Which were the two AP bodies that survived?"

"One was Sifa's," Milena said. "The other was yours, it happened to be in having a standard medical exam. Sifa's survived through more dumb luck. It was at the far end of the room, the initial small shockwave dislodged a broken wall panel which knocked it down behind some exercise equipment and then served as a shield while the fire burnt itself out. But Sifa's brain is beyond salvageable at this point."

Ram felt as mindless as his own blank. Just numb, more than anything.

"What about using the surviving APs for one of the other subjects?"

Milena sighed. "There has to be a genetic match or the grafting between human and AP will not take."

"I see," Ram said, just as a blinding flash of headache rose and faded behind his eyes. He winced until it passed. "How can we carry on without Mael or Alina or anyone?"

"That is what they will decide right now. Chief Executive Zhukov has called a meeting in the crew ring and we will go there immediately. But obviously, things are not good. Not good at all."

"I have to be there?" Ram asked.

"You're not invited," Milena said. "But if you don't step up now, they will disregard you. If you don't step forward now, you'll likely not get another chance and humanity needs you. So, get your giant ass up and let's go."

The medical personnel helped him get to his feet, though his head spun enormously and he had to hold on for some time before anyone dared let go. His first step, he fell against the wall. His second, he found himself bent at the waist, dry-heaving and sweating.

"You've had a lot of anesthetic in the last couple of days," Milena explained. "It will wear off quicker if you get your heart rate up. Come on, we'll be late."

By the time they got to the huge communal mess hall that the crew shared, Ram felt much better, physically. Emotionally, he felt little more than a sense of wonder. A sense of awe at how badly things had gone. Clearly, Milena was pumping him full of something or other to keep his grief and guilt from overwhelming him. He was grateful.

Director Zuma, on the other hand, looked awful. She stood at the far end of the mess hall, which was the full length of the ring section. As far a distance as someone could see onboard the *Victory* and yet even from that distance, Ram could see she was defeated.

The mess was full. Every person on the ship, surely, was there. They had never told Ram how many crewmembers there were, nor exactly how big the ship was and he had never pushed for answers. But he guessed there were a hundred people in that room or more, sitting in tightly packed chairs and at tables that faced a clear space at the far end. It was so full that people stood at the sides and back of the room.

Ram noted a handful of marines, fully armed, dotted around the room, two of them flanking the people up at the front of the room. Milena saw him looking at them.

"Don't worry about them," she said quietly, as they took the last spaces at the rear of the hall. "They are just a precaution."

"Right," Ram whispered. "Against me?"

"No," Milena said. "You are innocent of any wrongdoing, either in the run up to or the execution of the event."

"Do they know that?"

"That's their commanding officer down the front," Milena said, pointing out a big, blond, grizzled man sitting slumped sideways in his folding chair, one arm slung over the back of it. "He knows he messed up as much as anyone. No one is looking to blame you."

"Who's the badass in the shiny uniform?" Ram muttered. An immaculate, naval style uniform and perfectly groomed hair couldn't disguise how much the man at the back looked dangerous.

"That's Commander Tamura, the ship's captain," Milena said. "His rank is Commander of the *UNOPS Victory*. We don't see him, he is never involved in ludus activities but him and his crew are responsible for getting us where we need to be. Commander Tamura is senior to the Captain of the Marines.

The crew loves him but he scares them, too."

Zhukov was there next to Commander Tamura, standing back from Zuma with his head bowed like he was at a funeral.

Director Zuma, about to address the crew, looked worse. Her shoulders rounded, her whole being sagged as if pulled down by a heavy weight. Simply standing before them took almost all the strength she had. Her richly brown skin had a gray pallor. Before speaking, Zuma took a deep, shuddering breath.

"Many times, I spoke of this mission as a spear thrust, aimed at our enemy's heart. I said that our spearhead was made up of our subjects. That our crew was the shaft, that we were aimed by all of humanity. Hyperbole, clearly. A handy metaphor and no more than that. But a few days ago, we lost the point of that spear. All our subjects, dead. The redundancies built into this mission have been overcome by a combination of malicious acts of terrorism, murder, chance and human error. I take full responsibility for the tragedy. It was my decision to pursue the policy that we pursued. It was my plan to forgo ethical concerns to increase the performance of Subject Alpha. It was my..."

Zuma broke off and rubbed her face.

"We must go on. Somehow. But how, exactly, will not be up to me. I resigned my commission a few minutes ago and Chief Executive Zhukov will take up the Managing Directorship from now on. He will take us onward from here. Whatever our personal and professional failures, they are irrelevant and I will continue to advise and support with whatever expertise I can provide. But stepping aside will mean a fresh start, a new approach. We have asked you all here to hear what we propose and to discuss it. Only critical crew are not in attendance and they will have the opportunity to comment later. In a few hours we will hold a memorial service for the fallen. But now I will now hand you over to the Chief Exec and Director."

She slumped away and stood with her head down. Shrunken, reduced. Defeated by her failures.

Zhukov stepped forward.

"This is not a democracy. We will not be taking a vote on courses of action. But I wished to look you all in the eye when I tell you this. The mission goes on. We all go on. And we will succeed. Anyone expressing a contrary view will be regarded by me in most unfavorable terms. Now. You know what happened in the ludus three days ago. The footage, from every angle, has been made available to you all for at least twenty-four hours so there's no need to go over the specifics as it unfolded. I have heard many of you asking how this could have happened and this is the question we also asked ourselves. There were a number of factors. The subjects' drivers were designed to support the subject in combat but also to provide personal psychological support and assessment. The drivers also met with the Chief Psychologist and the Director, with written reports evidenced by recordings of conversations and footage of the subject.

"In this case, however, Noomi had been deceiving us for some time. Filing reports that drastically misrepresented her conversations with Alina as well as deleting, obscuring and editing the recordings of their conversations. We believe many of the recordings she submitted were concocted purely to keep us off their track."

A pale hand near the front shot up.

"I wanted to keep questions for the end but I will take one now, go ahead."

"Sir, we carry out regular audits and random inspections exactly so that we can avoid this kind of deceit."

"Thank you, Beaumont. Indeed, we do and yet because of technical assistance from Diego, they were able to hide the secret conversations that they did have. We are not clear on how they did it but we will uncover full details. It may be they had help and that there are other people on this ship, in this room, who helped them. If you are out there then hear me when I say this. We will find you. It would be better if you give yourself up now. Just like Diego, you will not suffer punitive punishment and if your skills are required for this mission then you will carry on with increased oversight. Punishment will have to wait until the mission is complete, perhaps when we are back on Earth. On the other hand, it may be that Alina, Noomi and Diego formed the complete cabal. Between the three of them, it is entirely possible they could have carried out everything that they did."

Ram leaned down to Milena as subtly as he could, heart thumping. "No mention of us?"

"Zuma is an idealist," Milena muttered. "Zhukov is a

pragmatist. He can see the big picture."

Ram let out a breath. Plainly, she had made a deal with the man.

"What did they want?" A voice called from the center the audience.

Zhukov sighed but he allowed the question. "They did not want this. They did not want to kill everyone and destroy the mission. They believed in the mission so much that they were willing to kill for it. They believed that Director Zuma was wrong with her Alpha First mission design. They discovered, through Diego we believe, that each of them was on the list for potentially sanctioned targets for Mael's homicidal incidents and they were unwilling to be so. The group believed, for many reasons that were perfectly valid, that Alina would make a better subject Alpha than Mael. Better in terms of our ultimate outcomes on the Orb. The only barrier, as far as they could tell, was the continued existence of Mael himself. The plan that they carried out was designed to kill Mael alone, yet Alina was willing to kill more subjects, should they oppose her. She was willing to kill non-vital crew, such as the drivers and marines if they attempted to stop or harm her."

"So she lost her mind?" Someone shouted.

Zhukov had clearly decided to let his audience vent a little. "No. Why would you think that? Did you not hear what I just said? She considered herself the best chance for this mission to succeed. We had demonstrated, over and over, that the lives of individuals on this ship were unimportant compared to Subject Alpha. Her willingness to kill to protect herself made perfect sense. But it was not only to kill Mael. Noomi euthanized most of our Artificial Persons and all backup subjects through improvised explosive devices. A day before, Alina allowed herself to be beaten so severely by Mael in order to gain access to the switches that would paralyze Mael and the other subjects that she felt would physically protect him. Noomi set the explosives while Diego controlled the security for all of them. He blocked our cameras and microphones. He locked the door to the barracks and our security team worked to counter his lock. When the lock was overcome, the individual in the team who was responsible for hacking the hack believed he had overcome Diego's program through his own skills. And we believed him. Of course, it was a trap. Four marines were sent in with nonlethal rounds to subdue Alina but they each had four magazines of expanding hollow point, each magazine with ninety-six rounds. That meant when Alina killed the marines, that she had over fifteen hundred live rounds. It looks as though well over a thousand rounds were fired between Alina and Eziz and the second team of marines fired some two hundred to bring them both down."

"Why didn't Team Two use the nonlethal rounds?"

Zhukov glanced at Captain Cassidy, sitting in the front row. Cassidy waved a hand at Zhukov, declining to comment.

"They tried that," Zhukov said, clearly he had been fully briefed by the Marine Captain. "The rounds had practically no effect on the enhanced bodies of the subjects. It was our prior belief that they would work, based on laboratory tests. Evidently, there are cascading errors going back months and even years, even to off this ship back on Earth and to before we left orbit. There is still much we don't understand. How did Diego access ship control and fire the thrusters to stop the ship spinning? That should have been compartmentalized. Why did Noomi murder herself during the detonation of the device? Was it accidental or intentional?"

"Were they terrorists?" Someone shouted.

"Certainly, Noomi seems to have felt strongly enough about Artificial Persons to be willing to destroy them. I am not an expert in pro-human terrorism but I believe they release the sims, when possible or kill them if not. What is more confusing is why she destroyed the backup subjects kept in deep coma. They were all heads without bodies and so would require an Artificial Person if they were ever to be used but I do not know what problem she may have had with them simply existing in storage, unconscious and unaware. Not offending anybody. Diego claims to know nothing of any bombs. Noomi's motivations may forever remain unknown. Is it even important? All we can do now is recover and move on."

"Move on? How can we move on? All our subjects are gone. It's all over."

Ram stood up straighter at the back. He felt Milena glance up at him. Being discounted to such an extent, after all his hard work. After all he had fought for. He wanted to wade into the crowd and lay waste to them.

"I know it seems that way," Zhukov said. "And perhaps you are correct. But we cannot allow you to be correct. And this is what I want you all to hear. We must leave this room, feeling and knowing that the mission is not over. That we do have a chance at victory. Because we must do so. We must or the alternative is too difficult to contemplate. So, a way forward. We have options. We have opportunities. There are still people on board this ship who would stand against the alien. We have Bediako. The only human to survive battle with the entity."

Bediako stood up straight, looked around the room once, slowly and nodded at Zhukov.

"It would be an honor," Bediako said. "To fight once more would be an honor. I have decades of combat experience at the most elite levels anywhere in the Solar System. You all need not worry about my skill and my fitness. Trust me. I am an expert."

A few people chuckled and Ram sensed a certain relaxation spreading through the room. A small collective sigh.

But not everyone was placated.

"Oskar?" Zhukov said to a hand sticking up in the center of the room.

"No offense, Bediako," a red-faced man with blond hair said, standing and addressing the room as well as the instructor and Zhukov in turn. Ram recalled that Sifa's driver was called Oskar. "But you had an attempt thirty years ago. And you failed."

Zhukov waived down the mumbled protests then invited Oskar to continue. Bediako's face was thunder.

"There is no one alive with more experience, that is indisputable. But we all know why you were not part of the intake for this mission and instead were lead instructor. Your body is simply not capable of achieving the required standard. Your second fusing with an Artificial Person body has seen to that. And an old model body, one that was not suitable for a primary candidate. I am sorry but you are too slow. Too weak."

"You impudent little twerp," Bediako said. "Who are you to judge me? You know nothing of combat. If you did, you would know that timing beats speed. Experience and skill make up for strength. Who would you prefer to fight the alien? You?"

"No," Oskar said. "What about one of the marines?"

All eyes in the room turned to the large Captain Cassidy sitting slouched in a chair at the front, who climbed to his feet and looked down on the seated audience.

The marine officer had lost a squad of his precious men and he looked like he had not slept in days. His rugged, bony face was deeply lined, with a weathered ruddiness seemingly undiminished by years in space. Still, the menace in his eyes was like a pair of lasers he was shooting around the room at everyone, one after the other. He looked like a man who wanted vengeance and, with the way he exuded competence, he knew how to get it.

Ram hoped that Milena was right and the man did not hold him responsible for the massacre. Captain Cassidy of the UNOP

Marine Corps looked like a bad man to have as an enemy.

"Hell," the Captain said. "You got to have rocks in your head, Oskar. There's no way me or any of my guys can face that thing without our augmentation. Look at me, for Christ's sake." The Captain held his arms out. "We're all so full of augments that we're practically cyborgs. You take out enough that we can get below the Zeta Line and it would ruin our physical abilities right away."

"Obviously," the driver called Oskar replied. "I know that, I just thought you could select the best hand to hand fighter from your company, I mean, of the survivors and have their augments removed."

The Captain was clearly horrified for a moment, then recovered to shake his head. "You don't understand, Oskar. Our augments have been part of us for years. They are a core part of our training right out of basic, everything we do relies on those components, from synchronized communications to neurochemically enhanced reactions. And we're just not trained to fight as individuals, we operate as part of a team."

"I understand all that but I have seen your marines training one on one, with knife fights and grappling. You do know how to do this."

"Don't presume to tell me my job, Oskar, you're, what, a medical doctor?"

"Biochemist originally but I also have a doctorate in human psychol—"

"Well, doctor, that's damned impressive but I've been a Marine for over twenty years and I know what I'm talking about." The Captain sighed and Ram saw for a moment a commanding officer who had just lost four people in his company. "Look, I understand, alright, you see my company and you see the finest killers humanity has ever produced and you think, why not throw them into the Arena? But you will also remember, that our predecessors in UNOP tried that in Mission Two. We simply do not have the mass to compete with an entity that size, nor do we have the reaction time without our augmentation, we just don't."

Oskar threw up his hands. "Fine, of course, I know. I know."

Captain Cassidy threw Ram a quick look from across the room. Ram's heart skipped a beat.

Was the Captain going to denounce him?

"However," Cassidy said. "I do believe my expertise can be of assistance to us all in making a decision here today. And I honestly can't believe none of you has said it so far. I'm certain we must all be thinking it. We all know that there was one survivor of the massacre in the barracks room. A man of utterly extraordinary physical ability. Demonstrably the strongest man the world has ever known. A man with thousands of hours of simulated combat in over a dozen highly competitive arenas. Just a few days ago he received multiple bullet wounds, including two rounds to the skull. And yet I hear that he has already made a full physical recovery. He was built for this, in every way." Captain Cassidy held out his hand, indicating the back of the room. "Thank you for joining us, Rama Seti."

Every head in the room turned to point his way in a suddenly rustling and chair scraping mass. Dozens of faces. Not one of them seemed to be impressed. Many of them turned back to the front.

Bediako's looked like he wanted to murder Cassidy and Ram both.

"Hi," Ram said. "How are you all doing?"

Someone near the front raised their hand.

"But he's not a real subject," a woman said. "He's only here for cannon fodder. I'm sorry but it's just the truth, isn't it?"

Another crew member he had never seen replied. "That's right, simulated experience has no bearing on real world experience."

Someone unseen called out. "He's only even been awake a few days, really."

People started shouting, speaking over each other.

"He just got shot to pieces and Fo has rebuilt him from scans."

"There's a certain mindset to champions that he just does not have."

"If you're going to consider him you might as well put one of the Artificial Persons in the arena, right?"

Ram thought it was mainly the drivers calling out. They had all lost their subjects and they were hurting, angry. Despairing. A few people then objected to the general consensus. Not many.

It was pissing him off.

"I'm sorry," Oskar the driver shouted. "I really am but he honestly does not have the mental fortitude. I've read his progress reports. He's a loser. He quits when things get tough, it's a deeply rooted pattern of behavior that cannot be excised, even with digital brain surgery. To put it bluntly, he will never have what it takes. This is a waste of our time."

Ram straightened up and strode down the center of the room toward the front. He wasn't entirely sure why he was going or what he would do when he got to there but he was angry at being dismissed out of hand by those people. Who were they to question him, to doubt him? What did they know about him, really? About what he knew he was capable of, deep down in his soul.

He towered over everyone. He overtopped even Bediako. The normal sized people were like children to him.

Sitting beneath him, the driver named Oskar seemed to shrink further into his seat, glancing up at Ram as he walked past. He stared down at Oskar with loathing. Sure, him and all the drivers were all ludicrously intelligent, accomplished and competent but, for fuck's sake, so was he. There was no reason to be intimidated by any one of them and not even by the group of them all together. A deep anger welled inside him. Anger at Alina and Mael.

And at himself.

Allowing that anger to come to the surface meant he could

face them down with little room left for self-doubt.

Zhukov nodded up at Ram when he drew near and Ram returned the nod. The sea of faces looking back at him when he turned to the audience was a little overwhelming for a moment but then that familiar feeling of unreality flooded in. He'd addressed crowds bigger than this before. Those times he had been in-game and he'd been in his avatar speaking to hundreds of other avatars, not real people but it amounted to the same thing, really. A few years back when he started building his co-op he'd even gone on a three-day business course called *Delivering Powerful IRL and Avar Presentations*. Little in that course had been of long term use but there was one tip that had always stuck with him.

Open with a joke.

"I'm hurt," Ram said. He watched the faces frown back at him. "I'm hurt real bad. I'm hurt that you guys didn't think of me right away."

It was a lame gag but a few people chuckled. Captain Cassidy even grunted.

"I shouldn't joke in these circumstances," Ram continued. "Obviously. Like someone just said, I haven't been here for long. Well, not conscious and attached to a body, anyway. But in the last seventy days or so since I have been a member of this crew, a willing participant in this mission, I have made friends here. Comrades, if you like. It has not been long in days and hours, perhaps but the ludus is an intense place and you live it, fully, day and night. I guess what I'm saying is that I really did count a handful of the other subjects as my friends. And they were murdered."

He looked out at them. They looked confused, saddened. It wasn't what Ram wanted to say at all.

"But look," he said. "I have experience. Lots simulated, yes. Some real world. And I have this body. This old model body, sure but it's one with modern features, recently installed. So, you know, as much as I hate to step up here and say this, logically, I'm really the best chance we have of winning in the Orb Arena."

"You?" Bediako shouted from across the room. He laughed. It was a sound like a chainsaw ripping through a bundle of rusty barbed wire. "You're a patsy, son. You're a lamb to the slaughter that fluked getting away from the slaughterhouse. Go sit down before you hurt yourself."

Ram shook his head. "And I say that putting you forward would be the worst mistake humanity could make. Let's face it, you went in there once before and you lost. And now you're old as fuck, you're riddled with radiation and your mind is full of holes. I'm sorry for you but you're a fragile old has-been and you wouldn't have a hope."

Silence. Bediako's eyes popped out of his head and veins at the man's temples and forehead shone.

Bediako strode forward, throwing chairs and people out of his way.

Ram prepared to fight, feeling the epinephrine surging

through him. He hoped Milena would dose him good.

Chairs scraped on the floor as people, especially in the front row jumped to their feet and scrambled aside, out of Bediako's way. He strutted with his head down, like a bullock making a run at a gate.

"Stop," Zhukov roared. The volume was such that it made Ram's ears' ring. He stepped into the Chief Instructor's way with his arms spread wide. "You cannot fight in here, this is the Mess Hall."

"Fine," Bediako said, coming to a stop, his face contorting with the effort to control himself. He towered over the new Director. "Not here. I will kill him in the ludus."

CHAPTER TWENTY-FIVE
BEDIAKO

RAMA STARED ACROSS the sparring room at Bediako. The chief instructor was busy slapping himself in the face and growling to psych himself up.

They had the huge room to themselves. All support staff had been ordered into the Ludus Mess or the PT Room, ready and waiting to pick up the pieces should anything go badly wrong. Whoever won the fight, both men were valuable resources, so Zhukov said beforehand.

"It has been my goal, throughout my careers, to always choose the best individual for the job," Zhukov said from ship's speakers, broadcasting throughout the *Victory*. "As much as it pains me to risk either man, we must determine who will provide humanity's best chance. Will it be technique and experience winning over strength and relative youth? We will know shortly who will be Mission Four's Subject Alpha. And may the best man win."

Zhukov had broadcast his message from the safety of his office. The camera feed from the sparring room was shared live with every screen on the ship.

"What did he mean by relative youth?" Ram muttered to Milena. He looked across the width of that tubular room to where Bediako jumped on the spot, slapping his chest now. The old man's physique really was remarkable, his muscles were smaller that Ram's but they appeared to be incredibly dense and the man moved like a ninja.

"This is it, now, Rama," Milena said from inside Ram's inner ear. "This is the fight that will decide all life as we know it."

"Don't say that," Ram said, flexing and stretching to warm his muscles. "What the hell's the matter with you?"

She laughed. "Just attempting to lighten the mood."

"Do you really think I can beat him?"

"I know you will beat him. You're stronger, younger, faster. He probably knows every trick there is to know but that didn't help him when he fought the Wheelhunter, did it. No doubt he will strike you, hard. No doubt he will get you in arm locks and leg locks and he will attempt to choke you. Your escape techniques are basic, yes but you have the strength to remove his holds. You have trained constantly, every day, all day, for months whereas he has been doing weights in his spare time. All you need to do is catch him, hold him still and pummel him. Or perhaps break his limbs until he cannot move any longer."

"Simple, really."

Across the room, Bediako completed his preparations and strode out to the middle of the huge space, his shoulders relaxed, like he was promenading around Nehru Park.

"If you are really afraid, you do not have to do this," Milena said. "You know that. A few days ago you were fighting only to stay alive as long as you could, your goal was simply to live. If you let Bediako fight the Wheeler, then you won't have to fight the alien. And you will live, certainly, maybe even make it back to Earth one day. So why don't you just give up right now?"

Ram laughed, watching the way Bediako moved lightly on his toes. He knew Milena was playing devil's advocate, was trying to remind him why he had stepped up.

"How long would I even live for if he loses against the Wheeler? Years, probably but we don't know, years when humanity is under a sustained alien attack? If I am the best fighter, then it has to be me in the Orb arena."

"You're going to crush him," Milena said. "Look at him, dancing about like an idiot."

Ram took a deep breath, watching Bediako's silky movement.

The instructor smiled when he saw Ram staring at him.

"He's one of the most elite fighters in human history," Ram said, rotating his hands to loosen his wrists.

"So are you, you moron. Give it your all. You will win this fight. His brain is seventy years old, all patched up with a downloaded mind. He's on his second body. You going to smash his skull in."

"Fine, Lena, take it easy," Ram said to her. "I hear what you're saying. I'm overpowered and he's been nerfed all to shit."

The massive training room seemed even bigger than usual, with no one in it but for Ram and Bediako. Almost everyone on the ship would be watching live, through the multiple cameras arrayed in the walls and ceiling all around the room.

"You're thinking of backing out, fat boy," Bediako said from the center of the room, holding his arms out like he owned the place. "And you should. Do yourself a favor. Do the mission a favor. You could still have uses, you can be my training partner. But you're no good if you're too broken to function."

Trying to intimidate me, Ram thought.

"He's just trying to intimidate you," Milena said. "He's asserting dominance, reminding you that he's the instructor. Demonstrating that this is his territory."

"Obviously," Ram muttered. "Stop talking unless it's practical advice."

"Come on up here, coward," Bediako shouted, laughing. Ram ignored him, rolling his head around to warm up his vast neck muscles.

"Roger that. First, try to keep away from him for as long as possible. Let him tire his old ass out."

Ram took a deep breath and walked out onto the mats, approaching the center of the room where his opponent waited.

Despite his advanced years, Bediako was a monster of a man. Almost as tall as Ram, big boned and with long, dense muscles like a sprinter in the Cyborg Olympics. His legs were long, powerful. He looked like he'd been sculpted from the finest Italian black marble.

"I'm not going to outrun him, Milena," Ram mumbled, speaking as low as he could without being overheard.

Bediako chuckled from the center of the room. "Taking combat advice from a psychologist? You are ignorant. You are naïve. You have no idea what those people have done to you when you have been unconscious, how much they have reconstructed your mind. Who even are you, now? You haven't learned a thing since these last two months, not from me nor from anyone, and you certainly have learned nothing from your driver."

Ram was itching to ask what the hell he was talking about but he knew that's what Bediako wanted, to unsettle him.

"I've learned enough."

The instructor laughed, looking around the room as if to invite the watching crowd to share in his laughter. "You're about to get a real lesson," Bediako said.

Ram wished he could think of a brilliant response, some brutal trash talk that would cut him to the bone.

"Shut the fuck up, grandpa," Ram said. "Let's do this."

Bediako grinned and hunched over, his arms out and up, palms down like a praying mantis. Ram turned sideways, leading with his right leg, bent his knees, put his weight on his toes, dropped his hips down to lower his center of gravity and held his hands at the ready. He knew Bediako was a champion grappler who liked to take his opponents to the ground and pound them into submission so Ram had to be ready for that. He wanted to keep Bediako away with punches and kicks, to use his reach advantage to strike Bediako.

He's expecting me to be defensive, Ram thought and aimed a low, fast kick at Bediako's knee. Bediako shifted a fraction and Ram hit nothing but air.

Bediako charged in, shooting for Ram's knees to take him down. Ram reached down to grab his opponent's back but a fist came out of nowhere and cracked him on the nose. The surprise of it distracted Ram for a moment and then Bediako had his arms entangled in Ram's knees. Ram punched down onto Bediako's back, a powerful blow into his kidney. He felt the man grunt as they both went down in a heap. The fall was hard but Ram was covered in muscle and it didn't hurt. Yet Ram felt a rising panic at the fact that he'd been taken to the ground. Right where Bediako wanted him. That was where Bediako's experience would win out.

It was all going wrong.

On his back, Ram fought to keep the older man at bay by grasping his wrists but Bediako twisted his arms out of Ram's grasp and grabbed one of Ram's elbows. Bediako pushed himself forward, pinning Ram's legs with his own, wriggling forward like a snake and mounting him, pinning Ram's hips to the floor. Bediako was going for an arm lock.

Or an arm break.

Ram had practiced enough grappling to know the proper techniques for countering all the holds and arm and leg locks and the chokes but he had not performed them enough times to do them without thinking. He had not had enough time for muscle memory to be established, so when his heart was racing and his mind whirring, he couldn't quite bring the techniques to mind, couldn't quite get his body to obey. He fumbled and struggled but couldn't free himself. All he could do was hold on for as long as possible and hope for a mistake, an opportunity. Both of them were panting with exertion, both slick with sweat and roaring with heat.

The force on his arm was incredible. Bediako pulled with the inexorable force of a machine.

"You're stronger than him, Ram," Milena's voice came through. She sounded perfectly calm. But then, she would, Ram thought. She was not the one about to get her arm broken. "I'm increasing your testosterone and cortisol uptake now. They're already naturally elevated but you can handle more. You must resist, pull his arm back. You are the strongest man who ever lived. Act like it!"

Ram wanted to shout at her to shut the fuck up but he needed every breath of air he could to get the oxygen he needed to fight. His heart was hammering in his chest, pounding so hard he could hear it throbbing in his ears.

Bediako's black face shone with sweat, his eyes popping as he strained against Ram's arm.

I'm the strongest man who ever lived, Ram thought. I can beat this old fuck. I have to.

Ram's arm flexed as he brought it in toward himself. Just a little.

Bediako presumably saw that his method would fail and so he changed it. Before Ram could react, Bediako, keeping firm pressure on Ram's arm, rolled off his hips, away from his body and threw both his legs across Ram's upper body.

Armbar.

Ram knew the technique. It was a classic. One that pitted the strength of a whole body against a single limb. Bediako was using his legs, buttocks and torso as well as both arms to attempt to overextend Ram's arm and break it. It would snap at the elbow unless Ram gave up or else could somehow free himself.

Bediako's massive, muscular leg was across Ram's throat and lower jaw.

The tendons on his arm were stretching. He could feel them. The bone at the elbow joint would be compressing the tissue in between, using the compressed tissue as a fulcrum to pivot his upper and lower arm in the wrong direction. Pain shot up to his shoulder and down to his fingers. Bediako arched his back and heaved, his tendons and veins popping out all over his skin. Someone was growling through their teeth.

Ram knew enough to know it was a difficult position to free himself from. But he had to. There were ways of doing it, he wracked his brain for the videos he had watched, the techniques he'd practiced with Te and Sifa.

Sifa. A surge of anger coursed through him at the memory of her body in the barracks, laying in a pool of blood. Killed through the culture of the ludus and the practice of favoring a single subject over the others. A culture encouraged and enforced by his opponent.

Ram squeezed his arm, contracted his chest, his back in fighting against the forces pulling it apart. His biceps strained against the might of Bediako's whole body.

And Ram overcame it. He pulled hard, so hard that Bediako was pulled slowly up off his back. Both of them breathed heavily, panting and sweating with the effort, throats raw and constricted. But Ram was stronger. He was doing it. He was winning.

Bediako changed position again. One moment Ram was straining, his arm curling back in toward himself and the next the pressure was released and Bediako was sitting upright, straddling him, high on Ram's chest. The first blow came before he was even in position, smacking into Ram's eye. He saw a field of a million silver stars, cascading inward. The next blow was harder, smacking into his nose and then a mighty great blow to his mouth, mangling his lips against his teeth.

Ram got his hands up to protect his face and many of the punches hit his forearms. Some glanced off and missed, other glanced off and hit his face with less power than they otherwise would have. But more slipped through or around his arms and smashed into his face, over and over.

He knew he'd fucked up. He'd lost. He'd allowed himself to get swarmed immediately and he didn't know any clever techniques that came from years of practice. He had no muscle memory to rely on, it would never have worked, he could never have beat a man with decades of experience. The punches smacked into him over and over.

"Ram," Milena was shouting. She'd been speaking for a while without him paying attention to her voice in his ear. "Ram, he is not hurting you. Can you hear me, Ram? Pay attention. You're not experiencing any pain, are you? Can you hear me? He's not powerful enough to hurt you."

She was right.

Ram was astonished but she was right. The blows that smacked into his face and head felt dulled. Almost numb. The impact rocked his head. The crack of Bediako's knuckles against his skin was a sharp, high note of pain, sure. But it was not terrible. It was not debilitating. He could compartmentalize it, lock the pain away from his awareness. The realization filled him with a sudden joy.

He laughed.

The punches stopped for a fraction of a second and Ram looked up at Bediako's sweating, confused, offended face, the old man's chest heaving with effort. And he laughed again.

Bediako grimaced and threw down punch after punch. Ram kept laughing. He'd never felt so invincible. The harder Bediako worked, the more Ram laughed.

"I'm sure you're enjoying yourself," Milena said. "But do you want to win now?"

Bediako was tired. It was obvious. While Ram had been resting on his back, Bediako had been fighting to stay on top and had expended a huge amount of energy in his punches. Ram reached up and grabbed Bediako's upper arms, pulling him down and reaching both hands around the back of his neck and head. Bediako tried to wriggle away backward but Ram held him fast. He pulled him in close then rolled over so that Ram was on top and in the guard position. Bediako was tired and Ram's strength could not be denied.

Bediako grasped Ram's arm and twisted, trying to break Ram's hold but Ram simply twisted back the other way and bent Bediako's own arm at the elbow joint. Bediako roared in pain and Ram carefully snapped the old man's elbow. The crack was so loud that the pop echoed off the walls and Ram kept twisting so that the joint crunched and ground against the cartilage inside. Bediako punched with his good hand but there was little strength behind it now. Ram threw his own fist into Bediako's contorted face, knocking the bastard's head back.

It felt good. He hit him again and felt a surge of joy, of release, when Bediako's nose burst under his fist. It felt right when Bediako's lips split and when his teeth tumbled down his throat. Milena was shouting in his ear again but he couldn't hear her. Bediako's cheeks split over his cheekbones, the red blood splashing up with every blow, raining down onto the black ceramic floor. He wondered how long it would take to cave in the skull and smash his head into pulp.

Ram's body went limp.

He fell straight down onto Bediako, his eyes landing next to his instructor's ruined face. Close enough to get the blood smeared across his eyes. Ram could not move a muscle and had to watch his instructor spit out a blood clot filled with teeth.

They had switched Ram off. Paralyzed him again to save Bediako from being beaten any further. Bediako lay under him, struggling to breathe through the mess of his face, panic in his eyes.

I won, Ram thought, grinning.

I bloody well won.

CHAPTER TWENTY-SIX
SUBJECT ALPHA

TWO DAYS LATER, they sat in Ram's new quarters around the meeting table, with Ram at the head.

Newly promoted Primary Subject Operator Milena Reis was in attendance and the joint Chief Executive Director / Managing Director of Mission Four - Zhukov to his friends - had come all the way over to Ram's swanky place to organize the plan for the final two months they had until the fight with the Wheelhunter.

"He would have killed him," Zhukov was saying to Milena. "We would have lost yet another asset and it would have been your fault."

Ram liked his new accommodation.

Without asking Ram they had assumed, correctly, that he would not wish to stay in the barracks any longer. The place where so many had died would be an empty and constant reminder of the violent tragedy so they'd converted the ludus counseling and medical rooms. Why stay in a barracks space designed to provide just the right level of conflict between twelve subjects? Now he lived somewhere that was designed to provide him the maximum level of comfort and recovery time. There was a bedroom, a shower and toilet room but also a living area, a small kitchen and a meeting room.

The whole place took up half of one ludus ring section. The ludus was still the best place for him to stay, after all, that was where he trained every day. Also, Zhukov and the other mission leaders did not want to take any risks with their last, best hope being the victim of any crazed attack by unknown elements in the crew.

In the days since Alina and Noomi's attack, every crew member had undergone intense scrutiny but the investigation had uncovered no further planned breaches of security. Still, it would not do to take the chance of a lone wolf sleeper terrorist or psychotic break or a person with an undetected hacked behavioral implant being set off. Marines were now posted at all times at the entrance to the ludus and at the entrances to his section and entry was tightly controlled.

Ram found that being Subject Alpha led to a number of privileges. Not just in the accommodation but also in the way he was treated by the bosses. As the sole surviving subject, he could exert more influence even than Mael had been allowed.

And he meant to exploit his new power. He sat in his large chair at the head of the meeting table and decided to push Zhukov to see how far he would bend.

"It's true that I may have overcooked the testosterone during the fight," Milena. "It only takes an increase by a little to start the feedback mechanisms to start a cascade of release and uptake."

"Your job is to know what you're doing," Zhukov said, gripping his screen in both fists. "If you're not capable of doing your job correctly then I will have you replaced with Nurul."

"You won't replace her," Ram said, staring across and down at Zhukov. "In fact, you will make sure that Milena is my only driver, from now until the mission is complete."

The Chief Executive was now taking Zuma's place as the Director of the mission itself and being completely hands on. Before, his job had been to provide on-site oversight of Zuma and to liaise with the UNOP HQ back on Earth. As the mission was so close to completion, he claimed he could do both jobs effectively and there was no need to promote someone internally.

"Oh?" Zhukov said, sitting upright, his top lip curling in disgust. "You are named Subject Alpha and twenty-four hours later you are throwing your weight around? Forcing your commanding officer to comply with your wishes? It is notable how those who were once weak abuse their power once they have it."

Ram scoffed. "Hey, at least I'm not a fucking serial killer, right?"

Zhukov colored. "What do you imagine that you going to do to compel me to do what you demand? Go on strike if you do not get your way, just so you can keep playing with your little friend?" Zhukov pointed at Milena. "If this woman had told us about Alina's plot to kill Mael then none of this would have happened."

"That's bullshit, you know that. You're trying to make me angry. That would be a mistake."

Zhukov's face flushed red and he grew so rigid he almost shook.

"Director Zhukov believes that anger improves performance," Milena said, looking at Zhukov. "This is because he has a large well of deep rooted anger of his own and has a selection bias when observing successful individuals who also experience their own anger issues."

Zhukov snorted, shaking his head at her. "And you, Milena Reis, would never have been selected to be an Alpha-level driver without this tragedy taking place. Your stepping aside for someone more competent would benefit this mission."

Ram answered before she could respond. "We've had almost three months to get to know each other. She's steered me through every crisis I've experienced on this ship. It's not relevant that she's the only friend I've still got. She's completely competent in every way. This Nurul must have encouraged Mael's insane and aggressive, violent behavior. I'm not working with someone like that. Only Milena."

Zhukov's top lip curled up, ever so slightly. "Your new-found arrogance is a result of your elevated testosterone, nothing more. Although, perhaps the parts of your brain responsible for humility were corrupted during one of your procedures. I could have your behavior surgically modified if I wanted to, so do not think for a moment that you are able to threaten me with anything, do you understand?"

Ram did what he thought would anger Zhukov the most.

He ignored him and addressed Milena. "Remind me again what would happen if you just cranked my hormones all the way to the top? Maxed them out?"

She glanced at Zhukov before answering. "You are thinking for the combat with the alien in the Arena?

"You said you turned them up further than you intended but it made me fight harder, better. So, when I'm out there in the Orb arena you can just crank me up as high as it goes because I don't need to save anything for the way back."

"It's not that simple. Obviously, hormones have a wide range of effects. Physiological effects, cognitive and behavioral effects. I list those as if they are different things but of course, they are not. Forgetting for a moment the complex feedback effects, if I could saturate your blood with testosterone and enable the uptake of it, flooding your cells with as much testosterone as is possible, it is likely that you would lose the ability to think clearly or even to think at all. You would be unable to fight. Unable to win."

Ram leaned back in his nice big chair. "That's a shame."

"And even if you survived the combat, there would be long-term effects on your body and mind."

"Come on, we can stop pretending I'm ever coming back from this. Even if I did win, what happens to me is irrelevant."

"Agreed," Zhukov said, immediately, taking back control of the meeting. "Milena will take you close to the edge of the maximum your body and mind are capable of achieving in that final battle. It is your driver's job to manage your performance and she will do so. To the best of her ability, at any rate. But there are others here who will help you in their own ways. You will take full advantage of their services and yet we have so little time left to us. Now, I have sent the action plan to your screens, please review this closely. It has been developed with the utmost care and is designed to be the most efficient process possible, taking us from today right up until the Orb arena itself."

"Hold on a second, don't I get a say in this?"

Zhukov chopped a hand in the air to cut Ram off. "This is the plan and if you can control your arrogance for one moment, you will listen to it and you will agree to it and we will have your full cooperation, do you understand? Having consulted with my teams over the last few days, my recommendation is that you see Dr. Fo to schedule in your medical enhancements. He will upgrade every biological component that we can fit under the

Zeta Line. He will give you the standard of augmentation previously reserved for Mael, swapping out your comms and endocrine support systems for the best, most reliable devices ever created. That should immediately result in nanoseconds improved response time. The day after, while you recover from the keyhole surgery, Captain Cassidy will set your physical training goals in consultation with the other drivers and experts. When you are not working on your physical fitness, I want Milena and you to research the Wheeler, come to understand everything about it, how it moves, what it is capable of. I want you to be humanity's greatest expert on the alien. And you will pick up your training with Bediako, practicing the techniques you will need to fight the alien. I have instructed that the Mission Three device, a real life simulacrum of the alien to be brought from storage. Bediako will teach you how to use it."

Ram pursed his lips and blew through them, wondering what it would be like to work with a man who he had humiliated and tried to kill. "How's his recovery coming?"

"He's had worse," Zhukov said.

"Enough to instruct you in IRL combat," Milena said.

"Is he okay with that?"

"He does not have a choice," Zhukov said. "None of us do. The *Victory* is set upon its course, as are all onboard her. We must each of us play our roles to the best of our ability. We can do nothing else."

"Bullshit," Ram said. "Haven't you learned anything from all that's happened? You thought you could control everything that happened on this ship. You had psychological profiles, advanced algorithms and AIs projecting behaviors, you had process charts and backup systems. And despite all that you came a hair's breadth from complete disaster. Shit, if I lose then it will have been a complete disaster. And still, here you are dictating to me every minute of the next three months. Don't you understand that's not the best way? People in real life are more than a few variables. Things change, you can't predict everything just because you have the computing power to do it. That's something that gaming has taught me. No matter how tightly controlled the parameters are, humans and the universe always finds a way of doing something surprising."

Zhukov was flushed red again. He rubbed his mouth. "A fine sentiment." He clearly wanted to argue and yet he hesitated, as if getting himself under control. "And I take your point. What about this plan would you like to change?"

Ram sighed with satisfaction. "I want more time in Avar, for one thing."

CHAPTER TWENTY-SEVEN
MISSION THREE

THE WHEELHUNTER CARTWHEELED toward Bediako, accelerating until the sound of the huge footpads thudded like a continuous drumroll on the floor of the arena.

A young Bediako ran from the alien at a full sprint, parallel to the curving wall of the enormous space. Dressed in a thin, skintight black outfit, his astonishing musculature shone in the ambient light, contracting and expanding like the pistons of some organic machine. He ran like an elite sprinter on the track, back straight, head up and arms and legs pumping with perfect precision.

Yet the Wheeler gained. It flung its legs over and over, the momentum of the heavy footpads swinging through the arc at the top, forward and down into the floor, where they drove off again, one leg pushing after the other in rapid succession. The arms sticking out on both sides of the central hub twirled around, the three-fingered hands at the ends flexed their wicked claws.

Bediako risked a glance over his shoulder as the Wheeler drew close to him. That glance lost him a fraction of a second and the Wheeler surged the final few meters. But the human prey swerved away, toward the wall. The Wheelhunter swerved to compensate, leaning over and using the arms to provide balance. Bediako changed back, dropping a shoulder one way, feinting a turn to the left again but instead charging to the right, his thigh muscles standing out in bunches as he stamped his foot to absorb his enormous momentum before accelerating again.

The Wheelhunter swiped a massive hand at the human, missing his back by a centimeter or two. After shifting again, leaning to the right, it gained on Bediako.

He turned, spinning with remarkable agility for such a huge man and charging at the alien, hoping to catch it by surprise.

The Wheeler lashed out with a long arm, throwing its claws at him like a whip. Bediako had the fastest reflexes the best minds in humanity could engineer into a body, he had a lifetime of combat training and real world experience. He blocked the alien's attack with his arm while charging. But the strength and mass of the creature could not be denied by skill and experience. The force of the blow threw Bediako to the side and the momentum of the alien continued.

Bediako's arm was ripped off at the shoulder in a shower of blood. His war cry turned into a scream of agony and fury.

"And I'll hold it there," Milena said.

Bediako froze, his scream cut off. His face carved in twisted horror like a grotesque statue. The blood droplets and mist from his wound stayed suspended in the air and the final few strands of skin still stretched between the severed arm and the gaping hole in his shoulder, elongated beyond what seemed possible. The Wheeler loomed above, tilted at a wild angle, frozen in motion at an angle that would have caused the alien to fall over if it tried to stay like it in real life.

In the Avar replay, Ram walked closer to the two figures and peered at the wound, frozen in time.

"Brutal," he said, wincing at the sight of it.

Milena thought it important that he observe every tiny detail of every combat replay over the previous three missions, especially the last one. She was in his ear, as usual, urging him to immerse himself in the simulated reality of it all. Over and over again.

"Do you see how the middle claw got stuck between the radius and the ulna, right up in the radioulnar joint? If it wasn't for that chance occurrence, who knows what might have happened. The anterior and posterior claws caused massive tissue damage in their own right, obviously. The anterior claw passed through the triceps and Bediako would have lost the ability to straighten his left arm. The posterior claw sliced through a number of the extensor compartment muscles of the forearm, which would have immediately impacted his ability to make a fist or to grasp with that hand and it also severed the radial artery. Blood loss from that wound alone would have been significant but with the enhanced coagulant function in that body, he could have fought on."

"Right," Ram said, leaning in through the paused blood spray to get a look at the huge alien hand and the relatively short but evilly sharp claws where they hooked into the man's flesh and blood. They were a darker shade of yellow than the mottled skin, almost brown. "But this one caught and the force was enough to tear his arm off. Makes you wonder if they should make our bones weaker and our tendons tougher. Break my bones but hold me together long enough to make a fight of it."

"The connective tissue in your generation of this body form has been significantly enhanced from the Mission Three models, I assure you," Milena said. "Skin, fascia, ligaments, tendons, all of it has been toughened and your bones are denser. Still, the force capable of doing this can't be denied. Your best course of action will be to avoid getting hit at all."

"That joke doesn't get any funnier."

"I agree but it's the truth. Avoid being struck by it at all, for as long as possible."

Ram sighed. "That's what they told this guy."

"What do you think he could have done differently in this moment?"

"I don't know, I'm not sure he could have survived from this point. If he had avoided blocking with his arm, he would have had to lean even further to the side from his turning maneuver. There's no way he could have kept his feet leaning far enough to avoid the trajectory of the claws and once he was down, the Wheeler would have him just as much as it did here. I think as soon as he decided to turn and face the alien at this point, it was only going to go one way."

"So you think he should have kept running?" Milena said.

"Clearly, he couldn't keep it up for much longer. These bodies can't sprint for long. I know that he was lighter than me but look how much he was sweating after just a few seconds, the heat he must have been generating was enormous. What's the air temperature again?"

"The arena is 19.6 degrees Celsius."

"Right, so he had to turn and fight soon but I think he should have done more twisting and turning. Maybe destabilized this thing." Ram couldn't keep the disgust out of his voice. He hated being near even a simulation of it. The lack of eyes, mouth, a head, in general, might have been the worst thing about it. The worst out of a long list of horrible shit.

"Alright so we'll keep trying to find efficient angles for your own fight," Milena said. "But what do you think he should have done after suffering this mortal wound. I'll play it and we can discuss it after. Tell me if you want me to pause or rewind at any point."

Ram danced back just as the scene came back to life. Bediako's shriek of anguish and terrible agony filled his ears, the blood spattered across both man and alien and the Wheeler thrashed its claws, flinging Bediako's arm away, spinning through the air in a grotesque parody of the alien's own locomotion as the two enemies clashed.

Bediako threw himself against the leading two legs of the alien, crashing against it with a fury and speed that rivaled that of the monster he fought. He hit it so hard with his body that the creature rocked with the impact, twisting itself, pivoting on the two feet it had on the floor. Bediako staggered with it, trying desperately to hold on with his one remaining arm. He failed.

The Wheeler moved so quickly, rolling and twisting so that Bediako, surely in agony, slipped on past it, just a little way. Claws whipped out again, raking down the man's back and side tearing two gouges through him from the shoulder blade to the kidney on one side. Blood gushed from the wounds and it was all-but over.

Still, the man, his face twisted beyond all recognition, charged back at the Wheeler, heaving in air through the ragged breath of his chest. Heart and lungs inside, giving it their all. Bediako's strength of will unfazed. Yet it was not enough, could never have been enough, in Ram's opinion.

"Freeze it," Milena said, just as the alien's claws took out Bediako's throat.

"What can I say?" Ram said. "We've been over this so many times. I think the bosses back then messed up when they gave him a brief to prolong the fight as much as possible in order to provide data. That's a crazy thing to do. What hope did he have when he stepped through the plasma screen and into this place, if he was thinking that he was far from the Alpha for one thing and that even his own commanding officers ordering him to deprioritize winning. Madness, surely you can see it."

"Of course," she said. "That's not something you will have to worry about. Winning is the only objective for you. And at least, with Mission Three, they got us this data. We know the top speed, or believe it to be thirty-one kilometers per hour. We got a good portion of the alien DNA from parts of Bediako's remains. We lost this fight but we gained a lot besides."

"Then I don't see how much more I can learn from watching this," Ram said. "I need to run additional simulations to try my own tactics, not watch failure over and over."

"I agree but I do think this is a valuable exercise. More even than you know, perhaps, this will prepare you for the violence you can expect, win or lose. I want you to feel at home inside the arena, so that when you walk out there, you will be used to what it's like and so you won't be distracted by the environment. We'll run our simulations, as many as we can per session but you need to see this also."

"The blood is pretty striking against the dark background," Ram said. "I know you guys said that the lighting in here comes out of the floor and walls and stuff but I don't really get it. The light comes out of the dark floor? That doesn't make sense."

Milena sighed. She had little time for questions that she thought were pointless or that distracted from his specific mission goals. "It's not so strange as you might think. The surface seems to be some strange silicon alloy, presumably, it conducts energy and throws off photons. Whatever the mechanism, it creates this even light of about four hundred lux, which is something like dawn or dusk on Earth. Actually ideal lighting conditions for human visual acuity."

"Right," Ram said, looking round. The ceiling was so far away, for a moment he felt as though he were looking down into a vast crater. He closed his eyes until the disorientation passed. "Do you think it's a coincidence that the light is so good for us?"

"How can it be? Of all the potential lighting conditions you could have on all the planets that could harbor life, from different types of stars and the proximity of the planet, to different atmospheric compositions, possible dust and particulates suspended in the air. That many variables result in a staggering number of possibilities. The chance that it just so happens to be Earth-like?"

"Alright but it's still pretty dark. Why not make it full daylight?"

"The hypothesis is that the environmental conditions in the Orb Arena are an averaging of conditions on Earth and the Wheelhunter home planet. It might explain why the simulated gravity is point-nine g, why the lighting is so dark, why the atmosphere is composed of this mix of gasses and under this specific pressure. If we're correct, then we can make a rough guess at the Wheelhunter's natural environment or at least the planet that they originated from, if they are in fact engineered lifeforms."

"So their homeworld is probably darker than ours." Ram stepped up the horrifically lumpy hub in the center of the alien and ran his hand over the rough skin. "And that explains why they don't have any eyes."

"Perhaps. It's hard to draw definite conclusions but that is consistent with the hypothesis. We also assume that their planet experiences approximately 0.8g. Lighter gravity is assumed to allow lifeforms to evolve to be taller than they might otherwise be, although that's not necessarily the case. And perhaps that helps to explain their notable form of locomotion. Cartwheeling this massive body around on a planet with lower gravity than Earth's might be easier. And it might not be such a dangerous thing if they fall over."

Ram grinned, poking at the skin of the paused Wheeler. "But when they're here on the Orb, they are fighting in higher gravity than they're used to. That gives us an advantage."

Milena hesitated. "In principle, yes. In fact, as you can see, they do seem to perform quite well, no? No doubt they are training in the arena conditions, just as you are."

"Right," Ram said. "The *Victory*'s artificial gravity is 0.9g so that the Subject Alpha plus the boarding party are acclimatized when they get on the Orb."

"The lighting and dark walls in the ludus have been designed to be similar, to ensure a feeling of familiarity or at least reduce the shock of the change in environment between ship and arena. We have a twenty-two point four percent oxygen level in the ludus which is higher than we would prefer and means we have to manage increased risk of oxygen toxicity, however limited that may be. Of course, if we are meeting the Wheelers halfway in terms of atmospheric oxygen in parts per million by volume that means that they are breathing a lower level than they would prefer. Again, though, it doesn't seem to have impacted their performance."

"Maybe if the fight went on long enough?"

He could almost hear Milena shrug. "Speculation."

Ram poked the hub again, pushed on it. It was a tough surface and it barely gave at all. "The briefing notes say it breathes through its skin. Doesn't seem porous."

"It can be semi-rigid and still have microscopic pores, Rama."

"Right, sure."

"One thing we must prepare you for outside of Avar is the smell of the atmosphere inside the Arena."

"It stinks of sulfur, doesn't it?"

"Quite strongly so, yes. As Avar is incapable of simulating the olfactory experience, we will begin to fill the training rooms periodically with sulfur dioxide of ten parts per million."

"Is that why they're yellow? They're from a stinking, volcanic, sulfuric world?"

"It's possible, though the pigmentation could come from anything. Are tigers full of sulfur? Are lions or giraffes? It could be that the Wheelers or the species that made them live on a world with yellow vegetation and yellow skin is an adaptation for camouflage."

"Have you considered that their volcanic world might be constantly spewing out great lava flows like on the Deccan Traps? There might be vast plains of basaltic rock which would be perfect for the rolling around on."

Milena sighed. "Of course they've considered that, Rama.

"Do you think when we face future races on the Orb, we'll have to deal with atmospheres more poisonous than we can deal with without breathing apparatus? What are we going to do about that?"

"It's not something that you'll ever have to worry about."

"Good point." Ram laughed. "Come on, inspire me about what the future holds again." He knew by now that if he made it psychological, he was more likely to get his way with his driver.

"Do you really want to discuss this while a man is frozen in the midst of being torn to pieces?"

Ram leaned in and looked closely at the claw which was

tearing the young Bediako's throat out. The claws were about fifteen centimeters long in total and razor sharp, slicing through skin and soft tissue like a scalpel. Partly serrated along the cutting edge and partly axe-like in cross section where it joined the knuckle. A truly horrific weapon and there were three on each hand.

Ram really wished the Zeta Line would have allowed him his own weapon. Even a combat knife would go some way to evening the odds.

Bediako's body had been ripped to shreds in mere seconds. Every swipe with those evil claws had opened up a new wound deep and wide enough to ruin his combat effectiveness and most of them would have been killing blows on an ordinary man. There was blood everywhere, in the air, on the floor and on both combatants. For once, Ram felt grateful there was no taste or smell in the simulated world.

"No, this doesn't bother me at all," he said to Milena, running his finger along the back of a blood-spattered claw. "It's just Avar. Tell me about the future."

"Fine, well, you know that after Mission Two the Orb told us we would have to fight with weapons and other equipment in the future. It didn't really make sense, we'd just seen our great champion forced to remove his weapons and armor before being slaughtered in moments, why was the Orb telling us that? Did it know how we must have felt? Was it monitoring what we were saying and telling us what it thought we wanted to hear? Or would that have been its message anyway, does the Orb have a pre-set sequence of messages that it sends out to every civilization that it encounters?"

"And?"

"Personally, I think it's the latter. Taking everything that it's told us so far, after every mission breaks orbit, it seems like it gives us a little bit more context each time."

"Why does it wait for us to leave? Is it afraid of us, maybe?"

"Hardly," Milena said. "It allows our boarding parties inside its structure with no hesitation, even when our people are carrying projectile weapons, energy weapons, high explosives and all the rest. Perhaps it waits until we leave to ensure that we are following its instructions. It says hard luck, you lost now come back in thirty years. That's a hard pill to swallow for us, let me tell you. In the transcripts from previous missions you can see how many of the marines and others on the ships and at Earth HQ are keen to board the Orb and try to penetrate deeper inside."

"To what end?" Ram looked around the arena. "There's no one home, right?"

"We really don't know. It seems obvious to you and me that the Orb Builders are not present in the Orb itself. All indications are that the space station is run by automation. Advanced AI, perhaps or just a series of possibly quite simple algorithms. I could imagine it's possible that the Orb Builders are operating it remotely from somewhere else in the galaxy, maybe with the faster than light communications that everyone says is impossible. But some people in UNOP are convinced there's a man behind the curtain. If only we could blast our way through a few corridor walls we could find the control center or the alien queen's throne room and force them to give up the secrets of the universe."

"You're not convinced then," Ram said.

"I just think they would have more important things to do."

"You know what I think? I think they're a long extinct race. They built the Orbs, spread them through the galaxy to impose an order on the constantly emerging, warring civilizations and then they disappeared."

"A popular theory inside UNOP but I don't see why they would have to be extinct."

"They evolved into a higher state of being, becoming pure energy or pure consciousness, maybe. Or they traveled to Andromeda so they had room to expand."

"Room to expand? You spend too much time in Avar, those guesses have no basis in fact or even in basic reason."

"Wow, take it easy. If they're still around, where are they? Why not speak to us directly instead of through this... place?"

"Maybe they're busy. Maybe there's not many of them and the galaxy is a big place. The Orb indicated that there are many levels to our staged conflicts. Right now, we are fighting the Wheelhunter civilization. Us and them must be the lowest of the ranks. Maybe there are dozens or thousands of others at this level, fighting for a way into the Orb network. And then there's a level above that we might reach one day, maybe in a thousand years, maybe never. In that level we have well-established cultures that are in direct contact with each other, trading and learning from each other. That's what the Orb hints at, at least. And also that there is an elite level, perhaps just two or three alien races that run the whole show. Maybe the Orb Builders are one of those? Maybe all three of them designed and established the Galactic Orb Network together?"

Ram sighed. "I wish I could be around to see all that."

Milena smiled inside his head. "Is this not wondrous enough for you, Rama?"

He laughed, looking around the vast chamber and at the paused image of the alien in front of him. "Sure. I just wish I had a weapon so that I could actually slay this demon."

"I'm afraid it's not going to happen. During the Mission Three final selection, the previous subjects were prevented from entering due to large organic structures integrated into their bodies and brains. Dr. Fo's predecessors implanted all manner of pumps and hydraulics and whatnot to enhance performance, increase efficiencies. All quite brutal and mechanical but constructed from human tissue. It seems that additional organs and limbs are unacceptable for the Orb when surgically implanted. How it is able to discern such fine detail, without invasive investigation and in less than one second, we have no idea. Yet it does."

"But I have implants. I have an inner ear speaker, microphone, receiver. I have the hormone regulators and stuff like that."

"Indeed, which is a relief. Clearly, the Orb allows us this much, for these combats with the Wheelhunter, at least. The Mission Three Alpha had a number of enhancements. An artificial eye, a backup heart with a tertiary one intended to activate when the other two had failed, alloy rods molded to his major bones. Our Beta had fewer alterations on her body and in her brain but they were enough to trigger whatever systems the Orb uses. And so on down the subjects they went until they reached Bediako. That gave UNOP the Zeta Line which we replicated in our new designs for the next generation."

"You mean the Artificial Persons," Ram said. "You made the Artificial Persons like that and stuck our heads on their bodies. And you stuck me on one of the older generation's body."

"We had enough of that kind of talk from Noomi. The Artificial Persons were grown to exact standards and then harvested, just as you'd grow and harvest a pumpkin."

"What other augmentations are in this body, exactly?"

"Just the ones you know about and a number of microscopic remote release drug capsules at various places throughout your body. Many capsules will be downstream from your heart and upstream from your head so the blood brain barrier gets flooded as quickly as possible. They are single use only, so we will use them only during the combat itself, if needed."

If needed, Ram thought. As if they wouldn't be needed. "What drugs?"

"Oh, nothing particularly special. Various cognitive enhancers to aid decision making, reaction times and visual acuity. Many varieties of amphetamines, methylphenidate, armodafinil, caffeine, theanine, nicotine, that kind of thing. All small as they can be made while retaining functionality. Our Subject Alpha during Mission Two got through with his inner ear implants, drug release capsules and hormone regulators so we were pretty confident back in Mission Three. We would guess that we are allowed a certain amount of artificial implants as a percentage of biomass, seemingly under one percent. Surely, it's usual for species all over the galaxy to have biologically integrated tech as standard. As always, these are conclusions from suppositions and extrapolation but all we're really saying is that the Orb has given this as the Zeta Line and we will, therefore, have to abide by it."

"Why have a Zeta Line at all, I wonder? Why not just let the most technologically advanced species win? That's a competition, of a kind."

"We assume the Orb attempts to create a balanced combat between the races."

"Balanced?" Ram said, pointing at the scene before him.

"Again, consider the range of possible matches. Perhaps it has different rules for the Wheelhunters, they may have a different Zeta Line to us. They might not be allowed communications implants and so on while we are. It's only logical to conclude so, seeing as how we expect our own Zeta Line will need to change when we face new alien races in the future."

"If the Orb allows all kinds of cool tech in the future, I wish I could be one of the guys who might fight in here then."

Milena made a disapproving sound.

"What?" Ram said. "I'm just demonstrating a keen attitude. That's what you want from me, right?"

"You are fantasizing about a future that you will not possibly see. All you are demonstrating is more resistance to your current reality."

Ram threw up his arms. "I can't win."

"Just focus on what you can actually do," Milena said.

"Alright, how about this?" Ram said. "What if Dr. Fo or someone could make me a spear constructed from rhino horn?"

"Great idea, I'll just get the extinct animal tissue selection box sent up from storage."

"I mean, rhino horn was made from fingernail cells, right? Why can't you make a weapon from my own cells? It's biological, just not physically attached."

"We tried that during the subject selection process at the smokescreen. The subject before Bediako, a remarkable woman named Aelfrith Smith, had bone claws grafted to her hands. Brave of her to do that but she was not allowed. Then Bediako stepped up with a knife made from human bone tissue and the Orb did not allow him through. When he handed it over, the

Orb chimed and then you see the result right here."

Ram shook his head. It was unlikely he would be able to think of something that thousands of genius scientists, engineers and AIs had not come up with before. Milena was right. He should focus on his own task. Getting good enough to have a hope against the alien.

"Fine," he said. "Let's play this out, shall we?"

"Agreed. Stand back a few paces?"

Rama backed away and the scene jerked back into life. The Wheeler tore Bediako's throat out, flinging blood and gore across the arena, right where Ram had just been standing. Bediako's body tumbled with the force of the blow and the alien followed up with a flurry of additional blows that ripped the human into pieces. The monstrous yellow beast stomped Bediako's viscera into the floor.

Bediako's skull was knocked skipping and spinning across the arena leaving a smear of blood behind. His jawbone was gone, his face a skinless red pulp and a few ragged vertebrae trailed from the base.

The alien rolled around, splashing in the guts for a few seconds before it rolled away back the way it came.

Ram looked down at the shining red lump that was Bediako's head with its precious brain inside. It was hard to believe that the quivering tissue, leaking blood and pink-gray matter, held the man's consciousness. Enough of it, anyway, for the UNOP doctors to transplant it into a new Artificial Person and save his life.

"Rama?" Milena said. "Do you want to watch the Mission Three crew come out into the arena and collect the remains? I'm not a medical doctor but I can explain quite a lot about the processes that saved his life. Such as it is."

"No," Ram said, watching the cartwheeling form of the Wheelhunter rolling away, its feet slap-slapping into the distance. "It's irrelevant. All I need to do is avoid the mistakes that Bediako made. Restart the simulation."

CHAPTER TWENTY-EIGHT
MANEUVER

OB STATION ZERO FILLED the screen. An obsidian disk hanging in the darkness of space, reflecting starlight like a black mirror.

"There it is," Zhukov said, pointing at the huge image on the meeting room wall in Ram's quarters.

As if any of the crowd needed the words to be spoken. Already many weeks into the long breaking maneuver, they were finally close enough to the Orb that the forward telescopes could pick out detail on it, resolve it in such definition that it was like looking out of a window.

Zhukov, Milena, Captain Cassidy, Commander Tamura, Dr. Fo and other crewmembers had joined Rama in his quarters so that they could share the special moment.

And it was special.

Ram sat quietly, his body and mind aching with the most intense eleven weeks of training anyone has ever gone through. Only with the most advanced medical and psychological care ever devised had he been able to train so hard, at such an intensity, without suffering a physical or mental breakdown. When he was not training his body, he was training his mind. Even when he slept he was taking in intravenous nutrients and drugs. Having a few moments to simply sit in a chair and watch his crewmates was a remarkable luxury.

Zhukov, a tumbler full to sloshing with vodka, stood beside the wall screen with his chest puffed out. He didn't seem drunk but he had sunk a fair few of them and Ram could hear it in his voice.

"Many of us have spent the better part of our lives in this project and working on this mission particularly. We have together faced an enormous number of challenges, some of them, indeed, existential. Solar flares, stray streaks of gamma rays and hull-damaging random impacts from asteroids and fabled teapots." Some people chuckled but Ram did not get the joke. "After our recent, almost-catastrophic internal attack, many of us had despaired. I know. And yet we pulled together. We worked harder. We worked better and we have each of us contributed to bringing us here today.

"Not least of all we have to thank our Subject Alpha, Rama Seti, for fulfilling his genetic destiny, just in time. If he had not given it his all these past weeks then I'm sure many of us would be feeling despair instead of the hope that we each of us now carry. In just two more days, Commander Tamura will perform the final maneuvers to put us into orbit around this magnificent artificial member of our solar system, right here. This thing that is an object designed and built by an alien civilization. An alien civilization that traveled to our home system by an unknown means of transportation but one so advanced that our best physicists struggle to even understand how it can be possible.

"But make no mistake. Orb Station Zero is humanity's gateway into a future so profound that we can scarcely even imagine it. And that future is within our grasp. Because of you. Because of all of you, we will make that future a reality. So raise your glass. Or your cup of coffee or pop your capsule. And let us all drink to each other. We made it this far and here's to being the first crew that will take humanity far into the future. Here's to each of you and every member of your teams. Here's to the *Victory*."

They cheered and some of the crew smiled but many were grim as they sipped their drinks. Something was troubling Ram but he couldn't quite place it. Maybe it was the crew's attitude that he found irritating.

Despite Zhukov's words, Ram knew the crew felt they were still heading for defeat. They did not believe in Ram. He was not the hero that they had been expecting and they were sad that all their hard work, years and decades of it, the commitment of their lives, was being entrusted to him, a nobody. A replacement sacrificial lamb who had been prepared for the slaughter only to find himself the last chance of humanity. And who was he? An Avar player with no combat experience before he was taken, had his body removed and his head shoved in storage for years before being chosen from a stack of other heads, almost at random. It was no wonder they had doubts. All that planning and it was dumb luck that Ram ended up the last subject standing.

What had Zhukov said in his speech, something about Ram's genetic destiny? What the hell did that mean? For some reason, he thought of Sifa's dead body, lying in a pool of blood under the tables in the barracks, the wet stink of metallic blood and the acrid propellant filling the air.

The crew filed out, quietly, back to their stations, some saying goodbye to him and smiling. Others ignored him. Director Zhukov stayed by the screen to speak quietly and informally to a couple of low-ranking marines. Ram noted that they were carrying sidearms only. What did genetic destiny mean? Just doing his best?

"There's one thing I haven't been able to shake this whole time, a question I keep asking myself," Ram said to Milena as they stood in the empty room watching the image of the Orb

Station on the big screen behind Zhukov. "Why me? Out of everyone on Earth and everywhere else in the system, why am I the one who is representing the human race?"

"You know why," Milena said. "A number of events beyond your control brought you here, step by step. Ultimately, it was Alina's actions that brought you the final way."

"She only did what she did because you people screwed it up," Ram said, harshly. "But I meant that first step. Why I was even selected into the Project in the first place."

"We told you. The Project algorithms picked you up in Avar. You tripped a number of automated systems that brought you to our attention and the more we studied you the more we saw your potential and we brought you onto the *Victory* right before we broke orbit. There was no time to recruit you properly." She was acting strangely. He was sure he knew her well enough to know she was uncomfortable when she was being evasive. He'd seen it enough times.

Ram nodded, looking at his hands. "It always seemed far-fetched but reasonable enough, I suppose and it was phrased just right, as if it was my own skills that did it. It played on my own narcissism, my ego. I was such a great Avar gamer that the United Nations thought I could be humanity's champion. I mean, how could that not make me feel good about myself? I bought it, I believed it."

Milena bit her lip. "And you don't anymore?"

His genetic destiny.

Ram was realizing it as he spoke the words aloud. "I remember when Noomi's bomb destroyed the Artificial Persons and you or Dr. Fo said that my AP and Sifa's AP were the only ones that made it."

"That's true, they did."

"And then when we met with Alina and Noomi right before they went crazy, you showed me the recordings of the APs. You guys said we carried them onboard to provide replacement body parts for the subjects. But only for the ones with a genetic match. So, that means the APs shared a genome with the subjects."

"That's right," Milena said. She swallowed, her eyes flicked to Zhukov.

"You also said, I'm certain, that the APs were grown in womb tanks before the *Victory* left Earth. And that they took a year in the tank to grow as much as would a normal ten-year-old human. I remember now. You said the words genetic destiny before, months ago, when you told me about the APs. I can't believe I never thought this through until now. If you didn't know that I was coming on board until the last minute, how come there was a genetically identical AP waiting for me? No, holy shit, no, there must have been *two* of them. One that I'm wearing now, the one you culled for me when you woke me up. And a second one that survived Noomi's blast. But how can that be possible? How can my genome match theirs?"

Milena hesitated for a long moment. "You had better talk to Director Zhukov about this."

"Talk to him?" Ram said, his voice shaking.

He strode over to Zhukov, knocking support crew aside. The Director turned just as Ram reached down and pushed the man against the wall, knocking his tumbler of vodka against the screen where it smashed into pieces. Zhukov's eyes glazed with the impact. The image of Orb Station Zero dripped with alcohol.

"Subject Alpha," the closest Marine shouted, "Release the Director immediately or we will use force."

Both Marines had their pistols aimed at Ram's head and they shouted at him.

"Put him down. Step away, now. Do it now, step back."

"No," Ram shouted over his shoulder, his voice coming out in a roar that shook the room. "You won't hurt me, you need me. Tell them to calm down."

Zhukov raised a shaking arm and waved a hand downward at the marines. Both slowly lowered their sidearms. Still, they stood ready.

Ram stuck his nose right down into Zhukov's face. "You and Zuma told me when you woke me up that you have a policy of full and complete honesty. It got obvious pretty quickly that was all a lie. Even still, you do nothing but conceal and deceive. Even now, when we are at the end of the mission you're still lying to me. It's time to talk, Zhukov. All I want to know is what is so special about me? Why am I here, really? I need to know."

Zhukov clawed at his neck and Ram released him a little. The Marines hovered behind, muttering reports into their mics. No doubt a whole squad was on their way as backup. Ram expected to have his paralysis switched on at any moment.

Instead, the Director decided to talk. "Yes. You are right. You are special, in a way. You always were."

Ram eased off but kept one hand on Zhukov's shoulder. The Marines stood tensely at the edges of Ram's peripheral vision.

"I understand that you are feeling emotional," Zhukov said, glancing at Milena.

Ram grabbed Zhukov and shook him once, hard.

"Stop that," Ram said. "Milena, if you or anyone else tries to dial down my testosterone or switch me off or anything like that then the next time I am conscious I will pull a fucking Alina on the Director here, right? I'll tear this ship apart."

He was banking on them needing him. He hoped the gamble would pay off.

"I understand," Milena said, though Ram wasn't sure if he trusted her.

"Now," Ram said, leaning in close to Zhukov's furious eyes. "Talk."

Zhukov's eyes shone. He was not a man used to being threatened. Ram wondered if he had, in fact, pushed his luck a little too far and then Zhukov's eyes took on the glazed expression of someone using internal communications systems. Was he giving the Marines an order? Would Ram find himself paralyzed after all? Would he ever be rendered conscious again?

"I will do better that explain things to you," Zhukov said after a moment, pushing Ram's hands away and straightening his own clothes. "I will show you."

CHAPTER TWENTY-NINE
REPLACEMENTS

HE WAS LED - OR ESCORTED - TO a part of the ship he had not been in before. Six Marines accompanied him, Zhukov and Milena as they went. The corridors were empty, the route cleared of crew. Ram experienced a thrill at his own power and influence that these men were afraid of him. That he was influential enough to affect the operation of a priceless, vast spaceship just by threatening violence or noncompliance.

Still, he was afraid of what he might find out about himself.

The group stopped by a doorway into the next ring section

and Zhukov turned to look up at Ram.

"You should prepare yourself for an emotional shock," he said. "One that will have an impact on your sense of identity."

"Just get on with it," Ram said, attempting to radiate confidence.

Zhukov set his mouth and nodded to the Marine next to him. The door hissed apart and Ram ducked through, following two Marines and Zhukov through a short connecting passage and into a room he recognized. It was like a day care center or a mental health ward in a hospital. All tables everywhere with toys and coloring pencils on them.

One was a black woman sitting on a sofa being read to by a normal sized crew member. The 7-foot woman looked a lot like Sifa. It was not her, because she had the slack-jawed, blank expression of someone severely lacking in mental faculties and her head was in proportion to her body. Intellectually, he knew it was not Sifa, nor had it ever been her body and yet it was deeply disturbing seeing someone who had been full of life and passion now being nothing more than a shell.

The second giant in the room had his back turned so Ram approached the table. The Marines held back but they watched him closely. Zhukov and Milena stood behind and either side of him at a respectful distance.

The AP was receiving instruction from an older support worker on fitting colored, shaped blocks through a box with shaped holes in it.

Ram looked down on a face that was remarkably similar to his own. The man's skin was paler, his short hair a lighter shade of brown than Ram's own near-black stubble. His head was huge and in proportion to the body but otherwise it was a familiar face. The man struggling with the puzzle game looked up at Ram for a moment with a distinct lack of interest before looking down again. He had shown no recognition. It was like looking into the eyes of a baby.

"Is he a clone of me?" Ram asked Zhukov, still looking down at the figure struggling to fit a square block into an octagonal hole.

"You are both clones," Zhukov said. "Or rather, you are genetically very similar. As close as identical twins gestated in two different wombs. There are a number of differences with regards to gene expression."

Ram wondered how many more looking glasses he would have to step through. "But how is this possible? I have a mother and a father."

"You do. And yet they are not genetically related to you."

"I have seen the video of myself being born and it was my mother I came out of, not a tank."

"That is correct."

Ram looked down at Zhukov then. "Did they know? Did you put a fertilized, cloned egg in my mom?"

Zhukov's shoulders were hunched. He nodded once, sharply. "As I recall, your parents were granted a license for a single child but after trying for some time they discovered that both of them were infertile. UNOP has for decades had standing arrangements with thousands of clinics all over the world. Your parents were offered an egg that your mother would bear. The agreement was that they would be free to raise that child to adulthood as their own with no interference from anyone else."

"They told me they had fertility treatment but they always said their genetic sequences were combined in a donated egg. Why didn't they just do that?"

"I'm afraid I do not know the details of your particular case, just what is on file. I must say, that in most cases a large lump sum was offered to encourage the parents to make the right decision."

"They were bribed." Ram couldn't believe it. It seemed so mercenary. He remembered that his parents had moved to Delhi around the time of his birth and then his father had been able to get his engineering job building the new airport.

"I don't know their reasoning, I am afraid, only that your mother was impregnated with you. Despite being an abnormally large baby, you both survived the labor and then your parents were free to raise you however they saw fit."

Ram did not know what to say.

He pulled out a chair at the table - a table and chair made to fit his huge body - and sat. The support worker smiled a greeting across the table. His newly discovered identical brother carried on jamming a red trapezoid against a square hole. Ram picked up a yellow tube shape and held it out to the clone. It took a long while for the clone to notice it. When he did, he swiped it from Ram's hand and gave him a quick, lopsided grin. The clone jammed it against the square slot, grunting in frustration.

"How long has he been learning this?" Ram asked the support worker.

She looked at Ram over the box. "Oh, they can't learn," she said. "Not in any meaningful sense. We are very careful to stop any mental development beyond a certain level. Manipulating objects like this is simply a way to maintain the fine motor control that a subject would require should the body be needed."

A subject.

Ram laid a palm across his eyes for a moment. The body he now occupied had belonged to a clone just like the one sitting beside him and that clone had been euthanized, had his head and central nervous system removed, to make way for Ram's own to be transplanted. It was hard to not feel bad for the guy, mindless automaton or not.

His years of alienation with his parents suddenly seemed to make sense. The arguments and conflict must have come from them, not from him as they had always asserted. It suddenly made sense why he was so much taller than anyone in his mother's or father's families.

"That's why you knew all about me," Ram said. "Why you were recording me, following me in Avar. Not because of my achievements."

"Actually," Zhukov said, standing behind and to the side with his hands clasped together. "It was both. Your genome was developed decades ago, along with many others that had the right mix of traits for the project. And we could create these incredible bodies in ectogenesis pods with no serious problems. But you cannot raise a person in a laboratory and expect them to become a hero. Only the real world has enough randomization, enough variables and challenges to create a truly rounded individual with what the old American astronauts called the Right Stuff. And so we sent you out into the world, dozens of each clone type, and waited to see what you would become."

"There are dozens of clones of me?"

"Your genome was one of the earliest and best performing but it was gradually supplanted by others as our engineers perfected the processes involved. Still, yes, there are dozens of your brothers out there. Almost all of them on Earth, some here and there elsewhere. And we brought fifteen of you onboard this ship when we left home. Unfortunately, Noomi destroyed your brothers with her explosive device, the damned fool."

"And this one," Ram said. "And the other one you grafted me on to. They've got the same genetic code, only they're eight and a half feet tall."

"Precisely. The differences being that certain of the gene sequences were switched on, others switched off and other processes were done to them from birth through to adulthood in order to grow them into these vast specimens we have here. But they are not human. As you can see, they are not self-aware at all. They have no consciousness. They were raised simply to be host bodies for you, the fully rounded humans with your great life experience."

Ram handed the AP a red pentagonal shape. It took it and eagerly tapped it on the box, twisting and turning it. "And there are dozens of clones, just like me? What are they like? What jobs do they have? Where do they live?"

"They are not just like you, no. I don't believe there are many left on Earth, if any, and we brought all the potentials we could locate onto this mission because we had the spare bodies of this model. But environmental factors played a huge part in the individual variation. You, Rama, achieved much with your time. Your parents had the right socioeconomic background and geographical location to allow you a number of options. We hope that our potential subjects will achieve not only great things with their lives but great things that will be relevant to the project. In your case, as with the others, we selected for Mission Four, you had the Right Stuff to be brought along as one of our backup models."

"We weren't good enough for the final round?"

Zhukov jerked his head in a nod. "As you know, your model is actually rather old now when compared to the others. Thirty years ago, you would have been in the top ten, certainly. Top three, perhaps. But now? You saw the report that Diego obtained. We brought you into the ludus mainly to be sacrificed to Mael's insanity. And yet here you are. Our Subject Alpha. Bearer of our hopes and our dreams."

Ram looked at the other Artificial Person in the room. "Were all the subjects also clones? Did they know?"

"We think Alina knew. None of them had official disclosure but word gets around, who knows for sure?" The Director tilted his head while he gazed at the Artificial Person. "UNOP needed huge bodies to fight the Wheelhunters. They started the program decades ago, growing fighters instead of recruiting them. But tank-grown warriors never had the real world experience needed. You have to have experienced traumas growing up that shape you into an adult with the drive and ambition to give this Project your all. Only the real world provides that. We created controlled environments and ended up with people who had no depth of character. We tried downloading minds into these bodies but there is so much loss of fidelity. When the information is mapped onto a new brain we see errors and losses creep in. Stands to reason, really. Everyone has an opinion about why but none of them really knows the reason that the data is lost. They have tried with synthetic brains and with Artificial Person brains but the personality that comes back is not quite right. I mean, think about it. There are 620 trillion synapses in a human brain. 90 billion neurons and over a trillion glia. Processing this volume of data strains our most powerful computational and storage systems so it's no wonder we see memory loss and personality changes after overlaying the data back into biological brains. We can allow a certain amount when we fill in gaps, as we did with Bediako after Mission Three and like we did with you when you were first revived and then again a few weeks ago. But an entire mind leaves us with a person without any verve. Transplanting the nervous system of clones that became fighters."

Like we did with you...

Ram shook his head in disbelief. "What's that? You downloaded parts of my mind, too? What other revelations are you going to spring on me?"

"That's the very last one, I promise this. After Alina's incident, you received a wound to the brain. Dr. Fo replaced the damaged cells and mapped your lost synaptic pathways onto it."

Milena spoke up from behind his shoulder. "And when you were first woken."

"Indeed," Zhukov said. "It was discovered that almost three years in a minimal-temperature coma state resulted in some mental degradation. Dr. Fo overlaid your brain with the data gathered from a scan before you were recruited."

"I don't remember being scanned."

"A side effect of the process is that you do not remember the process. Your memory is wiped by the scans before they can be stored long term."

"How many scans have I had?"

"Oh, I do not know this. Perhaps four since you were woken."

Ram rubbed his face and sighed. He almost laughed as he got to his feet. His cloned, Artificial Person brother paid him no attention. "Why even hide this from me?"

Zhukov half-turned to Milena. She glared at him but answered Ram calmly. "They felt that since your main problem is self-confidence, revealing your cloned nature would have adverse effects on your performance."

"You didn't think that, did you, Milena?" Ram said.

"I think I know you better than that." She shrugged. "I was overruled."

Zhukov looked confused. "Are you not feeling a loss of identity in this moment? You have had a lot to process and no doubt you will need time to come to terms with this. But you should remember that our genetic potential and even our own personal experiences are not necessarily the sum of who we are. If you so choose, your actions and decisions in the moment can be the way you define yourself in the future."

"You never met my parents," Ram said, looking down at his idiot clone, fumbling around with a green cube. "My dad is a violent asshole and my mom is a coward. Remembering my childhood, you know, this makes a lot of sense. I actually used to hope that I was adopted. Truthfully, I think this whole clone thing is pretty cool."

"Cool?"

"Wait, did you tell my mom and dad to make me take up wrestling?"

"Part of the UNOP agreement was that the children would be encouraged to take up combat sports and sport in general.

Not mandatory but I think they would receive a range of financial bonuses depending on the engagement.

"I can't believe this. My dad beating me for years, trying to force me to take up wrestling and go to cricket. I thought he hated me but he was just trying to earn himself some money." Ram laughed, bitter but relieved. His childhood suddenly made more sense.

Milena smiled along with him. "I'm glad we could provide you with closure."

Zhukov seemed confused.

"This is like the last piece of the puzzle for me," Ram explained. "I always knew something was up, that there was something no one was telling me. My parents were hiding all this. Then you guys, no matter how much I learned there was always the feeling that there was something else. I told myself I was being paranoid or that it didn't matter but it was always there. And now it isn't. You've told me everything and who I am makes sense. My life, since before I was born, was on rails. Some of those rails led to me living in Avar, in my apartment and dying young and fat and lonely. Another rail led me here and I might have been a victim of Mael's or Alina's. I might have been Subject Omega and made it through until after the Subject Alpha fought, maybe heading back to Earth until the joints and organs in this ridiculous body started to fail. How many years can these bodies take all these growth hormones and training, three? Ten at the most? Anyway, this is the rail that I found myself on. This was always somewhere I might have ended up, back when my genetic code was stitched together forty years ago. I know that now. I know who I am. Knowing the constraints of my life has freed me. I can focus now, a hundred percent."

Zhukov looked at him warily, as if suspecting he was being lied to or that Ram was being sarcastic. Then he jerked his head in a brisk nod. "I am impressed with your attitude. Now you know where you came from, yes indeed. The full story, nothing held back. Good, it is over. Now, we are only days away from the final battle and there is much to be done."

Ram pursed his lips. "The mind scans stuff, though, I don't like the idea of losing my memories to a loss of fidelity. And, I have to know, are you sure you're not adding in a little extra stuff here and there? Or taking things away on purpose? I don't quite feel like myself all the time."

The Director wrinkled his nose. "No. We do not know how to do that. One day, we will and then we will do so. But no, we only use it to fill in the gaps, to make you back into who you are, not take you away from it."

Ram drummed his fingers on the table a few times. "Alright, I believe you, Zhukov. Sounds like it helped me out and I'll be dead in a few days anyway, right? So what does it matter if I've got a few extra glitches?"

Zhukov stood up straight as an iron rod. "We believe in you completely," he said, with undisguised impatience. "I wish that you would do also. Now, can we continue with your training?"

Ram clapped a hand on his clone brother's shoulder. "We can finish it."

PART FIVE
CONQUEST

CHAPTER THIRTY
ORBIT

THE *UNOPS VICTORY* ACHIEVED final position in orbit around Orb Station Zero with less than 36 hours remaining before the Orb's deadline.

All the crew had to do now was wait for the Wheelhunter ship to appear through the Orb-generated wormhole. The meeting room in Ram's quarters had once again become the de facto location for the department heads to witness the momentous appearance as well as agree the final plans for Ram's boarding the Orb. Zhukov, Dr. Fo, Bediako, Cassidy, Milena and a handful of key personnel.

Ram needed the meeting so that he would feel prepared to fight a giant alien to the death the next day. He knew that he had a limited number of hours of life left to live. 35 hours and 24 minutes, roughly, until Zero Hour so he was keen to get the meeting finished. And yet it had not really begun. The officers could not relax until the Wheeler vessel popped through the wormhole into the Sol System. On the other hand, no one knew precisely when the alien ship would appear and so they sat staring at a screen showing an empty region of space.

"How do you know it will come from the spot where the telescope probes are pointing?" Ram said, watching the screen while he ate. He still had five thousand more calories to get through before the end of the day and his pile of brown rice and kidney beans was unusually unappealing. Especially as it was likely to be the last proper meal he ever ate.

Some last supper.

"The alien vessel always appears in the same area of space, relative to the position of the Orb and the Sun," Zhukov said without turning away from the screen. "Five thousand kilometers on the dark side and that's where we have the probes pointing. One in orbit, another on a flyby of the wormhole area." He was holding a glass of the Stolichnaya vodka he had been saving for this moment. Marine Captain Cassidy had declined a glass as his Marines were on high alert. Bediako, grim and lurking at the back of the room, had sneered at the offer. Milena threw a few down her neck right away. Ram was not allowed any.

"How big is the wormhole?" Ram asked, just to be speaking. No one else was talking much and the silence was putting him off his food.

"We do not know," Zhukov answered. "One of the Mission Four experiments will be to measure the size and shape of it. UNOP scientists back on Earth developed it but too late to go on Mission Three. We have a mission specialist who will analyze the electromagnetic distortions and capture the dimensions, almost immediately."

Ram nodded, chewing his rice. "What do you think would happen if the *Victory* tried to fly through the wormhole from this end?"

"Don't be ridiculous," Zhukov said. Bediako snorted from the corner.

"Mission Three sent a probe into the area when it was in orbit," Milena said. "The wormhole wasn't there, we believe that the Orb creates the wormhole for the Wheeler ship each time it comes and goes. Otherwise, all we can detect is the particular environment that exists everywhere within the Orb's powerful magnetic field."

"Just a thought," Ram said, shrugging. He wondered if it was worth trolling them any further. "Do you guys think it'll be the same design of ship this time? If they've kept the exact same design ship every year for the last hundred and twenty years, what do you think that says about their technological development? Are they so advanced that they don't need to upgrade, their ship design is perfected? Or are they just really slow to make adaptations? I know you guys enjoy hiding all this stuff from me but our ships have definitely gotten bigger, way bigger, with every mission. Don't they want to be in an arms race with us? Are we so far behind them technologically?"

Zhukov tutted.

Milena sat in a chair, leaning forward with her forearms on her knees. She looked like she didn't want to even blink in case she missed what they were all waiting for.

Bediako lurked at the back of the room, a massive, brooding presence that Ram felt confident enough to ignore. He knew that he was better than Bediako, stronger. He was not afraid of the man anymore. But he did appreciate him as a trainer and Ram respected his advice.

Dr. Fo sat at a small table in the corner, tapping furiously on a screen and speaking rapidly but quietly to his team back in the medical ring. They were running tests continuously on Ram's body and mind, tweaking everything toward optimal performance.

Captain Cassidy of the UNOP Marine Corps stood at ease, arms behind his back near to the wall and beside the door, as if he was ready to run and join his company, should any shit go down. He had a slab-like face with a nose that looked like it had been broken and smashed flat a dozen times. A faint lattice of scar tissue, like claw marks or burns, covered the right side of his weather-beaten face and neck. He was a scary looking guy.

"We ain't so far behind," Cassidy said. "We're packing some serious—"

"Quiet!" Zhukov snapped, spinning around so fast that he spilled his drink, glaring at Cassidy.

Captain Cassidy cut off what he was saying but Ram thought it was from surprise rather than respect, raising his eyebrows. It was like watching a mastiff growling up at a tiger.

Behind Zhukov, the screen flashed and whited out as the cameras were hit with a soup of particles and radiation that washed it out. When the whiteout cleared, the alien ship was there in the blackness of space, filling the screen. Ram froze, spoon halfway to his mouth.

It was the same design of ship recorded by the other missions. The alien vessel was in many ways remarkably similar to a human one. It was not bulky like the *Victory*, with a diameter almost equal to the length but it was long, wide and with a low profile. Engines at the rear in two clusters, he knew they would be glowing with a pale blue exhaust. It did not spin, as their own ship did and the surface was pale and bright, shining with reflected light from the distant Sun and stars.

"Why's it so shiny?" Ram asked.

"Clearly, they are not interested in stealth," Zhukov said, angry that he had missed the moment. "It must be a function required in the operation of the craft."

"It's combat shielding," Bediako said. "Protection against lasers and the like."

"Ablative armor," the Captain said, nodding his savaged block of a head. "Polishing increases efficiency. Precisely like a reentry heatshield."

"We have physical shielding on the outside and inside of the *Victory*," Dr. Fo muttered without even out looking up from his screen. "The main function of which is to protect the crew from solar and cosmic radiation. No doubt the reflective outer layer is a substance which performs such a function for the Wheelhunter species."

"Perhaps they just like the way it looks," Milena said, winking at Ram.

"Yeah, like the Orb," Ram said. "Maybe that's the unifying aesthetic valued by every civilization in the galaxy. Everyone loves shiny things."

Zhukov grunted, conveying contempt. "That vessel contains our enemies. One of the aliens on that ship will be the creature that you, Rama Seti, will fight to the death in a few hours. Need I remind you that the lifeforms onboard that ship are also prepared to invade and colonize our entire system, should we lose."

"I hadn't forgotten," Ram said, putting down his spoon and pushing his plate away. Training every day, all day, with violence in mind and body, made it difficult to resist throwing his plate at Zhukov's head or jumping over the table to punch him in the face. He took a deep breath, getting his anger under control because he didn't want to kill him.

"Keep eating," Dr. Fo said.

"I'm not hungry."

"That is irrelevant, you must—"

"I'll finish it later. You all need to get on with this meeting or get the fuck out of my quarters. I have real preparations to get on with." He glanced at the Wheelhunter ship up on the screen.

The others bristled, to one extent or another, but they settled down at the meeting table without objecting.

"It has already begun," Zhukov said. "Perhaps you can advise us of the security situation, Captain?"

"We are at our fullest level of alertness. Our weapons are charged and armed, from personal defense weapons for all relevant crew members trained in their operation, to our elite marines with the most advanced and deadly weapons yet developed by humanity. And of course, our ship to ship weapon systems are fully powered and armed and ready to destroy anything that makes a move to attack us."

"Wonderful," Zhukov said. "Thank you very much, Captain. It is a relief to know that you are all here ready to fight and die to protect this ship. Now—"

"Wait a sec," Ram said, looking around him, confused. "What was that? That was a security briefing? What's going on?"

Zhukov's face reddened and Bediako smiled to himself. Dr. Fo looked down, as if embarrassed. The Captain stared straight ahead as if he was a statue.

"What am I missing, here?" Ram said.

"It does not concern you," Zhukov said. "We may move on."

"What is this?" Ram asked. "It's like you're programmed NPCs in Avar."

Milena stared at Zhukov with a look loaded with meaning. After a moment he sighed and nodded at her.

"We're sorry, Ram," she said. "I suppose there's no harm in explaining. You see, we are unsure of the Wheelhunter capabilities, as a species. Bear in mind that this is a completely alien animal, something with a biology that we barely understand, that could be capable of abilities that we cannot conceive of, or at least that no human or AI has hypothesized. Having said that, an early UNOP risk assessment highlighted a low probability, critical risk that the Wheeler is able to read your memories in some way. We don't know how it might work, biologically, and some of us don't believe it can be done but perhaps it can remotely scan your brain, biologically or take a sample from your body."

"Like, if it takes a chunk of my brain back home with it at the end of the fight?"

"The concept is most unlikely," Dr. Fo said. "But not biologically impossible."

"And if the Wheeler was able to read your mind, what would it know about *Victory*?" Captain Cassidy said. "And what would it know about Earth?"

Ram sighed and leaned back in his chair. "That's why you hide stuff from me. That's why you never tell me how many

Marines are on board. That's why the ship's design and systems are all redacted on the network. That's why you won't tell me what Earth's preparations for the invasion are. You think I'm a fucking security risk."

Milena spread her hands. "Like I said, a very low probability but a critical level of impact."

"I understand."

The Captain spoke up. "We don't know how it will work if the Sol System is awarded to the Wheelers. Imagine if the Orb grants permission for the alien vessel to open fire upon the *Victory* immediately upon your loss of the fight. We would be in for a fight for our lives."

"I said I understand."

"We have to prepare for every eventuality," Milena said. "It does not reflect our beliefs about your chances for success."

"Sure," Ram said. "So, what does my final medical say, Doc?"

"That Rama Seti is a miracle of modern science improving on nature," Dr. Fo said, clapping his hands together once. "Bearing in mind that he is not designed for longevity, I could not be happier with his current health and strength. What would have taken days to recover from, even in someone as fit and augmented as the Captain here, is fully healed in a matter of hours for our dear Rama. His mind and knowledge and experience are dreadfully valuable now and we have a final upload to perform first thing in the morning. One day, when the methods are perfected, we can bring him back in a new body or so I hope. What is more, we have made remarkable advances during this mission and I cannot wait to apply these methods to future subjects when we get home. Assuming we need future subjects, that is. Perhaps I will be designing drone soldiers to fight waves of Wheeler invaders. Sorry, Rama, I don't mean that."

"You are years away from getting back to Earth, Doctor," Zhukov said, irritated. "Just be sure to submit all your data in time for it to be encrypted for our final communications with Project HQ."

"Final?" Ram said.

"Another precaution, not a prediction," Zhukov said. "We'll send a last communication back to Earth before the boarding team departs for the Orb Station. We'll send petabytes of data protected by unbreakable encryption. There will be all our final reports, our medical data, final fight data, science experiment results on the Wheeler vessel, Avar records, the last personal logs, every second of our recorded video and audio from every camera and microphone on the ship, all the drone swarm images and data recorded since the last upload. That way, none of the knowledge and experience of this mission can be lost, should the Wheelers attack immediately."

Ram hadn't considered that his loss in the arena might mean the immediate destruction of the *Victory*. Not something he wanted on his mind. It felt more real than the almost abstract idea of the Sol System being invaded.

"Bediako," Zhukov said, indicating the huge instructor. "What is Rama's combat and training status?"

"He has come a long way in the last few weeks. While I fundamentally disagree with your and Dr. Fo's policy of building his mass at the expense of agility and flexibility, his reaction time has continued to improve at a remarkable rate, shaving off nanoseconds every day. The outcomes of his sessions within Avar and with the IRL combat drone continue to improve, even as the parameters of the simulations are increased. I would never have expected him to reach this level by this point."

He can't even bring himself to say he thinks I have a chance.

Zhukov smiled, nodding patronizingly at Ram, as if he was proud and pleased. "Thank you, that more than anything, gives me great hope. And Milena? What is Subject Alpha's mental state?"

"It could not be better," Milena said, even though she knew it was not true. "Most people would be unable to stand the emotional stress and yet Ram is coping well. As everyone else says, his performance continues to improve."

Zhukov was about to carry on but Rama could not take it anymore.

"I need to say something," Ram said.

"Of course," Zhukov said, a benevolent smile on his face. The Wheelhunter ship filled the screen on the wall behind him.

Ram cleared his throat. "It's obvious that you held this little update meeting for my benefit. You're all trying to be positive so that I keep my spirits up. And that's great, I appreciate it. But there's no need. We all know that for all my improvements, I'm not as fast as the Wheelhunter is. I'm not as strong. I'm not as big. I still have no way to hurt it other than to try snapping its limbs one by one at the joints. And I'm not being negative about myself as an individual, I've seen the stats and I doubt Mael or Alina would have been able to achieve the required speeds and techniques either. I actually feel pretty great about myself. I was designed for this, genetically. I know that I am possibly the strongest, most physically powerful human in the Sol System, maybe more than anyone who ever lived, crazy as that sounds. I know what's at stake here. I'll give it my all. I don't doubt myself. But I'm certain, just as you all are, that when I go up against the alien that's in that ship, I'm going to die."

No one spoke for a while. Ram felt tired.

"Well," Captain Cassidy said. "Just make sure to kill that fucker before you do, alright?"

Ram laughed. "Alright." He yawned.

"You need to rest," Milena said. "Everybody out," she ordered and her boss and colleagues obeyed her, wishing him a good night's sleep as they went. After a while, it was just him and Milena, alone, in the meeting room.

Ram nodded at the live image on the wall, the enormous Wheelhunter vessel, thousands of kilometers away but closing on the Orb Station Zero with every second. "It's funny to think that this will be my last ever chance to sleep. In the morning, I'll take my last ever shit. At least I've had my last ever bowl of rice and beans."

Milena looked at him for a long moment. She carefully folded her screen away. "You must focus on positive thoughts, Rama. And you need sleep, eight hours at least, ideally twelve. I have to go."

"These aren't negative thoughts, Milena," Ram said, standing and moving over to her slowly. "Just observations. It's a strange thing to know your time is up. Countless millions of people must have felt like this. Guys before battle, you know, when they knew they were walking straight into machine guns the next day. Or people going in for surgery that they know is hopeless. So for me, in the morning I have the final medical, the final briefing and then we board the shuttle. This might be the last time I'll ever be alone with anyone. I don't want you to go."

Milena smiled up at him, placing a hand on his stomach. "You need sleep more than you need physical intimacy."

"Hey, come on. You're only saying that because you've actually experienced physical intimacy before."

Milena sighed. "You had intercourse with Alina multiple times and with Sifa also. I was there, in a way, helping you enjoy those moments on an emotional level."

"You turned up my oxytocin but that doesn't make it real. With them, it wasn't about intimacy. Even with Sifa. You know, the subjects all believed that the barracks had no cameras in it but it did, didn't it. You saw everything I said and did in there."

"Of course."

Ram sighed. "You know everything about me. You know my history, you've seen me at my worst and you know what I'm feeling and you know what decisions I'll make even before I make them. You know me better than anyone. Better than anyone else in my whole life. But I never know exactly what you're thinking. I don't know what you really think of me. Forgetting all this, all the project, the mission, all that bullshit."

"I do know you. Yes, better than anyone ever has. Better even than you know yourself, and that is not hyperbole, that is a fact. And I always told you that this would not be an equal relationship. But, Ram, you do know me. We've spent hundreds of hours together. Do you really think all our conversations could be scripted? How could I maintain an act for so long? What about when we make each other laugh, does that feel real to you?"

"Sure. Yes." Ram said it and he thought that he probably meant it.

She unfolded her screen again and tapped away at it.

"What are you doing?"

"Turning off the cameras and microphones in your bedroom. Come on, we'll have to be quick. Tomorrow, you fight."

Ram followed her out of the meeting room, glancing one last time at the Wheelhunter ship, burning into orbit around the Orb.

CHAPTER THIRTY-ONE
BOARDING

COME.

The Orb beamed the boarding instruction at the *Victory*. They were prepared, with the shuttle inside the shuttle bay fueled, crewed and raring to go.

"Boarding Team shuttle ready to depart," Captain Cassidy said, from his seat inside the shuttle crew compartment. As the officer responsible for crew and mission security, the Marine Captain was in overall command of the boarding mission. The reply from the pilot was sent only to him but the shuttle immediately began to shake as the engines were fired up and the air inside the bay, essentially a huge airlock, was violently sucked back into the ship's air systems.

Positioned in the center of the rows of seats, Ram reclined in a reentry chair designed for eight feet tall subjects. Even then, he was bigger than the seat had been designed for and the strapping cut into his shoulders and chest. The passenger section of the shuttle held the support crew that would be joining him on the Orb. There was a lot of them. Twelve Marines in three squads plus Cassidy in full combat gear and a range of weapons that they almost certainly would not need. Still, Ram was glad to have them backing him up. Their easy confidence made him feel calm. Their demeanor reminded him of the other elite Avar gamers in his co-op when they waited in a pre-game lobby. A relaxation that came from certainty in your own abilities and a familiarity and trust in your teammates. And he knew the Marines had run the operation in Avar a hundred times so they were drilled to perfection.

As well as the Marines there were eighteen crew members plus equipment crammed into the crew compartment. The cargo hold in the shuttle's belly was so packed with their gear that some of them carried extra stuff on their laps.

Milena seated herself beside him. He was happy to have her there but he had been confused about one thing ever since he had woken up that morning.

"Milena," he whispered. "Last night, did we...? You know. In my bedroom?"

She raised an eyebrow. "Have you forgotten?"

"It's the strangest thing, I remember heading toward my room with you but then there's nothing. Did you drug me?"

She closed her eyes. "You had your mind scanned and

uploaded this morning, do you remember your medical schedule? Sounds like the process interfered with your memory storage going right back to last night."

"I can't believe this. That's the worst thing I ever heard." He looked down at her. "How did I do? Was it good? I'm pretty sure there's no way we could have, you know, physically performed a full docking maneuver. Did you, like, achieve your key objectives?"

"You're an idiot." She reached over and placed her hand on his arm. "But tell you what, you beat the alien and we can make new memories."

"Oh man," Ram said. "I thought I was motivated to succeed before this moment but I think I just found a whole new gear."

Dr. Fo sat behind Ram, despite Director Zhukov pressuring the doctor into staying on the ship. He was too valuable an asset to humanity to risk being trapped on the Orb should anything go wrong. Dr. Fo had laughed him off.

"Rama Seti is my patient," Dr. Fo said. "And, perhaps, if I may be so bold, my friend. I wish to be there to oversee the final preparations which will ensure his victory and also so that I may immediately perform any necessary medical procedures upon his corpse."

Ram was glad the doctor would be there. Although he was a medical genius, his skills would most likely not be required. And it was probably because almost everyone else who had liked him was now dead or six billion kilometers away but Ram was starting to think of the man as a friend.

The shuttle shook with growing intensity and then the vibration lessened, replaced with a steady hum as the engines settled into a cruise state.

"We are clear of the shuttle bay," Cassidy announced through internal comms. "Our pilot is stabilizing our spin and we are heading for Orb Station."

Bediako sat beside him in the other huge reentry chair. There was no final training assistance that the old guy could advise on but he was there as a backup. If Rama was rejected by the Orb, for some reason, then Bediako could take his place. No one wanted that to happen, not even Ram.

Accompanying the heads of departments were selected members of the training, medical and intel teams. Medical personnel were there to give Ram his final injections and to scrape up his remains from the floor of the arena. The communications personnel and intelligence officers who would record everything from inside the Orb for later study and perform their own experiments in a quest to better penetrate the depths of the structure with their scanning equipment.

Milena looked calm as she always did, leaning back in her seat, peering at the screen in her hands. Ram knew he should be mentally preparing for the fight but all he could think about was Milena and how much he wished he could remember the night they had spent together. He felt like he'd been robbed.

Ram closed his eyes and focused on his breathing. Still, the thoughts that bubbled up were of death and violence, blood and a giant yellow monster. Three-dimensional red words shot up at him from the darkness. HUMANITY and FUTURE and DESTRUCTION and LOSER. He allowed the thoughts to flow through him, observing them and passing no judgment, granting them no emotional power over him.

Kind of.

Who was he kidding?

Captain Cassidy called out. "We are coming up to the outer hull of the Orb now. I recommend that you check your screens for the live feed from the forward cameras. I'll throw it up on the cabin monitor."

"Look at this, Ram," Milena's breathless voice next to him as she held up her screen. "What an incredible thing to witness."

It was just like watching the replays of the earlier missions. Ram had viewed them so many times that it was like a replay all over again.

The Orb was exactly the same as it had been in Mission Three, Mission Two and in Mission One. It was only their approach angle that was slightly different as the shuttle eased its way through the roughly hundred-meter square opening at the equator. The shining black shell reflected the shuttle lights as well as the ranging lasers and illumination from the *Victory* before she went over the horizon.

Even though he had seen it so many times in replays and he was watching the images through a wall screen rather that with his own eyes, the alienness of the thing was never more apparent as when the shuttle flew inside the open bay. The black mirror exterior was inhumanly perfect and seemingly timeless. Even knowing that the outer surface was capable of changing to white, to a silvered reflective shine, to red and blue, it didn't seem possible.

"I still wonder whether the Orb Builders are hiding inside," Ram whispered to Milena.

"A pleasant fantasy," she said. "But honestly, best guess is that the Orb Builders are busy overseeing the galactic network of empires. I have to go along with the common UNOP conclusions that they operate the Orbs remotely or perhaps the Orbs are run by some form of AI."

"Another part of me likes the idea that the Orb Builders are themselves AI."

"A common hypothesis and a reasonable one. There's no way of knowing at the moment. In time, if and when humanity works its way up through the ranks of species in the arenas across the galaxy, we may meet the Orb Builders themselves. But not today. Now, you need to stop intellectually and emotionally avoiding the fight and start focusing on the Wheelhunters."

Ram imagined that the alien shuttle would be entering an identical hole on the opposite hemisphere while the *Victory* and the alien ship continued to orbit opposite the other, each hidden from direct view by the Orb itself. Ram wondered what the Wheelhunter was feeling in that moment, on its own shuttle.

Was it afraid? Did it even feel anything like emotions at all? There was still so much about them that no one knew and yet Ram had to kill it.

"Do you think I have a chance?" Ram asked Bediako.

The instructor turned to Ram and looked him in the eye. "You have the best chance of anyone. We can say no more than that."

Thanks a lot, asshole.

"Doctor Fo," Ram said. "You believe in me, right?"

"Oh, absolutely, yes, of course I do. Yes, indeed. You are most impressive, everyone says so. And well done for thinking positive thoughts, good for you, that's the spirit."

"Quite the vote of confidence, Doc."

Milena patted his forearm. "That's what you get for requiring external validation."

Ram looked at the vast Orb filling the screen. The shuttle was almost at the surface.

"I wish I'd learned to meditate," Ram said. "I'll never get the chance now."

"The main thing is that you resist being a slave to your emotions. Decide what you would like your thoughts to be about and think those thoughts."

Ram nodded, looking at her. "I know what my last thoughts are going to be about." He raised his eyebrows.

Milena smiled back at him, though there was a sadness in the corners of her eyes. He was glad to see it. He hoped that she really did feel something for him and the whole thing hadn't been purely for the sake of the mission.

Crazy, really. He was facing his own death, the failure of the mission and UNOP itself and being responsible for the destruction of humanity and yet he was feeling smug because a beautiful woman seemed to care for him a tiny bit. His gratitude for her was completely pathetic. And yet, he could think of nothing better to be his last thoughts than her tits and her ass and her lips.

He wished he had more time.

On the screen, the black hull of the Orb filled the screen. The shuttle, descending along the equator, came up to the vast, square, open door of the shuttle bay.

"Three minutes until landing," Cassidy drawled, as if he was on a pleasure cruise.

The craft's engines vibrated heavily right before they shut down and the shuttle pilot used the monopropellant thrusters to arrest their speed in relation to the surface until they coasted over the hundred-meter square opening.

Thirty-one people in the passenger compartment held their breath as the pilot rotated the shuttle, maneuvered inside and set the craft down on the floor of the huge space. A short series of thuds sounded on the hull as the shuttle landed and everyone let out a huge sigh of relief.

"This is your pilot speaking. Solid landing is confirmed. Welcome to Orb Station Zero."

Ram slapped the quick release on his harness and grinned at Milena.

"Alright, let's do this."

CHAPTER THIRTY-TWO
ARENA

THE INSIDE OF THE ORB hangar was a featureless black cube. The shuttle lamps illuminated the solid surfaces around them with bright blue-white light and the walls, ceiling and floor emitted their own soft glow. The hangar bay was one hundred meters on all sides with a fifty-meter opening on the wall opposite the outer door.

Silently, they watched on their screens as the outer hull doors slid shut behind them with a smoothness that no human machinery could touch and air howled around the outer hull of the shuttle. The breathable gas mixture produced by the Orb was heated and the action of the hot air on the frozen outer hull caused the passenger compartment to ring with the sound of expanding metal panels.

Ram stood, stretching his legs and back. The epinephrine in his blood hummed throughout his body and he itched to be moving.

The pilot's voice came through on the shared channel. "Outer door closed behind us right on schedule. Air inside the shuttle bay showing as the standard Orb mix. Sensors show gravity nominal. Radiation within safety parameters. Filters are picking up no contaminants or life signs. We are green across the board. Alright, over to you, Captain Cassidy."

"Okay, listen up," Cassidy said, standing by the side door which would open into a loading ramp. "My Marines will exit first and establish a perimeter. I will then call the teams out in the prearranged order. We're all excited and we're all afraid but we will do this calmly and we will do this professionally. There is plenty of time before Zero Hour and so we will not rush or make mistakes. We will do this exactly as we have drilled it." Cassidy paused, looking around at the Marines and crew staring at him over the seat backs. "Having said that, if anyone sees or hears or smells anything that is unexpected, anything that you feel may be a threat or simply something you notice that you have not seen in the previous mission replays then you will let me know immediately. And for Christ's sake, don't touch anything weird, alright? Okay, let's make history, people."

He punched the door release code and the side of the shuttle opened with a banging, whirring noise. The external air whooshed in and mixed with the shuttle air. Ram instinctively held his breath, unwilling to trust the alien air. But there was only so long he could do that.

The Marines flowed down the ramp even before it locked in place. They worked quickly and efficiently and they covered the exits of the shuttle as the boarding party teams unbuckled themselves and prepared their equipment.

Ram started toward the exit. Bediako stopped him with an open palm on Ram's chest.

"Wait until the Marines have cleared the area," Bediako said.

Ram couldn't stand being cooped up on the shuttle anymore. He wanted to set foot on the alien space station, if for no reason other than to be actually doing something. He took a breath and controlled himself before he smashed the instructor in the face and ripped his head off.

"Come on, man," Ram said, through gritted teeth. "We know there's no one here. The Orb Builders are not here. The Wheelhunters are embarking on the opposite side of the Orb Station and there's no way for them to get to us. I mean, there's no reason to expect anything has changed since the last mission and the one before that and the one before fucking that."

Bediako looked up at him. "Rama Seti, you are currently the most important human being in the Sol System. We cannot afford to make any assumptions or take even the slightest unnecessary risk with your person."

It couldn't have been an easy thing for him to admit, even though it was technically true. The real truth was, Ram couldn't bear to think about the fact.

Ram controlled his breathing and tried to make light of things. "I guess I should enjoy my status while it lasts."

"Indeed."

While they waited for the equipment to be unloaded on their wheeled cases and for the Marines to sweep every millimeter of the hangar bay, Milena took Ram's right hand in both of hers and held it to her chest. "You must cultivate a positive mental attitude, Ram."

"I am positive," he said, automatically placating. When she didn't respond he looked down at her. "Seriously, I'm looking forward to you dosing me up with some of your homicidal maniac cocktail. It will be great to be out of my mind."

"I'll be there with you," Milena said, meaning of course that she would be there in spirit, in his head. "But with the advances that you have made the last few weeks, I expect that you will be able to achieve victory with minimal support from me."

"You don't need to bullshit me, Milena. I mean it. Don't hold back with anything. Use everything you have on me, turn it all up as high as it goes. It will take everything that I have, everything that you have plus all the luck in the world. Burn through everything, don't save a drop and neither will I."

Her head was a meter below his own but she looked him square in the eye. "Agreed."

Of course she would. Only a psychotic would put the wellbeing of a single man before the existence of all humanity. A dead man walking, to boot. It was a completely unnecessary thing to urge her to do but he was nervous beyond words and his mouth and mind were running wild.

He had to get himself under control.

The Captain's voice called out for the last of the boarding teams to disembark.

Milena squeezed Ram's hand for the last time and let it drop.

Ram followed Bediako down the side ramp and into the Orb hangar space. The shuttle sat in the center of the huge cuboid like a stocky, remote control airplane in a toy box, engines still cooling at the rear. The ceiling, 300 feet above, was vertigo inducing. Ram took a deep breath of the alien air. It smelled just fine, other than the chemical stink of the shuttlecraft and the animal sweat of the hardworking boarding team.

I'm on an alien space station.

"This way," the Captain said. He and his Marines moved the group through the space to the fifty-meter open door in the wall in front of the shuttle's nose. The corridor was a straight line through the center of the Orb toward the arena, a kilometer-long cuboid leading to the heart of the station.

They went in relative silence, in the order they had in their own simulations. Everyone seemed to know where their place was and where they were all going. A squad of four Marines guarded him and Milena, even though it was unnecessary. There was nothing that would harm him before he got into the Arena. Two Marines in front, two behind, with their weapons ready and Bediako positioned himself in front of the Marines, as if placing himself in potential harm's way. If Ram wasn't feeling so psychotically aggressive, he would have been touched by his concern. By his display of duty over his personal feelings.

Ram allowed himself to be brought along by the mass of bodies and the trundling of the alloy trolleys while he focused on staying calm and attempting to retain his own center.

He looked around at the smooth, black walls far away on either side and considered where he was. His mind ran immediately into the astonishing fact of the thing, which set him off wondering again what the Orb Builders were like and whether they were still around anywhere in the galaxy. Whether any of the hypotheses so far dreamed up about them even approached the truth. He imagined the network of galactic civilizations that maybe collectively created some kind of super culture, an information and trading and even political network of cultures that humanity was potentially going to be a part of, one day. That humans might be given access to distant star systems, technological advances or, at the least, gifted advice or information which would enable humanity to join that galactic community.

But only if humans could win a fight against a giant yellow wheel-shaped monster.

Only if Ram could win. Today, right now. He was out of time, humanity was out of time. It was now or never.

It was too much for Ram to take in. The responsibility of it too great. His hands and lips tingled with the adrenaline coursing through his bloodstream.

Milena could sense his rising anxiety. Just seeing her face as she glanced up at him calmed him a little and he remembered to control his breathing.

He remembered that he was made for this. Designed for it, decades ago, bred for it and ultimately trained for it. Ultimately, he was the only person, out of the billions of people in the Sol System, who even had the remotest chance.

I can do this, he told himself. A mantra, repeated in time with his footsteps on the black floor.

I can do this. I will do this. I can do this.

Together, the boarding team followed the route through the Orb. The team were generally quiet, although there were plenty of fraught whispered discussions about equipment and with verbal updates amongst the Marines and between Cassidy and the two Marines, shuttle pilot and crew left back in the shuttle bay. Two of the crew stopped in the corridor behind the group to set up some sort of scanning experiment. Bediako was silent. Even Dr. Fo barely spoke, other than to hurry his medical team along.

There was not far to go but Ram paid less and less attention to his surroundings. Mostly, he focused on his breathing. Feeling the air rush in, cool and yet warm, in through his nostrils and filling his chest. His lungs expanded to enormous proportions and his chest grew with every breath in. Controlling the air as it left his body, he modulated the flow so that it was as close to perfectly constant as it could be. No doubt, to the boarding team around him, breathing with such precision made Ram sound like a machine or perhaps a lunatic.

Instead, his guts were filled with the wriggling worms of anxiety. And just the thought of having a panic attack was enough to start him down the road to having one.

"Milena," he said.

"I know," she whispered. "Here."

A moment after she tapped her screen, Ram sighed a huge, juddering sigh. And then breathed a little easier.

"Orb Arena staging chamber, right ahead," the Captain reported as the corridor ended in a translucent swirling, smoky gray wall. "Set up, people. You know your routines. And make sure, for the love of Jesus Christ, that you stay away from the smokescreen."

While the Marines held Ram back momentarily, the crew trundled their equipment to their areas around the open space and unpacked with practiced efficiency. Machines started up, blinking and whirring into life. After a couple of minutes, Cassidy nodded that Ram was clear to enter.

Just like on the footage he had watched, just like in the Avar he had walked through a dozen times, the end of the corridor came out into a hundred-meter cube space that had, decades before, been labeled the staging chamber. It was the same dimensions as the huge shuttle bay. Walls, floor, ceiling made of the ubiquitous black metallic-ceramic but the wall opposite the corridor opening was different.

That fifty-meter square section over the one wall of the staging chamber. The semi-transparent film of plasma that was impenetrable apart from when the Orb turned off the plasma flow. That flow would be stopped only twice. Once to let the champion into the arena and then to allow the champion to leave at the end. If the champion was unable to leave, the Orb allowed the support crew to go and collect the remains before being asked to leave again almost immediately. Some crew said it was a force field but most called it the smokescreen because of the way the surface of it swirled as if it was filled with smoke.

Beyond that square was the Orb Arena itself.

One of the biotechnicians screamed and jumped in amongst a clatter of empty aluminum equipment cases. While his team cursed his idiocy and incompetence and helped him to his feet, he took off his still-smoking helmet and inspected the way that the camera and flashlights on the front had been sheared off by the line of plasma.

"Close shave," someone said.

Dr. Fo, for once, did not look amused. "If anyone else stumbles into that wall of deadly plasma beams, please ensure you kill yourself in the process or else I will do it for you."

"Ram," Milena said. "Please remember to stay away from the

smokescreen. This side and the other."

"I'm out of my mind with all these hormones," Ram said. "But I'm not a fucking idiot."

Ram's throat was constricted and his voice sounded weird. His sense of self was diminishing from the growing anxiety. He focused again on his breathing and tried to bring his awareness back to the ever-changing moment to moment consciousness rather than his impending painful death.

"There's only a few minutes to go," Milena said. All he could do was nod his acknowledgment. He marched back and forth near to the smokescreen, shaking his arms and trying to keep himself under control, every breath a conscious effort. His hands and face tingled.

While the technicians busied themselves setting up their equipment and everyone else gave Ram space, Bediako stepped up to him.

"You know that I was not selected as the Subject Alpha on the third mission, yes? Did I ever tell you about coming here, to this room, thirty years ago?"

"No." Ram did not stop marching up and down past where Bediako stood, listening while the instructor spoke.

"They packed Subject Alpha's body and brain with so much tech that he was basically a cyborg. Augmented to fuck, he used to say. That guy, an American named Duncan, he had metal fused to his bones, he had lenses grafted to his eyeballs. And we all kind of knew that he *might* not be allowed through the

457

smokescreen. We'd seen what happened on Mission Two with the weapons and body armor. And yet there was the expectation that he would go through, be the one to face the monster in its lair. But it was always strange, how old Duncan had been selected as the Alpha but his performance was only better than anyone else's because he had all the augments. Without that, he would have been down the list, maybe not even in the top ten or the top twenty. So I stood here, right here in this chamber, ranked as the Subject Zeta, while the others waited their turn in front of me and others behind me. None of us knew for sure which of us the Orb would let through that smokescreen right there. We had been training for years and we knew we had to win if our chance came. And we all believed that there was a good chance that, if we fought, we would die. At least, I did. We never spoke of it, would not have admitted it. Then the Orb turned the Alpha down and he had to walk away. Old Duncan was crushed. All of them before me, Alpha, Beta and so on. One after the other, they all felt like they'd failed, that they had let everyone down, even though they never had a free choice about how many augmentations they were given. Fighting in this way is an idealistic activity, it attracts people who are obsessed with themselves, with bettering themselves. That is the nature of fighting. In a lot of ways, I let my spirit be defeated by my sense of self. I was young, then. Even though I was fighting for humanity, my selection and my failure, it was all about me. I was ignorant to the fact that I was no more than a tool, a weapon for all of humanity. We all were. But you know, now, standing here again and thinking about it, do you know what I feel most of all?"

"No."

"Anger. I feel a deep rage, right down in my guts. Rage at this Orb for doing this to us, for having the arrogance for forcing us to fight in this way for our existence. But most of all I'm feeling a murderous rage at that fucking alien out there right now. That hideous freak out there right now, that is our enemy, humanity's enemy. Sure, the Orb is facilitating our conflict but the Wheelers want to take over our planet, our home. They want Earth. They want to colonize us. *Us*, humanity. How dare they, Ram? Can you feel the disgust? Can you feel the outrage? The anger? The rage?"

"Yes," Ram growled, his body shaking, vibrating. "Fuck, yes. I need to kill. Get away from me."

Milena walked up and Bediako stepped back to the safety of the medical officers.

"Can't control myself much longer," Ram said to her, hearing his heartbeat racing in the shaking of his voice. "Dial me down or I'll wreck these people."

"Focus on your breathing. Look at me, Ram. You know me. You truly know me and I know you. You know I trust in reason and honesty. Now, listen. It is my honest belief that you will win this fight. It's not wishful thinking. It's not my feelings clouding my judgment. It's the facts and my knowledge of who you are. I'm not dialing you down because I know that you can control yourself perfectly for a few more minutes. And then you will unleash everything against your enemy."

Ram stopped in front of her and closed his eyes. Colors swirled behind his eyelids. He looked down at Milena's beautiful, strong face.

"You helped make me the best version of myself. This moment, I'm the strongest, fastest, toughest human who ever lived. Because of biologists, engineers, administrators but also because of me. And because of you. I'm going to kill that thing out there. But if I die, know I'm happy I got here. And I don't care if no one else ever knows I existed. I know who I was. And you know. And—"

The Orb chimed three times. The clear pings ringing out and stopping everyone in their tracks while they sounded.

"That's your cue," Milena said.

Ram leaned down and kissed her soft lips. My last kiss, he thought.

He stepped toward the center of the smokescreen wall and the technicians, the Marines, the doctors stopped what they were doing. And they applauded. They nodded at him as he walked by, clapping their hands all the way.

"You can do it, Rama."

"Thank you, Ram, thank you."

"We believe in you, Rama."

"Kill that thing."

"Rip it to pieces, man, come on."

"Go, Rama Seti, you go."

Ram's throat constricted with emotion to such an extent that he did not trust himself to speak without bursting into tears. He was not afraid. He was wound tighter than a coiled spring, his limbs quivered and everything in him was urging him to fight, to move, to shout and he knew he had to keep control of himself until he got through the fizzing smokescreen before him. He could not risk touching the thing nor could he risk hurting any of the crew around him.

The Orb chimed twice. The clapping died away and the technicians and everyone got back to work on their own tasks. Resuscitation machines and sensors, weapons platforms and communications. Recording equipment stood on tripods either side of him. Ram forgot them all and stood looking out through the swirling barrier at the vast space beyond.

"I'm with you, Ram," Milena said, her voice sounding in his head. "All the way."

He turned to take one last look at her but before he did so, the single chime sounded.

The swirling, deadly barrier parted, revealing the vast space beyond.

He took a deep, shuddering breath.

And stepped into the Orb Arena.

CHAPTER THIRTY-THREE
WARRIOR

THE FLAWLESSLY SMOOTH, SHINING black floor of the arena was a perfect circle with a 400-meter diameter. A huge space, as big as a sports stadium emptied of the seats. Above, the geometrically precise half-circle dome of the roof was a dark point two-hundred meters above the center of the arena. The walls all around curved steadily up toward the top. Light enough to see by came from a clear white glow that was thought to emanate through the black surfaces or perhaps even from the air itself. It was bright enough to see clear across the plane of the floor to the other side of the arena.

It stank. The air inside was just as he had been trained to expect and his head filled with the heady, high oxygen content, the vile stench of the sulfur dioxide. Expecting it didn't make the stench any less appalling.

And there it was.

The Wheelhunter. Even from such a distance, it was a strange sight. That glinting sickly yellow, the smooth motion of the legs and hub contrasting with the jerking of the flailing arms with their wicked claws. It came on, lumbering toward the center.

Ram went to meet it.

He had run through the moment in Avar so many times that it was a familiar moment, like a recurring dream coming true. Almost a profound sense of deja vu. Layers of reality overlaid themselves. It was difficult to remember that if he died this time he would not respawn again and again until his Avar session was over for the day. Every move that he made would be the move that was set into reality, into the real history of the universe. There were no saves, no reloading.

The thing came on at a steady pace and he did his best to shake himself out of his dissociative state. This was happening, whether it felt real or not. The Wheelhunters advanced at a pace of around 1.6 meters per second which would bring it to the center of the arena in two minutes.

He would have to avoid the blade-like claws on the arms for long enough to get close to the thing. There was nothing he could do to cut the creature in return so he would have to use brute force to break the Wheelhunter's limbs and then beat it to death. He would have to work out the detail in real time as the combat played out.

In the previous mission, Bediako had been ordered to prolong the combat by evading the Wheelhunter, testing its speed and agility. By retreating and hoping to draw it away, all he'd done was allow it to get too close and then found himself on the back foot as the encounter proper started.

Ram had options. He could charge the Wheelhunter first, attack it like it had never been attacked before. The surprise might work in his favor. It was the tactic that Bediako favored more than any other but that was only because the success of such a move would vindicate his own past failures. Still, it was the one approach no one had tried and so it was what Ram intended.

His other option was to back away immediately. To not go to the center and to keep away from the alien for as long as possible. Perhaps it would tire, perhaps it would be confused or unnerved. But it seemed like a long shot and the only attraction really was that it might prolong the moments until the combat was joined.

It rolled closer and Ram had his first indication that something was wrong. Something was different.

Ram stopped walking forward. He had about a hundred meters to go to the center of the arena.

"Milena, can you see this?"

"What should I be seeing?"

"It's bigger, I think. Yeah, I'm sure of it."

"Hold on, we're checking the cameras." She went quiet for a long moment as the Wheelhunter came closer. "You're right. It seems to be around ten to twenty percent taller than the Mission Three entity."

Ram swallowed. "That's just great."

He started backing away from the Wheelhunter, giving himself more time. His opponent did not appear to change its own speed or react in any other way. It just kept rolling on.

Milena's voice remained steady. "It doesn't matter, Ram. We discussed this as a possibility. The strategic options remain the same."

"You're right, I was screwed anyway so what's the difference."

"Ram, you must stay positive-"

"No, I know. It's fine. Really. I'm relieved, if anything."

She paused. "You are relieved because now no one can expect you to win. But you're just setting yourself up for failure. Stop retreating. You must go forward."

Ram kept backing away from the alien. "I'm not setting myself up to fail. Honestly, I'm not. This fight was always all or nothing anyway, right? One of the lies you guys told me when I first woke up was that you wanted me because I was an all or nothing gamer. I thought I would win for a while. I think I'm better than anyone ever has been. But I've been holding on to the hope of survival all this time. Now I know there's no chance of that and so there's no reason to hold back anything at all."

Milena said nothing for a moment. "I want you to survive this. But you can only do that if you win."

The Wheelhunter came on as Ram backed away continuously but it was catching up, slowly.

"I intend to win."

"You can't do that if you keep running away until it chases you down. Don't avoid this, Ram. It will close soon, it will accelerate faster than you can react to. You've seen it a thousand times. You know what your best hope is. Fight on your own terms. Remember the training."

Ram watched the yellow monster growing larger and larger. The air stank, he expected that. But he thought he caught a whiff of the smell of the alien. A musky, strange, chemical stink wafted through the arena by the cartwheeling motion of the massive footpads.

"Bediako was told to run away around the circumference and that took him away from the smokescreen."

"You intend to push it into the forcefield and kill it that way. How many times did we try it in Avar? It is too fast, too heavy. If you can get hold of it, you will be unable to move it and you are almost certain to be thrown into the screen instead."

"Have you got any better ideas? How else can I hurt it? Anyway, I'm not going to push it in. The Orb's rules are that I have to kill it by my actions and it doesn't matter if I die in the process, right? So I'm going to drag it in with me."

He looked over his shoulder and saw the murky square of the smokescreen about thirty meters behind him. He kept edging back without taking his eyes off the Wheelhunter. It would surge forward at any moment.

"The rules are not clear, there could be other interpretations. We may be losing nuance in the translation."

"It's within fifty meters now so this is it. I'll draw it close as I can. Oh, man, it's huge. It must be close to four meters tall. Oh, man."

The creature's feet slapped into the floor, over and over, the arms twirling. He recalled how many times his head had been crushed by those feet in Avar training.

"Ram, quickly, attack now before it rushes you."

"No. I can't do that, I need to use its momentum against it, I need it to be rolling fast."

"It's at thirty meters, this is it."

"Goodbye, Milena."

The alien stopped.

CHAPTER THIRTY-FOUR
CHAMPION

IT STAYED MOTIONLESS. TWO HUGE oval footpads on the floor, one behind the other. The base of the leading footpad pointed right at Ram, with another unseen balancing behind and the final two pointed up in the air, fore and aft. The two arms stuck out from the hub to either side.

"What's it doing?" Milena said.

Ram was about to joke that perhaps it was afraid of him. But he was too unsettled to speak. His heartbeat thudded in his ears.

Milena spoke softly. "We've never seen one motionless

before."

Ram looked closer and could make out the arms and hands moving slightly, up and down. The hub itself was expanding and contracting.

"It's breathing," Ram said, his voice close to a whisper, afraid to do anything to change the situation.

"We think it's your proximity to the smokescreen," Milena said, after a pause. "That's the only possible variable. It knows what you plan to do."

"At least we know it's wary of the plasma, that means it can be hurt by it."

"Only if it went near it. Clearly, it is wise enough to stay away."

Ram swallowed, his mouth dry as cotton wool.

"What would happen if neither of us moved? Is there a time limit?"

Milena all-but sighed. "You know we don't know that. Perhaps the Wheeler would tire, weaken. Perhaps not. But we know that you would. You cannot maintain this heightened metabolic rate for much longer without losing combat efficiency. All you can do now is attack."

Rama knew she was right. The thing was monstrous in the flesh, the wafts of sulfurous stench growing stronger.

"I can bait it into rushing me, double back," Ram said and yet he found it impossible to move, almost paralyzed with fear. He was safe in that moment and taking any action would lead to agony, failure and death.

Milena's soft breath in his ear. "You should take the initiative before you lose it."

"I know."

He had to move. He had to.

His body shaking with the adrenaline flooding his system, Ram took an experimental, slow step sideways, to his left.

The Wheelhunter remained motionless. As if it were rooted to the spot by the two flat footpads against the black floor.

He took another step leftwards and froze when the Wheeler shifted its balance toward him.

Each of the six legs had three ball and socket joints. One joint at the hub, another at the ankle so the foot could pivot at any angle and the final joint in the middle.

As Ram took his next step, the ankle joints on the Wheeler's two grounded feet bent sideways. As if preparing to tilt over in a turn should Ram run away beside the wall, as Bediako had done in Mission Three.

Instead, Ram turned back to the right and took a quick two steps in that direction. The Wheelhunter leaned the other way and even rolled forward by a few degrees, ready to chase him.

"Alright, then," Ram said. "This is it."

Ram tried to remember what he had prepared for his last words. He knew it would be recorded for posterity and it had to be something profound but he was numb with terror and the strain had made him mindless.

"Fuck it," he muttered.

He ran to his right for five steps, turned completely around and ran back to the left, not approaching the wall nor closing the distance to the alien, hoping that it would be enough to draw it in.

It worked.

The slap-slap-slap of the footpads drummed on the floor as the Wheeler accelerated toward him, closing on Ram, the sound growing louder behind him.

He ran on to the left as fast as he could for a few steps, knowing that he could never outrun the speed of his pursuer, expecting the blow to crash into his skull at any moment.

The drumming of its feet filled his ears.

Ram changed direction for the final time, crouching to take the momentum out of his pace, twisting completely about and running straight for the Wheeler.

It was right there. Almost upon him.

But the changes in direction had had the desired effect. The Wheeler was off balance as it swung a vast hand at Ram's head, leaning and twisting itself out of shape trying to match Ram's movement.

He ducked and weaved away from the blow and, changing direction again, jinked beside the enormous monster looming above. A massive yellow footpad stomped down where he'd been just a millisecond before but Ram was already up and moving, coming up on the other side of the Wheeler's hub. The thing pivoted and the other arm with its powerful, clawed fingers flashed up toward him with mad power.

Every instinct screamed at him to run, to duck and to curl into a tight ball on the ground.

Instead, Ram leaped forward and crashed into the Wheeler's central hub.

The claws raked his face, head and shoulder. Agony seared through him as the claws sliced deep enough to cut open his scalp and grind against the hardened bone of his skull. Blood gushed out and down his face before the coagulants in it stemmed the flow.

As he grappled the Wheeler's hub a great anger flooded up and into him, the deep, primal revulsion at it overwhelming his reason.

The hub was so wide he could barely grasp it but he wrapped his arms around it and pushed as hard as he could. The ball and socket joint of the alien's arm on that side was over his shoulder, giving him a point to heave upward.

His face pressed jammed against the yellow, knobbled, lizard-skin that covered the whole creature and it reeked like nothing he'd ever smelled before. Like a rotten food, fungus stench mixed with stomach bile and raw sewage.

The claw on his side raked Ram's back from his neck to his kidneys with shallow but long and savage cuts, slashing and tearing away at him. The sickly-sweet metallic stink of his own blood filled his head.

There was no time to think, only to feel. And the feeling was hate. An all-consuming hatred for the wrongness of it, for the unearthliness of it. His disgust gave him strength.

Ram pushed against the hub, his shoes sliding on the black floor underfoot, pushed it sideways with everything he had.

It began to fall, tilting over to what seemed like the point of no return and Ram felt a momentary thrill of victory.

The Wheeler pivoted, fast and threw out its clawed hand on the far side to hold itself up.

Ram kept pushing but it would not fall further. It writhed beneath him, twisting to free itself from his grasp. Ram punched the hub hard, with an uppercut down low.

It was like punching a slab of greenwood. The blow crunched Ram's knuckles. He hit it again, breaking the bones in his hand but the hub's skin did give a little, quivering with the force of the blow and the alien ceased writhing for a fraction of a second, as if it was stunned. Ram hit it again, mangling his hand and the pain made him cry out, half a whimper and half a roar of fury.

It tilted further. But no more.

The Wheeler had greater leverage than he did, could transfer more of its strength into the struggle. Ram's feet were small in comparison but the alien had one huge footpad providing unrivaled friction to the floor, plus the tripod-hand worked like a bike's kickstand, stopping it tipping. And its strength was enormous. It twisted, pivoting on its many joints, still raking his back over and over while Ram cried and heaved, his tendons stretching and muscles tearing from the effort.

Ram's red blood spattered everywhere, smearing the Wheeler's body, spraying the air with a red mist.

He couldn't do it. He wouldn't push it over. He wasn't strong enough. The realization almost defeated him as the Wheeler forced itself back to upright, bending and using the mass of the other legs to force Ram back. So much so he was afraid his back would be broken by the weight of it.

So he pulled.

He wrapped one arm over the Wheeler's shoulder joint, the joint of the alien's arm where it came out of the hub. And he pulled, heaving backward, pulling the gigantic mass of the Wheeler down on top of himself.

They crashed to the floor, the legs thrashing to free itself from his grip.

Milena was shouting warnings in his head but he was beyond understanding language, he had become an animal, fighting for its life.

The arm that had shredded his back was now caught under his body. The claws stabbed into his body and carved up his kidney and guts on one side. The agony of it shot through him. But he wrapped his legs around the hub as best he could and he held on. He held the arm to him and he punched it in the shoulder joint. The Wheeler shuddered and Ram knew, he *knew*, that he had hurt it.

A thrill of joy surged through him, even as the massive

creature squirmed, crushed and stabbed him. Ram punched it again feeling the soft tissue under the skin give a little. He hit it again and again while the alien writhed and twisted but Ram held on. He jabbed a series of blows at the arm then pushed it, levering the long, thin bone of the upper arm using his own shoulder as the pivot point.

Ram felt and heard the shoulder socket pop.

The alien moaned.

A horrific, muffled shriek from inside the hub like a gagged banshee and Ram laughed as he punched and twisted the arm again, trying to tear it off.

The skin was too strong. Though the arm was dislocated inside and had suffered internal soft tissue damage, the yellow lizard skin exterior was too tough to tear through.

It bucked and rolled and it was all Ram could do to hold on. The alien reached through its legs with the other arm and grabbed ahold of Ram's knee where he had wrapped his limbs around the hub.

Though Ram yanked his leg away, the alien stuck its claws in deep and pulled, ripping his calf muscle to pieces. Ram screamed as the agony tore through him and he punched the hub repeatedly in a blind rage. The pain and the fury filled him and he stamped up at the arm, kicking it away. The remnants of his calf hanging in tatters from his knee.

The weight of the Wheeler, writhing on top of him, compressed his chest so much that it was hard to breathe, impossible to take a full breath. As the creature struggled to right itself, kicking all its legs, a cascade of Ram's ribs popped. The sharp agony shot through his chest like a hundred knives carving into his lungs.

The Wheeler rolled itself half off him, the enormous footpads swaying and hammering to drag itself away.

Ram held on to the dislocated arm, terrified of losing his only possible advantage. He couldn't let it get upright again, get mobile.

The alien's arm was not attached internally to the hub and had little strength but it was not completely disabled. The thirty-centimeter-long fingers scraped their savage claws down Ram's face, puncturing his cheek and slicing between his molars. The alien pulled and Ram's cheek came away in a tearing shred and a shower of teeth that splatted onto the floor.

Ram screamed. He turned his head over to clear his airway of teeth and he coughed the blood out of his throat.

The Wheeler crawled away, righting itself but Ram staggered over to it, threw himself against the hub and stamped on its ankle with his one working leg. The thing shrieked again, shaking and Ram pushed it over.

Ram felt himself weakening. His heart was racing so hard it was like an assault rifle on full auto, his face was torn and between his crushed chest and facial wound pumping blood down his throat, he struggled to breathe.

The Wheeler was disoriented and injured also but Ram knew,

with complete certainty that broken bones and dislocated joints wouldn't kill the beast before Ram died from his own injuries.

He had only a few moments left, he needed a new plan, a better course of action, something, someone to help him.

Milena was yelling in his ear.

"Get away from the screen, Ram," she was shouting, barely discernable over his racing heart and tattered breath. "Watch out for the smokescreen."

Ram glanced behind. Their grappling had brought them to the edge of the arena, the wall looming up over him. The deadly smokescreen was within arm's reach. The murky gray plasma swirled right there behind him, the shapes of the boarding crew beyond.

The Wheeler kicked with a powerful foot, knocking Ram into the screen. Ram knew whatever part of his body touched it, he was going to lose. And yet the unstoppable power of animal instinct took over deep within his brain, far beyond the control of his conscious mind and his hand shot out to brace himself against the wall.

He yanked it back as he fell onto his face, landing just centimeters from the screen.

Too slow.

His reaction came after it had already happened. He snatched his right hand back only to find he'd lost all four fingers. The stumps were just above the knuckles, the glistening red wounds sheared off with molecular precision. As he watched, blood welled in a dozen tiny points then poured out over his skin.

The Wheeler kicked him again and Ram rolled sideways, straight into the claws that reached for his face. He grabbed for them with his ruined hand, his missing fingers meaning all he did was thump into the alien's tough skin and the razor sharp claws lacerated his face, tearing through the remnants of his already shredded flesh.

One claw slipped into Ram's eyeball, catching on the lower rim of the socket and whipping out the eye itself. Ram screamed, blood pouring from his missing face and into his throat.

He threw himself against the hub, half blind and mad with pain, punching and striking with both hands. Expending everything he possibly could, all he had left. The Wheeler shook and flailed. He was hurting it but not enough. Ram was fading fast, his strength leeching out along with his blood.

There was just no way to hurt it.

He needed a blade, a spear to get through the armored skin. But he had nothing. One hand was useless, punching with his missing fingers weakened the structure of his fist and was effectively pointless.

He wrapped his arms around the hub and heaved it backward, twisting, trying to throw or roll the thing into the screen but he couldn't shift it.

His strength faded with the effort. All the alien had to do was to survive a few moments longer and Ram would die.

The Wheeler had braced itself with a foot right underneath

him and, blinking away the blood and tears from his remaining eye, Ram saw the limb stretched under him. Ram stamped down and felt it crunch and snap with a resounding pop.

Ram wished he could use the alien's shattered bone as a blade to spear through the thick yellow hide.

But there's no way to get the alien's bone out of its body.

The hub was heaving, struggling for breath, it seemed but it bucked and threw Ram off again. The smokescreen was behind him, there was nothing he could do to stop his momentum and the sheet of swirling plasma burned through his hand up to the wrist.

Ram screaming through the tatters of his face as the pain and horror shot through him. He pulled back his right arm, glistening pink bones at his wrist, sheared off completely flat at the ends, like some sort of biological tool.

And there it was. Right there in front of his face. The way to make a spear.

While the Wheeler thrashed itself upright behind him, Ram laid his arm at an oblique angle against the searing agony and rotated it, rolled it around to burn his wrist bones into sharp points. He had to peer through his tears in his eye. The horror of it twisted his guts, the wrongness of burning his own limb away, of searing through the skin, the muscle and the two bones of his forearm. He was screaming, shaking as he pulled it back and inspected the damage.

Two perfect chisel points.

As he turned to drive it into the Wheeler's body, which was hanging back from the smokescreen, it lashed out and slashed its claws across his abdomen, low down, ripping three gashes through his body from hip to hip, from his genitals to his ribs.

It was a killing blow. But Ram didn't stop as his guts tumbled out under his feet in slimy, shit stinking ribbons. He knew he was dead as he charged raggedly forward, treading on his guts, dragging more of them out of the gaping wound with each step as he closed on the Wheeler. Its next swipe, Ram caught under his left arm. Still, the power of it crushed more ribs and knocked Ram to the side, forcing more of his entrails out of the gaping holes across his belly.

But Ram held on. He had only seconds of life left.

Roaring through the hole of his face, he fell against the Wheeler and drove his arm into the creature with every gram of strength he had.

His chisel-bladed arm punched through the skin and his arm thrust deep inside the hub. The thing screamed and shook, rolling away. Ram held on to the hub's shoulder joint with his other arm, drew out his bone-spear in a spray of dark red, stinking, gelatinous blood and slammed it back in again, tearing through more of the tough yellow hide. Inside the hub was a mass of tissue. Gristle and soft, pulpy organs that he stabbed through, over and over again. The Wheeler rolled and bucked, cartwheeling around. He held on but Ram had no idea which way was up or how long the fight had gone on for nor how long he had left to live.

All he knew was he had to finish it.

He reached his left arm inside the hub and grabbed hold of a slippery string of sinew and pulled, snapping it. The Wheeler screamed and bubbled, belching out horrifically foul gasses. He stabbed his sharpened wrist into the inside, mincing whatever tissue he could and he dragged out fistfuls of foul yellow mush with his hand and yanked out red chunks of quivering alien matter and he knew that he was drowning in his own blood.

He couldn't get a breath through his windpipe. His vision, already half gone, darkened from the edges. He went on fighting, punching and thrashing at the Wheeler which shook under him, quivering and writhing.

Milena was shouting in his head but he didn't know what she was saying. He didn't know anything anymore. He had been destroyed. His body was ruined. His face was gone. He couldn't move a muscle.

Far above him, the half circle dome ceiling of the Orb arena curved up into a shining darkness, like the endless blackness of interstellar space.

CHAPTER THIRTY-FIVE
SPOILS OF WAR

THE VOID. LOST IN DREAMS and voices in the midnight dark, packets of data swirling in the ether. Time passed.

And Rama Seti woke.

"Ram? Can you hear me? Ram?" A woman's voice. He recognized it, perhaps. A voice from far away. "Come on, Ram, wake up, hurry."

Another voice spoke, close by the first. "He should be conscious right now. Look at my display, it says he is awake."

"Then why is he not responding, doctor?" the woman said. A rich, confident voice.

"Milena?" Ram asked. "Milena, is that you?"

"He moaned, did you hear that?" Milena said, a smile in her voice.

"I think you are imagining things." It was Dr. Fo, he knew it now. "Still, no harm in moving things along. Here, let us give him a little jolt of the old wake-up juice."

White light seared into Ram and he cried out.

"No!" he screamed, trying to leap up.

Figures moved in the whiteout. He was on his back, on a bed. Lights above at the edges of the room made his eyes ache.

He could not move.

"Ram," Milena said. Her hands, the cool touch of her palms, pressed against his face.

"What happened? Where am I?"

"You are disoriented," a voice said in his ear. It spoke English but the accent wasn't Indian. "Do not be alarmed. You are perfectly safe."

His bed hummed and it sat him up. He couldn't open his eyes properly but they put a straw in his mouth and he drank down a beautiful draught of lukewarm water.

"Everything is alright," Milena whispered. "You're safe now."

"So bright," he muttered. "Can't see."

Dr. Fo spoke to someone unseen. "Can you dim the lights, please?"

"Your eyes are new to you, Ram," Milena said. "Your brain needs time to adjust."

Ram blinked away some of the glare. He was in the clinic. The white tile walls too bright to look at but he could see the people around him. Milena, Dr. Fo and his familiar team, beavering away.

"What happened?"

Dr. Fo's face loomed over him. "What do you remember?"

"I don't know. The Orb. The arena. Oh, god. Dying. Oh, god."

Milena's voice smiled. "You won."

Ram didn't think that sounded right. "I can't have done. I remember how it felt."

Milena spoke gently. "Your life signs continued and the Wheelhunter's did not. The Orb stated that you won and here you are."

"How do you feel now?" Dr. Fo asked.

"Not sure. How do I look? How should I feel?"

"It may take time to adjust to your new body but it is largely the same in outward appearance as your last one."

"Another one?" Ram said. "You used that poor Artificial Person just to bring me back?"

Dr. Fo cleared his throat and adjusted his collar. "That Artificial Person gave its woeful existence so that you could be reconstructed. That was its entire purpose. Do not mourn that animated collection of tissue. We salvaged as much from the shreds of your brain and spinal cord as we could. It was a challenge, what with so much of your nervous systems essentially pulped by the alien but we scraped out rather a lot of good material from your remains to integrate into your new body. And then we plugged the gaps with pieces of downloaded memories. You may feel a touch of dislocation for a while."

Ram felt like his head was submerged under a ton of water. "How long have you been working on me? How long has it been since the Orb? Where are we?"

"It has been ten months since you killed the Wheelhunter," Milena said. "The doctor was taking his time, being sure to do it thoroughly. But our timetable has recently accelerated somewhat."

"I've been in stasis?"

Dr. Fo answered. "A chemically induced coma, you might say. You were in rather a bad way so it might be better to say that you were simply mechanically unable to achieve consciousness for much of the time. I've lost count of how many surgeries we have performed to transform your tattered remains into this fine specimen. Dozens of procedures, certainly."

Ram assumed they were keeping his hormones at semi-sedation levels because he felt emotionally numb at the revelation. "You brought me back from death. Why?"

"Why?" Milena said, grinning. "What do you mean why? Rama Seti, you mad bastard, how can you ask us such a thing? You are the greatest hero of the age. How could we possibly allow you to die?"

Ram stared at her for a moment. "I'm the what?"

"Can you stand? Come on, you should be able to with the amount of augmentation in you."

Ram climbed to his feet with ease and his head spun only a little. "I feel different," he said, looking down at his hands and body. On the outside at least it seemed to be the same as the last one, perhaps a little less bulky. "What augmentation is in me?"

Dr. Fo clapped his hands in joy. "As much as we could print off and cram into you."

"What about the Zeta Line?" Ram asked.

Milena walked to the door of the clinic, speaking over her shoulder. "Re-fusing your nervous system lost you a few milliseconds reaction time so you cannot compete on the Orb again." She stood by the door, waiting for Ram to join her. "But we more than made up the losses, as the doctor says, with a fully integrated suite of military-grade augmentations. Biological, cybernetic and neurochemical, you name it."

"What the hell for?" Ram said, walking unsteadily toward her.

"We'll get to that but right now we are on a tight schedule," she said, her smile dropping momentarily. She thumbed open the door, revealing the familiar white corridors of the *Victory* beyond. "Thank you, Doctor Fo," she called as she left.

Ram ducked after her. "Where are we going?"

"I want you to see this on a nice big screen."

She led him to the Intel room in the medical ring. Ram had been in it before when they'd run him through the Disclosure process. The room was kitted out the same as before but this time, no Intel Officer waited for them. Just the big screen on the wall and an empty desk chair where he had been.

"So I guess Diego is still confined to his quarters?"

Milena settled in the comfortable seat. "Actually, no. In fact, he has been given the opportunity to repay the damage he helped to cause. But forget him for a moment. This is the time to celebrate you, Ram."

"Celebrate me?"

The screen snapped into life and displayed a flamboyantly-coiffed Avar news reader in an old fashioned style studio handing over to a reporter who was recording a segment from within an Avar projection.

"Thank you, Andro," the reporter said, before launching into the rapid-speak required to cram audio information into as tight a time frame as possible. "Yes, I'm right here in the latest must-visit Avar destination which has recorded over half a billion unique visits in the last forty-eight hours. The new Rama Seti commemorative square in New Delhi which has opened fully two months before the first annual celebration of his great victory in the Grand Arena of the Solar System Orb. As you can see behind me, the statue of Rama in his famous pose at the end of the already-legendary battle is one hundred meters tall. Cast from a hundred tons of copper, assembled on site and coated with a hundred kilograms of gold, the unconventional pose of the statue has been hailed as a marvel of Indian engineering. Although, of course, as well as praise, it has also attracted controversy. The building site was attacked by pro-human terrorists objecting to the UNOP's use of Artificial Persons in its program which last year successfully staved off the potential of an invasion of the Solar System by a race of hitherto unknown wheel-shaped alien lifeforms. As well as IRL assaults, Avar users have also come under attack, with viruses, horror suites and doxing being the primary tools Avar terrorists and conspiracy theorists have used in efforts to keep people away. A huge security effort has been put in place on site as well as throughout the Avar network to reduce the threats but, either way and, as you can see behind me, the danger has not put off this unprecedented torrent of visitors from paying their respects to the man that many are now calling humanity's greatest champion, Indian Avar gamer and IRL superhero, Rama Seti. Back to you, Andro."

Milena paused the replay.

Ram sat staring at the screen and the image of a statue of himself with his face half torn off, his jagged wrist held aloft and ready to be plunged downward into where the Wheeler's hub would have been. A statue of Rama Seti, in Delhi.

"Is this real?" He looked at her carefully. "Is any of this real?"

"There's ten months' worth of it, from all over the world. Articles, books, Avar, you name it."

"How is it possible? How did they find out?"

"We sent all our data, all our records back to Earth. In light of your victory, that is to say, humanity's victory, the Project decided that the time had come for Full Disclosure. So they released it. All of it. Well, most of it. And the world went crazy. It has taken them a while to go through stages of denial and adjustment. Currently, they seem to be ecstatic about the whole thing. And now you are the greatest singular hero since, well, anyone."

Ram rubbed his hands over his face and laughed. "It's like a dream come true and yet I don't feel much of anything. It still doesn't seem real, any of it."

"You have a new body to get used to, all over again. This time, I hope you have a longer opportunity to enjoy it, to feel part of yourself, part of the world again."

"You don't sound too hopeful," Ram said. "Do my chances of death have something to do with that stuff about the pro-human and pro-Artificial Person terrorists and conspiracy theorists waiting back on Earth?"

"It's just the usual brand of extremists who are willing to murder people in order to protect the sanctity of human life. But there is a significant minority who believe the entire Project is a fake. That all the footage is staged, acted and computer generated. There are all kinds of videos supposedly proving that this is the case, demonstrating inconsistent shadows and utilizing elements of our conversations taken out of context. When you have so many thousands of hours of footage in the public domain, you can edit it to show any version of reality, of history, that you wish and many of these lunatics seem to be doing just that. But none of that is any of our concern, not in the least, so put it out of your mind."

"Okay, sure, I understand. To be honest, I just hope I get the hero treatment rather than being targeted for assassination when we get home."

Milena nodded. "As I said, it is none of our concern. Either way."

Something in her brisk tone alerted him. "What do you mean? How long is it exactly until we get back to Earth?"

Milena stood. "Director Zhukov is waiting for you in the forward observation deck. He would like to tell you himself precisely what comes next for Mission Four."

Ram had never been allowed out of a few key areas of the *Victory*, namely the ludus ring, certain medical and admin sections and parts of the crew quarters.

But Milena led him quickly through a long secure tunnel that ran through the ludus ring and into what she called the Forward Observation Deck, a section of the leading ring. A central strip along the floor of the room was a series of six rectangular windows joined side by side. Standing on the center of one of the middle windows was Zhukov, wearing his incongruous gray business suit, looking down past his toes and out into the blackness of space.

"Director," Milena called out. "Ram is here."

Zhukov waved him over while Milena hung back.

"Congratulations, Rama Seti," Zhukov said, taking great care to dramatically emphasize his consonants. "Come here to me and look upon what your victory has bought for us."

Ram stood beside the Director, towering over him, and looked down into the absolute blackness of space.

"Is this supposed to be some sort of metaph—"

He broke off as the blinding blue and white of curve of the planet Earth rotated into view beneath him. The ship rotated fully once every thirty seconds and so the planet moved quickly beneath him. Swirling cloud covered the globe and the sunlight reflected off the water. Ram was confused. He knew there was at least another year before they would be near Earth's orbit, probably longer.

And something seemed wrong about the planet.

Most of the surface he saw was covered or at least partially obscured by the cloud cover but still there was something disturbing him until he realized what it was.

Then he was afraid.

There was very little land. None of it was shaped like Earth's continents and what little land, in the shape of chains and clusters of islands, he could see through the cloud, was all shades of black and gray rock. No green at all.

"I know what you are thinking," Director Zhukov said, peering sideways up at him.

"That isn't Earth," Ram said, watching the planet move as the ship's ring rotated him away from it.

"We are calling it Arcadia. The light reflecting off the surface of this planet and into your heavily augmented retinas is coming from a star called 55 Cancri, which is forty-one light years from Earth. A gift, to humanity, from the Orb Builders. A reward for your victory against the Wheelhunter almost a year ago."

Ram's voice came out in little more than a hushed whisper. "Funny, it feels more like an hour ago to me."

"After your victory, the Orb told us it would maintain the doorway into the 55 Cancri system for us for one cycle. That means a period of thirty years. To keep it open longer we shall have to win the next battle on the Orb Station Zero, assuming that the Wheelhunters wish to challenge us for the system. The Project HQ ordered us to proceed through the wormhole and to take possession of the system while we could, with UNOP colony ships to follow us as quickly as they could. With continuing improvements in propulsion technology, the first of those ships should be here in a couple of years. We proceeded through and arrived in orbit around Arcadia sixty-two days ago. We landed probes immediately and a few days ago sent down the first party of marines, engineers and researchers to begin humanity's first extrasolar colony and take our place in the galactic civilization. Ex-Director Zuma is in command of the landing party. Her military background and semi-expendable status were an irresistible combination for HQ, it seems."

Ram could not tear his eyes from the blue gleam of the planet as it passed beneath his feet once more. "The Orb Builders just gave us a whole system? With a habitable planet?"

"An immediately habitable planet, Arcadia here, plus what seems to be a habitable moon and two other terrestrial planets suitable for underground or enclosed colonies, as we have on Mars and so on, not to mention asteroids and dwarf planets so far unseen. A system so clearly attractive and yet uninhabited until the Wheelers were granted it thirty years ago, after we failed our Mission Three."

"And they've had to abandon this whole system to us? They've just gone because the Orb told them to?"

Zhukov was grim yet that amused him, somewhat.

"We assumed that they had gone. We initially detected no Wheeler ships in the area although we have no idea what kind of stealth technology they may have. But we have a problem. A Wheeler ship is heading this way. It was in orbit around the sixth planet, on the far side of the star, when we arrived but it is now coming for us. It will be here in only a few days."

"It's coming to fight. And we're not going to run? Can we beat it?"

"The *Victory* has some armament but it is not a warship. Nevertheless, UNOP orders are to protect our landing party and continue establishing an outpost on the surface. The good news is that we have reinforcements heading this way, executing an extreme breaking maneuver to join us in orbit and fight the alien ship. UNOP's flagship, the battleship *Stalwart Sentinel* under Admiral Goro Howe had already crossed Saturn's orbit when it was rerouted to the Orb wormhole and so to the Cancri System. Its true power is classified, even to me, but it is the most powerful vessel humanity has ever constructed. There are hundreds of crew, it has fighter complement, UNOP Marines, projectile and energy weapons of enormous power. If humanity has a chance of keeping this system, we will have to fight for it."

"I thought the Orb Station had gifted us this system as loot. Can it step in and help us?"

"It does not work that way. The Orb grants us access with the wormhole and, we believe, it cut off access to the system for the Wheelers. But it has given us, in effect, the legal rights to the system. If the aliens can fight us off, then they will do so. And fighting, they are. The Orb Builders never intended to stop conflict with their Orb Station Network, merely to control it, shape it. Even encourage it, but only on their terms. For us to join the galactic empire, we will have to fight for our place, in the Arenas and in the star systems all across the galaxy."

"You picked a great time to wake me up."

"I will be frank, Rama Seti. We need you. I admit that I was wrong about you, about what you could do with converting all your Avar experience into real life results. You have extensive experience in squad and tactical combat Avar gaming. Even before we arrived at Arcadia, we invested so much of our precious and dwindling resources in bringing you back because I knew you would be valuable. But since we arrived, I ordered the installation of as much military grade augmentation as Dr. Fo could possibly graft into your replacement body, some of it experimental and some of it, I am sad to say, currently untested, uncalibrated and inactivated. Because, Rama, we discovered that the Wheelers are still on the planet. Those filthy yellow monsters were deliberately concealing themselves in bases underground on the same landmass that we selected to land upon and our outpost has been attacked twice in the last four days. We have lost a number of people already and we believe the last attacks were only probing ones. Our satellites show the Wheelers are massing a few kilometers away for a full-out assault. You will be attached to Captain Cassidy's Marines company as a special advisor."

"You want me to advise the Marines on how best to fight the Wheelers," Ram said, itching for combat for himself.

"They're not going to *fight* them, they're going to shoot them and blow them into small pieces. Your designation will be as an advisor but I want you to kill the Wheelers, Rama Seti. We need you to join Cassidy's reinforcements, go down to the planet and help our outpost hold on to what you already won."

Ram nodded slowly. He wanted this. "When do I go?"

Director Zhukov held out a hand for Milena, passing Ram off to her once again. "Shuttle A is fueled, stocked with Marines and waiting for you. As soon as you get to Shuttle Bay 1 and we are over the entry window for the LZ, you will be on your way. You may well be landing in the middle of a war zone. Our engineers have printed you an assault rifle and body armor suitable for your stature. The armorer reviewed your weapons proficiencies and provided equipment to match. He even made you a gigantic replica of the sword you used in an Avar called *Shield Wall*. You must hold against the Wheelers on the ground while the *Victory* holds in orbit, until Admiral Howe's *Sentinel* arrives. Good luck, Rama Seti. If you manage to live through this next mission, who knows, perhaps you will have a long career fighting aliens for the UNOP Marine Corp. Now, Rama Seti, time to go to work."

"Yes, sir!"

AUTHOR'S NOTE

Rama Seti's story continues in *Earth Colony Sentinel* Galactic Arena Book 2. Out now.

If you enjoyed *Orb Station Zero* please leave a review online! Even a couple of lines saying what you liked about the story would be an enormous help and mean that this book is more visible to new readers.

You can find out more and get in touch with me at dandavisauthor.com

BOOKS BY DAN DAVIS

The GALACTIC ARENA Series

Inhuman Contact
Onca's Duty
Orb Station Zero
Earth Colony Sentinel

The IMMORTAL KNIGHT Chronicles

Vampire Crusader
Vampire Outlaw

GUNPOWDER & ALCHEMY

White Wind Rising
Dark Water Breaking
Green Earth Shaking

For a complete and up-to-date list of Dan's available books, visit: http://dandavisauthor.com/books/

Printed in Great Britain
by Amazon